The Parentectomy

The Parentectomy

A MEMOIR

A Perspective On Rising Above
Parental Alienation

Kimber Adams

To order additional copies of this book, contact:
Xlibris Corporation
1-888-795-4274
www.Xlibris.com
Orders@Xlibris.com
59322

The Parentectomy is one of the most captivating books I have read in years. Kimber Adams did a magnificent job of describing the unfortunate decisions that too many parents make during divorce; to use the children as pawns. But she did an even better job at describing the emotions and thought process behind the sacrifice only the bravest of parents are willing to make in order to protect their children from the emotional scars of Parental Alienation: letting go. Thank you Kimber, for touching my soul with such an inspiring novel.

Beverly Morris
President & Founder
The National Association of Non Custodial Moms
www.nancm.org

The Parentectomy is a true illustration of parental alienation. It sets the stage showing that divorce can turn into a war based on revenge. A parent's worst nightmare becomes a reality when the children are brainwashed into erasing half of their identity. This memoir is the representation of a father that uses anger and revenge to punish his wife for terminating the marriage. We divorce our spouses, but in some cases the alienating parent weaves a web of lies and manipulates a child to believe their other parent divorced them as well. As a child who was alienated from my mother, I can feel the pain of these children who manifest these hateful behaviors. Kimber Adams allows us to relate and know as parents who mourn our children that we are not alone. This book is an eye-opener for parents and professionals to witness the breakdown of parental bonds and revenge. You will find comfort in this emotional roller coaster as a mother finds her way in the world while battling her ex to continue to be what she always was—a ***mother***.

Chrissy Chrzanowski
Founder-Parental Alienation Hurts
http://www.parentalalientionhurts.com

The Parentectomy is not for the faint of heart. Parental Alienation is a real subject where one party chooses to disrupt the lives of all parties involved while going through a divorce. It's hard to believe that one human being will do everything in their power to distress, intimidate, and alienate the other party; but it happens. What's equally disturbing is when the children get involved, and through misinformation they sometimes choose sides and alienate one parent. I read this book with both curiosity and amazement. Kimber Adams tells a story that is worth sharing with both men and women who have experienced a difficult, post-divorce transition and then overcame those obstacles and found personal triumph. I recommend *The Parentectomy* for those Single Parents who can relate to this subject and want to find a good book with a meaningful ending.

Richard "RJ" Jaramillo
President/Founder of Single Dad
www.singledad.com

In *The Parentectomy*, Kimber Adams vividly illustrates the heartbreak, frustration and hopelessness that parents experience when their children are manipulated and turned against them in order to fill the other parent's unhealthy emotional needs. *The Parentectomy* is a novel and Adams is a gifted story-teller; however her lessons are very real. Parents, legal and mental health professionals would be well-served to use Adams' experiences to protect children from becoming one parent's weapon and crutch when a child's only wish is to have normal, loving relationships with both his or her parents.

Mike Jeffries
Author, A Family's Heartbreak: A Parent's Introduction to Parental Alienation
www.afamilysheartbreak.com

I found the book to be highly enjoyable. It presents a good example of the unfolding of an alienation situation from the perspective of a targeted parent. I am sure that other targeted parents will gain comfort and insight from reading the book.

Amy J.L. Baker Ph.D.
Author of *Adult Children of Parental Alienation Syndrome: Breaking the Ties That Bind*

The Parentectomy clearly explains the sudden, destructive nature of Parental Alienation; how family can inadvertently, or in some cases, intentionally, make it worse and how these behaviors are, ultimately, most damaging to the children involved. A riveting novel.

Sarvy Emo
Founder of Parental Alienation Awareness Day April 25th and
Parental Alienation Awareness Organization
www.paawareness.org

Breakthrough Parenting has been helping parents in difficult custody situations for more than 25 years.

When it came to moderate and severe Parental Alienation cases, it was always a major challenge to get family members, friends and even many licensed family professionals to understand what it was like to be on the receiving end of PAS. Until this book came out, those who hadn't experienced it first hand could not even imagine what PAS was like. This lack of understanding led to a large number of family tragedies across the U.S., even all over the world.

As professional educators, we were pleased to find the book so clear and easy to read that we can even recommend it to every-day parents without an academic background. We will use this in our own practice as much as possible, and we will also recommend the book to the family professionals for whom we provide training throughout the year. These are primarily clinicians ranging from Marriage & Family Therapists in private practice to Social Workers at government agencies like DSS, DCFS, etc. Our hope is that this book can help them learn to identify Parental Alienation cases more quickly, and recommend effective interventions based on this understanding.

Ms. Adams' writing is very clear and focused. Her storytelling flows, and the key details that are so important to understand in PAS cases are lucidly described in a way that makes the whole situation come alive.

We have helped many thousands of parents in difficult PAS cases, and are glad to have this additional resource to educate those who need to gain a better understanding of PAS and its impact on family dynamics.

Bjorn Ahlen, Co-Founder & CEO
Breakthrough Parenting, Inc.
http://www.breakthroughparenting.com/PAS.htm

FOR TARGETED PARENTS ~

As long as your child is in this world, there is reason to be hopeful.

As long as there is hope, there is reason to press forward in your life.

FOR MY CHILDREN ~

Read this in a spirit of forgiveness, with a vision for progress.

Read this knowing you are loved by many in as many different ways.

And the king said,
"Divide the living child in two,
and give half to one, and half to the other."
Then the woman whose son was living spoke to the king,
for she yearned with compassion for her son;
and she said,
"O my lord, give her the living child, and by no means kill him!"

1 Kings 3:25-26

≈≈≈

Run to our friends. Go. See what that will get you. Ridicule.
I am to them what I originally was to you.
They believe what they see and that's what they see,
and they also see the very mixed up person that you obviously have become.
After all, it really is you who have thwarted my progress,
tainted my reputation, thrown me off course.
There is an escape from the frustrations you cause me and,
fortunately, my reputation provides enough insulation from the outside world
so I can indulge in this escape with impunity. What escape?
Those eruptions of anger you dread and fear, my rages.
Ah, it feels so good to rage.
It is the expression of and the confirmation of my power over you.
Lying feels good too, for the same reason,
but nothing compares to the pleasure of exploding for no material reason
and venting my anger like a lunatic,
all the time a spectator at my own show and seeing
your helplessness, pain, fear, frustration, and dependence.
Go ahead.
Tell our friends about it.
See if they can imagine it, let alone believe it.
The more outrageous your account of what happened,
the more convinced they will be that the crazy one is you.

Excerpt written by Ken Heilbrunn, MD
From the Forward of *Malignant Self Love: Narcissism Revisited*
by Sam Vaknin, PhD

Acknowledgements

Vlado, my love, you breathed energy into my spirit, and taught me a better way to *be* in this world by demonstrating a new approach to life. Your love empowers, inspires, and renders me able to live fully. It is not possible to express in words the gratitude I feel for all you've invested into my well-being. As my partner and father to our children, you personifying the qualities you teach as agent and life coach. Your phenomenal ability to improve the lives you touch is an endless blessing to me. Thank you for letting me pass *you* forward.

Mom and Pops, Don and Katarina, I am deeply thankful for your undying love and support throughout the entirety of this ordeal. All things considered, you lived it *with me*. Be that as it may, at the end of the day, you valued me as only a parent could. I am indebted. Mom, thanks for your editing tips, for the confidence you've shown in me, and for believing in the importance of this project.

Buddy and Kelli, thank you for being there for me whenever I needed to vent or share a moment that gave me reason to hope. I'm thankful to have intimate and dependable friends in my siblings.

To friends and extended family that stood by me without judgment—you know who you are—I am profoundly grateful for our continued friendship.

I sincerely appreciate my readers and the invaluable contributions they made to this novel. Linda Levin, for adeptly pointing out a missing ingredient that prompted the floodgates to open; Anna Dunkerly, for your writing expertise and editing advise; Anastasia Pavlovic, for asking the right question; Carl Herrman, for vineyard conversations over new wine and for making this read your 'cup of tea' for a night; Marian Lind, for holding me accountable with near daily words of support as this project was launched and for sharing your point of view in editing; Donna Robin, for your quick, expert edit as well as finesse extraordinaire in delivering honest feedback and prudent consideration; and Ruth Siress, for your caring words of affirmation that blanket my life as well as this project. Your insightful encouragement to "Chose life—Chose love," generated a far-reaching positive impact.

And last, but not least, many thanks to the team at Xlibris for your professionalism; author representative Jason Paul; gatekeeper Reiona Appala; submissions representative Jade Navarro; editors Marian Lumayag, Joane Verallo, and Charisse Desabelle; the production team of Carolyn Gambito; layout and design team of James Mensidor and Judee Lou Sanchez; and the marketing team of Jo Arciaga.

Prologue

"Ready?" I asked, perusing the contents of my pocketbook. "Map, money, bankomat . . . I'm set."

"Let me use the restroom real quick," Mom whispered, with an emphasis on *real*.

My parents are from the Midwest and had never been to Europe. Our new life was shared via narrative over the phone. The stories usually began with, "I wish you could have been with me today!" I lived the life of an expatriate corporate wife in Vienna, Austria. My husband had accepted a global vice president position and we looked forward to the new assignment overseas knowing the experience would be invaluable for our children, as well as for ourselves. Finally, after a year of adjustment and transformation that comes from evolving within a new culture, my parents decided to join our adventure abroad for a couple of weeks.

"Dad? Where are you?" I yelled down the stairwell to their wing of our home.

"Waiting for you two!"

His voice came from the foyer, which I'd fashioned into a sunroom. He had settled down to bathe in the sunshine just down the hallway from where I stood. I joined him by the front door but didn't make myself comfortable as I knew Mom would zip past us soon, walking as quickly as she could to make up for the time we spent waiting for her. "You've got a beautiful home here, Toots."

"Thanks, Dad. The kids and I have really enjoyed this place."

Our rental home was over one hundred years old and overflowing with character. To me, it was inspiration. I'd measured every floor, wall, and window before we packed our belongings to be shipped overseas. Our forty-foot containers included not only seventeen years' worth of history from our marriage but window treatments, paintings, and new furniture to fill twenty-two rooms. Design and setup had been a ten-month investment of time, but as the pieces came together after arrival, our villa was transformed into a home. Every nook and cranny was complete. There were no house projects waiting to monopolize our free time because it was my hope that enjoying life and each other might be our focus in a new environment. I'd heard that Austrian society worked to live as opposed to our household, which tended to live to work.

True to form, Mom nearly sprinted past us out the door. Dad pried himself up from his comfortable sun-drenched lounge chair and I locked the door behind us. As my parents and I walked to the metro station, mother's excitement to see the Picasso exhibit in town became contagious.

"I can't believe I'm actually here!" she chirped, taking in the view of our district's city hall with its prominent clock tower as we walked toward the metro.

"Want me to pinch you?" Dad asked her.

I was amused by the familiar nonsense that goes on between them. They were high school sweethearts, homecoming king and queen, and still at the top of their game near the small town we all grew up in. I wondered if my marriage wouldn't have grown apart like it did if my life had been confined to that town. There is something about the accountability of a small town that is quite opposite the anonymity of living life as an expatriate in a foreign city. But for reasons I had yet to learn, life brought me to Vienna.

On the train platform, Dad and I waited with an open map, looking for the tram number we would need once we were downtown. Mom was milling about, "people watching" behind us. She'd spotted a couple of gentlemen descending the stairwell. I briefly noticed her intrigue, as she couldn't seem to keep her eyes off them.

The train *whooshed* into the station; the doors slammed open, and those passengers exiting made their way past those of us waiting to get on. As my parents and I sat down, the two gentlemen my mom had her eye on sat in the booth opposite us. My dad, being the kind of guy who waves to everyone he meets driving down the road whether he knows them or not, was unable to sit in the awkward silence of togetherness that two metro booths produce.

"Guten Morgen." He nodded in their direction, greeting them with his Midwestern accent.

"Guten Morgen," replied the taller of the two men.

I was amused by my father, but at the same time, feeling a little weak at the sight of the statuesque gentleman's dazzling good looks opposite me. He was five inches taller than me, with jet-black hair, midnight blue eyes, and striking chiseled features. He carried himself with ease and had an obvious sense of style. His voice was a deep baritone that resonated self-confidence and charm. The gentlemen with him beamed a gracious smile, and I smiled back, but I could barely lay eyes on the one who was speaking. He literally took my breath away and left me wondering how one achieves such elegance just going about a routine day.

"Are you traveling?" he asked. "I see you hold a map." It was broken English, but still better than any of us spoke the local German language of Deutsch.

"We are, and we're on our way to see the Picasso exhibit today," my father answered.

"Excellent. You will enjoy that. Where are you from?" he asked, in his operatic voice.

Dad flopped his finger between himself and Mom and told him they were from the United States. He paused for the announcement coming from the overhead loud speakers before he made his own broadcast. "She lives here!" he said, pointing at me.

"You live here!" he echoed, looking my direction.

I glanced his direction and, nodding, said, "I do! Just over a year now."

"Are you a student here?"

"No," I answered, nearly laughing at the idea of being a student traveling with my parents. I was unsure where to lead the conversation that was taking place over the roar of the train track and the screeching whistle of the brakes at each stop. "I work at the American International School." It was a seasonal position as swim coach, but it had become my identity of late. "What do you do?" I asked him.

"Many things. I'm a sports agent. I'm almost never in this part of town, but one of the teams I follow is staying at the Schönbrunn Hotel. We came out to see them off this morning." Gesturing to the gentleman with him, he said, "This is my brother. We're artistic photographers. Have you been to Museumsquartier? We have a gallery near there." Adding an afterthought, as he seemed to be analyzing me, he said, "I also enjoy writing."

"I also enjoy photography and writing!" He gave a knowing nod.

"Which sports?" I asked.

"Basketball and soccer. Do you play?"

"I did. I played basketball in college for a year before I focused on music," I answered.

"Wundershön!" he said, obviously intrigued that we had interests in common.

He asked my father what other sights we planned to see in the city. Dad mentioned those we had already seen before he told the gentleman of our plans to travel to Switzerland soon.

"Very good. I hope you enjoy the rest of your visit." He looked at me and asked, "Can I have your phone number?"

I had become accustomed to being asked for my number in the city. In fact, I received more appreciative attention from strangers on the street than I was given at home. But I had never accepted numbers from strangers, nor had I ever even considered handing out my phone number! Now, in front of my parents, one of the most impressive men I'd ever laid eyes on was asking me for my number. He was magnificent. I stalled, pretending not to hear over the loudspeaker announcing Karlsplatz was near.

Mom was telling me in ventriloquist fashion under her breath, "Take his. Take his."

So assertively nervous, nervously assertive, I asked for his number. He handed me his business card as he invited us to visit his art gallery. With that, the train began its screeching halt. We exchanged the customary "pleased to meet you" among the five of us.

As we all moved toward the door, the tall gentleman looked back, looked right *through* me it felt. The moment was sublime. I knew I was surrounded by dozens of other people, but under his gaze, nothing else existed.

"I'm Viktor," he said. "I hope to hear from you soon." Then he was gone.

I stepped onto the platform and walked a few steps away from the train before I stopped to take a deep breath. Mom was holding my arm as though I needed support. She was smiling as she pointed to his business card and said, "Put that in a safe place." Which, of course, I did!

Dad noticed my reaction to the encounter and said, "Be careful, Toots. You don't know anything about those men."

Was I just hit on in the presence of my parents? Maybe it was just wishful thinking, or an amusing dream. Perhaps my interpretation was just a need to feel noticed and alive? Was he married or divorced, available or taken? Perhaps his plight was similar to my own. The focus of seeing each other again had been around visiting his art gallery, so maybe he was hoping for a sale. No doubt, we weren't the first tourists he'd invited to his gallery. But there was more; I wasn't imagining. It was a gloriously palpable moment.

He mentioned he was almost never in that part of town. Mom used the restroom, putting us on the train platform five minutes later than we might have arrived otherwise. The trains run every five minutes on that metro line.

Yet we were on the same train platform to wait within the same five minutes in a city full of train platforms and two million people.

I call it a second birthday; the day destiny serendipitously intervened, because it's the day, I'd come to learn, that brought me back to life—the day that kept me alive.

∞ PART I ∞

In the still of the night and the quiet of his sleep, his little hand reaches out to pat my face. Beyond his five senses, there is a knowing in the gentle touch on my cheek. The boxing match going on in my mind causes my unrest. Earlier comments tear at my heart, ripping away every shred of hope I'd felt only two weeks earlier when my older son spent time with me.

"Looks to me like you're getting a sweetheart deal being able to support yourself on Dad's money," he'd chided.

Poisonous venom spewed through the phone line pounding body, mind, and soul. I try not to let it kill me even though parts of me died long ago. I refused to believe it was my child's own thought process. Hadn't he said only two weeks ago that I didn't deserve what had gone on? I know I heard him say, "I'm so sorry, Mom." But now, I sense a weakness, a conformed young man making his life easier. I simply cannot, will not, believe the hatred in his words is his own. He's an extremely intelligent person, so he can't actually believe that I am not entitled to anything after eighteen years of marriage. I didn't invest in myself, I didn't develop a career—I dedicated my days to the benefit of those around me. He and his sisters, along with their father and my role as spouse and corporate wife, were my occupation! Like his dad, he now viewed it as nothing. My contribution to their lives, to our family, all of it, perceived to be insignificant. My "sweetheart deal" doesn't even pay the rent. I live for the moment on assets I helped save.

His little hand touches my face. Patting me in his sleep, he is a beacon of calm hope in my corner. His caress seems to say, "Stay with me, Mom. I need you." I tenderly pull him closer. Yes, I deserve this—this connection, this love, this life. A hand, two years old at rest on my face, venoms antidote in the touch of a small boy. I'm sure I deserve this, knowing fully the sensitive child I hold deserves all of me too.

Chapter 1

After being in Vienna for only ten days, which was enough time for our shipment of containers to be unloaded into the house, my husband left the city.

"What's the problem?" he asked. It was a rhetorical question. "You know your way around now. You've been here almost two weeks! I'll be back in a month. You'll be fine."

It was late July. In the following month, my daughters and I buckled down to unpack and establish our home. We ventured out for groceries and very little beyond that. At the outset of life in a foreign country, surrounded by people who may or may not know how to speak my language, I was barely comfortable managing social interaction in our little neighborhood. The thought of getting lost in the city or needing help and having no one to call kept me close to home. Little did I know, at that point in time, how lucky I was to speak the international language.

My daughters, twelve-year-old Amanda, and eight-year-old Alexia, worked in spurts to help complete the unpacking, decorating, and painting. We even managed to clear out all the boxes and mounds of shipping material. Holding my hands, Alexia would take a giant step into a box piled high with papers then hop up and down to condense the mass. Bubble wrap was left out to be jumped on separately.

They amused themselves all day with their new surroundings, discovering all the little details. Our back garden with its manicured walking path, flowerbeds, and fruit trees, provided for imaginative journeys in the wild. Inside, the girls explored each room, holding hands to buoy their courage as they moved into new territory. The top level housed an attic they decided was haunted because there was an antique sickle hanging from the wall. There was no question in their minds; it belonged to the grim reaper.

The girls entertained themselves with elaborate fantasy, while I worked and fussed over the fine points of decor. Every break was spent catching up with a new "reality" that had unfolded in their minds. The house was inspiring, albeit a little daunting in size, which made it a tad spooky for me too. Settling in was a grueling month of sweat and hard work. I wanted our home in order before my husband, Peter, returned with our son, Adam, and our family was completely together inside. It was a big effort up front in hopes of a big payoff over time—enjoying life. I believed our lives would be different in a new culture.

During that month there were almost daily visits from our landlady who had one reason or another to stop by. She was full of spunk and energy at over seventy years of age. The house was full of childhood memories for her, as she had grown up there. She told the story of her grandmother passing away in the room I'd chosen for a study. Amanda and Alexia looked at each other with big eyes and frightened faces when they received that piece of history. Proof! The girls had all the information they needed. Now, they were certain the house was haunted.

There were bells to each bedroom on the wall near the dumbwaiter across the hall from the kitchen. Our landlady explained they were no longer useful.

"It's better," she added.

Agreed! I couldn't imagine my family having the ability to *ring* for me. The windowpanes throughout the home were doubled originals. She showed me how the inner layer had to be locked into place to keep the second windows handle from smashing through the first when both were open. This was especially important in the event of a breeze. I took in everything she was saying, hoping all the while her windows would endure our family. The formal dining room and living room faced the street. In the living room were four stained glass windows, but the dining room's stained glass had not survived the war.

"It's a pity," she said, still sounding as though the loss had happened just last week. Clearly, she cherished the home we were renting from her.

On we went, throughout the month. With each trip she made to our home, we listened to her reminisce, telling stories and receiving more instructions on the proper care of something or other in the house. I promised her I would care for it as if it were my own. When it was complete, it did feel like my own. Though I knew our life in Vienna was temporary, I could imagine living in that residence forever. It suited me perfectly. When the finishing touches were hung, our landlady gave the ultimate compliment.

"It's never looked better in my life," she said, patting me on the back as she spoke.

When my son, Adam, walked in and saw the finished version of the house he had only seen empty, his reaction was worth the effort.

"This is incredible!" he marveled. Pleased with the final results myself, I enjoyed watching his amazement as he wandered through his new home.

Somewhere in the distance, I heard Peter say, "You really worked hard."

Chapter 2

My soon-to-be-sixteen-year-old son begged to go out and explore the city. He'd been in Vienna for less than a day, but had been asleep since he arrived and was ready to be in motion. Having been uprooted in time for his junior year was a tumultuous event for him. He tried to convince us he was old enough to take an apartment and graduate with the class he'd known for the past three years. We had moved him to a private school forty-five minutes away in a bigger town during his eighth grade. We had a couple hours together every day while we made the trip through the mountains. Some days he would catch up on homework, and other days we'd just talk. The decision had been a good move for him academically as well as socially, and he couldn't imagine leaving his close friends behind. I was sure that I spent more time with my teenage son than most mothers did, simply because we were together on the road so much. Though my day was largely sacrificed to the drive, I loved our time together. But circumstances change, and ultimately, against his wish, Adam was forced to leave his beloved high school to follow his family. In the States, he had a driving permit for almost a year and was an excellent driver. But in Austria, fifteen-year-olds don't drive. Nor do sixteen-year-olds. He wouldn't have a license, but instead, would take public transportation. We all discovered soon enough, he had more freedom on public transport than he would have had with a car.

"I'll be fine, Mom. I can read a map."

"Be back by four o'clock. Know where you are and how long it will take you to be back . . . by four," I reiterated.

"No problem!" He smiled, letting the excitement creep into his voice.

"Be careful. Use your head. The rules are very black-and-white here, okay?"

"Got it, Mom."

He headed out the door for adventures I had yet to take. When we visited Vienna months earlier to look for a home and choose a school for the children, he surprised me with his knowledge of art and European history. Downtown, the sight of Stephansdom with its 450-foot spire and geometric roof tiles of black and gold stopped him in his tracks. He said, "Oh my gosh! That's the cover of my history book!"

Still uncomfortable with his new independence, I had to applaud his courage. Being the responsible person he is, he returned on time bubbling over about his discoveries.

"You've got to go with me tomorrow to see this. Have you seen the Gloriette?"

Worn and envious at the same time, I told him again, "We've worked all month. Seriously, we haven't been anywhere. We'll all go. It's a date!"

The next morning, the children and I walked to the Schönbrunn Palace. Completed in the mid-18th century, it was built in grand Baroque design to be the summer residence of the imperial family. The side entrance was near our home, just down the street a couple of blocks then across a bridge. We stepped through the gate into a lane of manicured trees that formed a beautiful green arch over our heads. There were rose gardens and paths running diagonally throughout the imposing landscape. We passed the largest, most intricate glass atrium I'd ever seen, and I made a mental note to revisit the site. Ahead, the covered lane ended, but I could see flower gardens inside the walking paths of a courtyard. As we approached the grounds that stretched out between the palace and its Gloriette, Adam made me close my eyes. He led me by the elbow to a set of stairs and we climbed them to a balcony joined to the palace. I wasn't allowed to open my eyes until he'd gently placed me exactly where he wanted me.

"Okay," he said. "You can open your eyes now."

He had centered me on the balcony at the sundial overlooking the perfectly maintained grounds adorned with scrollwork of colorful blooms. Both sides of the courtyard were lined with statues of lovers, maidens, and soldiers. At the end, a fountain with mermen riding horses rose up from the base of the hill, appearing to be chiseled out of natural stone. The sight of the Gloriette sitting on the mount in the distance took my breath. The Neo-Classical arcade was given its name because it was the crowning glory of the palace gardens. Bright blue sky shone through the columns. As the scene was fully absorbed, I knew it was a crowning glory moment of my own—a moment I'd remember forever. Adam had ensured that.

We stood looking at one of the most amazing landscapes we'd ever seen, and it was just a short walk from home. There on the balcony of the Schönbrunn with my children came a new awareness. The opportunities ahead of all of us were unlike anything we'd ever imagined or known before.

Chapter 3

I fell asleep that night studying transportation routes to the American International School. Orientation was taking place, and we needed to be on campus early the next morning. There were bus, metro line, and tram connections to coordinate. I decided we would leave a couple hours in advance even though it looked like it should only take an hour. That would leave time to gain the knowledge we needed to maneuver the system. Once the school year began, the children were to be riding a city bus turned school bus, but knowing an alternative way to get there was necessary.

Traffic travels on the right side of the road in Austria as well as the trains, trams, and bus routes. Posted above every entrance to the metro lines are the names of the last station on each line, which makes choosing your direction easy. We made all of the connections and had fun getting acquainted with a fresh and very different way of life. However, at the end of the tramline, we stepped off and found ourselves turning in circles. There was no school in sight.

Just then, a van pulled up beside us. The woman driving rolled her window down and asked in perfect English, "Do you need a ride up to the school?"

"Yes! Are we that obvious?"

"A mom, a map, three kids in American clothes . . . yep, you're obvious!"

"You're an angel. Thank you."

Inside the van was a teenage boy named Devon, only one year older than Adam. Their friendship blossomed on the spot and continued through Devon's graduation.

At orientation, it was evident that Adam, who stood six feet and three inches at that time, was the tallest boy in school.

"Are you a basketball player? A volleyball player?" asked potential teammates.

"I've played a little basketball. Isn't volleyball a girl's sport?" he answered. There were no boys' volleyball teams in any of the schools he'd attended. It was an honest mistake.

The group of boys that included Devon sniggered and invited Adam to the next volleyball practice. It proved to be quite a humiliating experience for him.

"I don't know how girls play that sport!" he contended, hanging on to his original thought as he walked into the kitchen where I was preparing dinner.

"Watch it, son. I played and I'm a girl." I reminded him, raising my eyebrows. "Men or women, it's all relative, you know. But you need to stop saying that!"

"Well, they kicked my butt. I'm going to try-out though."

"Great! I heard good things about the group of boys on that team. From what I've seen, I like them."

Adam's birthday was fast approaching and I knew that turning sixteen in a foreign country after he'd been driving with his permit for a year was not going to be the cornerstone birthday most sixteen-year-olds look forward to. He may have felt a new sense of freedom and responsibility, but it was in a new country, a new city, and a new school. With the unfamiliar came limitation. I recruited Devon and a friend of his from the volleyball team to get a group of kids from the school together to surprise Adam at our house on his birthday. They pulled together about twenty teenagers for a party that happened to be the night before the first day of school.

I watched for them as Adam showered upstairs. They arrived right on time. I brought them through a lower front entrance so they couldn't accidentally be seen. They filed in through our gym equipment, made their way across the hall, and settled into the den of our basement.

"Hurry up, son! Your dad's home." I lied to him to get him moving quicker. "We're all waiting for you downstairs!" Days earlier he was told we were going out for a family dinner to celebrate the occasion.

"Okay. Just give me ten more minutes."

Silently, this group of strangers waited. They hid themselves behind the sofa and around the corner in the dining nook to make the surprise more dramatic. As we waited for Adam to come down the steps, I whispered, thank-you to all of them.

They whispered back, "Thanks for the party!"

All we heard was the shuffle of feet at the door. Adam had come downstairs wrapped in a towel to ask what he should wear!

"Surprise!" roared the small crowd in our den.

Completely dumbstruck and speechless, Adam was in shock to see a room full of his peers. He looked around, spotted a few familiar faces, and secured the towel around his waist a little better.

"How did you do this?" he asked, looking at me in shock.

"I recruited help," I said, pointing out Devon. Adam gave me a one-armed side hug as he tightly clutched the towel with his other hand. "You guys have fun. I'll be in the kitchen," I said, pleased with myself.

"Be right back, guys." He ran up forty-two steps in the stairwell, got dressed, and was back downstairs in record time. His year was looking up. I beamed as I prepared snacks for them. The surprise was pulled off without a glitch, and the look on Adam's face was priceless.

Chapter 4

I knocked at the door of the school's athletic director and heard him shout, "It's open!"

"Hi, I'm Paige Sullivan." I stepped inside, extending my hand to shake his as he struggled to remove himself from the comfort of his chair.

"Hello! George Muston. What can I do for you?" He had taken my hand in both of his.

What was that accent? Scottish maybe, and it was thick. He was near retirement and appeared to be a former athlete himself, but the years behind a desk had not been kind to his physique.

"I wanted to let you know I'm a swim coach. I heard the school had a team, but there seemed to be some uncertainty as to whether or not you had a coach."

"Ah, heavenly days. You coach swimming!"

I was nodding. "For just three years now."

"What age?"

"Ages seven to eighteen—I was head coach to a hundred swimmers."

"Great day! Yes, we could use your help. But the position doesn't pay much."

"It never does," I said, giving an affirmative smile. "That's not why I do it."

"The fringe benefit is travel. Your expenses are paid. Our leagues are from London to Moscow and Munich to Egypt."

My eyebrows went up in disbelief. As a child growing up in the Midwest, I'd never traveled west of the Rockies or east of the Arkansas River.

"Awesome!" To be able to travel was exactly what I had in mind for our family when we relocated to Europe. It was an unexpected surprise to learn how much opportunity there would be to see the world while coaching. "How many swimmers do you think we'll have this year?"

"Twenty-five, maybe thirty."

"Well, that should be easy." I knew it was an upper school team and swimmers of that age tended to be a very disciplined group of young people. This would take little effort in comparison to my former team.

"We don't know which facility you'll practice in yet, but we will know soon. Do you have a minute? I could introduce you to the other coach."

I was confused. "Oh, so you have a coach?"

"Only one. It's better to have two on deck."

I knew that. "Of course. Sure, I have time."

As we wondered through the halls of the school, I became more familiar with its layout. We found my cohort in the lower gymnasium and George shouted across the class in progress.

"Heath! Come," he yelled, motioning him toward us with a wide nod.

A cute, beefy gymnast trotted our direction. "Hey, mate!" he yelled as he approached us, his Australian accent sounding exaggerated. He reached to shake hands while my new athletic director introduced us. I towered over his shaved head as we shared our credentials. Each of us expressed our excitement about the season and it was settled—we could work together. Transients of the world tend to bond quickly, and there in the gymnasium, a friendship was born. The season would begin in November.

≈≈≈

Adam made the volleyball team and traveled to places we hadn't considered visiting. In Budapest, he was picked up by his host family in a Ferrari and driven to the top of the Buda side of Budapest. As they rounded a corner, a mansion rose on the hill in front of him. When Adam asked his host what he did for a living, the gentleman answered, "I'm in the import/export business, son."

On the floor of Adam's guest bedroom in the manor lay a bearskin rug. There was no questioning whether or not it was real as it included the head of the beast. He dined at a family-owned restaurant that evening with the men of the house. There, he was introduced to his host's mistress. "We don't speak of such things at home," he was told.

As Adam recounted tidbits from each of his sports trips, I couldn't help but marvel at the insight our children were gaining into cultural differences. Their school, like other international schools, was comprised of eighty-one different nationalities. Attending class and spending days with friends from other parts of the world was an education in itself, but to be in the home of a host family on a sports trip was a bird's eye view of people in their own unique environment. Our home was opened to the interesting teenagers from other schools in our league when Vienna hosted a game or tournament. It was enjoyable sharing our American way of life with them and hearing their point of view about it. Altogether, the experiences gained would serve our children well their entire lives.

Chapter 5

Day by day, we settled into our new lifestyle. No longer were the days of dashing out the door at a quarter to six in the morning to make the forty-five-minute drive over the mountain. My newly found free time went to the gym in our basement to rid myself of the fast-food pounds that had accumulated while driving nearly two hundred miles a day in the States. A typical refrigerator in Europe is half the size of an American model, so I found myself at the market nearly every day as well. It was within walking distance, so I used a basket on wheels to do the shopping. It didn't take long to discover that buying in bulk was something of the past. Preservatives, I learned, were minimized; and one could only carry so much.

Most everything seemed minimized in fact. Our washing machine was less than a twenty-inch drum of space. It was front-loading, and each wash cycle took almost three hours. If I didn't wash at least three loads a day, I was behind. I tried to change the habits of my teenagers, but that proved impossible. If jeans were worn once, they were dirty. If the towel was used once, it was dirty. Laundry became the bane of my existence.

Time flew and before long, the holidays were upon us. We invited a small group for Thanksgiving dinner. Since the day is not a holiday in Austria, we had to schedule around work. The turkey was ordered and delivered *so* fresh it still had fluffy feathers in parts. Pumpkin, cranberries, pecans, and sweet potatoes could only be found at the Naschmarkt in town; so I ventured off to hunt for those necessary items. Fortunately, our oven was a large model, and the turkey fit—but that's all that fit. The menu had to be cooked in advance. As dishes were warmed, I'd send them up in our dumbwaiter so they could be placed on the sideboard in the formal dining room.

By the end of November, the dark of night begins to fall before four o'clock in the afternoon, so the lights on all the trees were aglow. We had a full traditional American Thanksgiving, visiting until the tall tapered candles on the table were stubs. As I prepared for bed there was a sense of accomplishment having managed that meal. In a country of minimized portions and variety, our super sized Thanksgiving feast was a feat to carry out. But I thought tradition was important to maintain. It was worth the effort.

Plans were made by my husband's family to join us at Christmas. His younger cousin, a single thirty-something bachelor arrived days before the others in order to do some sightseeing with us. Part of the agenda included taking in the Viennese traditions at Christmastime that cast a spell over the city. Part of the magic is the Christkindlmarkets. There were people standing around elevated circular tables with their friends, snacking on roasted chestnuts and drinking Glühwein, the seasonal hot mulled wine. Surrounding them were booths full of every handcrafted item you can imagine. That year, there was a blanket of snow on the ground. Icy flakes swirled under the enchanting lights of the season, and it was one of the most romantic settings I'd ever witnessed.

We were moving through it though, detached from the experience, as we didn't stop to order a drink or enjoy the moment. I was lagging behind, as the conversation taking place did not include me. From a distance, I heard my husband advising his cousin.

There we were, surrounded by a novel and embellished Christmas tradition with so many new sights and smells, yet none of it captivated my husband's attention. I wanted to indulge my curiosity and ponder the historic and imaginative setting we were in, but Peter just kept moving. To him it was another day and an opportunity to confidently impart his wisdom. Our differences were grossly magnified in a new culture.

Chapter 6

Swim season was in full swing after the holiday break. I took coaching a little more serious than Heath did and couldn't imagine "winging it" come time to assemble relays for the upcoming tournaments, so we created a mock meet in order to train parents and get some official times on each of our swimmers. It was a fun way to open the season, show the parents what had been accomplished to date, and let the swimmers know their standing in relation to their teammates. There was a lot of consideration given to making the experience a positive one for each swimmer and at the same time, as successful a season as possible for everyone involved.

When there was work to be done away from pool deck, Heath and I would work at my house so that I could be home with the children. He was a bachelor without a roommate. Often, we'd finish working and he'd hang around for lack of anything better to do. He'd been in the international school system for almost ten years and his travel stories were endless. Heath knew I enjoyed reading, so at one point, he gave me a leather-bound journal he'd kept that documented his expeditions. I was reading bits of it to Peter one night and mentioned that the journal would be great fodder for a novel. At that point Peter exploded, telling me if I wanted to write a book, it should be about him. After all, he argued, there weren't many men who had accomplished all he had in an equal number of years.

Entertaining as Heath was, my husband didn't appreciate his presence in our lives. One evening after a late arrival home, he offered to drive Heath to the train station. I grabbed my coat to ride along, but Peter stopped me. He said he had things to discuss with Heath. It was a long time before my co-coach returned to our home.

It was embarrassing. Our friendship was innocent, and I was protective of it. In spite of that, my husband showed up on pool deck one day at practice. Peter sat opposite us and literally glared at Heath the entire hour, even though he had a daughter in the water that he could have been watching. I wondered how he would react to me showing up in his office to make sure all his interactions were appropriate. He told me lively stories about the women in the office wearing sheer clothing and giving presentations without their jackets. Most of these same women were averse to bras as well. But marching into Peter's office or being anything like him was a fleeting thought. I had no desire to govern, police, or dominate my husband, however I resented him terribly for controlling and humiliating me.

≈≈≈

Like many disenchanted corporate wives, I discovered shopping. The currency exchange at that time was so good that every cash withdrawal from our account in the States warranted an extra 20 percent in schillings. Free money! I rationalized. Between the stress building in my marriage, walking nearly everywhere, and actually having time at home to use the gym equipment, there was little in my wardrobe that properly fit. In addition, Vienna has its own fashion rules and I wanted to blend in.

"I should have something in return for this deficient marriage!" I said to a friend over the phone one day. Her marriage seemed more doomed than my own, so she understood compensating the loss and loneliness with frivolous activity. She was the only person I confided in, as we were neighbors and her husband was absent almost as much as mine. We depended on each other for daily interaction with another adult.

"Hey, that's my motto. I'll go with you. Do you have a ball gown yet?" she asked.

"No, I really just need basics today."

"You need me. Basics are boring!"

"Maybe, but I need pants and some warm sweaters."

"That's easy, and I'm sure we'll have time afterward to look for ball gowns."

She was correct.

≈≈≈

"Two kids from the middle of nowhere, cruising down the road in their Mercedes, dressed for a ball at the Hofburg Palace in Vienna." My husband was full of himself. "Who would have guessed it?" he added.

I gave him a superficial smile. We had come so far from the days of walking at college because we couldn't afford gas for the car, days of using cloth diapers because we couldn't afford disposables, days of only dreaming about dining in a restaurant. Life is definitely easier with money, but it was true—money could not buy happiness.

Inside the palace, it was as if we'd stepped back in time a hundred years. There were floral arrangements that stood taller than the people walking past them. The foyer rose to a grandiose dome above us and was lined on either side by double staircases of marble. A trumpet sounded from the balcony to signal the opening of the ball. Girls in white gowns escorted by boys in tailed black tuxedos walked single file onto the ballroom floor then parted to make way for dancers that performed an accomplished ballet. Bouquets were presented to the chairman and his wife before the opening number began. It was a lively waltz that filled the space with gusto and the dance floor became a blur of black tuxedos and white ball gowns swirling all over the extravagant ballroom.

When the dance floor was opened to the public, Peter and I went for a walk through the building. At one of the restaurants, we ran into a couple whose daughter was on my swim team. I had spoken to them on pool deck several times, but it was the first opportunity I had to visit with them at length. The man worked for the embassy, and his wife assisted him where she could. We were discussing the Eastern Bloc and most of the discourse was directed to me, as I was the person they were familiar with. In addition, it was probably obvious that I was the only one interested in what they were explaining. Peter much preferred discussing topics in which he could contribute something to the conversation. His inability to add to the discussion seemed to bring out his demons.

Shortly after we excused ourselves from them, the night came to an end. My husband demanded we leave and proceeded to rage all the way home about how I was flirting with the father of my swimmer. His accusations were outrageous—two "kids" from the middle of nowhere, cruising down the road in their Mercedes, dressed for a ball at the Hofburg Palace in Vienna, completely unable to function as husband and wife.

It was a familiar pattern of behavior for us; the volatility in our interaction was nothing new. We'd only changed the backdrop in which to let it all play out. It seemed my husband had a sixth sense when it came to destroying the best of moments. I had such high hopes that the move and a change of scenery would infuse our relationship with a heightened sense of purpose. There were visions of us reconnecting in our need to depend on each other more, all those miles from family, friends, and home. The wish was ever so naïve.

≈≈≈

"You *will . . . be . . . on* my arm in Paris," my husband growled.

I was to be *on* his arm like a decorative handbag. We were discussing Paris, for heaven's sake! I didn't hear, "I want you *in* my arms . . ." My husband merely wanted me at his side.

"I can't! It's SCIS tournament that weekend, and I am going to be there for the team. I'm going to be there to watch our daughter! I'm not going to miss it."

"Yes, you are," he matter-of-factly stated. "Besides, I don't know why you think you need that job."

"I told you I'm not going to miss the meet. I'll join you and the group Sunday morning, but I'm not going to abandon the team that weekend." I was indignant, unwavering in my responsibility to the team.

It was time for the company's annual swanky weekend at a five-star hotel in a fabulous destination. It meant days of being with other corporate wives, being offered champagne throughout the day—beginning with breakfast and continuing throughout the day as we traipsed from one attraction to another. Listening to peers explain stories of their homes being built in obscure parts of the world—out of materials collected from more obscure parts of the world—while dining on extravagant meals was a long-established ritual to undergo. In general, the excursion meant being among competitive snobs. All that, every day, before we dressed for the evening to be at our husbands' sides. Maybe others enjoyed it, but I was uncomfortable, sensing a finely tuned ambiance of smoke and mirrors.

I did fly into Paris Sunday morning after a successful tournament for my team. The limo met me at the airport and drove straight to the museum our corporate group was touring. I couldn't go inside without a drink as I was parched from the flight and from being on deck at the heated swimming pool in Bratislava the day before. I walked to a café around the corner and asked the gentleman behind the bar for a bottle of water. I struggled to communicate and the proprietor shooed me out the door with the back of his hand. Welcome to Paris.

By my husband's side, the weekend pleasure trip wasn't much improved over my encounter at the café. We were in one of the most romantic cities in the world, but all we could do was go through the motions of pretending to enjoy ourselves. Happy faces for public viewing turned to silence and minor exchanges behind closed doors.

Peter was the captain of his team that weekend, and I felt like two extra points on his statistics sheet; an appendage that augmented his ego, while he controlled me into being an extension of his will, which registered with me as a round about way for Peter to love himself. I wasn't desired for an emotional connection. I was required for a depiction of completion.

We cruised the Seine one evening as a corporate group. Dinner on board was spectacular. It was after the dessert wine was served that I noticed out the window we were approaching the Eiffel Tower. My friend watched me inform Peter then excuse myself before I walked outside to the deck. Shortly afterward, she came looking for me, followed by her husband. The tower twinkled in the distance, and my nerves were pulsing to the rhythm of the lights. I was frazzled and angry. My husband sat below deck, discussing business while passing by the Eiffel Tower on shore. Just as inattentively over the course of our marriage, he had let *us* pass him by. I felt our marriage slipping away as quickly as the boat was floating down the river. My friend snapped a photo while I stood captivated by the sight of the tower and its sparkling reflection in the water. My face glittered in that snapshot too, with tears.

Chapter 7

Over the years, Peter had climbed the corporate ladder in distinguished fashion and was viewed as one of the company's best and brightest. For him to travel for extended periods of time was not something out of the ordinary. But during the eleven months we lived in Vienna, I had seen my husband less than a month full of days. Peter had tended to one corporate crisis after another around the world, but none of them in Vienna. Unfortunately, the days we did manage to spend in the vicinity of each other were not fond memories.

Peter had been absent so much since our move to Vienna that by spring, he requested the company pay travel expenses for me to spend some time with him in LA. It meant his parents flying to Vienna to watch our children for the week. Even though I didn't like the idea of being so far from them, my sister had agreed to meet me in California and the thought of seeing her lifted my spirits. I flew in for a long weekend and was met at the airport by the husband of Peter's assistant. We laughed and shared our stories of support, all for a good cause as the world needed the company's products.

I was dropped at the hotel that had become a second home to my husband over the past year. Anticipating my arrival, the concierge and his staff welcomed me, offering royal treatment while comfortably settling me into the room. They informed me that I was to be prepared for dinner in just over an hour—not long enough for some desperately needed sleep if I was going to be ready on time. Three hours later, I was still waiting for Peter to pick me up for dinner. Needless to say, the fantasy of a romantic weekend away with my husband was much better than the reality.

My sister joined us the next day. We decided to rent bikes for an afternoon ride on the boardwalk at Venice Beach. It was good to be in her presence, and whenever we had a private moment, the conversation turned from touristy small talk to the intimate details shared between sisters.

The following morning after breakfast, Peter was joking around, sarcastically asking what kind of rough day we had planned while he would be toiling away at work. He teased us about being ladies of leisure. We were all laughing when the telephone rang. It was the same cousin that had visited us over the Christmas holiday in Vienna. Immediately, my husband turned on his best woe-is-me voice for his relative on the phone.

He barely looked our direction as he waved good-bye to us. We left the room, gently closing the door behind.

"What was that all about? He was just joking with us and laughing a second ago!" My sister was stunned by the display of abnormal behavior she had just witnessed.

"Welcome to my world, sis." I stood near the door to listen for a moment. Peter droned on, portraying himself as the sacrificial victim. It was a familiar sound that I resented terribly as martyrdom had long been his chosen procedure for winning people.

Whether it was the head of his company or an aide, a dear family member or an acquaintance, my husband was making sure everyone knew he was at a loss as to how to deal with his private problems. He would thank people for asking or thank them for caring whether they asked or not, embellishing his gratitude for their concern. He wanted those around him to understand the extent of his commitment and responsibility to the company, which was to absolve him from any perceived wrongdoing in failing to make his family a priority. Peter understood the time and distance he spent away from home did not go unnoticed by outsiders. I'd received a beautiful bouquet of flowers from a colleague of his that I had never met. The gentleman wanted to let me know he recognized the hardship I had to deal with in Peter's absence. Even strangers to me understood, but my husband viewed the transparency of our marriage as a public dynamic to manage. It was just another challenge to Peter, rather than a red flag that perhaps he ought to send a bouquet of flowers to his wife now and then as well.

≈≈≈

It was June, nearly a year after our move to Austria. As I put away dishes from my thirty-eighth birthday party, Peter flatly stated, "I'll be leaving Sunday."

I took a deep breath. Sunday was three days away, and he'd just returned a couple days earlier. In spite of the chasm that was growing between us, I still harbored a desire to maximize our freedoms in a new location and take pleasure in life, and possibly even each other, if stress and tensions could be forgotten for a few weeks. It was summer vacation from the school routine. I had anticipated the break would be time for our family to explore Europe together.

"The problems in LA are a mystery. We've got to get them resolved," Peter explained. I knew he needed to get to the bottom of the problems in LA, but even as the reason for another absence was shared, I couldn't help but feel manipulated and second-rate. I'd supported every effort he made for every critical situation that came along; but lately, as much as he tried to make me part of his business team, my heart did not belong to the company like his did.

"I'm staying there until things are resolved," he announced. I was absorbing that much when he added, "Oh, I decided to take a one-bedroom apartment for the summer instead of staying in the hotel. You and the kids can visit anytime you want."

"The summer! It'll take that long? The company wouldn't pay for at least two bedrooms?" I asked.

"I'm sure they would, but I'm just doing my part to cut unnecessary expenses."

"I thought we were going to travel this summer. What happened to that?"

"It's my head on the chopping block for what's happening in LA. Do you understand?"

I was silent.

"Travel all you want! I don't care," Peter spouted as he walked away.

I understood perfectly. Our marriage was a paralyzed union. I was ready to admit that it had been for a long time. Neglect and indifference had replaced nurturing and love. Having known each other since third grade and been married days after we both turned twenty, we'd grown up together. Ill equipped and unprepared for a mutual life, we simply became the familiar and the secure to one another. We muddled through, outwardly successful but privately a disaster.

Problems had come early in the relationship. One counselor suggested I take an assertiveness training course. Naturally, my young husband didn't think that was necessary. Often he'd half-heartedly joke about our vows, reminding me that I promised to love, honor, and *obey*. I had deferred in order to keep peace, losing myself and a voice in the partnership in the process.

I was told to love my husband the way I wanted him to love me. But I had always done that. The more I gave, the less I got. To Peter, what we had *was* love because it met his needs. Often, he would pride himself or brag to his friends about his low-maintenance wife. I made many futile attempts to explain to him that I didn't exist in the marriage. He would tell me I didn't know what I wanted or that I was the kind of girl who was incapable of being happy. Or he would offer a lot of nice words to make me feel better, but eventually, I'd come to understand, the nice words were just insincere rhetoric as there was no action to substantiate them.

Our roles were clearly defined. As had chronically been our pattern, Peter would bury himself in work while I vacantly drifted through days of mothering, carpooling, laundering, cleaning, cooking, shopping, and volunteering. My children's lives were full, and with every activity or accomplishment of theirs, I found worth in my days. Between motherhood, our church, and coaching, a sense of fulfillment was accomplished. But there was an abyss between my husband's disposition and mine that was not likely to change at nearly forty years of age. I'd learned over the past year that a spirit of oneness or a sense of fulfillment from my marriage was idealistic fantasy given the personalities involved. Adversity throughout the years gave way to each of us simply being unable to meet the other's expectations. When the pattern of our lives together revolved around him, a pattern that clearly worked for him, trying to change it was like pulling the rug out from under him. I was as guilty as anyone for allowing it to be that way.

Our bookshelves were full of self-help books and marriage advice. I became addicted to reading everything I could in an effort to stimulate the change we needed. After finishing a particularly helpful book, I suggested he read it as well. He told me he didn't have the luxury of time that I had to invest in the relationship or in reading a book that might improve it. It was one of many indicators that we'd reached a stalemate.

Peter's drug of choice was praise, and I just could not give him all he needed. Even if I had been a good cheerleader, I was just a small part of his world—a part that was not important enough to fulfill the craving he had for admiration. Over the years, he had often been emotionally remote and mentally absent, even when he was physically present. My effort to communicate was rejected continuously. His life was too big and too important to bother with emotional frivolities. The pressures of his job and the scarcity of hours in his day just didn't allow for being burdened by anything that didn't warrant a big return for the investment of his time. Put simply, time spent on me, something he'd already obtained, was not a priority as it gained him nothing.

I was as unimportant to him as the employees he'd let go for one reason or another. He was the kind of man who simply didn't invest in those who disappointed him. He cut them loose. With the clearly apparent impossibilities in our marriage, we were avoiding the inevitable. My husband lived his life, I lived mine; and under the same roof, we just slipped into singleness.

Oh, I decided to take a one-bedroom apartment . . . you and the kids can visit anytime. His words still echoed in my mind. I apathetically contemplated who it was that might join him in that apartment-complex bedroom out from under the watchful eye of hotel staff. I felt a mixture of resentment and relief. He'd won his freedom. At the same time, there would be peace over the summer for the children and myself.

≈≈≈

During that summer, my mom visited with an attorney who was a friend of hers. She wanted to understand my legal rights outside United States jurisdiction. The failure of my marriage was apparent, but it wasn't discussed. Mother only briefly mentioned the conversation to me.

Adam found work in the States that summer. My daughters and I traveled back to Tennessee, which had been home to us for fourteen years before we were transferred to Vienna. Our time was spent in a frenzy of activity with old friends.

In our expatriate orientation classes, we were told that living in a new culture would forever change us. Our counselor described a scenario of round-headed people moving to live in and among square-headed people. Over time, the round heads adapted and began to form hexagons. However, the hexagon heads didn't fit into the society of round heads anymore, nor were they completely a square head. They were just different. Being surrounded by old friends, I fully understood that scenario.

We did visit the one-bedroom apartment in LA to celebrate Peter's birthday. It was close quarters compared to our home in Vienna, but the kids enjoyed the novelty of our time together there. Movie rentals at the apartment complex came from a vending machine that functioned twenty-four hours a day. Because the place was so small and there was no other bedroom, the children ate and slept in front of the television, which glowed night and day. Living in a foreign country, the English channels were primarily news, so they were eager to catch up with the American television shows back home. Between the swimming pool, cable television, and the movie vending machine, the kids were in heaven.

Chapter 8

We didn't call our time apart that summer an official separation. We conveniently allowed his job to be the reason for the distance between us. Having been back together under the same roof with my husband for only two weeks after our summer apart, I longed to return to the peaceful summer we'd had without each other. Tension filled the air and turned our beautiful home into an unpleasant dwelling at best. We had gone from walking on eggshells around each other to living under a cloud of imminent separation. I wondered, what were we teaching our children? Better to be married and miserable than divorced? On the other hand, how could I concern myself with my needs when their needs had been my life's purpose?

Autumn brought my son's senior year. As I snapped the traditional first-day-of-school photo of my three children standing at the door together, the thought struck me—my son would be gone the following fall. Soon, they'd all be graduated and on their own and then what?

Broken and depressed, I wasn't at my best for anyone. I was a festering infection of grief and anger. There was heartache for the marriage and all I knew it would never be, as well as sorrow for our family. But I detested betraying myself into thinking I'd get *extra points* somewhere for suffering and denying my needs in order to meet Peter's. Disgust consumed me, not only for the way I would shrink in the face of his rash cruelty in an attempt to maintain harmony, but for the injustice of his superior temperament in regard to me.

I could no longer bear allowing him to crush my soul into such a tiny space. I despised who I was in his presence. My feelings, my thoughts, and my being had been buried for so long that I finally comprehended the most significant void in my life was *me*! I simply did not exist in the marriage. One choice, so long ago, had rippled into years of emotional slavery. I desired a connection to my life's partner that I knew I would never have with Peter. Regularly, he'd chide the men in my family for being so simple in their desire to be home with their loved ones. Peter was a provider, and beyond that, I had come to expect nothing.

≈≈≈

The diversion of my parents' visit was welcomed relief. I threw myself into preparation and planning. I'd mentally listed places that I wanted them to see. Maybe it was a desire to experience the world with someone emotionally connected to me, someone who would share the wonder of the experience.

During one of Peter's trips to Italy, he mentioned being in Pisa. Like a child who expects a bedtime story full of fantasy, I expected marvel in his voice as he described the tower. When I asked if he'd seen it, he told me he had. I had to drag more comment about it from him, and finally he said, "It's leaning." No wonder, no speculation, just, "It's leaning."

The forecast promised heavenly temperatures as Mom and Dad packed their suitcases to visit us. We'd lived in Vienna just over a year, and the trip was much anticipated by them, as well as by our children and me. I drew up a loose schedule of the sights we could see on the days they were in town. My parents and I also planned a trip, just the three of us, to Lucerne, Switzerland, to meet the family of an exchange student my parents hosted fifteen years earlier. Peter had reluctantly agreed to let me accompany them as it meant he would be solely responsible for the children over the weekend.

As anticipated, the weather conditions were gorgeous while we traipsed around Vienna. Summer was evaporating away. In its place was an invigorating freshness with the feel of newness circulating on the crisp autumn breeze. A years' worth of discoveries were condensed into the week, but making our way around town, the main revelation for me was how edifying living abroad had been. I wanted to give them *all* of what I had taken in over the past year, but in only a handful of days that was not possible. Nevertheless, it was a pleasure introducing them to a different way of life in a new culture while showing them highlights of a city I'd come to think of as unparalleled in its splendor and rich history.

It was time for our Swiss excursion. To relax and converse uninterrupted with my parents, while enjoying a train ride through the majestic scenery of the Alps was a treat. When we arrived, we threw our bags into a waiting taxi at the station. I gave the hotel address to the driver in Deutsch. He looked at me and asked something in French! When I couldn't make him understand where we needed to go, I suggested we go into the hotel lobby so that I could show him on a city map.

Shock registered soon after the map was spread before me. On the map I needed to be looking at, there would have been a river running through the middle of town, but there was no river. My parents and I had been so caught up in conversation that the extra travel time went unnoticed. Dad was out of his element in Europe, especially depending on me as a tour guide. Before we set out, I convinced my father I'd be able to guide our journey by reminding him that parents entrusted their teenagers to me on swim trips. It made a good argument, but in the end, it was just hollow pride. Plunked in Lausanne, hours from where we were supposed to be, I was reduced to the equivalent of a mixed-up teenager who had let her father down. Fortunately, the hotel across the street from the train station had a room available, so we checked in. The concierge was chuckling as he explained we were not the first people to arrive in Lausanne, rather than Lucerne, by mistake. When we woke up, we were looking out over Lake Geneva instead of the Reuss River, but the sunrise view was glorious!

The train ride back to Lucerne in the morning was full of spectacular scenery, which, looking back, turned the embarrassment of the misstep into a nostalgic and amusing memory. It was the first time I could remember being alone with my parents for any length of time. We sat on the train, face-to-face for a few more than ten hours one way and again, ten hours back to Vienna. There was little sleeping going on. They knew I was not happy in my marriage. They didn't tell me to get out. They didn't tell me I had to stay. They just listened and offered their support. "Just be careful, Toots," were my father's final words on the subject. Our time together was everything I'd hoped it would be.

Chapter 2

I had dabbled in modeling over the years and reasoned that outside of the American school, it was employment I might be able to get abroad without a work permit. I sat with the phone book, reading through the list of agencies. There were some familiar establishments in the book, so I found their locations on the map and called to arrange meetings with each team of bookers.

The first agency immediately told me they had no need for a classic look. I thanked them and left. Outside, I remembered a period of time when my dad took up refurbishing "classic" cars. If memory served me correctly, an auto only needed to be thirty-five years old to be a classic, an antique. At thirty-eight, I had just been told I was an antique. In the modeling world, I knew that was true. Skimming the copied list again, I decided on a local agency that would likely have an active character division.

I made my way across the cobblestone streets in heels and wondered about the locals who managed that feat every day. It was a city full of elegantly dressed people that seemed to mirror the stately exteriors of the architecture they moved through. It was fascinating, but at the same time, it felt like home. I loved it.

Andrea, the owner of the local agency I chose, met me at her desk and took a quick look at my portfolio before she welcomed me to her team. She explained there wasn't a lot going on in the business until people had returned to the city from "holiday."

It was October before I heard from her. Andrea called my cell phone when she couldn't reach me at home. She had a casting for me to attend and it was for a television commercial. I thought the odds of landing a job like that were slim as Deutsch was not my mother tongue, but she said I should try anyway. I jotted down the address and phone number of the casting on the back of a business card I grabbed from my purse.

When we hung up, I realized it was the card from the elegant man on the train. A shiver ran through me when I remembered how stunningly handsome he was. I slipped the card back into my purse, making a mental note to transfer it to my portfolio when I got home, as I'd need the address for the casting with me.

Another deadpan telephone conversation with my absent husband and the familiar agitation left me in a state of hyperactive productivity. I needed to spend energy and there was no better way to spend it than cleaning the house. There would be quick results and, afterward, a sense of progress about something. Unlike my inability to communicate with him, I was capable of performing near miracles on a home.

I began cleaning in my husband's corner office, gathering books from the side table and from around the floor surrounding the recliner. The books were replaced systematically; and the shelves, adorned with sentimental memorabilia were dusted. There were mixed emotions as recollections of those proud moments on display came to mind.

I carefully moved the large crystal trophy from its lighted base. The photo on display beside the trophy showed jubilant success as Peter held the crystal high overhead for his admiring fans. He'd only been in the leadership position for a handful of months, yet true to form, he was happy to take credit for the accomplishment. There was a plaque, attached to the image of a soaring eagle that hung between our bookshelves. On it was the motto he had created for his business family and their future. The painting had been his "going away" present from the employees. I'd grown to begrudge the phrase. He had so much energy to create a "family" out of a work environment full of strangers, offering the very best of himself to them and their future. But the effort he spent on his own household was minimal. I wished it were our family, our future that mattered to him.

As I began sorting through the papers on the desk, trying to decipher what lists were outdated and what lists were yet unfinished, I came across a scrap of paper that instantly robbed my energy and left me stunned. In my husband's handwriting was a note he'd written to himself. It read—Call Paige Sullivan. Three words, utterly powerful in portraying the absolute void of connection between my husband of eighteen years and myself. I wanted to believe I was at least in his thoughts the mornings he didn't wake up beside me. I wanted to believe his family was on his mind before he drifted off to sleep at night. Yet there in my hand I held a devastating clue to the position I occupied in his heart and his thoughts. My mind swirled. How many wives does he have? Do husbands really need to write down their wife's first and last name to remember to call them? To call home? To call the mother of their children? Are we really to this point? Just a mechanical and obligatory task he needed to put on a to-do list, without any sense of hunger to be connected to my voice, our children, or our life together. I looked again. No mistake—Call Paige Sullivan. I crumpled it and wept.

My children, the church, social obligations, and a deep commitment to family tradition had prevented me from giving a strong voice to the emptiness in my heart. I was an object to my husband and the realization was profoundly dehumanizing. Peter's wife, just a piece of what completed the image of the man he made public. My marriage to Peter was miserable, but my life did not belong to him. Uncomplicated expectations of simply being loved, even if that meant loving myself enough to make a difference, paved the way now; and like the cobblestone streets of the beautiful city I lived in, each stone, each step would pave the way to better tomorrows. One way or another, things would change because I would make the steps toward change.

The "pumpkin shell" Peter had put me in was disintegrating, but in its collapse came a breath of fresh air. Living in Vienna had awakened me, had breathed life into me. For the first time in years, I could see. I understood what it is to be freed from a cage, and scolded myself for allowing captivity so long.

Chapter 10

"Are we going to make it?" he asked from a hotel somewhere on the other side of the world from his children and me. The question was put to me in a way that made me entirely responsible for the outcome of our dire circumstances.

"I don't know."

Silence.

"I think we should separate."

Silence.

"I want to know if it's possible to miss you because right now, when you're gone, our days are much better than when you are home."

The void on the other end of the conversation made me wonder if we'd lost reception.

"The bad patterns in our marriage need to be broken. Somehow things have got to change . . . it would be nice to have a friend in you, at the least."

"I don't want to be your *friend*! There will be no separation," he argued. "Things happen during separations that can't be undone." I suspected that was true. "If this thing ends, it ends." No discussion. No voice. He added, "I told you once not to talk like this again unless you were serious."

"I'm serious. Something has to change."

"People make their own hell," he taunted. I'd heard that before, and I knew well enough that he wasn't stating a fact; he was threatening to make my life hell if I left him. I wasn't intimidated by it anymore. I was near tears and unable to speak when I heard him say, "I guess that's it. I hope you've measured the cost of your decision." And he hung up.

I sat there feeling utterly hopeless. It had continually been up to me to do the right thing, to keep us together, to make sure my children had what they needed—above all, two parents. Even in his absence, I'd try to make sure the children understood that he was away because he was important to the company and he wanted to make a better life for us. At home though, behind closed doors, I let him know that what he was doing was for *him* and his ego. Being gone 90 percent of the time was certainly not *for* his family. We had enough material wealth. We had more than enough! We just didn't have him.

Peters' position in the company was his identity. His reputation was everything to him. On no account, that I was aware of, did he fail to come through for his superiors. They, along with his subordinates, provided the adulation he needed. His position at home as husband and father had, for the most part, been dutiful obligation. He'd give just enough pep talks to make sure we were all onboard with the direction his career was taking. He'd sit us down for family meetings and tell us about the next opportunity he had to further his career.

"If you can get behind me for just a couple years, I'll be home more after that," he'd say. "They expect me to get things in order if I take this position. They know I can do it. That's why they want me." He'd color the speech and paint such a bright picture that none of us dared speak up against his desires when it came time to "vote." In my imagination was an annoying little dog that wouldn't leave the spread on the picnic table alone. Like my children and I, the little dog jumped and jumped, trying to catch a bite of something savory. But it was Peter who would throw the bone as far as he could in order to reclaim peace for himself. He threw bones for his family often.

Once I had absorbed the finality of what was happening, I called a real estate agent. I didn't know if the apartment I was looking for would be Peter's or mine, but I knew one of us would be taking a different place near our home. While I was looking for an apartment, all the while thinking it might improve our relationship, my husband was consulting with a senior partner of one of the biggest law firms in the world. And . . . he hired her. I remained uninformed.

During his absence, my hunt for a new place proved to be easier than I'd expected. I found a small sixty-square-meter apartment only a few tram stops from the house in the same district of town.

I talked to my daughters about what was happening. They were not oblivious to the fact that their father and I couldn't get along, but like every child, they hoped we'd stay together. Adam was visiting colleges in the States. He told me later that his dad woke him up after our conversation and cried to him, "Your mother is leaving me." He appeared distraught, and in that moment, my son secured a place in his father's life that he had never known before. He became his dad's best friend and confidant.

Adam listened as his father spoke, "She's making the biggest mistake of her life. She'll kill herself before the divorce is final. She'll realize what she has done, and she'll kill herself."

Chapter 11

Amanda played on the middle school soccer team. They were in a tournament in Poland the weekend Peter and Adam were to return to Vienna. I chaperoned the team and took Alexia, my little snuggle bug, so that she could experience Warsaw as well. One of my vivid memories of that entertaining weekend together was watching Amanda, confidently and casually, walk across center field to shake hands with the Russian team after they staged an intimidating entrance. They were dressed in black and appeared a foot taller than our team when they burst onto the field with a startling chant. Amanda's teammates followed her—both teams mixed and mingled, shaking hands before the championship match. My daughter amazed me, so strong and confident. Her team went on to win that game and bring home the first place trophy from the tournament.

The girls and I, along with the team, arrived back in Vienna early in the morning after an overnight train ride. My husband met us at the station. I should say the girls' father met us at the station because the man who picked us up didn't acknowledge me. He had a big grin, long hugs, and promises of gifts waiting for his daughters, but he barely looked my direction. Pretending to be unaware, he let me struggle with the suitcase. He was there to pick up his daughters. I was just more insufferable baggage to him. Exhausted after spending the night on the train with the team, I considered, just for a moment, taking public transportation home. But that would have meant the girls traveling home alone with their father, and I wanted them to see that we would be able to work together where they were concerned. This was the first time they'd seen us together since news of the separation.

At home, the girls and I had showers running before we'd even undressed. It had been a long weekend in less than favorable conditions. I was in the master bedroom, and they were upstairs in their bathroom. Peter told me we were going to sit down and draw up an agreement, first thing. I rushed through my shower.

"Did you find an apartment?" he asked.

"Yes, it's right down the Fifty-two. Just three stops from here. I think you'll like it."

"I don't like anything about this, and I am not going to be the one who moves," he shouted.

"Why should I move? You are almost never here!" I reminded him.

"The company pays the rent for this place, and I am the employee. Do you really want to screw up your son's senior year?"

"But you're never here! We're all accustomed to life without you! I want our children's lives to stay as normal as possible. You going will not be a big change for them."

"If I go, we all go . . . . back to the States. Is that what you want?"

"Of course not." Naturally, I wanted our son to graduate first. My history with Peter had taught me that the situation I was in was explosive, and I desperately wanted to get through our "discussion" about a separation.

"Sit down. We're going to do this now," he ordered. He had pencil and paper in hand, and he'd obviously been counseled or given much thought to what would be written down in our "agreement" because the pages filled quickly.

He pulled up a page and titled his writing, centering the text.

Peter and Paige Sullivan
Marital Dissolution

- *It is Paige's desire to separate, leave the home, and end this marriage against Peter's desire.*

He also stated the date of official separation, adding that bullet point item to the next line. By this point, I was in tears. It was not my desire to end the marriage. But neither was it my desire to stay in it as it was. I let the tears fall freely while Peter continued to write.

With the exception of circumstances beyond his control, it is agreed that the children will finish the school year at Vienna's American International School. The children will primarily reside with their father at their current address.

Peter went on to list what I would receive while we lived in Vienna. His bullet point list included the exact amount I would need, in schillings, to pay rent each month. He also promised the security deposit, stipulating that it should be returned to him upon our departure from the city. He created blank spaces to recognize the amounts it would take to furnish the apartment and support me each month. Neither of us had any idea what those amounts should be. The intention was to forward our rough draft to an attorney who would be given relevant financial information in order to calculate an appropriate monthly spousal support.

Peter continued writing.

> *Paige will maintain her own accounts* (which at the time this was written, did not exist) *and not have access to any of Peter's accounts or vice versa.*

> *Paige will retain access to the primary residence at Peter's discretion. During this time, Paige will:*

> - *buy groceries,*
> - *wash clothes,*
> - *clean the house,*
> - *cook three to four meals weekly, and*
> - *stay at the primary residence to watch the children when Peter travels on business.*

One page had filled and the last item on the list was *all* I needed to hear. With my husband's travel schedule, my children and I would spend our days as usual. There would be nights that he was in town. That would mean the kids and I may not have breakfast together, but it was rare we all sat down to breakfast anyway.

Peter pulled up a new page and kept writing.

> *Child Custody*

> - *Until Alexia graduates from high school, Peter and Paige will live in the same school district. This district will be chosen around Peter's work to allow him to support the family and father his children on a routine day-to-day basis. Both parties wish to make this separation as easy as possible on their children and allow them complete access to both parents. However, should Paige decide to leave the school district all—*

I stopped him there. I couldn't agree to live at his beck and call or else, lose my children. That paragraph was never finished. But the agreement goes on to say,

- *Custody over decision making for the children will be shared fifty-fifty.*
- *Physical presence of the children in each parent's home will be largely at the discretion of the children but on the whole, should be even.*
- *Holidays*
1. *All holidays will be decided by the children and parents with every reasonable effort made to split holiday time evenly.*
2. *Christmas morning will rotate between parents each year.*

Peter continued, off the top of his head, to write what would happen with accumulated physical property, cash, stock, stock options, vested options, unvested options, the 401(k) account, retirement accounts, and incentive investment stock options. Two more pages filled in a matter of minutes as he listed percentages and specified what the calculation for division would be on stock options. Finally, we reached the point of determining support for the children once we were back in the United States. There was no discussion. Peter wrote:

Child Care and Spousal Support upon Return to the United States.

> *The intention is for Paige to be provided for while she develops a means to begin a career. This period will not exceed five years and the amount paid will equal $_____.*

Again, the line was left blank because he knew the amount would need to be determined by someone who knew more about dissolving a marriage than we did. To finalize our "agreement", Peter added the following, verbatim:

- *A COLA adjustment based on CPI will be made each year. If Paige remarries, this support will stop.*
- *If a job change by Peter results in a lower salary, the amounts will be renegotiated.*
- *Peter will provide for the children's college education. As a result, Paige will relinquish all right to Peter's bonuses.*

- *Peter will pay child support to Paige for her custody time. This will amount to $ _____/child and stop as each child leaves her home or turns eighteen.*
- *Health insurance until Paige has established a career with her own benefits.*

Peter handed it to me to look over, and I scratched out *leave the home* in the first line. It was not my desire to leave the home. I wanted to reword the entire top paragraph but didn't dare start fighting about details. *Paige's desire to leave the marriage* was not correct. The marriage was not a healthy relationship. I wanted it to change. The main point for me was that I would be in the home when he traveled, so I regained my composure and agreed; the rough draft was final. It would all be dealt with by professionals, but at least there was a basis in understanding of what to expect.

Eighteen years and as simple as that, we'd come to terms in going our separate ways. There was a feeling of security, as well as relief, in what was drawn up. At the same time, it all felt surreal. The agreement seemed fair; and life would, relatively speaking, remain the same. It appeared the only difference would be an official end to our marriage. I felt disposed of.

That night we slept in separate beds. I took the basement guest room, a space Peter had suggested I move into instead of getting an apartment. But I knew that would change nothing. I'd lived in the basement of his life long enough.

In the middle of the night, I heard him pillaging the house. I quietly stepped out of bed, closed the door to the guest room, and turned the skeleton key to lock the door. It was a relief to be this far in the process, but the situation was volatile. I wasn't safe yet.

My thoughts drifted to another time. Peter had only taken a swing at my face once, but I ducked and missed the punch. He'd been in an accident and was swinging from a temporary wheelchair as I tied his shoes. His "brothers" had arrived a little early for Bible study at our home. Earlier that morning, Peter told me that he wanted to answer the door in his wheelchair, by himself. The doorbell had just rung, but he wasn't ready, and that made him angry. In a fit of frustration, he swung at the nearest thing, which happened to be my head. I excused his behavior, feeling sorry for him and his circumstances.

I didn't get out of bed the next morning until I heard the children's voices in the kitchen. I knew Peter wouldn't do anything to me while they were in the vicinity. It was a relief when he left for work before the kids needed to leave to catch their bus.

Once everyone was out of the house, I wondered around in a daze, just soaking up the warm environment I'd created. It was picture-perfect. Why, dear God, why, couldn't our time spent together in this place have been better? Tears came, and I spent the day mourning. So much history, so much time and energy had been invested in him, in our family. I was actually walking away from our picture-perfect life. There was nothing more to hope for. The illusion would never become my reality.

Chapter 12

In his madness during the night, Peter had taken all my bankcards and credit cards as well as all the cash I had in my wallet, except a groschen, which at that time was less than a penny. In my wallet, I had phone numbers and business cards from friends I'd made around the city. They were all gone—every phone number, every slip of paper—gone. He even took the photos of our children that I had in my wallet! My rings were gone too. He'd given me a beautiful princess-cut diamond anniversary ring, and along with my wedding diamond, they had disappeared. Apparently, I no longer deserved them.

I called home to let my parents know we were separating and asked for the number of my mother's friend who was an attorney. We spoke briefly, and he asked me to fax the agreement Peter had drawn up. I called back after giving him enough time to look over it before we discussed the details. He assured me that with the faxed agreement he held and my circumstances being what they were outside the United States, my rights to custody of the children would not be compromised. He explained the trend in custody was equal time with both parents anyway, and there was little I could do to change that. On paper, the arrangement looked good to him, but he did have a laugh about my list of chores. "What are you? His personal servant?" he asked.

I laughed it off. He offered to fill in some of the blanks pertaining to finances, so I gave him some numbers. It would be little more than a second opinion as Peter was having his attorney sort out what I should receive on a monthly basis as well. All in all, the attorney assured me leaving the home under the circumstances would be no problem.

Throughout the day, I had no idea if securing the apartment would take place. I certainly had no way of making it happen. I was anxious remembering how crazed Peter sounded while he went through my things. A safe place to dissolve the problems in the marriage was definitely in order. Fortunately, Peter did come home with enough cash for the real estate agent but said he didn't have enough time to set up an account for me.

Our separation agreement was drawn up on Sunday. It was Tuesday when I received a key to the new apartment. It was also Tuesday that I received a phone call from our pastors back in the States. What timing! I spent most of the conversation in tears, listening.

"Is there someone else?" asked pastor.

I said no, thinking there had long been someone else. The company. Memories of home flooded my mind as I listened to their voices. I remembered how grounded I felt surrounded by the people in that church. They made up for all that was missing at home. We had been members of the church for fourteen years.

During the announcement inviting the congregation to join our farewell luncheon, our pastor said, "We know God has a plan for them in Vienna. It's an exciting time in their lives and a sad time for those of us who are left behind, so we celebrate their departure with fond memories and time together. Join us in the fellowship hall, and don't worry if you haven't brought a dish." I was holding my youngest daughter, fighting back tears, and trying to look happy while trepidation knocked at my heart. At that time, I couldn't imagine life without our church family.

It was a couple weeks after that conversation that we received a letter written by our pastors instructing us to work things out. They told my husband he needed to hear me and know how I felt. But he did and he didn't care. They suspected I felt that life had passed me by, which wasn't the case at all. I lived an amazing life. But in the vicinity of my husband, I was reduced to an inappreciable and nonessential thing. Shutting down was a natural response to an unnatural marriage dynamic.

When it arrived, Peter read it in his study before he handed it to me. The letter instructed him to stop neglecting his family and do the right thing. He was instructed to repent and ask my forgiveness for the wrong and hurtful words he'd used to demean me. There were many directives for him, yet when he handed the letter back to me, scrawled in his handwriting across the top of the page was, "It is your decision. The ball is in your court." I was supposed to do the right thing by myself. I wanted to cry, knowing even if I started shouting I wouldn't be heard. How could I be expected to stay for more mental and emotional abuse? I trusted my will to live fully—mentally, spiritually, and emotionally whole. There would be no more mistreatment. There was no way to make anyone understand that the man I lived with was not the man they knew.

≈≈≈

It was Wednesday before I had enough moved to the new apartment to sleep in it. Using plastic grocery bags, I hauled odds and ends from home, barely enough to be comfortable, because I didn't want gaping holes left in the décor of our home. The foyer became a foyer again. Wicker sunroom furniture that I could carry became my living room by day. By night, the cushions were thrown onto the floor for a bed. The first couple nights were lit by camp light and candles as I was without electricity. From twenty-two rooms down to two rooms, Mrs. Corporate Vice President yesterday and overnight I'd become a pauper.

Peter wanted to see the space he was paying for, so he came to look through the apartment. It wasn't settled before he arrived. There were grocery bags full of clothing, personal items, toiletries, and odds and ends from the kitchen still lining the hallway. In Austria, every plastic bag from the grocery store is paid for, and they are reused to go to the market until the day they become a trash bag. The cost is minimal.

Peter was looking around, making disapproving comments of the apartment, as he felt it was a better place than necessary. His concern as he took in the new living arrangement was that it not cost him too much. Perhaps one room would have been better than two, especially if two rooms meant I'd be comfortable.

"Where did you get those?" he asked in an accusatory tone, pointing to the bags piled haphazardly along the wall.

"What?" I didn't understand what he was referring to, as the plastic sacks were full of personal things and *extras* from the kitchen that would never be missed or even noticed.

"The bags!" he barked.

I wasn't sure when Peter became aware of the fact that plastic bags were paid for at the grocery store, but obviously, he'd been informed.

"I used the sacks from the house," I answered.

"Well, I want them back," he ordered.

The plastic bags from the grocery store were worth more to him than me. Peter never said to me in a rational frame of mind, "I want to go to counseling with you. I'll do whatever I need to do to work this out. I care more about this family than anything." Not once did I hear him say, "I want you back."

There were tears and more tears over my failed marriage. Yet in the calm of a new space, I felt hope . . . and there was peace. Blessed peace.

Chapter 13

"Everybody can see what an evil bitch you are."

I was back at home to pick up more household items that I needed, but after being badgered about moving half of a double mirror set, I eventually decided that I was not going to beg. I continued to pack more of my clothes. I noticed the photos of Peter and myself, as a couple, had been taken off the walls and removed from the shelves—a symbolic killing. I hoped he hadn't destroyed the photos. He had also turned off the answering machine the day I left. I hadn't been able to tell the children goodnight, even by voice message when no one picked up, so I turned it back on. He was following me.

"I can't believe you're leaving me," he whined. "I wish I could go back eighteen years and make a better choice."

"A better choice? I've given you the best of myself!"

He huffed, "If that was your best, you're a sorry excuse."

Completely closed and unresponsive, in silence, I continued to gather my things. He softened.

"Can't you see?" he asked. "No one is ever going to love you like I do."

His words didn't sway me. I knew I'd been a good wife. I knew I was a good mother. I knew who I was. There was no reason to cower or react to his roller coaster of tactics and emotions. If I was never "loved" again, it would be fine with me.

Before I left, he threatened me again. "We can get this divorce in the Dominican Republic. You better not contact any attorneys! And I want your new coat and those diamond earrings back!"

His instability was frightening.

≈≈≈

It was a few days after we returned from Poland that Alexia said to me, "I know Dad's trying to take us away from you."

"What? Why would you say that, Alexia?"

"Girls, I've got presents at home for you!" She was mimicking her dad word for word from the scene at the train station. Peter almost never bought the kids' gifts on his business travels, so Alexia astutely perceived his gesture as manipulation.

"Well, sweetie, we're not going to let that happen." I held her, trying to reassure her that things were not going to change much. I explained there would be mornings we wouldn't get to have breakfast together, but living without arguments was better than living without breakfast together every now and then.

She held me tight. I thought she was testing my commitment to her. I didn't comprehend that her assessment was a warning.

≈≈≈

It was Saturday morning. I had gone to the house to see the kids and do some laundry for everyone. It was only six days after we'd drawn up the separation agreement. I had finished my chores, and Peter and I were standing outside the gate of our home.

"I need your keys." Peter was nonchalant as he made his demand.

"What?" I asked.

"I said I need your keys."

Given the turn of events the past week, handing over my keys, even if he told me it was to copy them, felt wrong. "No, that was not part of the agreement. I need a key to come and go."

"You will be here when I say you can be here."

"There's no way to run this house without a key!" I argued.

"My parents arrive tomorrow. They'll need your key."

It was the first time he mentioned they were coming. Bewildered and exasperated, I pointedly said, "They can use yours. I'm not giving you my key."

He lunged for the key ring in my hand. I held on as long as I could, but he twisted my wrist, then my arm until I screamed in pain and let go. We were a spectacle in the street. As soon as he had what he wanted, he disappeared behind the gate. It was a gate that locked automatically and was part of what made the residence a fortress.

As I walked to the tram, not wanting to create a bigger scene for the neighbors, I convinced myself that once his parents had gone home, he'd calm down. I'd spent eighteen years trying to see the best in my husband, on every occasion putting a positive spin on the things he did. I wanted to believe I could trust him. Regardless, an attorney was drawing up the handwritten agreement we'd worked out. Soon it would be firm legal ground to stand on.

Two weeks later, I expected his parents to be leaving soon. Peter had not found the time to set up a bank account for me but, instead, would give me enough money to eat for a day or two. My dad sent a check to get me on my feet. We had incurred some travel expenses while they were visiting that Peter complained about, so the check served two purposes. Dad didn't want to owe my husband a dime and, unspoken, he wasn't going to have a daughter in a foreign country without funds—especially under the circumstances. He wanted me to have a choice. Being forced back to an emotionally abusive husband "hat in hand" didn't compute.

Peter and his father had finally taken the time to bring me a couple twin mattresses from a spare room at our home. They made a much better bed thrown on the floor than the wicker furniture cushions I was using.

"I'll try to get an account set up for you this week too," said my husband.

"Dad sent me a check for the travel expenses you complained about. I used it to set up an account for myself. I'll give you the account number." I could tell my father-in-law knew that his son holding out on setting up an account for me was wrong, but he said nothing. He sat there like a puppet beside his son, the puppet master.

"Ran to Daddy, did you?" Peter quipped.

With his parents' intervention in our separation, he had nerve to throw that in my face. But he knew that. He'd relentlessly known how to "push my buttons." He was looking for a reaction that he could fault. I turned and walked away.

It was good to be able to tell Peter and his father that my dad was looking out for me. I wanted them to know I had the support of my family because, together, they looked at me so smug and self-righteous. It was as if they were thinking what I really needed was to be committed to a mental hospital. The thought of ending a bad marriage seemed beyond their comprehension. To them, I was out of order. I was a menace to Peter's honor, his esteem, and the reputation he had created as being a family man.

I communicated with my parents by asking the toy store below my apartment if I could pay them to use their fax machine. It wasn't the greatest method, as my parents didn't have a private fax; but for the time being, it was the best way to communicate with them because I didn't have money to set up a hard line into the new apartment, and my cell phone didn't work internationally.

Peter decided that while his parents were in our home, my children could see me at the little apartment two nights a week and weekends whenever *they* wanted. The children had no clothes, no desks to study on, and no space to call their own within those two rooms. They had nothing in the apartment. Their lives were supposed to stay the same, in their own bedrooms after school with Peter traveling and tending his career and me at home with them when he was out of town. Things were not going to change much! It wasn't supposed to be this way.

My heart was breaking. The children and I had seen so little of each other since his parents' arrival. To be separated from each other when we most needed to be together was just a cruel trick. I was angry and frustrated Peter hadn't told me the day we drew up our agreement that his parents were coming for a visit. I reasoned he needed their support, and he might need to put some distance between us, but to eliminate me from my children's lives was just callous. His parents considered themselves the emotional crutch of the entire family. Whenever a crisis arose—whether it was aunt, uncle, or cousin—they were there; so their involvement in our troubled situation wasn't an unusual appearance for them. But I couldn't be around them and just pretend we were still a big, happy family. I consoled myself, knowing the children had a diversion for the time being and kept my distance, biding my time until they left.

Chapter 14

News of the separation spread fast throughout our network of friends at school and the company.

"Are you crazy? Stay for the lifestyle if nothing else!" my friend instructed over dinner one night. She was also in a less-than-happy marriage but had settled for "good enough." She and her husband each appeared to live separate lives, but their marriage suited both of them. We'd become close through our children's activities, as all three of her children were the same ages as mine.

"There has got to be more to life than a lifestyle. I think I could handle the absences, I just can't handle the way he acts when he *is* home."

She was listening intently, wanting to understand, so I continued.

"One weekend in October, he was home for literally thirty-six hours. It was barely enough time for me to launder and iron some of the shirts he wanted in his suitcase again. The time was spent listening to him rant and rave about every mistake he could find. Most of the fault he finds is with me, but Adam also gets it, and this time Amanda was being yelled at as well. He's frustrated with work, supposedly, but he comes home and takes it out on his family!"

"That's natural," she said. "When stress levels are high, there has to be a release."

"It has gone on too long, Carol. I just can't be the thing he kicks around after a bad day at work anymore. He'll come down on me for some minor detail and act like nothing ever happened thirty minutes later. He praises me one minute then blasts me for something else the next. I'm so frustrated! He leaves town and my children are left with an irritated mother. I hate it. Every family vacation we've taken is full of ugly memories. This has gone on for years! I've built layers of walls around myself for protection when he's around. I'm dying inside those walls. It's not good for him, and it's not good for me. It's really not good for our kids. When he left to catch his flight, Amanda collapsed into my arms in tears and said, 'Why does he act that way? He's home one day, and it's awful. Why?' What am I supposed to say to her? I don't want to lie to them anymore. I don't want to protect him by excusing his bad behavior any longer. I'm finished doing that. Heaven forbid I teach my daughters to accept this kind of treatment from their own husbands! I've told Peter something has to change. One way or the other, our marriage is going to change."

"What if it doesn't?"

"Then it doesn't." Pausing, I admitted, "It's not looking so promising. He wants the illusion he's created for his public persona in place, but beyond that, he doesn't want to spend any energy being a husband to me. He'll bring me a cup of coffee in the morning, say, 'I love you' then ignore me the rest of the day. Literally! He has no time for me when he's around. His priorities are his job and the company first. He says God is first, but from my viewpoint that claim is for exhibition. He's very good at 'talking the talk,' but God is a self-improvement program *for* him. It's not part of who he is. Next, are his parents and his children, followed by his friends and social obligations. On Peter's hierarchy of priorities, I'm just something that can be taken for granted when he's not viewing me as a duty. That marriage certificate? It's just a ticket to treat me any way he wants. I am yelled at more than I am spoken to. If he could just be kind . . ." I was getting very emotional, fighting back the tears as we were in a public place.

There was pity and understanding on her face, but she was saddened by my resolve to change our family's status. It was such a pretty picture for the people around us.

"Are his parents still in town?" she asked.

"They're here." I shook my head. "If he didn't have them to depend on, my children and I would have a normal life right now. I'm sure Peter would still be making more time for them, but he should have done that a long time ago. His parents are so . . . I don't know where to begin."

"When I met his mother, she seemed very domineering."

"She is. She's very controlling, but the things she does are so sugarcoated no one sees it as manipulative. The kids repeat her stories to me . . . she's reliving every memory she has of them. At first I thought she was just being sentimental because it's a difficult time. I guess I wanted to believe she was helping them remember the good times. But now I think it's more like she's trying to make them believe she's the one they've had to depend on all along. Like, their whole life, she's been there. My children have memories of things that never happened—good and bad! Along with Peter, they're exaggerating every mistake I ever made with the children. Peter's neglect, his cruelty, his absence in our lives is completely forgotten."

"I imagine Peter is feeling very guilty," she surmised.

Nodding in agreement, I said, "I think so too, where the children are concerned. But I think he feels no guilt whatsoever about the role he's played in all this as *husband*. He doesn't want this marriage any more than I do at this point. But it's much better for him to be the victim and win everyone's sympathy. To take his guilt over being absent from the children and turn it into a rescue, of sorts, is complicating our lives in a way I never expected. He was rarely home this past year."

"We all know how much you're on your own, Paige."

"Life was supposed to be the same for the children and me." I was getting emotional again.

We paid our bill and walked outside where I let my pent-up tears flow. "It's just so frustrating with his parents here. But the kids love having their grandparents here. It protects them from reality, I guess. I feel as though the whole agreement Peter and I had about me being the one to move was just a masterminded trick to remove me from his life, my home . . . just a way to remove me from my children's lives so he can punish me. But I can't go back. I just can't go back . . . to . . ."

She held me while I cried. "Well, his parents can't stay forever. You may be giving Peter too much credit. He's just angry, Paige. You left him. That's not an easy thing for a man's ego. Just give it time."

I shuddered at the thought of his parents staying indefinitely and forced myself to be positive. We stood in silence, and she rubbed my back, letting me cry it out.

Carol reached to give me a hug goodnight. "Thanks for explaining this, Paige. I just wasn't aware your marriage was in trouble." She shook her head and said, "You've got more courage than most people I know."

I didn't confirm or deny that sentiment but did feel strength I never knew I had.

"Hopefully one day, my children will understand that courage."

Taking a deep breath and trying to shake off the emotion consuming me, I changed the subject. "Come for basketball Thursday night. Joe's got me up there playing with the guys. It'd be fun to have a female on the court with me."

"Basketball is really not my thing, but I may walk up to give you some moral support." She lived a short walk from the school.

"Thanks for the visit. I enjoyed the company for dinner."

"Me too. I'll do what I can to see you Thursday," she said.

It was good to have someone to talk to, but reliving it all left my nerves raw. It was hours before I felt calm. Whenever I opened up about what was happening, I began to shake at the core, and it left me feeling utterly spent.

Carol didn't make it to the basketball game, but I had fun playing regardless. Adam's chemistry teacher invited me to join the group at the beginning of the school year, but I'd just recently begun to play because I hadn't had access to our home gym. He offered a ride home after the game.

"It's a little out of your way, Joe. I'm in the Fourteenth District."

"No problem. I'm happy to take you. It's raining!"

The conversation was small talk about basketball as we drove through the woods that isolated the school from most of the town, but then he asked, "Is what I hear about the separation true?"

"It's true."

"How are you doing?"

"Horrible, so far. Peter is extremely angry right now, and he flew his parents over to keep from needing me in the house. With them here, I've had little opportunity to be with the kids." I barely let the topic go below the surface, as my friendship with Joe had not grown to any depth.

"I've been through a divorce. It's not easy for anyone, but for what it's worth, your son seems to be doing fine. He had the highest grade on the last test."

"Super. Thanks, Joe."

We were nearing my apartment. "If you need anything, I mean anything, I'm just a phone call away. If you need a car, whatever, don't hesitate to call me, okay?"

"Thanks for being such a good friend," I said.

Before I got out, he gave me a peck on the cheek and watched from his car to make sure I was safely inside the building before he drove off. I realized the kiss wasn't the traditional kiss on the right cheek, kiss on the left cheek. We were two Americans living in a foreign country, and that kiss on the cheek was a kiss goodnight. Inside my apartment, I could still feel his hand on my back. I thought of him as a friend, but it was evident he hoped for more. For a moment, I was a little angry that a man would make a move that quickly after learning I'd just separated. I received a note from him in the mail that week. In a part of it, he wrote about the moonlight streaming through the raindrops on his windows as he drove home that night. It was then I knew I couldn't play basketball with the guys again.

Chapter 15

I moved quickly along the rock wall to the gate of our home when I saw our car approaching. I was thankful I wouldn't have to wait to be buzzed inside. I could just walk in, before or after the car. Normally, we parked in our courtyard; but that day, Peter didn't use the remote to open the car gate, which would have allowed me entry to our grounds. Instead, he pulled haphazardly into a parking space beside a neighboring apartment building. He burst from the car and raced across the street with a vainglorious look on his face, key in hand, arriving at the pedestrian gate before me.

As he searched for the correct key, he said, "You are not needed here today."

Dismissed like a failed employee, I could barely absorb the words. "We had an agreement! My children need to see me, and I need to see them. This is ridiculous. Your parents need to go home." My voice began to quiver, and I tried to steel my tears.

"You have no right to tell me who may or may not be in *my* home!"

My home? The house I made a home was suddenly *his*. During my parents' visit, he tried to present himself as the helpful husband when he inadvertently asked where the forks belonged as he unloaded the dishwasher. We'd lived there over a year, and he honestly didn't know where the forks belonged. Some of his antics were laughable absurdity. But the games he played now were anything but entertaining. The home he'd spent so little time in, the home that days ago belonged to us, the home my children lived in now belonged solely to him. Already, he'd been home longer than at any other time since we'd moved to Vienna the previous year.

During the month, there had been a number of days go by that I had not seen the children at all. On Thanksgiving, they were to come to my place. But Peter decided their dinner wouldn't be until five o'clock, and after they finished, it would be too late for them to join me for a little feast at my place. They didn't want to come earlier because they wouldn't be hungry for their grandmother's meal, which had, without explanation, taken priority over my dinner. When I knew I wouldn't see them, I decided to get out and enjoy the festive lights of our little district and do some window-shopping for Christmas ideas. On my way home from the metro that night, I passed the house around 5:30 p.m. and the formal dining room was dark. I stood in the street staring at the house, wondering if my children missed me as much as I missed them. I debated ringing the bell to wish them a happy Thanksgiving but decided not to interrupt and present myself as a nuisance. I remembered Thanksgiving the year before and the years before that in our home in the States. They were elaborate affairs.

Our baby son's birth date and death date had also come and gone, and I didn't get to see the children either of those days. Those were two days I thanked heaven for the healthy children I had and days that Peter knew were difficult.

We stood on opposite sides of the front gate. Peter stood in the courtyard holding the door half-closed and I stood outside, opposite him blocking my entry. It was the doorway to my children, my routine, my life, and my identity. Keeper of the keys, *Saint* Peter was in complete control.

"This is still the marital residence," I reminded him. "My children live here."

"You should have thought about that before you left them."

"I did not leave my children! I left you," I yelled.

The children were due home from school at any moment, and I believed the need to be in *our* routine was long overdue. I'd given Peter and his parents more than enough time together. He was an *adult* who still needed his mother, yet his own children were being denied their mother. It was beyond me how incapable he was of considering that his children might need both of their parents more than he did as a full-grown man.

"We agreed that I would be here until you came home from work, which lately, on average, has been around eleven o'clock at night . . . if you're in town! Adjusting to this separation was not going to be that difficult because you're hardly ever here anyway! You're making this so much more traumatic for our kids than it needs to be."

"I did not leave this family."

It was impossible to deal with Peter's ability to create his own reality. He honestly believed that tending his career was the same as being present to nurture his family.

"What are you doing here in the middle of the day?" I asked him.

"Demands at work have let up! I'll come home when I want."

"We had an agreement!" I yelled, unable to control my anger any longer.

"Don't talk to me about agreements!" He was seething. "You agreed to be married to me." The solid iron door slammed in my face, but the most prevalent barrier to my children was my husband. I couldn't stop the tears. I waited at the gate to see the children after they got off the bus, but when they saw that I was an emotional wreck . . . well, spending time with someone like that isn't very fun.

"Will you come see me tomorrow?" I asked.

Amanda answered, "It's hard, Mom. You don't have anything I need over there to do research."

Alexia chimed in, agreeing. "Yah, and I need to work on my science fair project. Tamarra might come over after school."

"I can help you with your science project. Ask your sister about her blue ribbon," I said, feigning a smile and looking for affirmation from Amanda. "Really, I'm not bad at helping with science projects."

"But Mom . . . . it's Tamarra. I want to make a good impression," she said, with a little roll of her eyes. My ten-year-old daughter needed to impress her rich friend with our villa. My little apartment, in contrast, was a shameful way for even my children to see me living.

"Just let me know, okay? I understand." It was all I could say. I wasn't their favorite person for leaving their dad, and every minute with them, I walked on eggshells. The dynamics rendered me powerless.

It was exasperating to be shut out of the house at a time when Peter and I *most* needed to be reaffirming the children of our love and devotion to them. We had not been allowed to establish healthy family dynamics for our separation. Walking to the tram, the words of my husband haunted me—*People make their own hell.* He knew exactly how to execute my punishment—take my children, my identity, and my life's purpose. He'd unrelentingly known how to make me conform. Only now, he confirmed to me the character that had driven the marriage to a breaking point. I was resolute in never returning to him.

Chapter 16

It was mid-December, nearly six weeks after their arrival, before my in-laws left our home. They needed to get their Christmas shopping finished as well as prepare for the holidays as the entire family planned to gather in their home. Finally, I was in my home with my children, as I should have been since the first day of the separation. Without his parents around, my husband was out every night, as usual. But now, I was thankful for the time his absence afforded me with my children. Business meetings, he explained. He still played me for a fool.

The first night on our own, Peter walked in the door around eleven o'clock with a grocery bag that he set on our hallway dresser. Inside the bag was part of a bottle of wine as well as some cheese and crackers. He'd gone downstairs, so I followed him. When I found him, he was standing in front of the washing machine with his shirt off, starting a load of laundry. I asked him about the wine and cheese. He said some of the executives who left the hotel that morning didn't want to leave it in the room and let it go to waste. No upper exec I knew cared about wasting a couple dollars' worth of food. They had so many other things on their minds they didn't give such things a second thought. I nodded . . . right.

During the year before our separation, my husband had begun carrying condoms in his briefcase. This was made clear to me one evening when we didn't have what we needed in our nightstand, so he ran to his briefcase! Trying to calm me, he explained it was just in case I ever flew with him and wanted to join the Mile High club. One night after making love, he pulled me close and said, "Tell me your real name." We'd been married eighteen years, so his question incited a frenzy of emotion. Shock, fueled by anger caused me to build another layer of protection around myself. He blamed that blunder on just being jet-lagged and disoriented. Memory or fantasy—wrong woman or wrong bed—he was definitely confused. The next day when I tried to discuss the incident further, he just defended himself by saying, "Why should I pay for hamburger when I can have steak at home?" It was Peter's version of a compliment, but I resented the inference that as his wife, I was only a little better than a prostitute since we were both being referred to as a piece of meat.

My memory flashed to four of us driving down a rather shady street while my parents visited Vienna. On three of the four corners of the intersection we were stopped at stood prostitutes looking for work. It was that moment Peter decided to break the silence in the car and ask my father, who had speculated in oil, if he'd done any drilling lately. Deliberately cavalier, the comment stunned me.

I had no proof of anything but knew all I needed to know. Trust was something of the past. Peter had badgered me and spent hours accusing me of having had an affair with Heath the previous year. I surmised he was projecting his antics as my own since he thought of us as being one-minded. Now he was walking in the door with wine and cheese, anxiously stripping his shirt to launder before I could see him and still lying to me about whom he'd been with. I observed him in detached amusement.

Chapter 17

Andrea called to give me the address for another casting call. I pulled out my book and added her instructions for the next day. The elegant man's card that I used to jot down Andrea's last set of instructions a couple months earlier was still inside my portfolio. I noticed the street was the same as the one Andrea had just given me, which meant I would be near the gallery he had mentioned. Not knowing if he would remember who I was, I sent him a text message reminding him we met on the U4 metro and I was with my parents. I asked if the invitation to view his gallery was still open since I would be in that area the next day. It seemed I had barely pushed the Send button before my phone rang. He was calling!

My heart began pounding as I heard that deep, beautiful voice again.

"You want to see my gallery? Or do you want to see me?"

His directness caught me off guard. "Could I meet you at your gallery tomorrow afternoon?" I emphasized *you* to let him know I was interested in more than his art.

"I'm not going to be in that part of town tomorrow, but I could meet you for a coffee the day after tomorrow." His English seemed to have improved a little, but it was still broken.

"Well, sure, that sounds great." I was giddy yet trying to keep my voice calm.

"Perfect. Where would you like to meet?" he asked.

Panic! My knowledge of the coffee houses in Vienna was limited as that was one part of the culture I had not embraced. My social life still revolved around the society of the American School and the American Women's Club in town.

"How about the Dommayer?" I suggested. It was a coffee house we were introduced to on our house-hunting trip—just across the bridge near home and in my neighborhood shopping area that bordered the entrance to the Schönbrunn. I enjoyed it for the ambiance.

"Yes! This is one of my favorite cafes. What time would you like to meet?"

"Is one o'clock all right?"

"One o'clock will be fine. I'll see you then."

"See you then," I said.

When I clicked off, my head whirled with thoughts. What was I doing? Technically, I was still married. I had told Peter on more than one occasion that I never wanted to act like he did. But it was a sign. So *many* signs! I was to be on the street of his gallery the next day. It occurred to me that the card I was holding had been in my purse with all my other cards and numbers. I moved it into my portfolio because I'd used it to jot down information I needed for casting. I couldn't remember dates, but I was sure it was only days before my husband emptied my purse, taking friends' phone numbers, business cards, credit cards, my children's photos, and cash. It was definitely a sign. I choose one of his favorite cafes. All signs. Not to mention the odds of ever having met him on the metro. Delighted, I tried to calm down as I searched my makeshift closet to figure out what I would wear to meet him. My heart was still pounding in my throat.

It seemed minutes from the time we spoke on the phone to the time I was walking into the Dommayer to meet him. He had arrived before I did and was settled into a corner booth facing the front door, reading a newspaper as he waited. I stepped inside, glanced right, glanced left, and there he was. He stood when he recognized me, and I beamed at the sight of him again. Our eyes stayed locked as I walked across the restaurant to join him. He extended his hand and traditionally kissed both of my cheeks, our hands lingering in each other for a moment.

We spoke at the same time. I said, "Hello." "How are you?" he asked me. Then nervous laughter.

He tried again. "How are you?"

My eyes were still locked on his, and I smiled. "I am very happy to be here with you."

"Good. Shall we sit? Do you like this table?"

"It's fine. Perfect."

He put away his newspaper, and we made ourselves comfortable. "So!" he said. "How was Switzerland?"

I was surprised he remembered my parents and I traveled to Switzerland, as it seemed ages ago to me. "Wonderful! Lucerne is one of my favorite places in the world." I told him about our train trip to Lausanne that turned out to be a memorable mishap. I was so comfortable in his presence I added what a joy it was to be with my parents over the long weekend and that I couldn't remember ever being alone with them.

"I'm glad you enjoyed your time. There are no accidents in life. It's very important to enjoy the life."

The life. I'd never heard it worded that way. English wasn't his mother tongue, I reasoned, considering his words.

"So tell me about yourself," he said.

This guy didn't mess around. But neither did I. Before I met him that day, I decided he would know everything there was to know about me from the get-go. No secrets. I took a deep breath and began.

"Well, I'm from the United States and moved to Vienna a year and a half ago. I work at the American International School part-time, but my family and I are here as expats with a big pharmaceutical company."

I paused. He didn't flinch, so I continued.

"I have been married for eighteen years, and I have three children . . ."

"What!" he shouted. "You're married?" Heads turned in the restaurant as his rich vocals carried like the booming voice of God speaking from the heavens. All eyes were on us when he added, even louder, "You have three children?"

I froze under the gaze of faces around the restaurant staring at us, and he then realized our conversation might be a little too lively. He raised his eyebrows and leaned closer to me. Speaking quietly, he asked, "You have three children?"

"Yes, I have three children. My oldest is seventeen, a boy named Adam, and my youngest daughter, Alexia, is ten. I have a thirteen-year-old daughter as well, and her name is Amanda."

"But . . . but," he stammered. Finally he asked the question he really wanted to know. "How old are you?"

"I'm thirty-eight. How old are you?" I was curious too.

"I can't believe it! We're nearly the same age. I'm thirty-nine. I thought you were younger."

"Well, I'll take that as a compliment." He wasn't laughing but asked me to continue, so I did.

"My husband and I are recently separated. He is married to his work. I am the one who left and live in a small place near my home. My children stayed in the big house because we wanted their lives to stay the same. It has been a difficult time." I let it tumble out in edited bits and pieces.

Two hours passed, and it felt like ten minutes. I learned that he too was separated from his wife of six years. Both of us had divorce looming in our future, but he and his wife had parted on friendly terms a couple years earlier. I didn't push for details but learned she was eighteen years older than him, and he had no children of his own.

The conversation transcended our circumstances; the experience transcended our histories. It was a soul-directed event. I was sure that in two hours, Viktor knew me better than my husband had known me in two decades. In fact, when he reiterated some of what I told him to make sure he understood, he was able to pinpoint feelings I hadn't voiced. He was speaking in generalities, so I asked him if he studied psychology.

"I studied economics. I just enjoy helping people," he explained.

"Lucky for me," I said as I winked. Then in all seriousness, I added, "I appreciate it."

It was time for us to part. He paid the check before we walked outside together. Standing on the sidewalk, he slowly and very deliberately kissed both of my cheeks as he held my shoulders. I reached up with open palms to his elbows; our eyes locked after we kissed good-bye.

"I'll call you," he said.

"I look forward to hearing from you," I answered, and with that, we released each other.

I hoped what he said was true, but there were no guarantees. I had to walk across the bridge to catch my bus, and as I looked down to the rushing water below, I felt sure I could fly. Euphoric! Exhilarated! Alive! I was smiling to heaven in gratitude, soaring as I made my way home to a new life.

Chapter 18

I felt more alive than I could ever remember feeling. Viktor and I were inseparable, spending every spare moment we could together. We sat for hours in the café, just talking, sharing our stories from the past as well as our dreams for the future.

"Eighteen years isn't eighteen months or eighteen days," he stated. "Are you sure the marriage will end?"

"I'm certain. The price I paid to please him is just too high. I didn't exist in our marriage. Life was about him. No matter how much I accomplished, nothing earned his respect. The character he's shown since the separation is something I cannot ever accept. It's very complicated to explain."

"When the children want you to return, what will you do?"

I decided to inform him of what I was dealing with. My children had become increasingly indifferent toward me and, at times, almost hostile.

"The children think I'm wrong for leaving. They are being used by their father to punish me, but they don't know that. They think God is on their dad's side because we've taught them marriage is sacred and divorce is wrong."

I listened to myself explain concepts that had been spoon-fed to me at one time—concepts I swallowed and tried to live by. I continued, "My children are enjoying the place they have in their father's life right now because he's been absent a lot while they were growing up. Since the separation, they have been his priority. He stopped traveling and started coming home in the middle of the afternoon."

Viktor nodded that he understood and continued to listen.

"My husband tells me that I'll need to go to university, then I'll be working, whereas he is established and can give the children all they need. He brought in his parents, so the children have had their grandparents in Vienna since the separation too. There is tension between my in-laws and me, as well as between Peter and me. While my in-laws were here, my children were telling me to stay away."

Viktor just listened as my words tumbled quickly. Tears began to well in my eyes. "My key was taken away. I see my children at school. Amanda is on the swim team, so I see her at practice. His parents have finally gone back to the United States though, so things are a little more normal for the children and me. But somehow I feel as locked out of their hearts, as I am locked out of the house."

"Okay, slow down," he said, patting my arm resting on the table. "You don't get to see your children every day?"

Embarrassed, I said, "No, not while their grandparents were in town." What might he think of a woman who didn't spend time with her children every day?

He took a moment to absorb what I said. "Well, in time they'll stop being angry. I'm sure they will realize the marriage wasn't working. They're old enough to understand these things."

I breathed a sigh, "I hope so."

≈≈≈

With my in-laws back in the States, Peter was dependant on me again to care for our children. For a couple weeks before Christmas, we functioned as a family in crisis, but nonetheless, as a family unit without Peter's parents' running interference. We were making the adjustments we should have been able to make six weeks earlier.

Without a key, I didn't have access to the home during the day, but I met my children after school for routine activities. I took Amanda to piano lessons and had Alexia with me between school and swim practice every day. At practice, she would walk the pool deck with me and cheer for her older sister or entertain herself reading. We were together in the evenings while their father worked and was out at night. It was business as usual. For me, other than afternoons with Viktor, life felt normal again.

It was good to be in familiar surroundings with access to a telephone. I had a chance to speak with my mother's friend, the attorney. He advised me to move half of our cash on hand to an account of my own. He was actually surprised I hadn't done that yet. Immediately, I called our little credit union in the town we moved from and reached a familiar voice. I explained I wanted our account divided in half—and to leave the extra penny in Peter's account. I faxed an application for an account of my own with my new address and waited for a faxed confirmation of the transfer. Eventually, it came through. I breathed a sigh of relief—until I looked closer at the numbers. There was a digit missing. What should have been a six-figure balance was a low five-figure balance.

I called back. "Hi, Dawn. Thank you for setting up my account. I think there's been a mistake though. There should be six figures."

There was silence on the other end of the line. It was the quiet of someone who didn't want to deliver bad news. She calmly and very slowly said, "Honey, he moved all the money into an account in his name on the first of November."

I was speechless. All I could manage to say was, "What!"

She explained again and added that it looked like the transaction took place at corporate headquarters. Then she asked, "Should I move the rest of what's here into your account?"

"No, let him keep it. I don't ever want to be accused of having the intention of taking more than my half."

We hung up, and I sat staring at an amount that summed up less than five percent of the cash we had on hand. It was just days earlier that I asked for a copy of our balance. My mother-in-law gave me the October statement explaining she hadn't received a current version. I felt defeated, afraid for the coming months, angry that I hadn't been informed and utterly betrayed by his parents. They told me on so many occasions what a wonderful *daughter* I was, how thankful they were to have me in their family, and how blessed my children were to have me as their mom.

I realized it was before Peter's phone call asking me "Are we going to make it?" that he had rearranged our bank accounts and moved the bulk of cash on hand into an account in his name alone. It was the same trip that he hired his attorney. Neither of these things was mentioned to me at that time.

Dawn informed me there would be a debit card arriving in the mail. At least I'd be able to withdraw schillings from an ATM if Peter *forgot* to fund my account. There was enough for necessities, but the total wasn't enough to last beyond the six or seven months we would be living in Vienna.

The next night back at the house, I used the opportunity to call the bank holding our stock to inquire about a loan. "Who better to loan me money than the people who could see what we were worth?" I reasoned. The gentleman I spoke with kindly let me know that without a "real" job, I was not going to be able to secure a loan. He looked through our assets and said, "Your name is on all the uncertificated stock. Would you like to sell some of it?"

"Can I do that on my own?" I asked.

"Of course," he answered. I saw light at the end of the tunnel again.

"How much do we have?" I asked.

He informed me how many shares we held and what the market value was that day. It happened to be the same amount as half of the cash would have been, so I ordered a sale.

"Sell all of it," I said.

"Every certificate?" he asked.

"Every certificate. Every share. Sell all of it."

He let me know the check would be in the mail. I relaxed knowing the days of being at Peter's mercy for financial support would not continue. Alexia and I made Christmas cookies that night. I cut Amanda's hair. Adam and I had time to talk a little, just like old times. He and Suzanna broke up over the weekend, and he needed some reassurance. It amazed me how normal my children acted with me outside Peter and their grandparents' presence. I was pleased with the normalcy of the evening.

When Peter returned home that night, I told him I needed my key back.

"No way! This isn't your home."

"This is the marital residence. I could move back in."

"I'll post someone at the door to prevent that from happening," he guaranteed me. As he turned to walk to the bedroom, he was mumbling something about consequences.

With that, I decided to hire a local attorney to get my key back—access to my children.

Chapter 12

Each time I prepared to meet Viktor, my problems seemed to disappear. It was pure delight to be near him. I could not pride myself in being a good judge of character, but with Viktor, there was no need to second-guess myself. I basked in his goodness and savored every conversation we had. There was great comfort in knowing he was a phone call away. Even though he knew the generalities of my circumstances, I didn't involve him in the details of the daily craziness. Our time together was sacred, and I needed the infusion of his stability and strength. He was a bright light in those dark days.

We met at the usual café near his gallery. Very little of our time together was spent on small talk. Curious to know more, he asked, "How much was your husband absent?"

"The past year has been the worst. He's been trying to solve a problem in LA. When he returns to us, he's got to catch up with the events taking place here, so even when he's in town, I don't see much of him. He comes home very late." I rocked my flat hand to indicate *more or less*. "For every ten days, I might see him one or two days. He tries to be home at least every other weekend."

He looked shocked, but nodded in understanding. "That's not good. Relationships need daily care, just like a plant that needs water and sunlight every day."

"We are not unique in the corporate world. Many executives divide their time between travel and home."

"Where is the quality of life in that? Where is the love in that? It's so mechanical, so unfeeling. There is no substitute for love."

I must have looked confused because he continued. "You neglect your soul without love. Your entire human existence is less than it should be."

The gulf I'd known between commitment and love came to light. "I never heard it worded that way."

"But it's true. Love has incredible power to give quality to your life. We must create love in our life, but if our priority is business, then we neglect our soul."

There was a depth of emotion in his profoundly simple words that helped me comprehend that he lived the life he spoke of. I felt my soul healing in his presence.

After taking a moment to absorb his thoughts, I revealed a little more. "The problem was not *just* his absence, it's the way he treated me when he was home that became unbearable. I am just a replaceable part of his life. He can literally pay someone for the things I do for him and there seems to be no more emotional connection to me than there is to the people he hires for service."

He drew me closer and gave me a kiss that let me know I was not insignificant.

"Are you seeing your children?" he asked.

"Yes, we've been together like we should have been all along." I told him about cookies and haircuts and breakups.

There was tenderness expressed on his face as he listened and said, "Good. Good. They need you. You're half of their identity."

Again, his words cut to the core of the matter. "I never thought of it that way, but of course, that's true. I'm the parent they've had every day." I was quiet a moment, remembering. "Peter told me several times that he was jealous of my time with the children, just envious of our relationship." I was shaking my head. "He chose how to spend his time, but he resented me for being so close to the kids."

"I'd like to meet your husband. I think I could help him."

I raised my eyebrows in disbelief. I was sure if anyone could help him, it was Viktor, but introducing them to each other was out of the question.

"I don't understand how someone can be so disconnected from his children."

"You mean because he's been absent so much?"

"No, I mean emotionally disconnected from his children. Keeping you away from them is destructive to them, and in the end, he is destructive to himself."

My spirit lightened when I knew he understood that I was good to my children. "Thank you," I whispered.

His face was full of compassion. Even though he hadn't told me he loved me, I felt it. We'd known each other a handful of days in comparison to the time I'd spent married, but I felt more content with him than I'd ever felt at any time in my life. We were comfortable sitting together in silence, just holding one another, our eyes locked in unspoken communication.

In the air of his expression was an appeal that I center myself on his ideals and put past offenses behind me. He was holding me tight. I felt an overwhelming sense of protection, as though I could have released the entirety of my being *into* him so that *he* could make everything better. He was extraordinarily generous with his emotional energy and intuitive to the point I suspected he knew me better than I knew myself.

He held my hand up and put his palm against mine. "Look how similar our hands are," he said. They were nearly identical in shape and size, only mine looked a little more worn. "We have artists' hands."

"I've been told I have pianist's hands, but never artistic hands."

"Music *is* art," he said. Our eyes were fixed on the likeness in our hands. "It's important to have similarities with your partner."

He was looking right through me again. I was sure he could see my heart dance at hearing him use the word *partner*.

Chapter 20

My cell phone rang while I was attending Amanda's piano recital. It was Alexia calling to tell me she felt bad and wanted to spend the night with me. I promised her I'd be there to pick her up as soon as her sister was finished. Peter was also in attendance. During the break we decided to wait in the restaurant, walking side by side as we made our way through the corridors, civil in public.

While we waited on our meal I told Peter I planned to go back to the States to start divorce proceedings inside U.S. jurisdiction. Our plan from the beginning was to be in Vienna for two years then return to the States where Adam would begin college and Amanda would be a freshman in a new high school. The Austrian attorney I spoke with about getting a key explained that anything decided in the Austrian courts could be modified if one day we were both back in the States. Recognizing that Peter hadn't embraced living abroad, I couldn't hope he'd settle in Vienna and be happy to abide by Austrian law. The attorney said he could help me get a key back to be with my children, but in light of the size of the estate, there was just too much at stake to divorce outside the United States under the highly charged circumstances. Peter had proven he couldn't be trusted as the agreement we had drawn up was ignored from the start; therefore, it was highly likely he would seek modification if he felt an Austrian judgment was unsatisfactory. I had decided proceeding with the divorce in Austria would be a waste of time, energy, and money.

"How do you think you're going to go back to the United States to file for divorce?" Peter asked. "You need money to set up residence in the States. You need money to hire an attorney!" His tone was haughty.

"I sold stock," I announced.

"You sold what stock?" he asked, superiority in his voice.

"You took all but a fraction of our cash and moved it into an account in your name." I let him know I'd discovered his secret. "I am not going to be at your mercy while this divorce takes place, so I sold our uncertificated stock, which totals half of our cash account. You should have just divided the cash with me."

When what I had told him registered, he screamed, "You sold *my* stock?"

"I sold *our* stock." I argued in defensive reaction. "And for a good price!"

It didn't matter to him the restaurant was full. He was center stage in his own show.

"You fucking bitch! I'll sue the bank. I'm not signing over any checks to you. You stupid bitch!" he screamed, a little louder. "You are such a dumb-ass. You have just created a war," he said, poking his finger into my chest as hard as he could. "This stock sale is all you'll ever get from me. You stupid fucking bitch!"

As I explained to him the financial limbo I'd been in, he was calling me a fucking bitch, over and over as I spoke. When I mentioned possibly starting a business, he laughed and told me I wasn't capable. Then he laughed a little louder, mocking me with a contorted smirk on his face, and said, "You're actually going to have to work!"

I remembered him telling me how he couldn't have accomplished what he did in his career without my support. The many times he'd told me how he depended on me, now forgotten. Trying to impress on me that none of what I'd accomplished as his helpmate was work, made me grieve for the years I'd invested in him.

He kicked away from the table, throwing a little bit of money to cover only part of his meal.

"From now on, you talk to my attorney," he seethed and stomped off.

I stayed through my daughter's performance, uncomfortable in public after the scene in the restaurant. Immediately afterward, I made my way to our youngest daughter by taxi. Before I arrived at home to pick her up, Peter had informed our son that I'd sold stock and ruined our family's financial future. Adam was angry with me for jeopardizing his college education. Nothing could have been further from the truth, but the things Peter relayed to my children were not even questioned. If their father told them something, it was perceived to be truthful, correct and "honest" of him to be informing them of my "bad behavior." Shortly after I arrived home, Peter arrived and ordered me, "Out!"

I told him I was taking Alexia with me because she wasn't feeling well. She overheard the argument going on, and stoic as ever, she said, "It's okay, Mom. I'll stay here." She intuitively knew that wanting to be with me that night would cause greater problems.

Our daughter was riveted to the stairs, not even coming close enough for me to reach her for a hug. My mind flashed back to the day she was born. Only moments after I'd given birth, *Peter* said, "I don't ever want to do this again!" Even childbirth was about him. I tried to ignore him, wondering what it was he thought he'd just done that might compare to delivering a nearly eight-pound baby. I brushed it off, determined not to let my killjoy husband destroy the most blessed of moments. He proceeded to give me a hundred-dollar bill that day—my keepsake for the birth of our daughter. He had earmarked the gift for *skinny clothes*.

Watching Alexia petrified on the stairs, I wanted so badly to just tune Peter out and take my daughter into my arms, just as I had the day she was born. Keeping her close after delivery, united eye-to-eye and heart-to-heart, her presence was my cocoon. Unfortunately, ten years later, there was no way to avoid or disregard Peter's mental state at that moment. Still eye-to-eye and heart-to-heart, we were petrified by a noxious force of adversity that undermined the very essence of our mother-child bond. Only now, there was no longer a cocoon for the two of us to escape to.

At six o'clock the next morning, my phone rang. I was told to be at the house in an hour because Alexia was still sick. Peter informed me he'd leave cab money, while he ordered me to take my daughter to the doctor as though I was hired help and not my child's mother. When I arrived, our friendly neighborhood doctor was examining her on the sofa. I suspected Peter didn't want to leave money for me or give me the ability to say to anyone that I'd taken Alexia to the doctor. Allowing me to do more for her that day than he might have been able to was not in keeping with a contrived competition he was insistent on winning.

When the doctor left and Peter had gone to work, Alexia asked me to fix her computer speakers, so I did. She let me know she was angry with me for destroying our family finances.

"Alexia, our family's financial future is fine. We have more money than we'll ever need."

When I tried to explain that what I had done was being exaggerated, she became defensive of her father. My little snuggle bug didn't want to snuggle in the rocking chair watching movies like she normally did when she was sick. I tackled some laundry as well as the dishes in the sink, then cleaned closets and made some chicken noodle soup with apple strudel to go with it for dessert.

The next morning I was called to be at the house by 7:15 a.m. I still had to ring the bell at the gate, before someone inside would buzz me into my own home. I waited . . . and waited, repeatedly knocking snow off my boots to kill time. Finally, the gate door buzzed. I pushed through against the snow accumulated on the other side.

Peter met me at the end of the hallway and yelled, "Take your shoes off when you come into my home!"

"Ass," I murmured as I slipped my shoes off, resentful of having to dance to his tune in order to be with my children. A few minutes later, he went outside to the car and came back in with his shoes on, tracking mud all over the white tile in the sunroom, across the hardwood floor, and down the beautiful carpet runner I had specially selected for the hallway.

Ignoring his provocation, I changed the subject. "I need your help with Christmas shopping."

Exploding, Peter yelled, "I've got too much going on at work right now to be home *early* so you can go Christmas shopping!" There it was—*I've got too much going on at work right now*—the old familiar catchphrase reserved just for me.

Before he left, he calmed down and told me he'd be home by four o'clock. He'd been coming home around that time since the separation, so I had no reason to believe he wouldn't, or couldn't, that day as well.

I worked around the house all day and decided, since Adam was home that afternoon, that I would leave a few minutes before Peter arrived to avoid another scene in front of the children. They didn't need to witness more of what occurred that morning. At 7:30 p.m., I called home to say goodnight and ask Peter what time he wanted me at the house in the morning. I was shocked and upset to learn he still wasn't home. I spoke with each of the children and told them goodnight. When I called Peter's cell phone, he was enjoying a spirited meal at a restaurant. I realized exactly what he'd intended for me that morning when he told me he'd be home by four o'clock. I was supposed to have spent my evening waiting on him, getting angry, and wondering how I would manage to Christmas shop.

I imagined in his weekend conversation with his parents he would complain about my irresponsibility. The thought of the events of that evening being misconstrued infuriated me, but I realized I needed to accept that Peter would disparage me from then on out. There was no changing him. All I could do was try to improve my reaction.

Peter told me he'd bring Alexia to the apartment the next morning at 7:15 a.m. By seven, the scent of her favorite breakfast muffins baking in the oven wafted through my apartment. It was seven twenty when he called to inform me he'd decided to take the morning off work. I ate blueberry muffins by myself. Alexia arrived at noon.

We played Labyrinth while a movie she'd brought along played in the background. The plan was to meet Amanda at home, so Alexia and I started early enough to have a hot chocolate at the bakery on the corner before we took the short tram ride. We arrived at the house before Amanda and therefore, had to wait outside in December weather because I still had no key. Finally, Amanda appeared, opened the gate, and then discovered *she* had no key to the house. I suggested we go to the apartment, but Alexia was cold and didn't want to walk back up to the tram. I didn't have enough money in my wallet for a taxi, so we looked for unlocked doors and windows. I felt like a prowler, looked like a prowler, in front of my daughters who watched me find a way into *their* home. We found a basement door that Peter forgot to lock.

That evening I put together outfits for their suitcases that I planned to pack the next day. They were flying, without me, to the States for Christmas. I would be on a later flight. As I cleaned up after dinner, the doorbell rang. It was our landlady dropping a Christmas present for us. While she was occupied with the girls, I quickly bagged a bottle of champagne on hand for her Christmas present.

When Peter arrived, I wanted to discuss travel arrangements with him. On the return flight, I was going to be traveling with our son and I wanted to have my credit card in the event of an emergency. Living abroad, I'd learned that not every card worked in every machine every time. It was better to have two options. I had a new debit card, but no credit card.

"I hate it for you," he said, his tone bitter with insincerity as his comment gushed with sarcasm. He didn't hate anything he was doing to me. "You created your situation. You have not been honorable. You've brought all this on yourself." It was sanctimonious and hypocritical rhetoric that rolled off his tongue as though it was a recorded message playing from the depths of his mind.

When I asked if the draft of our agreement was back from his attorney, he told me to stop harassing him. "Just get out of my house! Leave, now!" His voice was hostile.

Again, my mind swirled with his words as I trekked to my apartment. *Not honorable? Harassing?* All I did was leave him, and there was good reason for that decision. But I had stopped obeying him, so I brought his ironclad judgment and self-righteous vindication upon myself.

Adam flew to the States the next day for the Christmas holiday. After school, I met Amanda and Alexia at home where I'd planned to pack them for their trip. However, the laundry room door was locked so I had no access to suitcases. I presumed Peter wanted to pack the girls himself as they looked on—endearing himself to them in some way while earning the right to complain about me to anyone who would listen.

I discovered many other doors in the house were locked. My daughters watched my dismay at being locked out of rooms. I wondered what they thought or what their dad told them about why he might be locking the rooms in the house. Even if he said nothing to them, he was clearly sending them the message that I could not be trusted. I had taken nothing that didn't belong to me or hadn't been discussed before it was moved from the home. I concluded that trying to figure out what might have provoked a reaction like locking all the doors was a futile waste of time. From my perspective, there was little rhyme or reason to Peter's modus operandi.

I rationalized, thinking he was trying to make me the "bad guy" so that his loss wasn't such a big deal. He was cunning and quick to make sure my children, my in-laws, and our friends viewed me as the sinful, untrustworthy, vile creature he needed to envision. I had agreed to be married to him, and from his perspective, departing from that promise made me immoral and deranged. He'd spent his career manipulating his environment and coercing his way to the top. The tricks he used in our home were child's play in comparison to the brilliance it took to mastermind and control his corporate operation.

The girls and I didn't have long to be together that night as their dad *did* come home relatively early to pack their suitcases. I asked them to walk with me to the door where I hugged them good-bye and gave them big kisses. It was the first time they were making an international flight without me.

"I'll see you at Nanny and Papa's," I told them.

They were not willing to linger as being with me threatened the newfound place they elicited in their father's life. It was a place that demanded absolute loyalty. Heaven forbid they anger their father and receive the same treatment they watched me receive.

"See you there, Mom." And they dashed off to their father.

My flight was out on Christmas Eve. Peter's assistant made our travel arrangements using our frequent-flyer miles. I was told the date for my flight was my own fault because I didn't tell him I wanted to be with my family during the holidays. He pretended to assume that I wanted to spend the Christmas holiday in Vienna alone.

Chapter 21

It was three days before Christmas. My family had all flown to the States. Viktor was comfortable with that knowledge and agreed to come to my apartment for a little Christmas celebration of our own. I was nervous as I prepared dinner. For the first time, he would see where I lived—how I lived.

My little apartment had a short hallway that I filled with my photography. In the corner of the entrance was the stereo as well as a rocking chair. Through the door to the kitchen and living area was a view of the neighborhood through large picture windows. I had put up a Christmas tree that overwhelmed the room from the corner. The living room was a diagonal arrangement of white wicker furniture around a small television set, with a built-in VCR, that had the sole purpose of playing videos. There was no reception since I had not connected to cable. To the right was a small L-shaped kitchen with a folding table under the window. At the end of the hallway was a small bedroom with a couple mattresses on the floor. On one wall I set up a laundry organizer that served as my closet. There were sweaters stacked on a top shelf and shoes lined up on the floor underneath the hanging clothes, all of which was exposed to the room. I used the box from the Christmas tree and wrapped it in fabric to form a headboard of sorts. The apartment was temporary, but it was serene.

I got into my bathrobe and slathered a moisturizing mask on my face after dinner was nearly prepared. Minutes later, the doorbell rang. It was Viktor—an hour early! I buzzed him in and ran to the bathroom to remove the facemask. I didn't have time to dress before I needed to be back at the door, so I met him looking a wreck in my bathrobe.

"You're early!"

"No problem," he said as he kissed me hello and turned sideways to get all of the bags he was carrying in through the doorway.

I laughed at the sight of him. He looked as though he'd just come from Christmas shopping and bought for everyone on his list in one day.

"This is my place! Welcome," I said, all smiles as I motioned him to move down the hallway.

He looked around, showing interest in my photography hanging on the walls. "Very nice," he said. "Where can I put these?" he asked, raising his arms strung with shopping bags.

"The Christmas tree is around the corner. You can just put them under there for now."

He gasped as he rounded the wall and spotted the tree. "*That* is beautiful."

"Thank you."

"Did you do this yourself?" he asked, gently lowering his packages without taking his gaze off the tree.

"Of course," I answered. "I'm going to shower quickly and dress. I'll be right back."

When I returned, he was still looking at the tree. "This is the most beautiful tree I've ever seen," he said.

"Ever?" I asked, hugging him close. It had been days since we'd seen each other. I was starved for his touch.

"Tell me about the last couple days," he said.

"Are you sure?" I asked.

"Of course."

"Can it wait?" I asked.

"Of course." He was grinning at me. "It smells good. What did you prepare?"

"Have a seat. I'll show you."

I served hot mulled cider while we visited and shared the events of our last few days. The oven timer rang, signaling the stuffed Cornish hens I'd prepared were ready. There were fresh green beans topped with bacon and slivered almonds for a side dish. Earlier I prepared potato-dough dinner rolls, and for dessert, there was pumpkin pie with homemade whipped cream waiting in the refrigerator. I found the stuffing mix and canned pumpkin at the British grocery store in town, so it was an easy meal to put together.

As we ate, we shared Christmas memories from childhood. He explained his Orthodox Christmas traditions, which were completely different than what I explained of a typical Christmas for our family. He marveled at the effort my family made to ensure that on Christmas Eve at my grandparents' home we heard "reindeer" on the roof. One of my uncles would excuse himself to use the restroom, when in actuality, he was climbing up on top of the house to stomp around the roof, giving his best effort to sound like a team of reindeer attached to a sleigh. It was marvelous for the imagination of a child. But every time, before all of us could get outside, Santa had sailed into the sky, and the only thing we'd hear was a distant, "Ho, Ho, Ho!"

"Speaking of Santa, will you open your gifts now?" he asked.

"Sure!" I felt a little unnerved at hearing *gifts*—plural. I bought him a pair of black leather gloves. One gift.

He chose one of the packages from under the tree and handed it to me. Followed by another, and another. Before the evening was over, I had opened every package he carried in the door. I was overwhelmed. There were art books, jewelry, perfume, teas, and sweets. All of it was strewn about with wrapping paper dappling the room in festivity. Viktor was thrilled with the gloves I had chosen for him, graciously relieving my embarrassment at having selected a single gift for him.

There was one small package waiting to be opened. Viktor let me know it was significant in its importance. My curiosity was piqued. He handed it to me and watched every detail of my reaction as I opened an Anne Geddes journal he had chosen. On the cover was a black-and-white photo of strong arms holding a sleeping infant.

There were tears of joy in my eyes and a smile on my face. He didn't have children of his own, but I knew he wanted a family. Naturally, I had entertained the hope of being part of his future. But standing there with confirmation he wanted me, I was overcome with emotion, and my love for him could not be contained. He wanted me to be part of his life in spite of my circumstances. I knew I was blessed beyond measure.

≈≈≈

We had dessert, pumpkin pie with whipped cream, and coffee for breakfast.

"I don't know this taste. What do you call it? Punkin' pie?"

"Pumpkin. You've never eaten pumpkin pie? Do you like it?"

"It's delicious. I love it."

Smiling at his satisfaction, I was, indeed, coming back to life. My pumpkin shell existence was a thing of the past.

We spent the day traveling to a romantic little village outside of Vienna. As we walked through softly falling snow under Christmas lights that might have been the city's hand-me-downs, we held each other close. It was picturesque with narrow streets that wound in curves to the lay of the land. Every home was decorated in white lights, most with doors that nearly opened onto the street. We passed a silver shop where a cute little cream and sugar set caught my eye. Viktor noticed and insisted we step inside. He wanted me to have it as a keepsake of our day.

"You know my wife and I have been separated for over two years now," he said as we waited for our hot chocolate in the café.

I nodded, listening.

"In that time, I have dated many different women. I know in five minutes with them if I want to invite them for a second coffee. I am an experienced man, and I know what characteristics I want in a partner. I know you are who I have been looking for."

Like cream and sugar, I knew we belonged together too. I was smiling, nodding, and fighting back tears of joy.

"I am with you," he said.

His words stirred me. "And I am with you," I replied. Our embrace was long, and the kiss seemed endless. We slept at my apartment again that night. By the time I needed to catch my flight, we had been together forty hours straight. The time had been too short for both of us.

Chapter 22

With no credit card to secure a hotel room, I flew into Washington DC where my layover was overnight. I missed Viktor beside me in bed and wondered about how fast our relationship was progressing. I felt like I'd known him all my life though. Our connection was powerful and too good to be amiss. In my short experience with Viktor, I felt more married to him than I was to Peter. I had spent a lifetime in performance trying to gain Peter's love, attention, and respect. I sensed that with Viktor, he respected himself enough to just respect his choice for a partner. He was so grounded and stable. I loved that his thought processes were so healthy. I was sure there would not be a need to earn his attention, respect, love, or a rightful place in his life. I had become part of him just like he had become part of me.

I woke up on Christmas morning alone in a hotel near the airport. There wasn't a lot of time to think about it given that I needed to catch the early shuttle in order to make my flight. Puddle jumping from DC to the plains of the Midwest, I arrived early afternoon.

My parents stood waiting at the little airport in their hometown. It was so good to be home! It was the first time in ten years that our entire family would be together for Christmas. The children joined us for part of the day and opened some of their gifts from my parents. But they had arrived with the gift to beat all in hand—a new Play Station II from their dad. Adam brought his new MP3 player. My daughters brought their new jewelry and clothes. It had been a very extravagant Christmas for them from their father.

"Dad just thought we'd been through a rough year with you leaving," explained Adam.

The lexis of dialogue my children were being exposed to again in their grandparents' home surfaced in Adam's words.

"You know I didn't leave *you*, right? You know your dad and I agreed I would be with you every day. Our routine was supposed to be like it always was, except for the mornings he was in town."

"I don't want to be in the middle of this, Mom. Just stop," he said.

Trying to defend myself was impossible. In doing so, I implied Peter was to blame. The children would get very defensive of him because they viewed him as the victim. So I had no choice but to hold my tongue while Peter rewarded my children for rejecting me.

Adam and I arrived back in Vienna just in time for New Year's Eve. He paid the hotel bill at our layover. At home, I prepared for the group he was bringing home that night after the festivities. The stores were closed, so it was a creative cooking effort to manage with what was on hand. I made chicken noodle soup and rolls.

Viktor was relieved to hear from me. In a mindless split-second decision before I left Vienna, I had decided not to take my cell phone because it didn't make international calls, but I only programmed Viktor's number into my phone and had never taken time to memorize it. Before I left, he asked when I would return. I got out my ticket and read from it the date of departure without taking time to write down the airline or flight number. But the date of departure is not the day of arrival when traveling *to* Europe—you lose a day. I tried calling an operator for his number from the pay phone, but she found no listing. Among the mistake of giving him the wrong return date, along with the misfortune of our flights being cancelled, he waited for two days without word from me.

Needless to say, he had begun to wonder if my children had talked me into being with their father again. Or perhaps my family or Peter's family or even Peter himself had talked me into returning to him. He was relieved to see me, yet a little upset that I didn't take his phone number to call him in the event of an emergency. That kind of chaotic thinking was foreign to Viktor. I was annoyed with myself too.

I told him about my time in the States, explaining how supportive my family had been.

"I told my mom about us," I added.

"You did?" He was surprised.

"I did. I told her everything."

"What did she say?"

"First, she asked, 'Are you talking about that elegant man at the train station?' I confirmed it was you." He looked pleased.

"Your mother liked me," he said. "The way she watched me at Hietzing when I walked down the stairs made me think she must have been a client at my boutique."

"She told me that you were watching me!" I said.

"Your mother had a lot to do with us getting together."

I was smiling while I relayed the conversation I had with my mother. Viktor was pleased to know my family was aware of us. I went on to let him know I had a chance to sit up with my brother one night just visiting and reminiscing. My brother knew Peter well, but I hadn't elaborated about my marriage during conversations with him that had become too infrequent over the years. I explained to Viktor that my brother was one of my best friends through school. He liked that my relationships with my siblings were good.

Then there was the trip to my in-laws' home to pick up the children one day. Peter's family didn't move from their seats when I stepped inside to greet everyone. I might as well have been one of America's most wanted criminals standing in that living room. Having done nothing to any of the cousins or my sister-in-law, I had to remind myself that blood is, indeed, thicker than water. I was the same person I'd always been; I'd just mustered enough courage to change an unhealthy relationship, and they didn't like it.

"They didn't talk to you?" he asked.

"No, there was zero conversation. A few of them managed to murmur hello, but there was no talking, only glaring. I asked if the kids were ready and they were. We left."

"So you didn't spend any time with your husband?"

"No, none."

The days I described were different from what Viktor had imagined. I scolded him a bit for imagining so incorrectly but understood that if I had been in his shoes, my thoughts might have been similar. Actually, my thoughts would probably have been worse. His experience with people was far beyond mine, and it had taught him to trust his instincts about a person's character. He trusted me. But he wasn't happy with the turn of events he'd been subjected to in the days ahead of my homecoming. I hated having put him through the agony of uncertainty for two days.

I needed to go back to the house to prepare for the party Adam was having that night. But lying in bed, wrapped in Viktor's arms while we visited that afternoon, I was home.

≈≈≈

Functioning on very little sleep, the next day was a low for my son and me. I offered to help him prepare his college applications because they needed to be mailed the next day.

"Get off my back!" he yelled at me as he scratched the pen in his fist across our computer desk. He was angry and scowling at me.

"Son, I am finished being treated badly. I will not be yelled at by you!" His behavior matched the example he'd witnessed in regard to how I should be dealt with. I left to buy groceries for the group invited to the house for movies that night. Junk food at the gas station was all I could find as that was the only place open. I dropped the food back at the house before I met Viktor for a walk at the Schönbrunn. I hoped Adam would be responsible for his college applications since I was not being given the opportunity to help him.

Viktor was on a side path near the entrance, clandestinely waiting. Feeling lighter than air at the sight of him, I was giggling that he pretended we needed to hide. We hugged each other a long time under the trees. We'd just come through our first test the day before. Each of us reassured the other that "all was well" in our embrace. He had been to his mother's for their New Year's Day dinner, and I could smell her cooking in his clothes. I realized I was hungry. None of the cold cuts I bought for the kids that evening looked very appetizing. So when Viktor asked me which direction I'd like to walk, I suggested we head toward some apple strudel. He thought the restaurants were open, and he needed coffee too. So we strolled to a small glass sided café on the grounds of the Schönbrunn. I didn't even know it existed until that day, but it was charming, complete with live classical piano music playing in the background.

Back at the house, my thoughts were on Viktor. I wanted my children to know him but understood it was too soon to introduce new people. For the time being, I would live a double life. After I welcomed the group of Adam's friends for movie night, I went back to my apartment. My attorney, who happened to be single and attractive, invited me to a party, but I declined.

The next afternoon, Adam and I went to Donauzentrum, a large shopping mall, to exchange the ring I gave him for Christmas. We also needed to buy groceries for the meal Adam wanted to cook for his girlfriend that evening. I'd taught him over the years how to handle himself in the kitchen and he was eager to show his girlfriend his culinary expertise. We set the table before leaving the house. It looked very romantic with tall candles and a centerpiece atop the table runner. I folded the napkins into the water glasses like a lily—the finishing touch. I remembered folding napkins for staff dinners seating twenty or more. Menu planning and stocking the bar began in the weeks ahead of the event. Preparation began days in advance as I created centerpieces, organized table décor, and found the appropriate serving pieces. The day of, as well as the day before, I managed the cooking. Once I had an assistant, and another time the desserts were flown in from a bakery in Chicago, but other than that, I literally did *all* the cooking. Now, preparing the table for two was a snap. Adam and I visited all day while we were out and it felt like old times. The adversity we'd encountered the day before was brushed aside. We talked about everything going on in his world. Alone with him, I had my buddy back.

The girls wanted to nap and unpack after their flight back to Vienna. The nap transpired into sixteen hours of much needed sleep. It was the following day before they joined me at my apartment. We had Mexican food, played Scattergories, and made brownies. Amanda had a cold. Even at thirteen, she snuggled under the blanket to rest in my arms that night. It was so good to have them back in Vienna and even better to have them with me. But it was short-lived, as I didn't see them again until school started.

Peter was perfectly able to work from the home office that I created for him the first month we arrived in Vienna. His job was such that working from home was usually a viable option. Centered in his study was a mahogany desk designed to accommodate Peter's needs. A friend brought the idea I'd conceived to fruition, custom-building the desk to suit my husband. It was opened in the front so he could stretch his legs. The height of the work surface was taller than average because of his long torso. I'd put a lot of thought into making it an inviting home office for him, as the workplace I'd built for him in our previous home was a disappointment to him.

Five years earlier, I'd decided that for his birthday I would remodel the room near our bedroom that was supposed to have been a nursery. I purchased the lumber, sanded and prepared it, and was ready to cut and secure it into a wall of shelves I'd envisioned. I remembered calling my dad for instructions on how to start the circular saw.

"You realize that thing will take off fingers?" he asked.

"That, I do know, Dad. Just tell me where the safety might be."

He explained, and I shared my plans. When it was time to lift the bookcase up against the wall, it took two of my neighbors, along with my son, to manage it. The bookshelves surrounded the window and nearly reached our twelve-foot-high ceilings. The result was gratifying as our collection of books filled the shelves, budding into a small library that became the focal point of the room.

I refurbished the desk he used in college by hemming fabric that matched the curtains to the size of the desktop, before adding a new piece of glass to create a smooth work surface. Purchases included a new phone and fax machine, and beyond that, the expenses were minimal. When it was time to surprise him on his birthday, I opened the door to a room that had been closed for months. It was inviting with all of his keepsakes on display. I was proud of the room's transformation and what I had accomplished without Peter's knowledge.

Our children watched, eager to see their father's reaction, as they'd been a part of the project by keeping the secret and helping me when necessary. After Peter shared a few pleasantries of being surprised, he turned a hard-hearted and authoritative glare toward me and asked, "Why didn't you buy one of Woody's chairs to replace this?" He was tipping the chair that fit his desk. My bubble burst. Woody handcrafted every piece, and his chairs were pricey. In deciding on a budget for the project, I concluded that spending money on a handcrafted chair would have been an expenditure that upset Peter. I was sure he would have been displeased with the price tag. In the end, it didn't matter. He spent little time in that space, and almost no time in the study I had created for him in Vienna—until the past two months, anyway.

Chapter 23

The first day back to school after the holiday break I took public transportation to the school and rode home on the bus in order to spend some extra time with all three of my children. We picked up pizza on the way home because they were starving. It was getting late when I said goodnight to them and left for my apartment. I'd learned that leaving before Peter arrived was better for all.

The hearing for the return of my key was to take place that week. I met my attorney several times to prepare and learned one afternoon that Peter put stop-pays on the stock checks I had received. He wanted my signature when the new checks arrived at his address. I had fallen for that trick before, signing dividend checks because he promised half for my account; but of course, I never received half of any dividends. The "light at the end of the tunnel" for me, the sale of uncertificated stock, just blacked out. Defeated again, I was still at his mercy for funds. I wished the hearing in Austria could deal with financial issues as well, but that had to wait for U.S. jurisdiction.

Our day in court was terrible. Peter told the judge that my children did not want me around. That angered my attorney who then explained that when both parents were in the home, there was conflict. My attorney went on to explain that the father had implemented his parents to thwart my efforts to spend quality time with my children. He expounded on Peter's compulsion to insist on exclusive loyalty from the children, concluding the father's behavior was not good for his children. The judge was nodding as though he'd heard it all before—and I'm sure he had. Then, my attorney started speculating about Peter having an affair with his colleague in LA. I couldn't believe it. I was shaking my head no in an attempt to get him to stop talking because I knew that accusation would incite Peter's wrath.

Afterward I said to my attorney, "What he's done is bad enough! Must we discuss issues irrelevant to a house key?"

"It's good for the judge to understand the dynamics in a marriage," my attorney explained.

"But I have no proof he had an affair with her."

"Paige, did you tell me that he spoke tenderly to his manager in LA?"

"Yes, he does speak tenderly to her." I was idealistically defensive. "He tells me she's in over her head, she's emotionally fragile, and he needs to build her up so she can make him look good in the company. He's on the phone with her from Vienna between midnight and two in the morning because that's the end of her business day. I told you that. You made it sound completely different than what I told you."

My attorney stared at me in disbelief. "Please don't be naïve," he quipped.

I knew Peter had been consorting with a flight attendant, for one. Before we separated, he'd asked me if I happened to read one of the e-mails he'd received from her. Odd she wrote, he pretended. I thought it was odd he assumed I would read his e-mail and even more odd that he was handing out his e-mail address to other women. But by that point in our marriage, I didn't care enough to even feign a little jealousy.

A good friend tried to tell me there were inappropriate things going on during business trips. She dared me to confront Peter with some of the details she offered, but I never did. I knew more than I wanted to know the night Peter pulled me towards himself in bed as he was drifting into sleep and asked me what my real name was.

As far as his colleague was concerned, all I really knew was the man I listened to from our bed at night was a completely different man than the one I was subjected to of late. Even though I suspected he wasn't true to me, I didn't believe Peter would get involved with one of his plant managers. Too risky for the reputation he'd worked so hard to build within the company.

At any rate, I didn't think those offenses belonged in a hearing that would decide whether or not I should have a key that would allow me access to my children. I didn't want an issue made of either of us seeing other people after the separation. After all, my attorney had asked me out himself! I was thankful my dealings with him were nearly complete. We would wait for the judgment on the key and hopefully, that would finalize my association with him.

The next morning when I called the house, Peter barked into the phone when he picked up.

"Who is this?" Angry, angry, angry. He knew exactly who was calling, or he would have never answered the phone in a fit of rage. He was yelling at me again about my damn attorney. I apologized right after the hearing and again, found myself expressing regret over the deviation my attorney had taken. I assured him I didn't believe those matters belonged in court the previous day.

"Why would you tell your attorney that I'm having an affair with my manager in LA?"

"I didn't tell him you were having an affair. In our conversation about the marriage, he asked me about your dealings with other women. Since you're on the phone almost every night with Sarah, I mentioned it. You talk so different to her than you do to me. I didn't know he'd bring it up in a hearing about a key."

Our conversation about court had calmed before I asked Peter to have the girls call me after they had prepared for school. Instead, he yelled for them to come down from their rooms to speak to me. When I heard their footsteps approaching on the hardwood floors, their father began screaming into the phone, out of the blue, "Liar! . . . Liar! . . . Liar!" I was sure that to my daughters our exchange sounded like a legitimate two-sided conversation in which I must have been saying something upsetting to provoke their dad. Peter was giving me enough time to "speak" between yelling "Liar!" But on the other end of the line, I was utterly stunned into silence. His side of the conversation was for the benefit of those who could hear him in the house—my children.

I knew I wouldn't see my daughters until the weekend. Their father was still able to come home in the middle of the afternoon when they arrived home from school. The two of us being together in the house was impossible. Peter was making the separation as difficult as he possibly could, for himself, for me, and for our children. To say we had irreconcilable differences was understating the mess. Both of the girls had planned sleepovers at the house Friday night, so we agreed they would spend Saturday afternoon and evening with me.

Chapter 24

I met Viktor as often as I could but knew he probably wasn't feeling like he'd won the lottery in considering our relationship. Between legal dealings and approaching swim meets, our afternoon routine had been disrupted.

"It's no problem. You're here now. We'll make the most of the time we have." He was squeezing my hand, holding tight when he added, "I like that your children are a high priority in your life."

I was thankful for his understanding—thankful for his insight. We talked about the possibility of getting away for a few days together. Travel plans with Viktor happened so easily. But seeing other parts of Europe from Vienna *was* relatively trouble-free, so we decided to just be spontaneous. Uncluttered and uncomplicated, simplicity was a way of life for Viktor. It was a drastic change from our household's habit of setting hurdles in order to give life meaning and purpose. His internal depths were profound and the peripheral aspects of living barely fazed him. His identity was not in his career, his value was not in his bank account, and his purpose was not in measuring up for others. I wanted that. Oh, how I wanted that in my life.

We met at the train station the next morning, perused the board of travel destinations, and decided to set our course for Munich. It was a city he thoroughly enjoyed and when he learned I'd never been there, he wanted me to see it. He offered to take my overnight bag, so I handed it to him. Even though Viktor was built like a Michelangelo sculpture, he hadn't anticipated the weight of the bag, so it nearly hit the floor.

"What did you put in here?" he asked.

"Not much, really. I guess it's the books that are heavy." I was still holding my camera. He looked puzzled as he heaved my bag up onto his shoulder.

We spent the entire journey chatting and enjoying the lovely scenery. The conversation was electric and I was thrilled that he enjoyed and considered my opinions. It was wonderful to be wholeheartedly desired in an exchange of thoughts. In the past, train travel inspired both of us to write, but neither of us picked up a pen as the train rolled along. We had each other. Viktor never made a phone call, never picked up a newspaper, and never left me—mentally, physically or emotionally. We were *together* and my reading material was untouched. It was Viktor who lugged my bag, habits from my past. He laughed at me for thinking I'd need entertainment while I was with him. To be his nonstop priority in the middle of the week was beyond belief, certainly not something I'd ever dreamed of expecting.

When we arrived, he took me to a restaurant at the top of a building overlooking Marienplatz. The view across the plaza was dominated by the neo-Gothic architecture of town hall. Inside its center tower was the Glockenspiel. We marveled at the spectacle together. I sat directly facing the window with Viktor beside me. He was part of my view. As incredible as the structure was before us, the real miracle, to me, was Viktor.

He showed me Maximillianstrasse the next day, one of his favorite streets. We ate at a popular restaurant in town; a trendy, upscale hot spot, then moved to his preferred café for coffee and dessert. Both of us carried cameras, but our eye for a photo was so different we were seldom shooting the same point. My shots were those of a tourist with a dash of artistic flare, but Viktor's photography was undeniably art. It was fun watching him frame a shot and posing for him when he asked me to add a profile, a hand, or a footprint to the frame. His camera work made me look exactly how I felt around him.

Back in Vienna, I unpacked the books I'd taken to read. Not one of them had been cracked open the entire trip.

Chapter 25

On Saturday, the girls and I had a spa day, plucking eyebrows and painting nails. We did some cooking too, but when it came time for sleep, they wanted their own beds. My mattresses on the floor weren't very comfortable as there was nothing holding them in place. We would all lie down together on the bed, but the one in the middle would eventually slide in between the mattresses to the hard floor underneath. However, they did want to return to my place the next day for Sunday dinner, which was music to my ears. We spent Sunday playing board games and having fun in the kitchen. Amanda had written an impromptu drama that the girls acted out. I was applauding loudly when they finished.

"Hollywood, here she comes!" I cheered.

"Actually, Mom, I'm thinking Broadway."

"Now that would be your niche, daughter. You could give them the best of all of your talent." Amanda began singing in front of large crowds at the age of eight. As a little seven-year-old, I took her to watch one of her best friends in the local pageant; and that night, she decided she would wear that crown one day. She won Little Miss Congeniality the next year, but having poured her heart into her singing, it was a bitter defeat to go home without placing. It was fun for the two of us though, pulling together her wardrobe and choreographing her talent number. Every year, she begged to enter the competition, and every year, the outcome was the same. The last year she entered, parents, contestants, and sponsors had told her that she had it in the bag. Walking away that year without placing was confusion beyond disappointment for her. Finally, she was ready to walk away from pageantry.

All was right with the world during those brief time periods of bemusement. The girls mentioned over the weekend that their dad might be traveling that week. I tried not to get my hopes up but was relieved when he called on Monday to ask if I would move in for the week with the kids.

"Of course!" I wondered why he didn't call in advance. I guessed he still presumed my world revolved around him.

"I'll be back on Thursday," he said. That meant I'd have three nights with my children.

Our time together was ordinary, spent on our usual day-to-day activities. We came home after swim practice, stopping to buy roasted chestnuts and baked potato skins on our way. Adam and I had a difficult conversation one night. The girls were nearby, listening in.

"Every marriage goes through ups and downs though, Mom."

"Sweetie, this isn't part of a cycle. It's a bad pattern that doesn't work. I don't like what you and your sisters are being taught when you look at your dad and me as an example for marriage. What goes on in this house is not right."

"No marriage is perfect."

"That's true." I had to guard my words and was unable to share my heart with him because he had become his father's best friend. Adam was extremely defensive of Peter. I knew that trying to make him understand, I'd have to say adverse things about his dad. Deliberate discussion that overtly portrayed Peter, from my point of view, as untruthful, or his behavior as harmful, condemned me more in my children's eyes than the covert inferences he utilized to win their allegiance. Pointing out Peter's sudden capability to be home was met with fierce contempt from all three of the children. They liked having their dad home and viewed me as the curmudgeon who wanted him to start traveling again when my frustration with his constant presence was evident. I just wanted life to be normal for the four of us. Being separate from Peter was something we were all accustomed to, and our life with him popping in and out on weekends was not expected to change.

Adam had the last word. No marriage was perfect. It felt wrong not to communicate the depth of turmoil and anguish in the marriage, but I knew attempting to help him come to terms with how far from perfect his parents union was would help nothing. In fact, it would probably make matters worse. All I could do was hug him, while letting him know I loved him unconditionally. I couldn't even make him understand there was no need for him or his sisters to ever choose between their mother and their father; that we would forever, equally, be their parents.

Adam gave me a key to the front gate while his dad was out of town. He said he didn't need it back, grinning as he pointed out his footprints that went up and over the wall beside the gate. I told him he did need a key back because our landlady was not going to be happy about her wall! I rubbed the prints to see how embedded they were before shaking my finger at Adam, trying to keep a straight face while imagining our little landlady reading someone the riot act. At least I'd be able to leave the home during the day knowing the front gate was locked. The house just had to be left open.

I cooked a lot in those two days. The Christmas tree was still up, so I took that down as well. I used the phone to catch up with my parents, took care of the laundry, cleaned the house from top to bottom, and used our gym equipment to get in a workout. I spoke with Peter's assistant as well, and discovered that he would travel again for two weeks in February. Hanging up after that conversation, I breathed a sigh of relief. This is how our separation was supposed to be—very little change for the children or for me.

Once Peter was back in town though, he still managed to come home in the middle of the afternoon every day. Our court date for judgment on the key was that week. Peter's attorney came to court believing I already had a key. I explained it was the one to the gate and not the house, which meant I needed to leave everything unlocked when I was there, which wasn't completely safe or smart. I told them I wanted a complete set as the key I possessed belonged to my son, and he needed a complete set as well. I won a key that day. Peter hadn't bothered to come hear the judgment.

I spoke with my attorney at length over lunch at a beautiful restaurant downtown. He shared some of his experiences from his own two previous marriages. I appreciated his concern, but at the same time, wanted little to do with him. I paid for my part of the lunch before I went to school for swim practice.

My children and I all traveled home on the train together, but Amanda and I stopped for groceries on the way. She needed lunch food. We had a constructive visit about life and seeing both sides of things. I reminded her that her grandmother, Peter's mother, always said, "The simplest thing as a sheet of paper has two sides to it." She knew that was true, but didn't want me to elaborate about "my side." Her father was home when we arrived, so I went to the apartment to work on meet entries for the team.

Attendance at swim practice had been less than impressive the past week. But that night, there was a good turnout, so I gave the team a speech about being at every practice until our international school's swim tournament in Cairo the end of the season. In motivating them, I motivated myself. The upcoming meet for Prague came together easy enough as I worked at home. I didn't have an assistant, so there was no one making suggestions for each swimmer's events. There was also no one to argue with about relays. I missed Heath's shenanigans. After the Prague meet was complete, I tentatively put together the Zurich meet while my swimmers' times were in front of me and my work was scattered all over the floor. It was easier to do it all at once. I faxed my athletic director the entries the next morning.

Chapter 26

"I've decided to have my parents come back," Peter informed me.

He spoke as though he was the only authority that mattered where our children were concerned. Based on the separation agreement, the Austrian court decided I should be free to come and go, as needed, in order to care for the children; but Peter was going to do everything in his power to keep my access to the children to a minimum.

"Why? They don't need to be here! Our agreement is working."

"They're just helping me pick up the pieces." His tone was deceptively pitiful.

I was flabbergasted. It was January 23; only five weeks since they left in December and during that time, we had all been back to the States to be home for Christmas. I could count on both hands the number of unadulterated times I'd been with my children at home since the separation.

I met Alexia at the bus stop the next day, fixed dinner for everyone, played board games, and baked some cookies. I also took time to call my in-laws and beg them not to return to Vienna. I told them about the agreement Peter and I drew up before our separation and they informed me they knew nothing about it.

"When he's traveling, I'm going to be here with my children," I said.

My father-in-law piped up and said, "You will not be in the house if I have anything to say about it!"

Dismay, hurt, and extremely frustrated, I begged. "Please. You guys need to stay out of the middle of our lives right now. There is no way our family can make the adjustments we need to make with you interfering."

My father-in-law huffed, "Well, you never did appreciate us being around, Paige."

That wasn't exactly true, because Peter was pleasant when his parents were around. But the time they'd spent with our family in recent years was excessive.

"No offense, Dad, but I married your son, not you and Mom. I spend more time with you lately than I have with him." He didn't speak, so I continued. "Please, just let your son grow up and handle his life like an adult."

"Paige, I wish you could hear yourself." His tone was smart.

I was the child acting out because I'd taken a stand against the way I was treated by their son. I was misbehaving; therefore, the *punishment* being rendered was justified. I understood his mind-set, but how dare he presume to have any say over who could be in my home! It was beyond me why he felt he had any claim over my children and the house my belongings were in.

"I am begging you! Please don't fly over here. Peter will not work with me, and he has little reason to even talk to me when you are here. These are *our* children, and we are going to need to be able to work together to finish raising them."

"Well, we'll do whatever our son wants us to do."

I was out of words. My father-in-law hung up, and that was that. They were more than willing to help their son perform a parentectomy on my children. I no longer mattered to them and if their presence meant I was ousted, then so-be-it. I couldn't help but remember the times they would come to visit. Each time resulted in them helping me with my daily routine.

"We're exhausted!" my mother-in-law would say. "There are three of us doing what you do. How do you do this every day?" she'd asked.

Peter told me many times since the birth of our first child that I was born to be a mother. Now, the only mother he wanted for his children was his own. Unfortunately, she was delighted to be needed as my replacement. The dynamics in my in-laws' marriage weren't exactly heaven on earth since retirement. Consequently, their son's mess became their purpose. They were more than happy to let their lives revolve around Peter and our children.

Chapter 27

I purchased a cell phone that would make international calls. With my in-laws back in town there would be no privacy trying to use the house phone. That night, I called an international operator who gave me the name of three attorneys in the Los Angeles area. The first one I spoke with told me that he was not the one to handle my case, but his suite mate was the man I needed. He was so convinced I'd be satisfied with the attorney he was recommending that I didn't even bother calling the other two—I'd just been given a recommendation. The name he gave me was Jerry Lowenstein. I dialed again and asked for him. We spoke briefly and set up an appointment to talk the next day.

I went straight to the music festival at school the next morning. Lunch needed to be set up; then I was announcing player, piece, and instrument for the second session. Alexia played her flute beautifully. She was the judges' choice for the final concert of the day from her session. I happened to run into our pastor from the international church we were attending in Vienna as well. He had spoken with Peter and our children and advised we meet for a counseling session. Then he said the oddest thing.

"I'm worried about your children. I just want them to see you as their mother," he said. His words were poignant, and I didn't fully understand them until much later.

I called a taxi since I needed to be calling my attorney in LA the same time I left school. Public transportation was not conducive to important phone calls. We talked for an hour as the taxi drove to my apartment. To my amazement, we never lost connection. I told him everything. He let me know what steps I needed to take. First order of business would be residency in California since we'd never lived there. When we became expatriates, we sold our home and left the States liquid. Unless the divorce took place in the state where we were married, there would need to be a residence. California was the next location for Peter though, and the attorney who was counseling him was from LA as well. In addition, I learned it was a no-fault state.

"Nobody cares who did what. It's fifty-fifty here," my attorney told me. That's exactly what I wanted to hear.

Alexia spent the next two evenings at my apartment. We played flute duets, and I let her play my open-keyed Gemeinhardt. She managed a very mature sound her first try. I was proud of her for learning so quickly. When her father arrived for pick-up, he called from the car and ordered me to bring her down. In front of Alexia, he told me that he wanted to let me into the house two or three nights a week to help my relationship with my older children.

"You have fences to mend," he said.

"You should stop working on their heads," I whispered to him.

"I've had nothing to do with the way they feel about you."

Our daughter was climbing into the car. The conversation ended. As they drove away, I was afraid for my daughter. Her father was a crazy maker, and I wanted her away from him.

Alexia came to swim practice the next day and afterward, went home with me. Peter arrived forty minutes later than he said he would. Unsurprisingly, Alexia was irritated to be awake past her bedtime. My "structured" child was not very flexible about her nighttime routine. When she was finished for the day, she was *finished*. I worried the episode would taint her desire to spend evenings with me.

The next night at the house, Peter finally gave me my key. He presented me with an undated paper stating I had received the key. I dated it and signed. I wanted to discuss his offer for regular time with the kids because I felt that would do as much good for them as counseling.

"Where will your parents be when I'm at the house with the kids two or three nights a week?" I asked.

"They'll probably be right here. It's a big house. You guys don't all need to be in the same room."

"Your mother can't help but try to outdo me when she's here. I know how this will play out if they are in the house."

"They've postponed their ticket a week."

"So. That's just one week. They need to stay away. Are we buying these last minute tickets for them?" I asked.

"That's none of your business."

"Fine. The girls mentioned you were planning a trip to Italy with them during ski week."

"Yes, it's really a shame you chose to leave when you did. Things at work just let up." The lilt in his voice was forced, but the truth was, things at work could have "let up" a long time ago. Peter's lifestyle was his choice.

I had asked on more than one occasion throughout our first year in Vienna if we could plan a trip to Italy. It was a place I wanted very much to experience.

"Things at work could have let up a long time ago," I said. "If we were not separated, you would not be making a trip to Italy. Just so you know, I'm planning to be in the States during ski week," I informed him. Vienna's schools had a ski week as well as spring break, and ski week was a couple weeks away.

"Where in the States?" he asked.

I considered telling him for a moment then decided against it. "That's none of your business." I retorted, serving up a dish of his own medicine.

Furious, he yelled, "I'm trying here, and you're impossible. You did this! You started this when you left."

"I took a step to *change* our marriage. It takes two to make a marriage work and two to make it fail."

"No, it doesn't."

"I'm over here with barely enough cash to function. You are keeping me from being at home with my children with your sudden ability to stay in town and come home in the middle of the afternoon—not to mention dragging your parents into this. You can't honestly think you're trying to help this marriage survive. It takes two."

"This conversation is over," he declared and stomped off.

Alexia was missing her report card. She needed a signature on it from one of us, as it was due back at school the next day. I was afraid it had inadvertently been thrown into the trash, so I started looking through the rubbish. Peter found me.

"What are you hoping to find in there?" he yelled.

I explained our daughter was missing her report card. She needed a signature.

"Get out of my house! I want you out now!"

He followed me and wouldn't even let me go upstairs to say goodnight to the kids or let my daughter know I hadn't found her report card. He was physically ready to explode, so I grabbed my coat and shoes and put them on halfway out the door.

Chapter 28

The next morning my team met at the train station for our trip to the Zurich meet. The train ride through the Alps to Zurich was spectacular, as always. The coach for the Zurich team was a familiar friend among the coaches present for that weekend's swim meet. She took us as a group to have fondue on the medieval side of town the eve of our arrival. The meet ran right on schedule the next day, and relatively speaking, it was a successful effort as we came home second only to London. Their team was huge, so we were accustomed to them dominating every tournament. I was pleased with the results.

Back in Vienna, I moved into the house for the next four nights. It was Sunday, February 4; and for four wonderful days, my children and I were "back to normal." But in spite of my wishes, my in-laws were coming back. They were returning to rescue their son, thereby preventing us from dealing with our problems and our life on our own as mature individuals. I cleaned and prepared the house on Wednesday, before I picked them up at the airport on Thursday. With their son out of town, the only other option was for them to pay for a taxi to our home, but I was hoping their time in Vienna would be short and sweet. There was no better way to ensure that than to start off on the "right foot." It was an awkward ride home. We talked about the kids. I had to miss the yearbook photos for the swim team that day in order to be at the airport. Regardless, I still had to be at school to pick up tickets, money, the team phone, and stopwatches before leaving town for the Prague meet the next day. Because the flight was late, my athletic director had to stay an extra thirty minutes waiting on me. He was a gracious man and played down my tardiness.

I was in my apartment, packing for the meet when my cell phone rang. It was my father-in-law calling to tell me that Alexia was not going to be traveling with me to Prague the next day. I'd just picked them up at the airport, going out of my way to accommodate them, and this was my reward. Alexia already had a ticket, and the two of us had just discussed how fun it was going to be to see the city. I was furious, but what could I do?

Physically removing her from them would be a traumatic experience for her. It may or may not be backed up by my oldest children. When I spoke with her about it, she seemed fine with the decision that her father had handed down. Within a few hours of arrival, my father-in-law was more than happy to do his son's dirty work. Thinking of my drive to the airport, I came to terms with the fact that my in-laws were not going to think better of me, regardless of any effort I made, even if it was on their behalf.

The train ride to Prague was long, but I was able to sleep a little bit as I hadn't slept much after the news of Alexia staying behind for the weekend. The coach's dinner that night was delicious, followed by a walking tour through town. Host coaches, without fail, tried to outdo each other when it came to putting their school and city on display. Charles Bridge was covered in snow. I lagged behind the group trying to successfully shoot photos in the dark. Though she wasn't with me, I could almost hear Alexia saying, "Hurry up, Mom!"

The competition the next day was the highlight of my coaching career. Amanda won gold medals in each of her events. I knew as a *mom*, I may see her on the gold medal stand again, but to be *mom and coach* watching her step up to the gold medal stand three times that day brought me to tears. They were happy tears that completely embarrassed my daughter. Coaches were supposed to be impartial, and I usually was. But the moment was awesome, and I was caught in it as a mom. The train ride home was fun. We were all celebrating because our high school team came home champions and our little middle school team won third place.

Sunday, I took Alexia swimming, and we had a fine time in each other's company. It didn't make up for the time we missed in Prague, but it helped. Amanda worked on her homework all day, in light of the fact that swim team trips were not favorable conditions for completing one's schoolwork. My son was a typical senior. Time with his friends was more important than anything. When I'd suggest he come over, he had other things to do. He did have a lot to do, and I didn't want his social life to suffer because of what was happening at home. Under the circumstances, or should I say, relatively speaking, I just wanted him to have as normal a senior year as possible, so I let him choose where he wanted to be. It's how I would have handled him if we were under the same roof. Demanding more of his presence at my place felt like an unfair and superfluous expectation to put on him.

≈≈≈

I never signed the new checks Peter held for the uncertificated shares of stock. Instead, I put stop-pays on them after I found out it would be possible to direct deposit the amount into our joint account, which had not been closed. I called the credit union to let them know a large amount would be hitting that account soon and to *please* transfer it immediately to my account. I was speaking to Dawn, the woman who divided what little bit was left of our joint account, so I didn't need to share any history. She knew my circumstances . . . and she knew Peter. She watched her monitor. The minute the transfer hit our joint account, she reassigned the money to my account. I received word it had worked and nearly broke down on the phone with her.

"You have no idea how you have helped me." My voice was shaking with emotion.

"I think I do, honey," she said.

I called the florist from our old hometown and had a floral arrangement decorated with Lifesavers sent to her with a note attached saying "Thank You!" No longer was I at Peter's mercy for money. If it took years to settle the divorce, I'd be fine . . . financially, anyway.

≈≈≈

Alexia was home sick the next day. When she called, I went to the house immediately. There were dishes in the sink to put into the dishwasher before we played board games. My mother-in-law wanted my signature on our tax return that she had prepared. I wanted to copy them, but she insisted on doing that herself. We didn't have a copier, so she left with Howard to find a copy shop. I rocked my daughter while they were gone. They had apparently called Peter to ask if it was all right if they left the house because when they returned, they told Alexia to call her dad and let him know she wasn't alone; they were home from making copies. I was right there with her, right there listening to the whole conversation, and I didn't exist. She was to *let him know she wasn't alone*. What they insinuated without saying was, *alone with your mother*, as though I were a danger to my own daughter.

I packed for the States the following day. Alexia was still home sick and called to let me know, but I didn't hear the call on my cell phone. Later when I saw she had called, I dialed her back. Her grandfather answered her cell phone.

"Hello."

"Hi, Howard," I usually called him Dad, but I just couldn't bring myself to use that term of endearment addressing him anymore. "I missed a call from Alexia. I was just returning her call."

He yelled for her. "Did you call your mom?" His tone was accusatory.

I heard her come closer to the phone and tell him, "I never called her." She was defensive.

"Well, can I speak to her?" I asked him.

"Do you want to talk to your mother?" he asked. It was a jaded question and not a request for her to show respect to me. Normally, he would have said, "Your mother would like to speak to you." but now, showing consideration for me was optional. In his words and his tone, my daughter heard, "You may choose if you wish to speak to your mother. You may choose whether to respect her or not. She is no longer of any authority over you." All unspoken, of course, but communicated nonetheless. We'd come a long way from the days of "No, sir" and "Yes, ma'am" living in the South. "Honor thy father and thy mother" had simply turned into "Honor thy father."

"I don't want to talk to her," she said. I could hear in her voice that she was trying to please him—making sure she performed correctly for the people around her who didn't like her mother anymore. My little girl, "peer" pressured by her elders.

It was difficult managing to deal with the web Peter was spinning for my children, but to cope with the extra entanglements his parents were happy to weave into the mess was almost too much to bear. In the past, I'd appreciated Howard's low-keyed and easygoing nature, but now, I felt like I never even knew him.

After practice that day, I walked Amanda home. She darted away from me the minute we were inside. In spite of the fact that we were all departing the next day, our time together at the house was brief. I gave my children their Valentine's gifts before I told them good-bye. They followed me to the door. From around the corner, their grandparents appeared from the other room. They were all traveling to Italy with Peter the next day. I wished them a safe trip, but they just nodded, my in-laws keeping my daughters tucked under their arms. They knew I would be traveling too but offered no well wishes for my safety.

Chapter 29

Viktor was sanity in the midst of irrationality, kindness amid cruelty, and wisdom among the simpleminded. He exuded magnetic qualities, and our closeness made my problems seem to disappear. He wasn't without a sense of humor either.

"This must be the biggest village in the world." The plane was descending, and he was looking out his window at LA. He'd never been there, and was shocked at how flat and spread out it appeared.

It was February 15. Viktor and I settled into a hotel in Beverly Hills that was recommended by my attorney as it was in close proximity to his home and office. Immediately, our hunt for an inexpensive apartment to establish residency in California began. Although we didn't plan to live there, it would be good to have a place to call home while we were in the process of relocating. Finding a cheap but safe location in the area was not easy. We chose a studio apartment—just a temporary address that represented residency. It cost as much to rent as the house payment I remembered making on the manor-style residence our family moved out of in Tennessee. It took some time to adjust to Southern California.

I set up a bank account and wired some money from the stock sale. I was so thankful I had a way to pay the security deposit on the studio apartment along with a couple months' rent up front. There was also the matter of a retainer fee for my attorney, as well as the hotel and rental car expenses.

Viktor did his best to make sure we enjoyed life a bit while we were getting to know our new city. We spent a day at the Getty Museum, took in a Lakers ball game, and attended a Grammy party. It was fun being with a man people wanted to get to know. When I met him, Viktor spoke seven languages, so the barrier to forming relationships was broken among the international population in LA.

We met my attorney who instantly put me at ease. He reminded me of an uncle I loved dearly. A teddy bear at heart, but at the same time, I knew I was in competent hands. He was a seasoned Hollywood attorney, mentioning he would appear on Larry King the following week. As I told the story about finding him through the international operator, he shook his head in disbelief and had a good laugh. I gathered he was accustomed to being referred by satisfied clients and not being plucked from thin air.

≈≈≈

Peter had kindly assured me, while he had office staff listening to him, that I would be able to speak with the children while they were in Italy by calling his cell phone. "Just dial the same number you dialed now," he instructed in a very condescending voice. But his cell phone was turned off all but once during their vacation. When I did reach them, I spoke with Alexia first. She informed me they were in a restaurant.

"Are you having a good time with your dad and grandparents?" I asked.

"We were having a good time until you called. I just wish we could enjoy this without being reminded of you," she said to me.

Her words cut to my heart. I missed them terribly knowing we were a world away from each other. But they weren't missing me at all. In fact, they just wanted to forget me and enjoy their vacation with their dad. I didn't want to break down on the phone with her, so I cut the conversation short.

"Okay, I'll talk to you guys when we're back in Vienna. Please tell your brother and sister I said hello." I couldn't imagine allowing her to speak that way to her father had the scenario been reversed but suspected her cutting remark satisfied her father and grandparents on some level. I imagined they excused her behavior "because of the rough time" she was going through.

≈≈≈

The week in LA was exhausting and eye-opening but, overall, an enjoyable week. It was uninterrupted, heavenly time with Viktor as opposed to the hellish days I'd known. It was strange going back to Vienna. Viktor went to his apartment overlooking the marvelous Staatsoper—Vienna's State Opera House. I returned to my little apartment on my own. It was unnatural to be apart from Viktor. I called the children, but they weren't home from Italy.

I was at the house the next morning to see the kids. Peter and his parents hovered, watching every move and listening to every word. I knew they were curious about where I might have been in the States. Our visit was brief, but I learned that Alexia would not be going to Cairo with me as planned.

"They don't want you to kidnap me," she informed me as we walked to the door to say good-bye. She was testing me with her boldness in relaying the conversations taking place in front of her. The collective frame of mind of her father and grandparents, in regard to me, could not have been more toxic to my child.

"You know I would never do that, don't you?" I asked her. She gave a halfhearted nod. I sensed she did *not* know that she could trust me. In order for her to travel with me, they were going to have to hand me her passport. Apparently, they decided in front of her, that giving me both daughters' passports was not a good idea. Better to keep those locked away. I didn't know when kidnapping began to be discussed in front of her, but I suspected this was the reason for their decision to keep her from traveling to Prague with me as well.

Paranoia ruled their minds. There was no reason for them to think of me as a kidnapper! Imaginative indulgences became their reality, and my daughter's mind was fodder for their tortuous negativity. I was distraught and outraged that they could plant such ideas into Alexia's beliefs about her mother. It was true—evil sees evil in everything. Naturally, that realization made me wonder if Peter had considered disappearing with my children. I suspected his reputation meant too much to him to go through with something like that, so I put the idea out of my mind.

Chapter 30

Only a week after returning from the States with Viktor, I found myself boarding another plane with my team. It was February 25, and we were on our way to Cairo, Egypt. Alone with seventeen swimmers, I let the older ones know I really needed their help. There was a lot of discussion as to whether or not the team would even make the ISST meet that year because of its location. George, my athletic director, consulted with our host and was assured that the constant conflict in the Mideast was not a threat to Cairo; so together, he and I decided to proceed in spite of our sister team in Zurich withdrawing from the competition. Besides, I reasoned, we had kids on the team whose parents worked in Intelligence. They wouldn't have signed permission slips for their children to attend if there was reason to keep them home.

The flight crew from Paris to Cairo was all male, each of them much larger than myself at five feet ten inches. They wore suits, but their muscles showed through their jackets. They were fit. It struck me as odd, but at the same time, undoubtedly it was better security. It took two hours to pass through airport control in Cairo. The building was dirty, and the feeling of being outside my comfort zone commenced. My older swimmers felt it too. One glance from the team leaders was all it took for their younger peers to quiet down and stay near.

I counted heads a dozen times as we made our way through the airport to our hosts waiting for us in the lobby. Transportation awaiting us was a yellow school bus along with a large city bus. Our baggage was loaded onto the school bus, and the team and I were loaded onto the city bus. When we arrived at the school, my swimmers helped the drivers unload their luggage without being asked to do so. Amanda spent most of her time with her best friend; but on occasion, our eyes would meet, each of us checking on the other.

Following registration, the team was dispersed to their host families. I hugged my daughter goodnight and told her to have a good time. We were meeting the next morning for practice before a full day of sightseeing. My chaperone from Vienna was arriving later that night. I was thankful there would be two of us roaming around the city sightseeing with the team the next day, although I was not happy he had finagled the trip with my athletic director to comfortably make the journey alone, thereby leaving me alone with the team on travel days in the airports. I wanted to bring Viktor but hadn't suggested that in light of the fact that no one knew about him. In addition, I wanted my children to meet him at a time when they were all together.

First on our tourism agenda were the Great Pyramids and the Sphinx. As the pyramids came into view, the bus became silent—all of us in awe. The question for the day was, "*How* did they do that?" The stones were so massive it was beyond comprehending how an ancient civilization managed to build the structures. To hear the stories of speculation about the nose of the Sphinx being used as target practice at some point in history was pitiful. I thought the depth and history of Vienna's culture was so rich and too deep to ever absorb, but standing among the pyramids, Vienna seemed young.

The Khan Market was our next stop, and it was completely unnerving. Most of my female swimmers had blond hair. I later learned from people within the international school community, they probably should have been veiled. Most of them never took their daughters outside the school complex without veiling them. They explained it wasn't necessary, but doing so was just less provocation to the men in the city. I took the girls, making myself responsible for my daughter, and the chaperone took the boys, but we moved through the market in sight of each other. There were small passages I didn't want anyone disappearing into, so I counted heads continuously.

Thankfully, it was a short stop, as we needed to meet the other teams on the Nile for a sunset cruise. Our team was large enough that we were given our own boat. Its sails were tattered and sheer. Even though the vessel was old, it looked sturdy and seaworthy. I loved being on the water, having grown up with a boat. It was relaxing, even looking for crocodiles among the vegetation of the banks in spite of being told it had been years since any were spotted. My daughter snuggled with her boyfriend. It was on the Nile that Amanda received her first kiss. When I wasn't looking, of course.

The opening ceremonies the next day were a memorable event. I carried our flag as we paraded around the swimming pool, riding high on team spirit as we moved to music blaring from the loudspeakers. My team captain won a gold medal that day, and I happened to be the coach presenting medals when it was her turn to take the stand. She was a senior. I reached to give her a congratulatory hug, and we clung to each other a little longer, whispering sentiments of appreciation to each other, as it was the end of her swim career.

There was an Egyptian dinner served under the grand tent for all the swimmers and coaches following the competition that day. In motion among the tables were belly dancers shimmying to the music of the live band they had on stage. It was a festive atmosphere, especially with half of the competition behind us. That day, Amanda swam her personal best in every event.

Day two brought our team another gold medal from an outstanding swimmer who was new to the team. The first time he practiced with us that year, he asked if he could swim some extra laps after he'd finished his workout. After all, we still had fifteen minutes of pool time. He proceeded to butterfly a couple hundred meters before he cooled down. It was fun having someone to push the others on the team.

My daughter's day, however, did not go as well. She made a spectacular entry on her backstroke. Surfacing long after the other swimmers had popped up above the water, she was a full body length ahead of them. She'd dolphin kick underwater long enough to make us really search her empty lane, but time after time, she would surface ahead of her competitors. It was dramatic and sensational . . . and oh, so much fun to watch! Backstroke was her event, and she usually finished in front of the crowd too; but that day, she just missed her turn. She didn't want to be disqualified, so she struggled to hit the wall but had completely lost her momentum. It was a disappointment, but in typical "fighter" fashion, she bounced back and swam yet another personal best in her freestyle event. I was proud of her, and she knew it.

That night, a group of coaches gathered in the hotel lobby. We decided earlier to experience the bazaar at night. They were gathered around a large table, drinking beer when I arrived.

"Have a beer, Paige. We're still waiting for Chuck."

"No thanks," I declined.

"You don't drink?" one of them asked.

"It just doesn't sound good," I said, without adding the rest of my thought, *these days.*

The chaperone my athletic director sent to help me had already flown out. He was there long enough to attend the coaches' dinner, collect the keepsakes they handed out, and do some sightseeing. I knew the coaches from Brussels and Prague well enough to enjoy an evening out with them. Even though I was the only female in the group, they treated me like one of the guys—until we were in the market, anyway.

We wandered aimlessly, completely intrigued by the market. My senses were on overload with the sound of Egyptian music, the new scents of a variety of rich spices and perfumes, all in addition to the view of colorful wares on display.

A group of local men watched us walk by and began arguing among themselves before one of them grabbed me. My fellow coaches gathered around quickly and tried to understand what the man who had my arm was trying to say. When we understood they were trying to purchase me, we all laughed, but the man holding my arm was not laughing. We thought they were just having fun with the tourists, no doubt a game they played with many tourists. The other men involved with the man holding my arm had hemmed all of us into a ring. We were still thinking it was a joke they might be carrying too far. But they assured us they were not joking. Finally, my protectors made the man speaking to us understand that I was not theirs to sell—that I didn't "belong" to any of the men I was accompanied by. This raised an eyebrow on the man who had grabbed me. I met his gaze in a glare of equality without enough background or understanding of his culture to have any idea what he might deduce from the information he was given. He was taken aback for a moment and we boldly broke from the entourage around us, unwilling to stick around for more conversation as we moved quickly out of their sight. The rest of the evening in the bazaar, the group encircled me as we made our way through the narrow passages. None of us were there to shop. We just wanted to experience the sights, the smells, and the sounds of the market at night. Experience it, we did.

With seventeen swimmers, seventeen passports, seventeen visas, and seventeen tickets in hand, I was at the airport with my team. I watched as seventeen bags were scanned before we all made our way to the ticket counter. As I stood there waiting with the team, I realized I didn't have my handbag. About the time I looked back, a man waving a driver's license was wandering through the crowd, mispronouncing my name. I waved to him, and he walked me back to security to collect my belongings. I left my oldest swimmers in charge to keep a head count. It wasn't until we were on the plane that I discovered security had "misplaced" my debit card. Shameful to call themselves security, I mused.

The flight home was time to reflect. I knew Viktor was looking forward to having me home safe, as he didn't like the idea of travel to Cairo. I appreciated that he showed concern without trying to control me.

First order of business would be to cancel the bankcard that was lost. I calculated the hours it would be before I could do that and hoped there would be no need for damage control to my account.

My thoughts drifted to Peter who had traveled internationally for half his business career. Although my own experiences traveling were not life changing or completely fulfilling, I couldn't imagine ever complaining about having had the opportunities I did to see the world. I remembered a time he called after having been served a six-course meal in a French chateau. The children and I were eating grilled cheese sandwiches and tomato soup that night, and Peter was complaining about the amount of *time* it took to dine on a sophisticated gourmet meal in an historic chateau in France. He enjoyed the company he was in that night and the food was excellent, but all of it was negated by the *time* he had to give to the occasion. I was thankful for the distance I felt from continually juggling Peter's imbalance and trying to appease his inability to slow down and appreciate the good things in his life. I dozed off, exhaustion overpowering me.

Vienna never looked so good. I was so relieved and grateful to have the team home safe. There were songs of praise and thanksgiving flooding my mind as we made our way off the plane and through the airport to parents waiting in the lobby. The team was all that arrived. It was two days before our baggage was secured and delivered.

At the house I saw Alexia briefly while her grandparents hovered, watching us. It had been the right decision for her to stay out of harm's way and at home with them, even if the rational that kept her there was completely wrong.

Adam was playing basketball in The Hague that weekend, Amanda was exhausted and trying to catch up on her schoolwork, and my in-laws had set up a full schedule of weekend entertainment for Alexia. I didn't let it bother me much as I knew they would be leaving that week, but I missed my kids.

Chapter 31

Over the weekend, my attorney managed to serve Peter with divorce papers in LA. When I asked him how he accomplished it without addresses, he told me they caught him at the airport. Apparently, an assistant had given enough information about his arrival time. A limo always picked him up, so he was accustomed to looking for the sign with his name. Peter walked right over to my attorney's deliveryman. I cringed a little at the thought of that event but knew without his itinerary or business addresses, the week would have been an expensive wild-goose chase trying to serve him papers. My attorney had no time for nonsense. He just got the job done.

As soon as the shops opened on Monday, I was downtown to find a copy of a book Amanda had forgotten on the plane. She needed it to complete her literature essay. When I took it to the house after school, I sat down on the sofa with her, watching Alexia at the computer. My father-in-law was watching me, so I asked what time their flight departed the next day.

"We're not leaving!" he barked.

My heart dropped. "Why? Did Peter ask you to stay?"

"I can't remember," he muttered, nearly unresponsive.

I sat there holding my daughter as tears welled in my eyes. Rather than make a scene for them to witness, I kissed them good-bye, dripping on them as I left. I said nothing to my in-laws. But the next day, I had a long conversation with my mother-in law.

"You don't know your son! I'm sure you know me better than you know him."

"Well, I know enough to know I can't believe everything you say just the same as I can't believe everything he says."

"You don't need for him to tell you I'm a good mom. You don't need for him to tell you I've been a good wife to him!"

"I don't want to discuss this with you, Paige. I think we need to end this conversation."

"No, I think we need to talk. You need to go home, and you need to understand why."

"Well, as long as my son needs me here and the children want me here, I'll be right here." She started folding clothes from the table we stood beside, displaying her importance in the home with a haughty look on her face.

"Don't you understand that as long as you are here, your son does not need to work with me? He has no need for me while you are here to replace me. But my children's mother should not be replaced. They love you, but you are not their mother."

"I'm not trying to replace you. I never have."

I thought that was debatable, as she tended to take over the house, my kitchen, my routine, whenever she appeared, but I let it go.

"If you want what is best for the children, then you will go home and let us work this out as a family. Staying again, being here now, is about punishing me for filing for divorce. Do you realize how your son is using you?"

"You are not going to talk to me like that about my son."

I reiterated, "You know me better than you know him." We were quiet as we finished folding the pile of laundry in front of us. I broke the silence.

"I'd like to take Adam to the airport when he flies out for his basketball tournament in Athens this weekend."

"Well, I'll have to talk to Peter." She added, "You know he really encourages the kids to have a good relationship with you."

I wanted to explode. "Why? Why, from the beginning of our separation, did he feel a need to encourage the children to have a good relationship with a mother they *all* had a good relationship with? When Peter starts encouraging them to have a good relationship with me, he's insinuating they have a bad relationship with me. He's poisoning them! My relationships with my children were fine! Better than his have ever been."

"Oh, he's very close to *his* children."

"I am glad the kids have a better connection to their dad. They all deserved that a long time ago, but it doesn't need to be at the expense of their bond with me! I know he tells them as often as he can how much he needs them, loves them, and appreciates their support. It is so unfair of him to be aligning the children with himself and manipulating their loyalty like that. When he encourages them to have a good rapport with someone they had a healthy relationship with, he's subtly sending them the message that in spite of all *he* imagines is wrong with me, *they* should still want a connection to me. All the while, they're expected to ignore the fact that their father, a man they idolize, considers me the most unfortunate mistake of his life. Our life together—a mistake! That makes them *mistakes*!"

She said nothing and appeared to be indifferent to what I was saying. I wondered if she'd completely tuned me out, but I needed to continue.

"I know he's been told by someone what he stands to pay in child support. I know it's a lot. I also know he desperately needs his children's love and respect. But he'll have that! He'll always have that. This doesn't have to be a competition. It is so unreasonable for all of you to be making the failure of this marriage my fault."

"Paige, he poured his heart out to us one night. He broke down telling us how he failed you as a husband."

I was shocked she admitted it. "I'm glad to hear he's taken some responsibility, but he needs to say the same thing to our children."

"Well, I thought he was being way too hard on himself." Her voice was near to the mother-ease you hear used on a newborn. "Look at how much he's done for his family."

She was needling me again. "He has not been home. He has not been a husband to me, and when he was here, he was cruel!"

"I don't want to get into tit for tat about your marriage," she said.

I didn't want her in the middle either.

"Our children need two parents. I'm begging you to do what you can to convince him to work with me. Please, go home, and let us deal with this on our own."

She was beginning to shake, so I put an arm around her. Our history was long. From the outset of our relationship, I'd viewed her as a mother figure in my life. I left the laundry room to go speak with my children.

"Don't force this. Just give everything time," Adam told me. Sound advice from a seventeen-year-old, I thought. I let my daughters know I wanted their grandparents to go home. I told them their dad and I had an agreement about their lives staying the same, but it was not being honored. I needed to be with them, and I thought they needed to be with me as well. I hugged them goodnight and left, knowing they were probably feeling stuck in the middle, but I couldn't stand what was happening.

≈≈≈

My morning began with a phone call from Peter. He was still away on business, but I had no idea what corner of the planet he was calling me from.

"I will not allow you to emotionally abuse my children," he told me.

"Me! How do you think I have emotionally abused our children?" I asked him.

"Alexia felt guilt-tripped after you told them you wanted my parents to go home. Quite frankly, Paige, when you abandoned them, you broke their hearts."

"I just want our children to know I want to be with them! Stop saying I abandoned my children! You know that's not true!" I could barely contain my anger.

"Well, you left the house. The facts speak for themselves. I have suggested to the children that you receive counseling with them." His voice was holier-than-thou.

It was everything I could do to remain calm while dealing with his convoluted remarks. "I think if I were in the home with them as we agreed, counseling would not be necessary. Why don't you just have your parents go home?"

Disregarding my request, he said, "I'm willing to pay for counseling. Are you refusing counseling?"

"No, I'm not refusing anything. I just want time with my kids! Just get your parents out of our home, out of the middle of our lives, and let us make this transition. What's happening is ridiculous."

"The children really enjoy having them around."

"No joke!" I said, sarcastically. "Tonight your mother prepared three different pies for them. They are exhausting themselves to win the kids."

"Well, my kids know what they want. I'll discuss it with them. So . . . are you refusing counseling?"

"No, I'm not."

"No, I'm not going to counseling . . . or no, I'm not refusing?" he provoked.

I was reaching the end of my wits with him. "I'm not refusing counseling."

"I'm happy to hear that," he said. Before he hung up, he added, "You need to leave my parents alone."

I felt the grip of his exploits strangling my heart, my soul. He was manipulating my children to create their own boundaries in their relationships with me. Boundaries we'd never known before had become the norm, and it was killing me. They believed the divorce was my fault; therefore, they couldn't be angry with their father. In fact, he had their sympathy, and they had aligned their every thought about the divorce with his.

I viewed the issues with the children as a point of contention between Peter and myself, but the depth of malice I faced from all of them caught me completely off guard. The word *abandoned* was casually being thrown around. The message was subtle, but absolutely heartrending as my children began to believe that I left them. An old wisdom came to mind. *A lie told often enough becomes the truth.* I shuddered to think of the indelible scars that were dangerously being afflicted on my children's hearts and minds. They were living out the experience of treating someone they loved as nothing more than a piece of their history, a dispensable part of their life! Someone who made them, nurtured them, and was half of their identity, now just a part of themselves to detest or simply be indifferent to.

Amanda told me the next day not to come over. She said they were fine with Grandma and Grandpa. I didn't blame her for wanting to avoid conflict that day but reminded her I needed to see them too. The comment was met with silence. Shortly after, she needed to get off the phone. Alexia wasn't in the mood to talk either. I was informed I wouldn't be allowed to drive Adam to the airport. His grandparents would drive him. When we hung up, I was exasperated. I didn't want to put my children in the middle, but neither did I want to give up on time with them.

There was eventually a counseling session scheduled with our pastor, but cancelled at the children's request as, by then, they were tired of talking about the divorce. When we did, finally, see a different family therapist, one that had been hand-picked by Peter, the qualified expert looked at me and asked, "Why are you dividing your children?"

Chapter 32

My photos from the trip to Cairo were scattered across the table of the café. Viktor was intrigued with a black-and-white I shot of the Sphinx. A camel stood on the hill above it, giving the photo depth and perspective. He marveled at the wonders he looked at but admitted they were not on his list of prospective travel destinations.

"Nor were they on my list, but I'm thankful for the experience."

"We'll see a lot of places together," he promised, pulling me close as he gave a pleasant sigh at the thought of traveling. "Munich was nice, wasn't it?"

"Awesome," I agreed. I was ready to go again.

As if on cue, sensing my desire to escape, he asked, "Shall we go to the village this week sometime?"

His connection to me was extraordinary. He would also intuit when I was in distress. My phone would ring, I'd dry my tears to answer, and it would be Viktor asking what was wrong. His sixth sense made me feel exposed in a way I never had before, yet I marveled at the gift. Life was so much better loving and being loved.

We met at Hietzing the next day to board a tram to the small village, both of us arriving with cameras in hand. I still didn't want Viktor involved in the day-to-day insanity of what was happening with the children. I couldn't explain something I didn't even fully understand. The speed at which my relationship with my children deteriorated had me absolutely bewildered.

"How are you?" he asked.

Something so simple was so foreign, so refreshing to me. He asked, "How are *you?*" rather than "How was your *day?*" or Peter's favorite, "What did you *accomplish* today?" Viktor always asked about me first, then about the day. I seldom let Peter and Viktor enter the same thought process. To me, Viktor deserved so much better than sharing anything in the same realm of space with Peter. They just didn't belong in the same sentence or thought. But every now and then, an understated yet powerfully defining difference would strike me.

"I'm fine. How are you?" I asked, returning his greeting.

He was cheerful every day. Content and anchored, he was even stable in defeat. When a contract for a soccer player he worked with was snatched away by another agent his attitude was, "No problem. There will be more, and the next one will be better." I admired his strength of mind and character.

Answering my question, he said, "Happy." Viktor was looking right through me again. "I'm happy, but I can see on your face that you are *not* fine."

"How do you see this?" I was smiling. It was a well-rehearsed happy face.

"I see this," he said as he drew a line from my nose to the corner of my mouth. "And I see this," he continued as he drew a line across my forehead.

"You have to teach me how to do that—how to read faces."

"Oh, that takes years of observation," he said, shaking his head as though my wish would be impossible to grant.

I giggled, guessing he was exaggerating his talent and experience.

"Tell me. What's going on?" He was unmoved in his resolve to know.

I sighed. "Are you sure you really want to know?" He nodded, waiting for me to speak. "My in-laws are still here. Peter was served divorce papers the day before they were to leave, so he cancelled their flight out. I'm sure it's to punish me because with his parents here, I don't have normal time with the kids. But it's my children I'm worried about."

"Their grandparents love them. This will all calm down in time. Your children are safe," he rationalized.

"I really don't think they are. Physically, yes. But emotionally and mentally, what's happening is not good."

"They'll understand in time that people grow apart."

"I trust one day my children will know the differences between their father and I were more than just growing apart. But I don't know if they'll forgive me for being the one to end the marriage. They hate me."

"They don't hate you. They're just angry right now." He was trying to put a positive spin on the situation.

"It's beyond that. They are hearing things about me kidnapping them, and then they'll hear something about me abandoning them. I'm sure nothing is making sense to them."

"No," Viktor said in disbelief. "So extreme?" he asked.

"It's extreme." I felt ready to break thinking about it. Trying not to let my voice quiver, I said, "I feel like I'm in the fight of my life, but I have no idea how to defeat this."

"Be careful," Viktor warned. "Progress lies in harmony."

I considered his words, felt his peace, and knew he was right.

"But I don't think there will ever be harmony with Peter. Harmony is just not *in* him."

"He does seem conflict oriented."

"That's the right term," I agreed.

"I just don't understand how a parent can use a child to hurt their spouse. It is such a low thing to do. He has no feeling for his children's basic needs, emotionally and mentally. In fact, this tells me your husband has no feeling for himself. He isn't thinking right now."

"Oh, he's thinking! He's thinking about his bank account, his reputation, and the best way to punish me for leaving him."

"But the marriage wasn't working. It's not good for him either."

"He didn't really need the marriage, he just needed the appearance of being a dedicated husband and family man."

Viktor shook his head, trying to understand, but I sensed he was nearly unable to relate to Peter's approach to life and family. "I'm shocked," he said. "Just shocked! How did you spend eighteen years living with such a man?"

That was a question I'd been asking myself lately too. I'd concluded the years with Peter *did* eventually bring me to Vienna, and for that, I was extraordinarily thankful. We were silent a moment.

"I think I would have followed my mother if it meant living under a tree," he said.

My heart dropped. I thought he was blaming me for not having a bulletproof relationship with my children that was resistant to such adversity.

"It's not their fault. It has taken me years to leave him. You don't understand how cunning he can be. He makes such heartfelt promises that seldom carry any weight. When you hear them, it's hard not to buy into what he says. But now, every time he begins a sentence with, 'When your mother left us . . .' he's sending them the message I abandoned *them*. They are *us*, the family; and I am separate, the hardhearted person who left. He's as convincing as ever."

"What do you mean?" Viktor asked.

"Positive or negative, he's extremely skillful at influencing people to have confidence in what he's saying and to conduct themselves accordingly."

Viktor nodded, but I sensed he had little basis to understand how debase the situation had become.

"He's trying to erase me from his life, but he's too caught up in his own emotions to understand the impact he is having on our children. He's obsessed with negating me from that household."

Viktor pulled me close enough to kiss my forehead. In his kiss was a message to think better thoughts. I recalled memories of my little one.

"Alexia calls herself Sugar Spy. She loves to play detective and hide in corners to 'get the scoop' on what's happening. I suspect her dad is taking advantage of her listening ear while pretending he doesn't know she's there. It's all obscured, of course. I think he knows better than to bad-mouth me directly, but heaven only knows what she's hearing. It's all so subtle."

He looked perplexed, imagining adult conversations about the separation taking place within earshot of the children. There was concern in his voice.

"It's just so unnatural for them. You've been with them their whole life."

With that, I fully understood his earlier comment about following his mother to live under a tree. She had been his caregiver throughout his childhood. Choosing to break from that nurturing would mean choosing to be neglected.

"Is your husband planning to quit his job?"

"I can't imagine him doing that. His job is his identity."

"Then why is he doing this?"

I shrugged my shoulders, shook my head, and relayed an earlier conversation.

"He told me the other day that he was established and could give the children all they needed. I would be working or studying, trying to start a career, and I wouldn't have time for them anymore. It's just a head game he's playing."

This drew a belly laugh from Viktor. "He's not normal. You both began with nothing, and he expects you to start over after eighteen years?"

"Yes." I gave one big affirmative nod. "I don't know who it is advising him. When he told me he was established, it sounded staged . . . rehearsed. By winning custody, he saves between seven and eight thousand dollars a month, he keeps his family man reputation, and he punishes me for ending the marriage. Maybe someone is advising him to use the children this way. He told me shortly after we'd drawn up the separation agreement that his attorney told him I'd be begging to come back. It all just makes me wonder if he's getting bad counsel."

"Attorneys enjoy angry clients. They just have to pour a little oil on the fire to keep their paychecks rolling in," Viktor said.

I thought of my attorney. He told me we were taking the high road, the entire way through. I appreciated that but wished there had been a different way to serve Peter divorce papers. That event, no doubt, was like pouring oil on fire.

"I can't imagine an attorney in the judicial system actually advising a client to use their child, psychologically damaging the child, just to keep conflict going . . . all for money." I rattled on, putting it all together.

"You must do everything you can to keep your children whole," Viktor advised.

I liked his terminology, and even though I knew he was correct, I had no idea how to keep my children complete and unmarred in the tug-of-war they were caught in. So much was already broken.

≈≈≈

"I'm the only friend he's got," said my son. "Who else is he supposed to talk to?" he asked me, in defense of having become his father's peer.

"He's got his parents, your uncle, his sister."

"Mom, just stop. You're just jealous of my relationship with Dad now."

"No, I'm not. I'm pleased you and your sisters have a place in his life, but it doesn't have to mean the end of our relationship. Do you remember telling me before the separation that you all knew who did what—the Easter bunny, Santa, the doctor appointments, the ball games I videoed? Remember?"

"Yes, I just said that stuff to make you stay," Adam said.

Showing appreciation for me was no longer allowed. Adam was disconnecting from the positive thoughts and feelings he had about me, replacing them with the attitude that he was just pretending when he acknowledged the things I'd done. The memories I had created with him were being downgraded and washed away. Our connection seemed to be little more than fragments of history that were violently being tossed around on a dangerous current of disregard running downriver, far away from us.

≈≈≈

"Please don't come over today, Mom." It was Alexia calling from her new cell phone from the bus. She told me it had been given to her in case she ever needed help. I intuited that to mean if I ever tried to kidnap her, she'd always have a way to contact her dad. "Do you understand what you have done to my heart?" she asked me.

"I understand your heart is breaking because your parents are not together," I said.

"You're not a good mom."

Immediately, I began to recount the things I'd done for her and explain what I thought made a good mom.

"Don't you remember rocking with me for days at a time when you were sick?"

"Stop lying!" she shrieked and began crying into her phone.

I knew the conversation taking place needed to happen face-to-face. "Alexia, will you come over with your brother and sister on Sunday?"

Peter was returning the next day, Saturday, and he liked everyone at home when he arrived; so I knew better than to ask her to be with me then.

"I'll ask. I'll call tomorrow." She had turned off her tears.

How could she say those things? Believe what she said? *Feel* what she believed? I was at a complete loss as to how to deal with what was happening.

Chapter 33

When I called the house the next morning to speak with Peter about a consistent arrangement to see the children while my in-laws were in town, my mother-in-law answered the phone. She informed me her son was still asleep, but she would have him call me when he woke up. I was tired of waiting, tired of being the nice guy, while my children were being fed lies. I informed my mother-in-law while we spoke that I wanted the children the next afternoon for Sunday dinner.

"Well, I'll have to ask my son if that's okay."

"Your son is not their only parent."

She stammered, "I think there are some kids coming tomorrow to work on a school project."

"Well, the kids need to eat. They can do that with me."

"I'll have Peter call you," she said.

By 7:00 p.m., still, there had been no phone call; so I called to speak with the girls directly. Amanda had friends coming over. She thought that trying to spend time at my place, between church and everyone arriving an hour later, would be too complicated. For unexplained reasons, Alexia didn't want to be alone with me. Adam was still in Athens playing basketball.

Peter took the phone.

"Stop putting the children in the middle," he scolded.

"You won't return my calls. My children and I need to see each other. What else am I supposed to do?"

"Why do I need to return your calls? You can come over here and see your children any time you want!" he was raising his voice to be heard. I heard footsteps on the stairs; the girls were going back to their bedrooms.

"Fine. I'll be there tomorrow night. I want you and your parents to make plans to be gone while I'm there." I called his bluff.

"It's a big house. We're not going anywhere."

When I arrived the next day, my mother-in-law had started a double batch of cookies, making herself indispensable in the hub of our home. I spoke with Alexia and pulled out the photos from Cairo that I brought to share with her that night. There were friends from the team at the house with Amanda. All of us enjoyed reliving fresh memories from the trip. I offered to help them with the school project coming together in my daughter's room, but they said it was under control. I was rubbing Alexia's back before she mysteriously disappeared when I needed to take a batch of cookies out of the oven. I found her with my mother-in-law who held her tight while whispering something in her ear.

The cookies had baked. Everyone was ready for one of my chocolate-chip-specialty-milk shakes. My mother-in-law went to the cupboard to pull out the blender. I informed her I'd make the milk shakes.

"Would you like one as well?" I asked her. She hem-hawed about her weight. "Would anyone like a different flavor?" I asked of the group.

"Mom, Grandma's making them," Amanda informed me.

"I'll do it, sweetie."

No one argued. My mother-in-law hung around nibbling on cookies and pouring Coke. Adam arrived home from his basketball tournament and treated me completely normal, as he was oblivious to the nonsense littering the air. He gave me a hug hello and another big hug after I gave him his keepsake from Cairo. Before he left the room, there was a kiss good-bye.

"I'd like to take Alexia to the high school play tomorrow night. We could drive up after dinner," I suggested.

My father-in-law had entered the kitchen. I was unaware of Peter's whereabouts.

Howard piped up and announced to everyone in the room, "I'm not supposed to let you have the keys to the car."

"That's crazy. You know I drove almost two hundred miles a day, and my driving record is perfect. It's your son that almost killed himself with his driving," I reminded them.

I wished I hadn't said it the minute it popped out of my mouth, but it was true. His driving was offensive, and his tickets were too numerous to keep track of. It was a couple months earlier that a ticket had arrived in the mail. At that point in time, cameras photographed the license plates of speeding cars in Vienna. You received your ticket in the mail. Peter decided it must have been mine; therefore, I was not going to be allowed to use the car. It was almost sinister how happy his father was to comply with his son's wishes and deliver my penalty. I saw my father-in-law completely different than the man I thought I'd known.

I was able to see my older children at the musical the next night, but Alexia never called to let me know whether she would be going with me or not. I didn't push it. I just went alone knowing I'd be watching my little one in concert the next night.

At four o'clock the next day, my phone rang. It was time for the kids to be coming home from school, but my father-in-law was calling to inform me that my daughter had been home sick all day with a stomach bug. Even though I was angry that no one bothered to inform me earlier, I managed to thank him for not letting me make an unnecessary trip up to the school.

"Please, from now on, if she's sick, let me know in the morning. I could have been with her all day."

"We were with her all day!" he spouted.

I knew that. I also knew why I hadn't been informed. But I didn't care if they were uncomfortable around me or how thick the tension was between us. After I knew Alexia was sick, I picked up some groceries and called to let them know I would be there soon.

"Please, Mom. Don't come over here," begged Amanda. "Dad's here." She also informed me her sister was getting a back rub from her grandmother and Adam was sleeping. Imagining the scenario of my arrival amid what was happening there, I knew it was best to comply with her wishes and just stay home.

Later Peter called to inform me our youngest needed to be seen at the hospital the next morning.

"Be ready!" he ordered as though I had a problem managing my time. "I'll be there at six thirty tomorrow morning."

"Is she okay for the night?" I asked.

"We've got it under control. I think she's just under stress."

No kidding! It was unnerving not being with her. Even more unnerving not being able to reduce the stress she felt. I thought if she was sick, she should have her mother, but her father announced the conclusion she was stressed as though it was my fault.

Peter arrived to pick me up at a quarter to seven the next morning. He was driving fast to make up the time he lost being late. Our daughter was thoroughly examined and sent home with medication for her stomachache.

"I think she could just come to my apartment today?" I said during the ride home.

"There's nothing over there for her," he argued.

I thought I'd let my daughter decide. "Alexia, would you like to come over to my apartment for the—"

"Shush!" Peter snarled as he snapped his fingers in my face and pointed at me to hush.

"We could just go to the house," Alexia interjected. *We!* One little word, and it thrilled me. It was a day of board games, movies, cooking, and cuddling my little snuggle bug. Her grandparents were in and out throughout the day, looking in on us. Alone with Alexia, everything was relatively normal. She named the fifth-graders that were "going together." She and Mark were back to being an item as well. I wondered if other mothers knew so many details of the happenings in the fifth grade. I was in heaven listening to her, watching her open up, and share her life with me.

As soon as Peter walked in the door, Alexia jumped into his arms like a toddler. I no longer existed. I had gathered my summer clothes that day and asked for a ride to my apartment, rather than struggling with the bags on the tram. Peter obliged and gave me a ride.

"The girls tell me you'll be going to London with them during spring break," I commented.

"Yup."

"Well, I want to let you know I'll be in the States during that time," I informed him.

"What are you going to be doing in the States?"

Resenting the control in his tone, I answered, "I'll be spending some time with my sister." *Among other things*, I thought.

"You're such a lousy mother."

I fell for his bait and started defending myself.

"Because *I'm* traveling for two weeks during a time that you will undoubtedly be keeping me from having normal time with my children, I'm a lousy mother?" Exasperating me was one of Peter's favorite activities. "We need to talk about the girls going back to the States with me. They can finish their school year, and we'll fly out immediately after."

"They're not going anywhere with you!"

"Why do you think you're the only person who can travel with them?"

"They trust me."

He knew they trusted me too, but arguing with him was a waste of time. Elaborating on why I knew they trusted me would only spur more rivalry. As so many times before, I let his barbs silence me, which only fueled his need for a reaction.

"I don't intend to be a single parent," he added out of the blue.

I laughed at his nerve to throw that at me given all he had orchestrated to ensure our children viewed him as their only respectable parent.

"With the money you've got, I'm sure you won't be single long."

"You'll be begging to come back soon," Peter countered.

"Where are my diamonds? I'd like to have those back."

"Those are a reminder to me to never give my heart to another woman."

I was thankful we'd reached my apartment. I thanked him for the ride as I left the vehicle. The more time I had away from my husband, the more thankful I was to be away from his undulating words that had been peddled off as emotion over the years. I was slowly coming to terms with the toll eighteen years with him had taken on me. Pulling away from the curb, Peter squealed the tires of our M-class like an immature teen trying to display every ounce of the power he took pleasure in possessing.

My in-laws failed to leave the house the next day. I spent the day with Alexia in spite of it, and left a couple hours after Adam and Amanda came home. I wanted to be gone before Peter arrived. In my apartment mailbox was a FedEx package from my attorney. He explained he needed a declaration, so I began writing. When the sun rose the next morning, I was still sitting there.

I needed to give a coach's speech for the swim season at the high school awards ceremony. I saw all of my children briefly at school that day before riding the bus home with Adam and Alexia. Amanda had an activities night at school and afterward was staying overnight with her best friend.

On Saturday morning when I called the house to schedule time with the children over the weekend, Peter was asleep. Alexia said she'd have him call me back, but the call never came. I worked on swim records all day and went through old journals and sentimental letters. When I called back that evening, Adam told me he had too much work to spend Sunday afternoon with me. Alexia was spending the night with a friend and didn't know when she'd return home, and my older daughter needed to buckle down to homework, as she hadn't started any of her weekend work yet. I let Amanda know her swim times had become new school records. She was thrilled to know her name would be in the record books.

"I'm so very proud of you and all you accomplished this year, sweetie."

"Thanks, Momma." The lilt in her voice let me know she was smiling.

Sunday was spent organizing things around the apartment. I packed and sorted out what I'd be taking to LA, then drew up a list of necessities to shop for upon arrival. I had a long, and emotional visit with my parents. Peter also called about a doctor's invoice he had received in regard to me.

It was March 20. I bought groceries to cook at the house and called a taxi instead of carrying the bags on the tram. Peter was waiting at the children's bus stop as my taxi turned the corner onto our street. It still startled me to see him around home at a time that was habitually referred to as the middle of his workday before we separated.

Inside the house I started baking shortbread. Peter was taking his parents out for the evening, but only with the knowledge that our older son would be home all night.

"Call us if you need anything," he instructed the children as he and his parents walked out the door. As I busied myself with dinner, the girls settled in nearby, dragging what they needed from their book bags to the kitchen. My little one was painting an invention. Amanda worked on her math. Adam was sleeping in spite of being put into "protector" role that evening, and I rejoiced knowing my son was comfortable trusting me. I checked e-mail after dinner was prepared, then joined Amanda in the kitchen.

"Are you hungry, sweetie?"

"Starving and it smells so good. I love your cooking, Mom."

She was forever endearing herself. Sunshine in the room since the day she was born, she was my receptive one. She was continually looking out for everyone around her, taking it upon herself to be the peacekeeper. Her spirit was so strong there were times I'd just marvel at her capacity to put everyone at ease and her courage to do unthinkable things, like bebop up to the Russian team to shake their hands while she and her teammates were being glared down.

"I'm glad you love my cooking," I said, winking at her.

"Are you okay, Mom?" she asked.

"Yes, why?"

"You just don't look so good," she answered.

"I'm fine," I assured her as I took her hands in mine across the island in our kitchen.

She was studying me with every ounce of her perceptiveness. Then she nearly screamed, "Mom! Are you pregnant?"

∞ PART II ∞

I've opened again, I've trusted, and I've received—more than my wildest dreams could have ever imagined. The baby booties I picked out on the way home were placed gently on top of a letter in addition to a dated pregnancy test inside the sturdy little box. The lid was golden, just like the moment. I tied a white ribbon round the box and called him.

"Meet me at the café beside Bellaria," he said, adding it was at the end of the Forty-ninth, across the street from the Museum of Natural History.

Perfect, I thought. A beautiful view for the moment I'd deliver news that his life would forever change. I saw him through the window before I stepped inside. When the host met me at the door, I just pointed to the table he occupied. As I was escorted to be seated, I noticed the print hanging on the wall directly above his head. It was Klimt's pregnant woman. Uncanny he chose that table, I thought, as he had no idea what he was about to hear. He stood when he saw me and asked if the table was all right.

"Perfect. You have no idea how perfect," I said, letting my coat fall into Viktor's waiting hands. I unwrapped the scarf from around my neck but quickly decided to put it back on my shoulders as the chilly winter air was still lingering.

"What is this?" he said, pointing to the box waiting on the table.

"This is why I wanted to see you tonight." I was exuberant and all smiles, the tears in my eyes appearing naturally from transferring into the warm air.

"Please, go ahead," I said, motioning for him to open the box after we had settled into each other's arms at our corner table.

He opened very slowly, clueless as to what might be inside. When he removed the top layer of tissue, he saw the little white baby booties. There were immediate tears in his eyes as he asked, "Are you? Are you sure?" With tears running down our faces we kissed through our smiles and held each other tight. When our embrace broke, he kissed the booties in his hand and held them to his heart before he picked up the note I wrote.

My dearest Viktor,

With a heart full of gratitude, I want you to know you give my life new meaning. Moments spent with you fill me with hope and promise for the future. To be blessed carrying your child overwhelms me with joy. You told me when I met you, "There are no accidents." I couldn't agree more. I know we are meant to be. Everything I am is yours. I love you.

Paige

"I love you too," he said. Though he'd shown me a hundred different ways, hearing his voice say the words made it absolute, consummate.

As if on cue, the saxophone and keyboard began playing "New York, New York." We laughed, happiness filling the air for his little first-generation American I carried.

Chapter 34

Having no idea how she figured it out, my eyes just welled with tears, and there was no need to speak. I didn't want to tell anyone before I knew the baby was healthy, but I couldn't lie to her. I nodded yes, confirming to Amanda I was pregnant.

"Is it Dad's?" she asked.

I shook my head no and watched shock register on my daughter's face.

"Mom! How could you?" she cried.

"Please go get your brother and sister. We all need to talk."

She ran from the room and promptly brought her brother and sister downstairs.

"You're pregnant!" Adam shouted as he entered the room.

"I'm so sorry," I was crying. "I didn't want to tell you like this. I didn't want to tell you now! I can't believe you figured this out, Amanda." I buried my face in my hands, my children looking on.

"I can't believe this," Adam said, under his breath.

"I wanted to introduce you to your brother or sister's father before I told you about the baby."

"Half brother . . . or half sister," Alexia corrected, forever the pragmatic realist of the bunch.

"I wanted you to get to know him before you found out. We don't even know if everything is okay yet. There will be an amniocentesis this week."

"That's why you're traveling this week?" Amanda asked.

"Yes, my appointment is Monday. The baby will be delivered in the States."

"When will you know if everything's okay?" she asked.

"It takes about two weeks to get test results back."

"Whose is it?" asked Adam.

I took a deep breath and began. "His name is Viktor. He's a wonderful man with no children of his own. He asks about you guys every time I see him. He loves you already, because you're part of me. He's really looking forward to meeting you."

"I'm not ready to meet him." Alexia made no bones about getting her point across.

"How did you meet him?" asked Adam.

"On the metro."

"You met on public transportation?" he asked in disbelief.

"Yes, he gave me his business card. We met for coffee one day and have been together ever since. I know what has happened between us has happened very fast, but I assure you, I am very fortunate to have this man in my life."

"What does he do?" asked Adam.

"He's a sports agent. He represents athletes, motivates them, and finds the right team for them to play on."

"He's a Jerry Maguire?" said Adam, my movie savvy child.

"Exactly. He's a photographer too! He has a gallery near Museumsquartier. He actually takes more photos than I do."

"That's impossible," said Alexia.

"I really want you to meet him," I said.

"What does he look like?" asked Amanda.

"Well, he's tall, dark, and handsome," I said, trying to lighten the mood.

"How dark?" asked Alexia. "Does he speak English?"

"It's his hair that is very dark. Our skin color is the same. And yes, he speaks English. As well as German, Serbian, Russian, Italian, Spanish, and French."

They were unmoved.

"Where is he from?" asked Adam.

"He was born in former Yugoslavia."

"Where's Yugoslavia?" Alexia asked

"I think Belgrade is about ten hours from here by car. It's between here and Greece."

We all sat looking at each other for a moment. I wanted them to ask all the questions they had.

"I'm so sorry, you guys. I know the separation has been hard on you, and I know no one is ready for this. I know this will be an embarrassment for you with some of your close friends at school. I'm just so sorry it's happening this way for you."

My face was wet with tears. Amanda had tears running down her face too, and it crushed me to know I'd forever be viewed differently by my children. Shocked silence filled the room.

Adam came around the kitchen island reaching to hug me. "I'm not real happy with you right now, but I'm thankful you never considered having an abortion."

I clung to him, thankful for his insight, and I prayed that others would echo the sentiments of my seventeen-year-old son. Our roles had reversed in that I was sure I would have told him the same thing if he'd come to me with news of a pregnancy.

"Please let me tell your dad when he comes home tonight," I said to all of them.

Amanda left the room, and I saw her walking in the flower garden. Adam and Alexia followed her, and together, my children stood among the fruit trees in our yard and absorbed the veracity of my news. They were holding each other as I sat watching them from the kitchen window, tears still running down my face, the joy I'd felt telling Viktor he would be a father fading into the absolute turmoil of my children's lives. I'd taught them since they were toddlers to be nice to each other because one day, the three of them would be all that was left of our family. But watching them hold each other, that day seemed to have already arrived.

≈≈≈

"You fucking whore! You goddamned fucking whore! Get out of my house. Get out of my house *now!*" Peter was screaming at me over the phone.

Adam had decided not to allow me to tell his father in person. His decision was spot on.

"You fucking whore! I want you out of my house and don't you ever plan to come back."

I grabbed my things and walked outside as I put my jacket on. "Your dad wants me to leave. Adam, I was going to tell him myself. You didn't need to do that."

"It's better this way," he said. "Really Mom, it's better I told him."

I nodded in agreement, tucking myself under his arm and hugging him around the waist. "Thank you for your reaction, son. I raised an awesome kid." It was so apparent who had raised him when I compared his reaction to Peter's.

"Yes, you did," he said, readily agreeing with my assessment.

"Are you guys all right if I leave?" I asked.

"We're not all right, Mom," said Amanda. "But you need to leave before Dad gets here." She gave me a quick hug. Alexia gave me a reluctant hug, but I held on to her.

I wanted to reassure all of them that things would work out and we'd all be okay before I let myself out. As I walked to the tram, the weight of what had happened crashing in, I felt their utter devastation in my wake.

Chapter 35

I'd just given Peter and his parents something huge to "hang their hat" on. To be legally married and carrying another man's child was so far outside the norm of society's rules. It was a given—you don't do that!

I spent the next day on the phone, listening to people tell me it was too soon for me, too soon for the kids, too soon for the family, too soon for everyone. I knew on an intellectual level what they were saying was true; but on an emotional level, the child I was carrying represented hope, love, and everything correct in the world. With Peter demanding the loyalty of my older children, I desperately wanted to learn that the baby I carried was healthy.

The children were not talkative the next day when I phoned them. I knew I dare not try to go to the house to see them, so I text-messaged all of them goodnight, reminding them my flight was first thing in the morning. I promised to be in touch, told them to have a good time while they were in London with their dad, and that I'd see them in two weeks.

Peter sat the children down for a family meeting in the days that followed my announcement. From what I've pieced together, the conversation went something like this.

"We need to put your mother and her illegitimate child on our prayer lists. The Ten Commandments are very clear. Adultery is considered a cardinal sin, the same as killing someone. So, you need to pray for her and her new family. I want to discuss something personal with you as well. Since your mother is having an affair, I wanted to ask you kids . . . because you're the dearest people in the world to me, if . . . well, if you would mind if I began dating?"

It was agreed by all—their dad *beginning* to date would be fine. The children later told me, "At least Dad respects us enough to ask first."

Peter was clever. To ask their permission to begin dating, something he started doing long before, was simply brilliant. Having it out in the open would certainly simplify his life. What I had done was considered an adulterous affair and what Peter was doing was considered an appropriate "response." In requesting they pray for my new family, he was suggesting to them that *they* were no longer my family. I was a detachment, no longer considered part of *their* family.

≈≈≈

My layover in Paris was nearly too short. In order to catch my flight, I had to run through Charles de Gaulle with a carry-on. Toting a bag wasn't the best thing to be doing in my condition, but I was still jogging with the pregnancy, so it wasn't a complete shock to my system. Thankfully, onboard, there were hours to just relax and try to sleep, which came easy. The day wasn't less problematic in LA though. I couldn't rent a car with only a debit card, but I did have my checkbook, so I had the airport taxi drop me at a dealership near the apartment so that I could just buy one.

Viktor and I used taxis the first week we visited LA; but this time I needed wheels to establish the apartment, meet with my attorney, and make trips back and forth to the doctor. Depending on taxis in LA was a lot different than waiting between three to five minutes for a taxi in Vienna. We learned it could take an hour or more to get a ride in LA, a difficult inconvenience I couldn't manage during this trip.

The dealer agreed to let me use one of the cars he had on his lot until the weekend because I didn't come across anything I wanted. Saturday, he was going to auction and invited me to come with him. He promised I'd have a big selection.

Once I had an essentially-paid-for-yet-borrowed car, the next couple hours were spent choosing the items needed for the new apartment before making a trip to the grocery store to purchase some essentials. It was dark as I unloaded the car, hauling my goods through the complex. Music was blasting from several apartments. It occurred to me nobody would ever hear me scream if the need arose, completely different from Vienna where quiet hours are strictly observed and respect for your fellow neighbors is not an expectation—it's the law.

Once the car was unloaded, I secured the deadbolts, checked the windows and sliding glass door to our terrace, put away the perishables, then fell into the bed without setting an alarm. It was almost ten o'clock in the morning in Vienna, the day after I woke up at four o'clock in the morning to catch my flight. I'd been in motion almost thirty hours. My head was dizzy with exhaustion.

Viktor flew in the next day from New York where he had been scouting galleries for his art. He felt about New York the same as I felt about

Vienna—fascinated with a sense of having been born there. He relayed the events of his trip while we prepared for our doctor's visit. I was nervous about undergoing an amniocentesis in spite of its necessity.

My fourth child was born with a rare disorder and lived for only one day. After holding him in my arms as his complications suffocated him, I knew I could not give birth to another child that would only suffer then die. I'd feel criminal letting that happen again, and at my age, the odds of a successful pregnancy were diminished. Foregoing an amniocentesis this time was contrary to reason.

Our doctor was great. He and Viktor visited through the whole procedure, discussing philosophical differences between the United States and Europe. The amniocentesis was over before I knew it. Now, all we could do was wait. The next few days were spent resting. It was much-needed rest as the past week had been emotionally, as well as physically, exhausting. Time with Viktor was magic, whether we were in a small studio apartment in Culver City or sitting in an elegant café in Munich. It didn't matter; he was consistent, steady as a rock, and as upbeat as the day was long.

Saturday arrived, and to say there was a big selection at the car auction was an understatement. The selection was colossal and completely overwhelming. Viktor declined making the trip as he didn't drive and had no idea what to look for in an auto. There I stood in a sea of cars, with a Dealer ID tag hanging around my neck. Having no idea where to begin, I decided to look for the shape and color I liked. I was partial to a Lexus that the mechanic with us examined and found acceptable. For a moment I thought my dealer was going to lose it in bidding, but he came through. The purchase price was much better than I had hoped for, even adding the agreed-upon fee for the dealer.

The answering machine at the house in Vienna was turned off, so I needed to make three different phone calls to their cell phones in order to make contact with my children. Fortunately, they all picked up! Amanda asked about the test. She wanted to know the exact date we would have results. Alexia was less than cooperative. When I spoke to Adam, he told me she was being obstinate with everyone and not to take it personally. Then he asked if Viktor had any luck in New York. There was an impression of acceptance in Adam and Amanda that pleased me. Alexia, however, had always enjoyed being "the baby." I suspected she was having a difficult time with the idea of losing her place. I wanted to comfort her and talk to her about it, but I wasn't given the chance. It was good to hear all of their voices before they flew out the next day. I told them I'd call their dad's cell phone while they were in London since their phones didn't work internationally, and then wished them all safe travel.

Peter left his phone turned off the entire time he was in London with the children, but I left messages for them every day. When I reached them after they returned to Vienna, they told me they'd never received any of my messages. I let them know I was thankful I could call their phones in Austria since they were home. It was nine o'clock at night, and their dad was going out. Peter was liberated with the news of my pregnancy, so there was no need to disguise his extracurricular activities anymore. Alexia was waiting for a phone call. Amanda asked about the test results that hadn't come back the day they were supposed to, and Adam was getting ready to play Ping-Pong with a friend. I was at ease knowing they were home safe, each already doing their own thing.

≈≈≈

Conversations with them were brief until Viktor and I were able to share the news we'd all been waiting for. Nervous, and still quietly praying for a healthy baby, I called the doctor's office, gave them my name, and asked if there were any test results yet. The silent wait for the nurse to come back to the phone seemed an eternal black hole. She burst back onto the line.

"Do you want to know the sex of the baby?" she asked.

"Yes," I said, hoping she hadn't offered that much without just cause.

"You're having a healthy baby boy," she said.

"A boy?" I looked at Viktor. "It's a healthy baby boy!" I squealed.

Viktor squeezed my hand, smiling with tears in his eyes, and asked, "Everything is okay?"

The nurse heard him ask and answered, "Yes, it's a healthy baby boy. I can't tell you his IQ, but his chromosomes are in order."

"No extra Y or anything?" I asked.

"No extra Y or anything." There was amusement in her voice as she added, "He's perfectly normal."

"Thank you," I said.

She barely got out "Your welcome!" before the line went dead.

Viktor and I held each other, both of us overcome with relief.

"We're having a son!" he said, drawing me in for a momentous kiss. "I only wanted a healthy child, but a son! We're celebrating tonight. Let's go to Spago's." It was home to fellow Austrian, Wolfgang Puck, and he wanted the evening to be memorable.

It hadn't occurred to me how much my sports-minded partner would enjoy a son. His only wish through the pregnancy was a healthy baby. The only other grandchild in the family was a girl. A boy for the firstborn male in the family meant the family name would be carried on. Viktor was absolutely delighted, as was I, to know the child was healthy.

Until the news, I'd felt it was a girl. I wondered if it was because my little girl's hearts and minds were being stolen away from me and I so desperately wanted to finish raising my daughters. But another son! The news was just wonderful.

We were seated beside Bo Derek as we watched Evander Holyfield walk out the door. It certainly was a notable beginning. Neither of us stopped smiling all night.

≈≈≈

"You were right, Amanda!" I said.

"It's a boy?" she asked, excitement in her voice.

"It's a boy!"

"Is he healthy?"

"Yes, yes! He's healthy."

"Good," she said, drawing it out in a long, relieved breath.

When I spoke to Alexia to tell her she would have a healthy little brother, she corrected me again.

"Half brother," she stated.

Adam said, "Cool."

One son graduating high school, setting out into the world the same year another one was arriving. Cool, indeed! I was a very rich woman.

Chapter 36

"Since I'm over here already, why don't I just meet Adam in New York to look at colleges, rather than you taking vacation," I said to Peter over the phone.

"No," he flatly stated. "What else do you want?"

"To speak with my children."

Peter yelled, "Adam! It's your mom. Do you want to speak to her?" Adam was sleeping, but I heard him making his way to the phone. Once we'd satisfied our need to hear each other's voice though, Adam wasn't very talkative.

"Can I speak with your dad again, Adam."

"Sure. He's right here," he said. No doubt monitoring our conversation, I thought.

"I'll be back Wednesday. I want some time with the kids when I return," I told Peter.

He was silent, as if I'd said nothing.

"Peter? How are we going to establish time for me with the children?"

"No time with them hasn't bothered you for the past two weeks!" he snapped.

"Peter, that is not true. I could throw the same thing back in your face for the past eighteen years."

"No, you couldn't. It's bothered me," he retorted.

"Me too! Why do you think I call every day? Sometimes three times a day to speak with each of them."

"Liar. Such a liar. You are a master liar."

"I have phone bills that show the calls I've made. Call me a liar all you want, it doesn't make it true."

"Liar!" was all he managed to come back with.

With that I hung up, no longer feeling a need to subject myself to his continuous barrage of verbal abuse. I wondered which of my children was listening to him and how long his side of the conversation continued.

I drove to my sister's home in Phoenix for the Easter holiday. Earlier I shopped for Easter basket items that I would give the kids when I returned to

Vienna. When we woke up Sunday morning, it was depressing not watching the three of them hunt for their Easter baskets. The hunt, which had grown more elaborate with their age, was something they looked forward to that day. Viktor had flown back to Vienna, and as much as my sister did to make the day enjoyable, I still felt removed from all that was natural.

Back in LA, my pastor from the small town we left in Tennessee called me. It was an extremely difficult conversation, and I spent most of it in tears. We talked for almost an hour. It was four o'clock in the morning in Vienna, but Viktor woke in his sleep, sensing something wrong. He called and called, unable to get through because the line was busy. When he finally reached me, he could tell that I had been crying. There was panic in his voice, afraid something was wrong with the baby. When I told him I'd been talking to my pastor and the conversation was difficult, he relaxed.

"Please. Don't let people provoke you to tears. It's not good for the baby."

"You don't understand. I loved this man and his family. The church *was* my family while I lived there. It hurts to know I've disappointed them. There is no way to make anyone understand."

"They'll understand in time. Right now, you must think of the baby. Please!" he begged.

I was calm before we hung up.

"Please get some sleep," I told him. "I'm fine. We're fine. Your energy is coming through the phone line. Really, we're fine."

"You need to sleep now too. Think about me," he said.

"Always," I answered.

"Um . . . not enough."

"I'm sorry. It's a lot for everybody to deal with. I understand you. Now, let's get some sleep. I love you."

"I love you too. I'm sending love for the baby too," he said.

"Goodnight."

≈≈≈

That week I also received a letter from my mother stating that she thought it best for the girls to live with their father while they adjusted to someone new in my life. Perhaps in a year or two, they would want to live with me again. To the people who didn't know Viktor, it seemed as though I'd derailed my life. He was such a blessing to me, but in light of the void in their understanding, he was a blessing multiplied by zero.

Conflicting emotions ran parallel, somehow balanced in their opposition within me. My loved ones were as disappointed in me as Viktor was pleased. I was grieved to know I'd hurt my family, yet there was renewal in being deeply cherished by someone. My future with Viktor was bright. Emotionally, we were intensely connected, and in each other, we had discovered ourselves. Gratification was mutual, and together, there was confidence and hope bolstering our dream of a life together. Life with Viktor was much more than a sense of being *on track*. It was pure *joy*—at a very high price.

Chapter 37

When I arrived in Vienna, I called the house several times. No answer. Odd, I thought, since I told everyone I'd be home that evening. The kids were looking forward to seeing me when I spoke to them. I tried Adam's cell phone and reached him.

"Hi! Are you home?" he asked.

"I'm here. Where are you?"

"Dad decided we should have a Fun Day. We're all at the Prater."

The Prater is Vienna's amusement park, famous for its giant Ferris wheel that was built in 1896. It is sprawled out across what were originally imperial hunting grounds, and even with a map, it's easy to become disoriented on the many paths that run amuck through the woods of the enormous park. It's a marvelous place for a family to spend the *day*.

"It doesn't sound like I'll be seeing you this evening."

"Um, well . . . no . . . I don't know, Mom. I don't know what time . . . "

"It's okay, Adam. Just have fun. Enjoy the Prater. I'll call you all tomorrow." I couldn't blame my children for abiding by Peter's wishes.

"Okay," he said.

"I love you."

"You too."

I couldn't help but remember how Peter demanded that all our children be at home when he arrived after an absence from them. It didn't matter that our children were grown, that our son was dating, or that they received invitations to sleepovers. They were to be *at home* when he arrived so that he could see them.

I hoped he would eventually get over needing to punish me. I also hoped my children would see what was going on. Soon! Alexia answered the phone the next morning.

"I promised you a trip to Made by You. Are you ready to paint some pottery today?" I asked her.

"Grandma is taking me tomorrow." I was silent when she added, "I want to go there with her."

"Why? You and I were going to do that," I reminded her.

"Mom, just stop."

I didn't reprimand her for talking to me that way, as I wanted to have a conversation without conflict.

"Can we make arrangements for dinner at my apartment?"

"I don't want to make plans without Adam and Amanda."

"Can I talk to Amanda?"

"She's shoe shopping with Kelsie."

"How about Adam?" I asked.

"He's not here."

"Will you have Amanda call me when she gets home? I'd really like to see you guys!"

"I'll have her call."

As usual, the call never came. I wanted my mother-in-law to go home more than ever. How dare she make plans to do the same things I had promised to do with my daughter! My father-in-law had flown home because his mother was ill. I prepared to speak with my mother-in-law again about going home to her husband. After all, her belief in marriage being sacred had been expressed over and over lately. Her sick mother-in-law had lived just a two-minute walk from their house as long as I'd known them. For her daughter-in-law not to be with her at her deathbed was ludicrous.

It was the next evening that I went to the house to finally see the kids. I had just received confirmation they would be there. Once inside, we were able to express our happiness to see each other. Their grandmother and Peter were not in sight. Alexia tried to feel the baby move. She was so cute when her guard was down. I wondered if she felt safe getting attached to her little "half" brother knowing he was healthy. Her demeanor was delightful when we were in the room alone. Amanda and I had a long conversation about life, the separation, and about the agreement I had with her father to be in the home every day. I tried to make her understand that when I left, it was with the understanding that life was not going to change much since her dad was rarely home because of his business travel. I still had the original agreement in my purse because I'd taken it to my attorney; so I was able to let her see, in her father's own handwriting, how things were supposed to be.

"This is a horrible mess for the baby to be born into," she said. "I just hope he never has to go through the things I'm going through." She broke down and just sobbed while I held her. She expressed pity for the baby, but the despair she felt was for herself . . . for us.

"He won't." What I didn't add was how impossible it would be for Viktor to ever use his child like she was being used. Viktor's sensibility and emotional connection to the people he loved could not abuse that bond.

I played a game of Ping-Pong with Adam and asked him if he'd help me get his box of memorabilia to a taxi. It was time to sort through the collection of keepsakes and assemble the scrapbook I'd been saving for all through his school years. I helped him find his box, and he carried it to the taxi for me, no questions asked.

The girls were getting their rooms cleaned for new tenants to look through the home the next day when I said goodnight to them. It was the first confirmation I had that we were actually moving back to the States. All the curtains I'd made would come down, walls I'd decorated would be emptied, and carpets I'd chosen would be rolled up for use in another home.

I asked my mother-in-law for the car keys so I could take Adam to the airport in the morning. She firmly reminded me that she was still not allowed to give me the keys. So I joined my son the next morning in his taxi ride to the airport in order to spend a little extra time with him. We planned to have breakfast after he checked in, but there was no time. He gave me a big hug and kiss good-bye.

"I love you," he said before he took off running to his gate.

"I love you too," I shouted at his back.

Amanda told me she needed to work all day, and if I came over, I'd just sit and watch her study. Alexia wouldn't hug me that morning when I met Adam and his taxi. In fact, she ran to hide from me when the car arrived in order to stay away from any displays of affection that would be seen by her grandparents. I decided to let it go and give them space for the day.

In the days that followed, Peter's grandmother passed away and my mother-in-law needed to return to the States for her funeral. We were discussing the events transpiring and I was relieved to know the children and I would have a bit of normal time together as flying all of them home for the funeral was not sensible.

"Peter will not be going to his grandmother's funeral," my mother-in-law informed me.

"Why?" I asked.

"Paige! Your affair has turned this family upside down. He needs to be here with his children."

"My affair? My relationship with Viktor began *after* your son had put me through hell in November. I can assure you, I was the loyal one to this family during our marriage."

She was glaring at me. "I don't want to be in the middle of this."

"Then *stop* being in the middle of it! Go home and stay home! I will be here with *my* children."

"I'm not leaving until Peter tells me to leave."

In that comment, I understood she would return to inhabit *my place*—in my children's lives and the home all of my belongings were in. She was more than happy to be "needed." I gave up and walked out feeling too much stress. *This poor baby.* I was stroking my tummy, instinctively calming the life sharing my experience.

Chapter 38

"Just try to arch your back a little more as you cross the bar," I instructed her.

I was helping at the school track meet. Amanda was competing in high jump, which happened to be my field event back in high school. It would have been better to share with her what I knew in a practice session, but according to her, she was competing in the event without *ever* having really practiced. Public events were something I looked forward to as the children and I could enjoy the activities under a veil of normalcy. Away from prying eyes and listening ears, we could just *be*.

"You make it sound like that's a natural thing to do in the air!" she said.

"Well, sweetie, it takes practice. But you're doing great—this being your first shot at it. Keep it up," I said, winking and patting her on the bottom. The role of coach came natural with her.

Across the field, I saw our car pull up. Peter was home from his travels. Alexia was with him, but she didn't get out of the car. He left her in it, parked up near the highway. I suspected she was reading but didn't like her sitting in the car unattended, especially with it hanging out into the road, as he hadn't parked completely parallel. He'd nearly missed every event, and he was in a rush to get down to the field.

I waved to Alexia in the car when I noticed her staring in my direction. She pretended not to see me wave. After I'd finished working the long jump pit, I walked over to the car to speak with her, but she wanted to read.

"I'll see you Sunday."

"Why?"

"I've asked for all of you to come for lunch on Sunday after church. Amanda said you would. Didn't you all talk about it?"

She couldn't remember. I was sure they had.

There was a big Sunday dinner waiting for them when they arrived at my apartment. We looked at photos and laughed a lot. The three of them had visited with the pastor of the church we attended in Vienna. He told me later that all of them said they saw a change in me after Alan passed away. He was our infant son that had lived only eighteen hours. This made no sense to me as no one had ever mentioned seeing a change in me during the seven years it had been since his death. I suspected Peter was trying to help the children give reason to their own feelings of rejection toward me by pinpointing a time their mother became *less than* the mother they deserved.

"Why am I hearing this for the first time?" I asked them.

"We're just trying to figure stuff out, Mom," said Adam.

"I think Alan gave me a greater appreciation of all of you. To be blessed with a healthy, intelligent, beautiful child is a lot to be blessed with. And I had not one, but three!"

I let them absorb my words, but none of them commented.

"I started coaching after Alan." I looked at Amanda. "We were able to drive over the mountain every day." I looked at Adam. "You had my undivided attention when you were sick." I looked at Alexia. "I think if anything changed me, it was Alexia's illness. We'd been on the receiving end of everyone's sympathy for six years! After Alan's death, there was your dad's accident, and then, to top it all, my baby got sick. When Alexia couldn't walk—that was the final straw. I was ready to scream at God."

"I don't remember you taking care of me," said Alexia.

My heart dropped. I wondered what prompted her comment—if she intended to irritate me with it or if that was actually how she felt. We'd spent days in the rocking chair together, hours trying to walk and deal with the pain. There were countless books read to her in an attempt to keep her brain stimulated. Alexia and I had lived as one, attached to each other for months. I couldn't believe she didn't remember me taking care of her, carrying her when she was too big to be carried, and dancing in circles with her when she finally had the courage to walk on her own again.

"Who do you think snuggled you in the rocking chair and gave you medicine and helped you forget the pain? Who do you think took care of you, Alexia?" I asked.

"Grandma," she answered.

I made plans with Adam to sort through the papers in his bedroom and I also wanted him to let me shoot his senior pictures the following week. When I called the house to make sure the girls were there and not with friends, Peter answered. He didn't want me showing up at the house.

"We have things to work out, Peter."

"What?"

"I spoke with the company. We will definitely be going home in two separate containers. We need to go through the house and divide things. I'd like to know what the move date will be, and we should talk about prom and graduation."

"Moving back to the States isn't decided. I'll reverse returning in two separate containers. That's my decision to make. You don't need to be talking to people at the office and complicating an already complicated situation. Do you understand? Stop speaking to people at the company!"

"But—"

"I'm on another call. I'll call you back."

While I waited on his call, I spoke with my daughters. Alexia wanted to stay with her father as he had taken the day off work to be with her and would also be home the next day for the Austrian holiday. Amanda was studying with a friend. I told her to have fun.

Peter did call back. "Did you understand that you are not to speak with anybody in the company from now on?"

"You can't tell me that. I can make the arrangements I need to get home with my belongings. I have to be able to speak with the people taking care of that."

"No, you don't. I will be taking care of all of this. You will not. I will reverse anything you tell them. You will have a court order within the week in regard to having no communication with anyone associated with my company. Anybody! That includes friends we have in this company. Don't push this, Paige."

"When are we moving back?" I asked.

"Sometime this summer," was all he offered.

"So when do you want to divide things?"

"There's time for that," Peter said, putting me off.

"We need to talk about Adam's graduation party."

"It's Adam's graduation. If he wants to do something, it's all up to him. *You* need to stop emotionally abusing the children."

"What!"

"When you put them in the middle of things, you are emotionally abusing them," he said.

"Peter, I don't have to let you play your mind games with me anymore." I hung up.

Since it was a holiday, I waited until eleven thirty the next morning to call the house. Alexia and her dad were watching television. Adam and Amanda were still asleep. I let Alexia go so she could finish watching her program. When I called an hour later, Peter answered.

"What time can I see the kids today?" I asked.

"You can see your kids anytime you want!" he screamed.

"What time will you be leaving so that I can see the kids today?" I asked again.

"I'm not leaving *my* home," he said. After a long pause, he sighed and said, "I'll bring them over to you."

That day I spent six hours with my children. I suspected he'd made plans to be with someone else that day as his parents were both at his grandmother's funeral.

When he picked the kids up, I told him I'd be at the house after school at four o'clock the next day.

"You will not be there unless you are told to be there!" he barked.

My children were listening, so I refrained from arguing with him over the fact that he had just told me I could see my kids anytime I wanted. When I called after school, Amanda just said, "Talk to Dad." He was home again.

Same thing the next day, but the day after that when I called to meet them, I found out that in their grandmother's absence, her sister had flown in! The children's great-aunt was now in our home to do the things I was supposed to be doing. Peter's parents were returning in only two days, but to magnify the drama of my indiscretions among friends and family, they flew in another relative to cover the bases.

I kept making my evening trek to the house if the kids didn't ask me to stay away. In being there, I subjected myself to whatever my in-laws dished out. Many days, when I'd arrive, my mother-in-law had her pockets full of the skeleton keys to all the doors in our home. One day her slacks had an elastic waistband, and the keys weighed the stretchy fabric pockets down to her knees. It was comical, but at the same time, I suspected the kids watched her lock all the doors before my arrival. She was sending my children the message their mother could not be trusted with the belongings in the house, which happened to be possessions I had collected throughout the course of our lives.

Once inside, I'd make my way to the kitchen where she had inevitably started preparing dinner. If I offered to finish cooking, my father-in-law would snap that they were eating at the house too. I couldn't sit at the same table with them, pretending to be family when all I wanted was for them to disappear. I'd wait outside while my children and their grandparents finished their evening meal, then either the kids would join me in the garden or I'd join them in their bedrooms. It was softball season by then, so we were able to practice in the backyard before it was dark.

The evening I scheduled to help Adam sort through the papers in his bedroom, Peter came home and decided it was time for me to leave. It was around ten o'clock, but we had an hour of work ahead of us.

"I want you out of my house now," he said to me while Adam was in the restroom.

"Peter, why don't you just pretend like we're married and *ignore* me," I shot back at him.

"Why do you have to be such a bitch? I'm trying here, and you are just a bitch."

"We have an hour left. Just let me help him finish this."

"Then I want you out! Do you understand? Out!" he was screaming.

"Got it. Loud and clear."

"I hope you traded up. I really do," he said to me, shaking his head, his words dripping with insincerity.

I glowered at him, wondering how he could think it was difficult for me to "trade up" given his cruelty. I didn't say it, still feeling a need to protect everyone and everything from his fragile mental state, but on the tip of my tongue was, "Not hard to do." I was full of anxiety every time the baby I carried was anywhere near Peter Sullivan.

When we finished, Adam and I made arrangements to meet and shop for a tux the following day. Our search for Adam's prom attire proved fruitless, but we had time for some discussions about finances being sorted out in a divorce and how it's all decided by plugging numbers into formulas that are used. Trying to assure him his future was fine, I told him what his dad earned annually, adding the fact that a bonus was received each year as well. He was shocked. We talked about standard of living and returning to the United States while we walked what felt like the entire city by the end of the day. We set a date to travel to Sopron, Hungary, for a tux the next week because we heard they were easy to find and relatively inexpensive compared to Vienna.

That night at Amanda's softball game, I spotted Alexia sitting between her grandparents. She ignored me when I walked in, so I walked over to greet her with a kiss. My in-laws ignored me as well, except to express annoyance that I was blocking their view, acting as if they were highly interested in the game ahead of Amanda's.

I met a friend on the sidelines.

"Your mother-in-law is a piece of work."

"Tell me," I said.

"The other day I took Emilia to your house. It was the first time I'd been inside that place!"

"Serious?" I said, "All those sleepovers and you never came inside?"

"Never. Bob was inside one time when he picked up. I've heard all about it though! Emilia said you turned Amanda's attic space into a queen's room. Whenever she talked about your house, she made it sound like a fairytale." I laughed. She continued, "Anyway, the other day when I stepped into the living room with those stained glass windows and the blue velvet curtains . . . the grand piano in the corner of your living room. Honestly, Paige, I felt like I was standing inside the cover of a *House Beautiful* magazine. I just stood there, gawking, and said to your mother-in-law, 'This is absolutely gorgeous,' and you'll never believe what she did."

"Try me. I bet I will."

"She took full credit for the way that place looks!"

Daria was searching my face for a reaction that was only a nod. "That sounds just like her."

"Well, I just said to her, '*Paige* did a beautiful job decorating this home.'"

"Thank you . . . I know. She's taking full credit for raising my children too. Or should I say, trying to make them think she's been the one constant in their lives. She's *remembering*," I said, motioning air quotes, "things with them that are *my* memories with them. It's like their memories are being re-written, and they seem to have no good memories of me!"

"Of course they have good memories. They'll make more good memories with you too. I don't know how you're managing with his parents in the middle of everything . . . in *your* house!"

"I'm sorry we never had coffee there. It would have been fun to show you the whole thing."

"I would have loved to see it all."

There was a long pause before she asked more about the separation. She'd spent years in counseling for her marriage and continually contemplated leaving her husband. I knew she was asking what she could expect, more than she was being nosy.

"It has been hell." I leveled with her. "Exactly what he promised me before I left him."

She was shaking her head, trying to understand how Peter could be so emotionally detached. I was certain that topic could be discussed all day without shedding any light on my circumstances.

"I think it boils down to guilt. He wants to be there for his children now. Obviously it's too late to be there for our marriage, but I think he's just feeling like he can't lose everything at once. He's abusing his connection to them though. They're flattered by his *need* for them, but it's unhealthy . . . just not natural. Definitely unfair to me."

She gave me a side hug and said, "Hang in there. Give it time. It'll all calm down soon."

"Hopefully being inside U.S. jurisdiction will turn things around," I said, optimistic but doubting at the same time that Peter would change anytime soon.

Amanda wasn't very talkative after the ball game. She wasn't pleased with her performance. I watched her walk to the car with her little sister where they took the front seat together. Another friend caught me to say hello. Before I could reach the girls, they were being driven off in the front seat, strapped into a seat belt together with an air bag ready to explode in their faces should there be a fender bender, or worse. I never let them ride in front; but now, as they passed me on the street, they were doubled up in the front seat. I hoped in the event the airbag were to deploy, they were big enough to handle its impact. As they passed me, neither of them waved good-bye.

Chapter 39

Peter served me with custody papers in Austria, trying to get a quick decision out of the foreign courts that might tip the scale in the American courts. He was claiming status quo custody with the children after using his parents to take my place the majority of the time we'd been apart. My discussion with the family services evaluator was first on the agenda in the Austrian process. When I relayed all that I'd been through at the hands of my estranged husband and his parents while in Vienna, she just nodded in understanding.

"They do this," she said. "Fathers do this to keep from paying child support. They can pay a domestic employee minimum wage, which is usually a lot less than a support payment."

"I think in my case, it is to punish me as well. I've been a career 'mom' my entire married life. It's what I do . . . my purpose in life."

"I can see," she said, smiling as she nodded to my growing tummy. "Congratulations," she added.

"Thank you." I smiled, taken aback with her positive acknowledgement of my pregnancy. "I think it's important that you know divorce papers have already been served in the United States. We already have a court date for a hearing on custody." Unsure of the language barrier, I babbled on, "This matter is in the U.S. courts as we speak."

"Well, I'm throwing it out," she said.

"Completely?" I asked.

"Completely. We call this bond abuse. When a parent is skillful at displaying loving actions . . . or when they become very nurturing in the relationship with the children, while destroying the children's relationship with the other parent, it is bond abuse. The examples you have given me are clearly those of an abusive man. He has no regard for the stress he is causing his children or you and the new life inside you." She paused then added, "He is abusing my time too if this process has begun in the States."

I breathed a sigh of relief. The thought of expecting Peter to respect my unborn child had never crossed my mind. I'd been so focused on simply getting him to respect my relationship with *our* children. But the social worker in front of me cared about all the children involved. Her viewpoint was refreshing, as opposed to the righteous and puritan mind-sets I was dealing with. It was likely, due to the pregnancy, that I would need to travel before Peter and the children. My doctor wanted me to fly before the thirty-second week, and the airlines wouldn't let me fly much later than that either. It was reassuring to know Peter would be unable to manipulate the court system in Austria after I left the country—one less thing to worry about as we brought the school year to a close and prepared to leave for Los Angeles.

It was a busy time for everyone, but I felt caught in a revolving loop of being put off by my family over the next several weeks.

"Talk to Adam," Peter would say. But when I did, I was accused of emotionally abusing him by putting him in the middle.

"Talk to Dad," the children would say, unable to make a decision to be with me that *he* did not consent to.

The best phrase for everyone in the house to use was "I'll call you back" as it delayed having to deal with anything. Nine times out of ten, the call was not returned, so I'd call back.

"Talk to the girls," Peter would say.

"I'll call you back," they'd tell me.

In making Adam's scrapbook, I had become very familiar with the copy shop below my apartment. Viktor's photos from New York were still in my possession, as well as a handful of imaginative shots from LA, so I designed a couple catalogs of his art before I met him one day at *our* café. I presented him with ten books of each catalog that would make it easier for him to market his work while calling on galleries to exhibit his art. He was on his way to Munich with his brother, and I wanted him to have as professional a presentation as possible. It was fun putting them together for him, knowing he'd be surprised.

"What's this?" he said with a look of amusement.

"These," I said, presenting the fruits of my labor, "are your new catalogs. You can leave these in galleries that express an interest in exhibiting your work."

Viktor was amazed. He liked my American initiative, which led to a fascinating conversation about a progressive approach to life and work ethic in different parts of the world. It was one of those days I was still in awe of how much he enjoyed and respected my input into conversation, even when my opinion was completely different than his. Peter incessantly badgered me until I agreed with him, but Viktor was open-minded and considerate of my thoughts in every discussion. He held me in high regard, and it was incredibly validating. At the same time, he made me want to grow, to be more than I'd known or envisioned of myself before he was part of my life.

≈≈≈

It was Mother's Day. The children and I had planned to be together part of the afternoon in my apartment. The call to let me know what time they planned to arrive never came, so I called them. It was Adam who answered.

"Alexia is giving Grandma and Aunt Charlotte a Mother's Day flute concert right now. Mom, I really don't know how to get out of all they have planned over here for Mother's Day today." His voice was apologetic.

"What is Amanda doing right now?" I asked.

"She's working on her homework. She's really swamped."

"Well, it doesn't sound like it would be good for her to have to leave anyway. If it's difficult for the three of you to be here . . . well, I'd rather not complicate your lives," I said, trying to laugh it off. "Are we still on for tux shopping tomorrow?" I asked, looking forward.

"Definitely." There was an awkward silence before he added, "Happy Mother's Day, Mom."

So that was it, I wouldn't be seeing them. My children were expected to celebrate their grandmother on Mother's Day. After all, she'd done so much for them.

It occurred to me that *even Peter* would have a hard time living with himself if he behaved toward his own mother like he wanted our children to behave toward me. Adam, Amanda, and Alexia were expected to negate their mother, a part of themselves, yet like what they saw when they looked in the mirror. I despised Peter's egocentric ignorance.

≈≈≈

Walking through Sopron with my son was a delight. We could have easily been tourists scouting the tiny Baroque village all day, but we had business to take care of. Prom was the coming weekend, and Adam needed something to wear. We found a tux, shirt, and bowtie before we made our way back to the train station. As we waited, I was flipping through our passports and noticed Adam had a new visa pasted into his. My visa, however, had expired. No one from the company contacted me when my family's visa was renewed. I suspected the paperwork on all our visas was completed at the same time, and mine was renewed as well, but it just hadn't been handed to me yet. Peter had undoubtedly decided my visa was not his liability. I had a sinking feeling sitting on the wrong side of the boarder, knowing I had little ground to stand on, as my "papers" were clearly not in order. I prayed I'd be able to get back into Austria without complication, and my prayer was shortly answered. Maybe the agent saw the original family visa and then saw Adam's renewal. Or perhaps it was just because the cover of my passport read United States of America. President William Jefferson Clinton was in the White House, and it was a time when living abroad taught me how privileged I was to be an American.

Adam and I arrived at the house by four o'clock that afternoon. Peter was out of town on business, and I was home with my daughters and their grandparents. I started cooking dinner and Amanda joined me. We visited as usual. My in-laws told me they would be dining out. Progress, I thought, and welcomed a night of routine activities alone with my children. Amanda and I cleaned up after dinner, chatting while we worked. It was time to get Alexia into bed, but when I went to get her so that I could tuck her in, she was curled up under her grandfather's arm on the sofa. My in-laws had quietly slipped back into the house without making their presence known.

Peter agreed before he flew out to let me host our son's prom preview party that had been scheduled months earlier. Adam had drawn up the guest list with his girlfriend, and informal invitations went out by word of mouth. I hired a man that drove a white horse-drawn carriage to pick up my son and his girlfriend at our house. The day arrived, and I shopped for the groceries I needed to prepare platters of hors d'oeuvres. I nearly fainted getting it all carried to my apartment, while resenting the thought of the Mercedes sitting in our courtyard while Peter was out of town. A lot of the food preparation was finished before I called a taxi to go to the house.

I arrived in time to iron Adam's tux and shirt, prepare a punch, decorate the formal dining room table, and set out the platters. The evening was going as planned until Adam remembered he'd forgotten to order his girlfriend a corsage. He ran to the gas station to pick up a bunch of flowers that were customarily located in buckets near the register, while I went to my cabinet full of floral arrangement material and found what I needed to make a corsage, hoping I'd remember the things I learned working with my mother in her flower shop. My mother-in-law walked into the kitchen and saw me busy at work trying to rescue my son from embarrassment.

"Wow. Now it's not every mother who can whip up a corsage at the last minute," she said. I wished her flattery extended to our reality.

"I know," said Adam, giving me a quick kiss before he ran upstairs to get dressed because everyone was due to arrive in about twenty minutes.

There was a crowd of about thirty people milling about the garden and our formal living areas. Half were parents who had come to photograph their prom-clad child in our garden. After photos and snacks, the doorbell rang. It was the carriage driver letting us know he had arrived. I checked the buggy and didn't like the scent of the seat. With permission granted, I ran for some perfume to spray onto the blanket and grabbed the extra flowers to scatter in the buggy. When Adam's date saw the white horse-drawn carriage sitting in our narrow street and realized it was for her, she squealed and nearly burst into tears. The other girls heard what was happening in front of the house and flung open the windows to watch. In their prom gowns, they looked like ladies-in-waiting hanging out the stained glass windows, chins in the palms of their hands with their elbows on the window sills, wishing their prince would take them to prom in a horse-drawn carriage. It was a step back in time, and the appreciation Adam showed made the entire week's effort worthwhile.

My athletic director was calling. He needed a permission slip for Amanda to attend the varsity softball tournament in Brussels. She was the only eighth-grader invited to go but she'd already missed too much school. He let me know the team would be missing two days of classes and not three as originally understood. Though I couldn't give him an answer without talking to Amanda, it was nice to be acknowledged by the school as my child's parent. I let George know I'd get back to him, but I didn't think she'd be going as her last conversation with me about missing school to sit on the varsity bench, especially in a city she'd already seen with the swim team, made no sense to her.

At the house that afternoon, my father-in-law met me at the door. Alexia was out shopping with her grandmother, and Adam and Amanda were at practice. I stayed and played the piano until the children arrived. With every pregnancy, I had taken time to play the piano or the flute to expose the baby to music, but this was the first opportunity in months that I was able to just relax and play the piano. Whenever I attended the opera, the baby would kick as if dancing to the music. Sitting at the piano playing, he reacted much the same. It was the longest I'd felt continuous movement from him, and with every kick, I was inspired to continue. I played with a contented smile at the unspoken communication that went on between us, the same as his brothers and sisters before him. It was the universal exchange that goes on between every mother and her unborn baby.

When Amanda arrived with her friend, she asked if I'd peel some kiwi for them to snack on while they studied. I overheard Alexia asking her grandmother to help her with her homework.

"I can help you, sweetie!" I said as I worked at the kitchen sink.

"Grandma can," she said.

"Alexia, I'd like to help you tonight."

"Mom, don't start this," said Alexia. "It's been a perfectly good day."

I couldn't recall ever hearing a ten-year-old talk to their parent in that way; not where I'd come from anyway. My mother-in-law was smirking in the corner, her true colors showing.

"Alexia, don't speak to me that way," I corrected her.

Her grandfather reached to hug her, sheltering her from my discipline.

"Grandma, will you give me a cinnamon roll," Alexia asked.

I looked at my mother-in-law and said, "She's not helpless." Turning to look at my daughter, I said, "Alexia, you can get your own cinnamon roll."

No one moved. My mother-in-law and I were at odds, and Alexia was waiting to see who would win the battle of wills. I gave Alexia a stern look that pleaded for her cooperation. She stood to get her own cinnamon roll.

"Where is Peter?" I asked my mother-in-law.

"We're not allowed to give you that information," she answered.

"Why not?" I snapped.

"Oh, I think you know," she said in her syrupy sweet voice.

"Because I filed for divorce, I'm not entitled to know the whereabouts of my children's father?"

She glared at me without saying a word. There was no point in trying to have a rational conversation. I was angry with myself for walking right into an opportunity for my mother-in-law to incorrectly demonstrate that I could not be trusted, once again, in front of my children. Something so simple as knowing where Peter was had become top secret. All of them were "protecting" each other from me. My in-laws were at the crux of it, protecting their son and their grandchildren; but my children were following suit, withholding information they were taught to believe I would abuse.

I gathered my things and prepared to leave once the kids were in their rooms studying.

"Be here tomorrow at four o'clock?" I asked my mother-in-law who followed me to the door.

"Well, now, the girls don't want you telling me when you will be here," she replied.

"I'm asking."

"Just work it out with your daughters," she said, closing the door on me.

Overcome with disbelief and exasperation, I turned to walk away. Damned if I did, damned if I didn't, there was no way to correctly deal with the directives I was being given. If I tried to schedule time with the kids, it was touted as mistreatment and my children would tell me to stop abusing them by putting them in the middle. If I tried to discuss schedules with my mother-in-law or Peter, I was simply put off.

It occurred to me I couldn't expect to be *more* significant to Peter than I had been to him while we were married. But now, I was treated as either irrelevant . . . *or* as a threat to everyone in his household. It was as though my children, Peter, and his parents had circled their wagons and I was alone, outside, in the dark, and totally blocked from being a part of the warmth and safety their circle of wagons created. I was the hungry wolf, the *threat* that was just starving for a bit of normalcy in her environment.

It was the end of May, almost seven months after Peter and I separated, six weeks before we would all be back in the States. I couldn't wait. The nonsense I was dealing with had gone on too long, and no matter what I did, it was viewed as incorrect. I didn't want the children in the middle. I wanted them to have two parents! If I defended myself against the lies they were led to believe, I was bad-mouthing their dad. How do you say, "He's lying" without calling their dad a liar? The more I tried to work it out in discussion, the more conflict arose. I couldn't balance the insidiousness of the situation any longer. I just wanted to be on American soil, inside U.S. jurisdiction to end the absurdity.

Chapter 40

There was a package waiting for me at the post office, signature required. I needed help translating the letter telling me to go pick it up, but the content of the package wasn't easier to read, in spite of it being in my native tongue. It was a copy of Peter's response to the divorce as well as his declaration for the U.S. courts. My children were included as applicants on his divorce papers.

In his declaration, he claimed I was in Los Angeles twice a month—I had been there only twice that year. He claimed I didn't try to make contact with my children. After months of runaround from him and his parents, he actually had the nerve to say I wasn't trying to make contact. I was furious.

I called my attorney, wondering how Peter could have signed such a declaration.

"Isn't this perjury?" I asked. "Can't he get into trouble for lying like this?"

"We just have to prove him wrong," my attorney answered. "You've been journaling, right?"

"Every day."

"We'll show them the journal and copy every page of your passport to show you have been in LA twice this year, but that could get a little tricky with residency," he explained, trying to calm me down. "It's time you have a conversation with your children though, Paige. He's got them listed as applicants. It looks like he's got them in his back pocket. I need to run. Call me tomorrow or after you've talked to your children."

Stunned, I clicked off, remembering a Sunday lunch after church in Vienna. Peter was talking about his childhood with the children, remembering the days before cable television. Since we graduated high school together, our childhoods were similar, so I chimed in and began confirming that we only had two television channels to choose from. Peter bristled as I spoke and shot me a look that let me know he wanted to be the center of his children's attention. I excused his behavior because I was with the children all week, and he only had the weekend to spend time with them. But how could I have been so blind to see there was competition for their affection before the separation even occurred?

I arrived at the house that evening with dinner in hand. My children ate in the den with their grandparents while I sat in the kitchen alone. My meal was quick as my appetite was small, so I began unloading the dishwasher. Adam was on his way upstairs to study, so I asked if we could speak before he began his work. I knew he was on his way to London the next day. I didn't want the conversation to wait until he returned.

"Did you know you are listed on your dad's divorce papers as applicants in the divorce?"

"Of course," he said, very matter-of-factly.

"Why?"

"Mom, Dad asked us a long time ago who we wanted to live with."

"How can he ask you such a question?" I screeched, my voice a couple notches higher than normal.

"Well, he wanted to know. He's got to plan his future. We all told him we'd live with him."

I felt like I'd been kicked in the stomach. "Your dad has no right to have that discussion with you while I am not present. This is a matter for all of us to discuss together."

"You're not here. We have regular family meetings as usual, and he asks us every time, 'Are you sure?' He's not forcing us to do anything."

"He asks you if you are *sure* you want to live with him?"

"Yes, he asks almost daily, just to make sure he understands where our hearts are." I laughed at the reference to him understanding a heart, and Adam got angry. "You're just here today because court is getting closer."

"If you believe that, then you are blind to what is going on."

"Mom, I'm not blind!" Adam shouted, angry that I insinuated he wasn't thinking for himself. "When was the last time you were in church?" he asked me. I didn't try to defend myself or offer any excuses as Adam knew the last time I was in church. We sat there staring at each other. "*That* in itself is enough reason for us to chose being with Dad."

"You think your dad is a stronger Christian?" I asked.

"I know he is," Adam darted back. I was dumbstruck. With God on Peter's side, in my children's minds, what chance did I have? I could hear Peter's righteous discourse tainting the minds of my children. I suspected he used the power of suggestion, which kept the children believing the thought process was their own. At a complete loss as to how to manage the conversation taking place, Adam added, "What have you done to try to make Dad's life easier since the separation?"

"What?" I asked, unsure of what he was talking about.

"You just sit back, and let him put money in your account without even trying to lighten the load."

"I get my check from coaching soon, Adam. I'm using inheritance to supplement what little your dad shares with me." Shaking my head, unable to understand him, I asked, "I don't have a teaching license to work at the American school full-time, so what would you like for me to do in Austria without a work permit?"

"Clean houses! We always paid Elizabeth in cash. You know that wasn't reported. You could do the same thing."

Peter's tax return would be high six figures that year, and my son was telling me to go clean houses to lighten his father's load. "Your father wanted a family and a career. Without my undivided support, doing all I do for you kids, I don't believe he could be where he is in the corporate hierarchy. If I expected him to come home and deal with household chores, the effort he's able to give his career would be cut in half. If he wanted a single life with no family to hinder his career, that's a different story. But he wanted it all—and he has it all because I have helped him. He depended on me. There are no financial burdens in this house. I explained all this to you in Sopron. If you believe there are . . ." I stopped myself. I knew I'd get nowhere trying to make Adam see his mind was being controlled.

"Dad's doing fine since you left, Mom. He's even up for another promotion."

I nodded. "I know. It amazes me he's able to be home with you guys now and not miss a beat in his career." I wanted Adam to think! So many contradictions, so much manipulation, just a quagmire of facts that he wasn't adding up. For the past fifteen years, his father told us he'd be home in a year or two, after the latest promotion was under control; but now, he had total freedom to be home long enough to win his children. He'd consistently had my support, but it could have been anybody supporting him. His parents taking my place in his life worked just fine for him. As long as there was someone to take care of the daily responsibilities in regard to house and family, Peter was fine. These thoughts seemed to be foreign to Adam.

"Don't be sarcastic, Mom," he said, throwing a couple T-shirts into his bag. "I really need to finish here."

I watched him choose the jeans he wanted to pack. "Do you need any help?" I asked.

"I'm fine."

"Have a safe trip, okay? Use your head." He nodded, and we hugged good-bye. "I love you, Adam."

"You too."

Downstairs, I found the girls and asked if they would walk me to the door so I could speak with them.

"I just had a talk with Adam, and he explained to me that your dad has been asking you who you want to live with." They were nodding that was true. "The court papers arrived at my apartment today. Your dad's papers basically say you want to divorce me too." I searched their faces. Their poor, cold, and indifferent little eyes just looked at me, no emotion. "Is that true?" I asked.

"I can't stand the idea of living with two people having sex outside marriage," my ten-year-old explained. "I don't want to live with a new person. Besides, you'll have a new baby, so why do you want us?"

"Oh my gosh! Alexia, no one will ever replace you!" I was on the verge of hysteria. "Amanda?"

She hung her head and appeared torn. I was outraged their father had been asking for their assurance nearly daily that they wanted to live with him. It was his version of creating a broken record playing in their minds; and there I was, too late, too ineffective to protect my children's well-being. Eighteen years washed away, and all that mattered were the last seven months.

"Nothing is in writing yet, Mom," Amanda added.

"What do you mean?" I questioned.

"None of us have signed the papers about us living with Dad," she tried to clarify.

"What papers?"

"Just a letter to the court that says we want to live with Dad."

"A letter you would write, or a letter your dad has written and wants you to sign?" I asked.

Amanda was reaching tears and just cried, "I don't know! Okay! I don't know!"

I held her tight, thankful for the glimpse of hope she gave me. Nothing had been signed.

Chapter 41

I met the judge for the custody hearing in Austria. He assured me he would not allow a judgment for Peter since the issue was in the U.S. courts. His perspective matched that of the family services evaluator. Peter's misuse of the Austrian system was not going to be tolerated. Legally, as we prepared to leave Austria, custody was shared and my anticipation of returning to U.S. soil intensified.

Peter arrived home after a two-week absence. Our daughters had no desire to leave all the excitement his return had generated. They were having an important family discussion when I called. A few minutes after we hung up, Amanda called back, asking how to connect the video cables to the television so they could look at the houses their dad video recorded in LA.

He could discuss leaving the country with them but threatened me not to. And since he *was* discussing leaving the country with them, if I were to bring up the same conversation with them, it would have only torn the children in two emotionally and mentally. But I was infuriated by his presumptuous inference in showing the children a video of *their new home* while discussing living in LA with them.

Before Amanda and I hung up, I asked to speak with Alexia.

"How about coming over after you guys are finished looking at the houses?" I asked her.

"I waited all day yesterday to spend time with Dad, but he slept. I feel like I haven't seen him yet, Mom. I want to be with him today."

"I understand. Maybe tomorrow?"

"Maybe," she answered.

Maybe turned into a day at the cinema with their dad—a double feature and a long meal afterward.

After school on Monday, I called Alexia to let her know I was on my way over.

"Don't come! Dad's home. He picked me up from school at three fifteen."

The company and the school were on opposite ends of the outskirts of Vienna. To be at school at that time, Peter had to leave work after his lunch hour. I later learned that he had gone to school to make sure Alexia and Amanda were not released to me the remainder of the school year. He was spreading his kidnapping paranoia, and it was obvious to those who knew me.

≈≈≈

The school's annual athletic banquet was that night. For the first time in my life, I wasn't nervous about speaking in public. Beforehand, I visited with a friend who informed me of Peter's visit to school.

"I can assure you, Cindy, I will not be kidnapping my children . . . nor will I be asking you to release them to me!"

"I know you wouldn't," she said, rolling her eyes at the irrationality Peter displayed. Changing the subject, she said, "You look beautiful pregnant, Paige."

"Ah, you're sweet. Thanks," I said, giving her a sideways hug.

"Thank you so much for all you accomplished with Claire. You made her believe she could do anything. I just appreciate all the work you put into making sure she was recognized for her improvement."

"Cindy, it's my pleasure, really."

"It must have been a difficult season with everything you were going through privately."

"Actually, to be on pool deck every day was a nice escape. At least it gave me a chance to see Amanda."

"Well, you didn't let your private life show. I would have never guessed the things you were going through."

"Good!" I assured her.

When it was time for the swim awards, George asked me to join him in front. Extending a paternal hand to my shoulder, he began.

"This young lady walked into my office last year to let me know she was a swim coach, and I can tell you, we need more people in the world like her." I noticed my father-in-law, who had been video recording the event, turn the camera off and put it in his lap. Looking at me, his hand still on my shoulder, George continued, "Paige, you've done an outstanding job the past two years." Appreciating the praise, but embarrassed by it at the same time, I lowered a smile of satisfaction. He continued, "Our team took first place at SCIS and third place behind London and Cairo this year at the ISST. Paige has turned this swim program around, and she leaves very big shoes to fill." He began clapping for me. Applause in the audience broke out and the people in the room rose to their feet! I stood in front of a crowd of parents, teachers, and student athletes giving me a standing ovation for a job well done. Pregnant and all, they valued me for the impact I had in their children's lives and their swim team experience. Period. "We'll all miss you, dear." George gave me a pat on the back and handed over the microphone to call my swimmers up and distribute the awards.

"Ditto that. I will miss all of you too." I was blinking back tears. "Thank you all, very much. It has been my pleasure." There was a lump in my throat. "Shall we get on with the business of our evening?" I asked. A group of eager swimmers were nodding yes.

To top off the evening, Adam won the annual scholar athlete award. The two of us were in good spirits as we shared several victorious hugs after the banquet. Adam heard parents thanking me for creating a positive team experience for their children. I was ever so proud of my son and wondered if he could ever feel that way about me.

The following evening, the seniors were honored with dinner at the ambassador's house. I mingled with friends from school. Peter was off in the distance with other people he knew. But when it was time to sit down, Adam sat between us, the three of us representing our family unit. Adam's teachers described him as hard working, honest, and fair with a good sense of humor. I bumped shoulders with him when they finished talking about him.

"I'm proud of you," I whispered through a grin.

Before the evening ended, the heavens opened, and we were drenched in rainfall. I was in heels, plus the driveway was long and steep. Adam held on to me all the way down the cobblestone driveway before he asked his dad if they could give me a ride. Peter agreed, and I thanked them both for a memorable evening as they dropped me at my apartment.

Chapter 42

It was the first of June and my first-born was graduating from high school. It seemed unbelievable to me that the little baby I nursed as a college student was now on *his* way to university. When I called to arrange meeting him that day, he was asleep. Our first view of each other would be when he walked down the aisle.

I had arrived at Palais Ferstel early in order to get a good seat. The atmosphere was sacred and I was in awe of the fact that Adam was graduating in such an historic location. The ceremony was in a room off of a circular staircase that wound around the Danube Mermaid sculpture under a domed-glass-skylight. The attendees gathered were solemn, as was typical of European public in such places. As I marveled at the architecture and the intricacy of the ceiling, I heard something akin to a person pulling the needle across a vinyl recording.

"Hello, Paige!" my mother-in-law screeched in her loudest "I'm from the middle of nowhere" voice, while sidestepping her way through the line of chairs.

She was embarrassing as well as slightly comical. Since the separation I couldn't remember her ever being happy to see me. She almost never initiated the exchanges we did have. But there at Adam's graduation, she needed to let me know she was present. Each graduate was given four tickets. Peter, Amanda, Alexia, and myself were the recipients of Adam's tickets. I didn't know how my in-laws managed to secure tickets, but their presence was congruous with the past seven months of our lives. I sat alone. Peter sat with his parents and our daughters in a different section of the room.

The ceremony was a little offbeat. It saddened me, for Adam, that he was not recognized. He was always at the top of his class before we moved, but he joined his graduating class too late in the game to get his international baccalaureate, which automatically kept him from graduating at the top of his class. But as I watched my son receive his diploma, those details faded into oblivion.

When the ceremony drew to a close, the graduates stood and threw their hats into the air, none of them reaching the frescos on the ceilings high above. "Sittin' on the Dock of the Bay" started playing over the loud speakers, and the graduates dispersed into the crowd. Adam was still near his friends when I reached to hug him. We held each other much longer than usual, my eyes full of joyful tears.

I stood back to watch and take in the excitement filling the room. Peter and his parents were taking pictures with Adam, and as usual, they were shooting three or four shots each time. When the girls finished taking their pictures, I asked for a photo with Adam. Howard, my father-in-law, snapped one shot of me with Adam before I was even looking at the camera, then he turned and walked away.

They had reservations at the DO & CO atop the structure overlooking Stephansdom—reservations that did not include me. Adam informed me earlier that Peter just wanted to relax and enjoy the moment without the tension of having me in the same space. Trying to convince him I had as much right to be with him that night as his father, Adam cut me off, explaining he felt the stress when Peter and I were in the same place at the ambassador's dinner. He didn't want his graduation celebration to include any tension or conflict. I understood him. I knew the distance between Peter and I wouldn't have been a lot different if we were still living in the same house, but that night, watching our son graduate, the evening passed without one word between us.

The moment had come, and I thought I was prepared; but watching Adam walk away with his sisters, my in-laws, and his father, to celebrate the biggest accomplishment of his life, I broke down and sobbed. Twelve years of school, of being room mother, of chaperoning field trips, of running fund-raisers, of driving every morning—almost eighteen years of being the one who was involved in my son's day-to-day life—and I was shut out of the celebration to honor him and commemorate the culmination of all those years.

I walked down the stairs of Palais Ferstel on my own, hoping not to see anyone I knew while I wept. Turning the corner to walk down the corridor, I saw Viktor, who stood waiting at the end of the stone arches, ready to scoop me into his arms and ease my heartbreak. He helped me into the taxi and listened to my story of the day all the way to my apartment. Viktor was family to me, and I very much wanted my children to meet him. But they continued to express their hesitancy at being ready for that.

Adam and his girlfriend joined me for dinner the next night. I presented Adam with a letter, a song, his memory book, and a coupon for a new camera that I wanted him to select. He gave me what seemed an endless hug after he read my letter.

"This is a perfect graduation gift," he said.

Chapter 43

I met the children the next morning for breakfast and endured one of the most difficult conversations of my life. They were asking me not to put them through psychological evaluations and a court custody battle. The assumption was that if there *were* evaluations, it would be my fault because I didn't just agree to let them live with their dad.

"Please, Mom. Just let Dad be our primary custodian," said Alexia. My youngest was throwing around legal terms that shocked me.

"No, unless your father has told you he intends to quit working to stay home and be Mr. Mom, I can't agree to that. Who do you think will raise you, Alexia? Grandma?" My tone was getting sarcastic.

Adam jumped in to answer for her. "Mom, a nanny can do what you do. It's no problem for the girls to be with someone else while Dad's at work." Having completely adopted his father's view of my role in the family as just a replaceable, rather insignificant part, he was speaking on behalf of his sisters who remained silent. The maternal bond I thought I had with my children was not immune to Peter's caustic thought processes, and I felt like a complete failure as a mother.

"Adam, you are grown and going away to college. My daughters need their mother, so for you to tell me that a nanny can do for *them* the things that I did for *you* is completely unacceptable."

"I just think they're better off with Dad," he shot back.

Amanda joined him, saying, "Mom, it's easier this way. Please just let us choose."

They were old enough to know what they wanted, and I knew I needed to respect their stand. I was pregnant with another man's child and that alone was reason for them to reject me. I didn't believe I'd raised them to be so judgmental or unforgiving, but they were entitled to their feelings. However, trying to decipher their thoughts and feelings from their fathers' was impossible. There was only one train of thought allowed under Peter's roof, and that was his own, which was not a new dynamic to being a prized loved one of Peter Sullivan's.

I had no reason to believe Peter would win custody and continue to forego travel and time spent in his company office, surrounded by colleagues, by coming home early every afternoon. Without his parents stepping in to replace me, the bond I had with my children would have been in a completely different state. The children may have been angry, but none of them were so intolerant that our connection would have been shattered. I didn't want my daughters raised by a nanny or, worse, their grandmother. In addition, the toxic cloud of negativity and indifference toward me, surrounded by Peter and his parents, was not healthy for them, emotionally or mentally. I knew eventually they would need to be evaluated, but for the moment, I decided to respect their wishes, rather than try to explain what I intuitively understood.

"For now, you may chose where you want to be. You have the freedom to do as you please this summer. I don't like the idea of you being put through psychiatric evaluations either. I don't want you in the middle of a big fight, but I don't want the rest of our lives to be what the past seven months have been, either."

They were relieved, and there was little more to say.

"Do you guys understand why I don't ask you, 'Who do you want to live with?'"

They shook their heads, not understanding why I hadn't asked them the same question their father asked them regularly. To them, their dad cared more because he showed concern about where they would live.

"I don't want you to have to choose between your parents. I could never ask you to chose between your father and your mother. Your dad is part of you just like I am part of you. I want you to have two parents, like always."

They were looking at me like I was from another planet speaking a foreign language. As discombobulated as I felt, I might as well have been speaking a foreign tongue as the promises I'd just made to keep them out of the middle of a big custody battle were out of respect for them. But the fact of the matter remained—they were not themselves, and that made the promises terrifying. I just needed time with my girls. I trusted that once we were on U.S. soil I would have that time, then they would see, remember, feel our connection, and want their lives to return to normal again. They seemed to care deeply about their little brother I carried. I suspected that once they met Viktor, they would appreciate him as well.

Chapter 44

It was June 10, three months after my pregnancy was announced, before my daughters were able to come to my apartment for a Sunday afternoon dinner. Adam was in Greece on his senior class trip. Amanda and Alexia walked into my apartment with yet another set of new cell phones that worked *internationally*. I suspected my daughters were told the phones were purchased in case I tried to kidnap them, but I didn't ask questions.

The girls and I shared a meal over conversation revolving around school and friends. Unsure of what the week would bring in regard to schedules, I prepared a birthday cake of the average variety for Amanda, even though her birthday was four days away. In the past, their birthday cakes were time-consuming creations to match their mood for the year or their new favorite character. But without any of my cake-decorating supplies in the little apartment, I just made an apple Bundt cake drizzled with caramel.

At Thanksgiving when the children didn't get to have a meal with me, it was a normal Sunday dinner some days afterward that Amanda pointed to the chicken, Waldorf salad, and muffins and said, "There's the turkey, the cranberry sauce, and dressing!"

"What?" I asked, needing more explanation.

"You know, Thanksgiving dinner that never happened. Work with me, Mom."

I laughed at that time and now, standing there holding a pathetic comparison of past birthday cakes, all I could say was, "Work with me here!"

We laughed and enjoyed the flavor because the cake certainly wasn't anything to look at. Both wanted haircuts after that. While I worked on Amanda's hair, Alexia stuffed a pillow under her T-shirt to look as pregnant as me.

"You're a little young for that," I teased her.

"You're a little married," she countered.

I hugged her, thinking touché. I snapped a photo for her little brother's baby book before removing the pillow from under her shirt.

"Do you want to have children one day?" I asked Alexia.

"I don't think so," she answered.

"I want to have five," Amanda piped in.

"I hope you guys are older than I was when you start having children." They wholeheartedly agreed.

"I think twenty-eight is the perfect age to have babies," said Amanda.

"Yeah? How have you come to this conclusion?" I asked, curious.

"I don't really know. I just think it's better than twenty-one."

"Well, you're right. I hope you girls wait until you're around thirty."

They were so open with their thoughts and their hearts, just so normal with me outside their father and grandparents' presence. I looked forward to similar days once we were back in the States.

Alexia had been pleading with me to let her shave her legs. I was thankful she chose to ask me for help. Better to teach her than let her do what I did at her age and just surprise my mom with shaved and bloody legs. So I showed her what to do and supervised the first attempt. She was nearly finished when Peter called to say he would be waiting outside the apartment building soon. We rushed to complete our exclusive little mother-daughter moment and gather the girls' belongings before I walked them downstairs.

"I'll see you tomorrow!" I said. It was Amanda's junior formal; and she, along with her best friend, wanted me to do their hair and makeup.

≈≈≈

With hot rollers, cosmetics, and camera in tow, I ordered pizza for dinner from the tram en route to the house. It arrived in perfect time. Listening to Adam tell me about his class trip to Greece, I was ever so thankful he came home in one piece. It sounded to me like there were too many invincible teenagers planning the week's escapades.

Amanda's class spent the day outdoors. Consequently, she was so sunburned her skin nearly matched the color of her red dress. She was not a happy young woman getting all dolled up, but she managed to put herself through the torture. My mother-in-law hovered over the entire process. My spirit increasingly challenged by her, my thoughts swelling with cynicism, I concluded she was afraid I'd make a memory with my daughter that didn't include her.

Alexia was showing the ring she had received from Mark that day, and Amanda wasn't pleased. "I'm going to high school and have never received a ring!" she complained, rolling her eyes at her little sister's display of maturity.

"When did he give you that Alexia?" I whispered, trying to keep it a private moment.

"Today!" she squealed under her breath.

"What did you do?"

"I gave him a hug."

I thought it was sweet, but Amanda was annoyed with the entire idea of her ten-year-old sister receiving sentimental tokens of jewelry from a boy and offering public displays of affection in return.

"Mark wants a picture of me before school ends, Mom. Will you make some copies tomorrow?"

"Sure," I told her, knowing she'd probably never see Mark again in her life.

As soon as Amanda and Lizbeth were ready, they walked downstairs where they posed on the staircase for some photos. They looked much older than fourteen all dressed up in their formals. The roses were blooming outside, so I asked them to pose for some shots under the trellis as well. I loved photographing my children, but the girls were in a rush to be on time, so half a roll was all we took.

I ran another piece of pizza through the microwave oven and played a game with Alexia in the kitchen. In exhibition style, my mother-in-law made sure she left the door open to our home gym across the hallway while she worked out on *my* gym equipment. The weight she was lifting was so small there was no point in hoping she might injure herself and need medical treatment from a trusted doctor in the States. Anything that might cause her to leave! It was a fleeting thought that made me like myself less, but I had really grown to despise the woman's presence in the middle of our lives.

With the car sitting in the courtyard the next day, again, I paid four hundred schillings to run photocopies up to the school by taxi. Alexia was thrilled. I had taken time to frame her photo for Mark in gold and wrapped it in an I Spy Bag. While I was copying, I made extras for her to hand out to all of her friends since she was moving away.

≈≈≈

Amanda's birthday arrived. I was happy to learn she planned to be at my apartment at three o'clock. But an hour after she was to have arrived I called the house wondering what was keeping her and learned she had gone to the cinema. I was happy to know she was enjoying her day. I just wished she would have shown some courtesy and let me know she changed her plans because food was prepared. Alexia told me over the phone that she was going to be with Amanda when they stopped over. She was, but they left twenty minutes after they turned up because their father wanted to take them swimming. I prepared and waited all day . . . for twenty minutes. Just enough time to collect her gift. As usual, trying to keep peace since it was a special day, I said nothing.

My birthday was three days after Amanda's, so the girls were tentatively planning a sleepover. They wanted to play board games, watch movies, and spend the night, with the intention that I not wake up alone on my birthday. I thought it was considerate of them.

On the eve of my birthday Peter brought the girls late, arriving at eleven o'clock that night. The girls were tired after a long day of activities as it was well past their regular bedtime. They washed up a bit, slipped into their pajamas, and were practically asleep before their heads hit the pillows.

Amanda was still asleep the next morning when Peter called to say he would be picking the girls up fifteen minutes early. By seven o'clock in the morning, the day of my birthday, my apartment was empty. Adam never called that day, and I didn't call him either. I picked out a book from my shelf and read it from cover to cover, enjoying the luxury of escape.

Viktor arrived looking dashing as ever, again, laden with gifts. He took me to dinner at a quaint little Italian restaurant before we walked to the Dommayer for coffee and dessert. It was fun to spend an evening inside the place we first met, but sitting there knowing it could be years before we were able to sit there again made the evening bittersweet. It was less than a month we were scheduled to fly to LA.

Chapter 45

The dreaded task of dividing our marital possessions had arrived. With the detailed inventory list I made when we became expatriates, I sat down and divided things of equal value into two separate columns so that Peter and I could take turns choosing from a column on the list. Peter stipulated that he would come to my apartment to divide belongings from that place before we divided the house. He was half an hour late, but the system I'd envisioned worked fine. However, Peter only had about forty-five minutes for the task of dividing nearly two decades' worth of accumulated property.

From my apartment, Peter took pens and pencils, my sleeping bag, a Paris travel book, half of the dozen or so movies I brought with me, and a rocking chair that was given to us when Alexia was born. He wanted to see my storage space as well, so we went down to look at the box of Christmas ornaments. It was there an argument over custody broke out.

"What do you want?" he growled.

"I want my children in my life every day, like it has been their whole lives!"

"Well, that's not going to happen." Peter was nearly chuckling when he added, "When I've finished with you in court, you'll be lucky to see the kids at all. What else do you want?"

I didn't respond, knowing whatever I said would be twisted into something that suited him, used to his advantage with the children and attorneys, then thrown back at me like it was all my idea. We drove to the house to continue the division. Peter couldn't help but refer to our house as "my home" as often as he could.

The photo albums I'd put together throughout our marriage, as well as all the videotapes of the children growing up, were nowhere to be seen. My lone college photo album remained, more of a reminder to me that the photo albums that should have been on that shelf had been hidden by Peter. I remembered him complaining about the expense of film, the expense of development, the expense of the albums; but now, the photo albums were another of his treasured possessions. I videoed the children's activities for Peter when he was out of town on business so that he wouldn't feel he'd missed so much when he returned. There were dozens of videos to be copied, but they had disappeared along with the photo albums. His office door was locked.

When we opened a cabinet full of baby clothes, Peter asked if he could keep all of it because he had hopes of one day having another child. There I was, about two months from delivering a baby and in that moment I just felt sorry for Peter. He seemed so small. I gave no argument over baby clothes since I was pretty sure Viktor wouldn't want his son in hand-me-downs anyway. Before we closed the door to the cabinet, Peter tossed me a receiving blanket.

He kept our daughters near him as we divided things.

"Go ahead," he said, prompting the girls. "Take the movies you want to have at *our* house." Peter was presuming again, and clearly sending the message to Amanda and Alexia that they would be in his custody when we arrived in the States. When I tried to make the point they would be in both homes, he was accusatory in front of the girls. "So now you want to take *their* stuff?"

Peter had a date and kept checking his watch as he rushed me through the house to complete our chore. There were items that needed to be tagged for his shipping container or the one that would be carrying my things, but he assured me it may not all be divided perfectly into two different "his and hers" containers. I knew I wouldn't be around to oversee any of the move, so there was little I could do but *hope* anyway.

Amanda was to babysit for the daughter of Peter's date, Heidi, and her excitement was bubbling over. With less than an hour to divide belongings stemming from eighteen years of marriage combined with Amanda's eagerness to meet her father's girlfriend and care for her two-year-old daughter, when they were still expressing their reluctance to meet Viktor, the day was a double dose of toxicity.

Viktor was closing his business, preparing to leave family and friends, and moving to a country whose language he was learning to speak. He wanted all of the children involved to have both parents. He also wanted me *whole* and knew that meant having my children in my life. It was a bold and brave move for him, but he felt it was the only option. My desire for the children to meet him grew, becoming almost desperate as Viktor began to express his point of view about the increasingly long wait. For his birthday the end of June, again, they refused to meet him at my apartment. When I tried to explain to them what he was giving up and why, the speech fell on deaf ears. I knew they were mirroring their father's sentiments, but still, their decision was offensive and hurtful. Viktor concluded that forcing such things would not bring good results, so we continued to wait for the children to come around on their own.

≈≈≈

Alexia called from the playground wanting her friends to visit with me. It was an unexpected, pleasant surprise. She asked if she could come over the next day, and I readily agreed. Adam brought her, then the three of us snacked through light conversation before we pulled out some board games. We chatted more than we played, and a couple hours had gone by before my son asked Alexia if she was staying or going. It was time for him to shower and get ready for his date.

"Staying," she said.

Adam was gone long enough to make the trip home before the phone rang.

"Mom? Hey, I forgot she wasn't supposed to be alone with you. Can you please bring her home?"

"That's ridiculous, Adam!"

"Mom, please! I don't want to be in trouble."

"I don't want you to be in trouble either, but you know this is nonsense."

"Please, Mom."

We were both silent as I concluded that keeping Alexia with me would only hurt Adam and future "visits." Even the term *visit* being thrown around separated me from them in a very basic way, as though we were guests around each other and our parent-child relationship was different. It suggested I was no longer a mother to them in the same sense that I was before the separation. That destructive idea had been part of Peter's game from the start. Trying to process all the ramifications of my children being taught that I was someone they could not trust, or should not be alone with, was overwhelming distress. Peter's mind-set and influence on them was demented. But what I perceived as ruinous behavior, my children understood as devotion and care. They may have had the feeling it was a little twisted, but nonetheless, their father's conduct was perceived as protectiveness.

"I understand the position you're in." In a sigh of frustration, I let him know I'd bring Alexia home.

Chapter 46

We had planned to meet over the weekend to shop for the camera I promised Adam for graduation. Amanda needed underclothes, and Alexia was usually able to find *something* she needed. The outing was wonderful—just the four of us, eating pizza, chatting as though the last eight months were a distant memory. Until . . . I was informed the children would not be coming to the States all summer.

Adam was on his way to university and lamenting the fact that he was not going to be allowed to work or earn any spending money the summer before he started college.

"Why can't you work?" I asked.

"Because I have to stay in Austria."

"Why do you need to stay in Austria?"

"Dad might need my testimony for the courts here," he explained.

"For what?" I asked.

"He wants something that says he has custody of the girls before he goes back to the States."

I took a deep breath, remembering the promises of the judge as well as the family services evaluator, and hoped they'd remember as well. My attorney in Vienna had not sent his final bill, so I figured I'd let him know what might take place after I left town. I felt comfortable Peter would not succeed with his plan to secure custody before he left Austria, but to learn he intended to keep the children throughout the summer unnerved me. Every one of the signals he'd sent the kids about me kidnapping them suddenly gave a crystal clear view of his paradigm. All the while, it was Peter planning to keep them in Austria.

≈≈≈

Adam and I planned a last mother-son date before I left for the States. He'd be going to Indiana when he returned and I'd be in California. Our time in the same vicinity of each other was drawing to a close, and I felt a tremendous weight of sadness about it.

Adam had mentioned wanting to see the opera house. Spending an evening with him there sounded like a wonderful way for us to say farewell to Vienna together. He brought his new camera, and we watched Neil Shicoff give an incredible performance. We enjoyed just wandering around the historic and opulent building during the break.

"Thank you so much for bringing me, Mom."

I'm not sure how many times I heard that throughout the evening, but I assured him each time, I was thrilled to be there with him. Before we walked across the street to enjoy a late dinner at the Sacher Hotel, Adam had to call Peter to let him know he wouldn't be meeting him at the Hietzing train platform. It was eleven o'clock, a couple hours before Adam's curfew. Peter hadn't met our son to walk him home from a train station the entire time we lived in Vienna, but he set it up with Adam that night "in order to spend some time with him." I heard Adam getting frustrated as he explained to his father that we still had plans and he'd be home in a couple hours. Peter's derisive tactics were never ending, and I wondered what life could have been like if he'd spent as much energy being a kind husband and attentive father as he now spent being contemptuous.

Adam and I enjoyed our conversation over dinner so much we decided to walk up Kärntnerstrasse when we left the Sacher Hotel. Many times during our visit, I needed to bite my tongue, but I was determined to have a memorably enjoyable evening with my son, the graduate. I learned that Peter had expressed his regret to Adam over taking my rings and the things from my purse. *How endearing of him to confess to his son that he felt bad about stealing from their mother. If only he felt bad about cheating me out of time with my children. If only he regretted stealing their hearts!* Adam reiterated his sentiments on just giving up the custody battle to make things "easier for everybody" and letting a nanny stay with the girls after school. *So my daughters can grow into wild, neglected teenage girls looking for love in all the wrong places? And don't think they wouldn't without a parent around!*

I kept my thoughts to myself and civilly heard Adam out on every subject from his childhood to our future. He resented some of the spankings he'd received as a young boy. He and his sisters attended a school that used corporal punishment when deemed necessary. It was a way of life that everyone in our social circle accepted, but Adam had begun to refer to the "beatings" he received. One time Peter used a belt on him that left both Adam and I in tears, but my son couldn't remember that incident. What bothered him were memories of a frustrated mother who was easily upset. I knew that was true as I had not been a happy person a lot of the time. It had been over seven years since any of the children had received a spanking, but I still regretted they ever knew what that was. I apologized to Adam for the way he was raised. He realized it was the norm where we lived, but that didn't erase the experience of being spanked. My parents had raised me with the same method and I never considered myself abused. When Adam was born, I determined to do better than they had in regard to discipline, and I believed I had. Regardless, it was Adam's spirit that needed tending to. I held him while he wept over childhood offenses. I wondered if it was the first time he let himself cry since our family fell apart.

In regard to our present circumstances, he began a defensive explanation for his thought process.

"Mom, it only takes one mistake to erase everything you ever did for me."

I knew he believed that with all his heart. Ever since he was a little boy, Adam tended to monitor his surroundings, seeing things as right or wrong without a lot in between.

"Adam, we're not talking about my reputation or public image . . . 'A lifetime to build, a second to destroy.' We're talking about a mother-son bond! We're talking about love. It's unconditional. Have I completely failed to teach you to love that way? No one will ever convince me that my biggest mistake, my crime that must be punished, is loving and being loved."

"Dad loved you as much as he's capable of loving anyone."

There was a poignant question in Adam's answer. I gave him an affectionate pat on the arm, determined to keep the sordid details of my marriage to his father under wraps. Protecting Peter and his reputation was a deeply ingrained habit as well. I wasn't sure how much longer I could, or should, do that in light of the situation; but the dark and quarrelsome times Adam had witnessed in person were far more than a child should endure. As we walked in silence, I was offering quiet prayers that my son would grow into his own person with over two thousand miles separating him from his father when the fall semester began. We walked up and down the street three times before we were ready to call it a night.

≈≈≈

Departure for LA was a week away and the girls wanted to spend the night with me. They arrived late afternoon. We spent the evening eating, visiting, cooking, and just having fun while a movie played in the background. It was an early night to bed, but Peter called minutes before midnight to say goodnight to the girls. They were already asleep, but he wouldn't hang up until he'd heard their voices. His paranoia was evident in his voice.

We spent the morning doing facials and *girly* things before we went shopping. There were a few things I wanted to take back to the States, and Amanda wanted another bra. She didn't feel comfortable shopping for those with anyone else. Alexia found a couple swimsuits she thought she had to have because the house their father purchased had a pool. Amanda also informed me that "their new school" was within walking distance of "their new home." I reminded her that no decision about custody had been made. Her eyes filled with tears, and all she could say was, "Stop, Mom!"

I hated the little time we had together to include discord, but at the same time, just giving up my daughters to a man who intended only to replace their mother and continue life tending his career was absurd to me. I gave her a long hug, and agreed not to discuss divorce before we were together again in the States.

My cell phone rang. It was Adam calling to tell me the girls' grandparents were missing them, as it had been nearly twenty-four hours since they'd seen them. I didn't know if it was a guilt trip to bring them home or a safety check to make sure I hadn't disappeared with them. Both options left me perturbed. I was thinking my in-laws needed to adjust to time without the girls because their days of being in the middle of our lives were numbered.

≈≈≈

Packing up the apartment and cleaning it to Austrian standards in order to receive the security deposit consumed most of my time during the last week. There were the added little details of turning off utilities, stopping automatic payments, and closing my bank account. Simple things, when you speak the same language!

Three days before my flight out, I received confirmation that Peter's attempt to gain status quo custody from the Austrian courts was denied. The case was officially closed. I breathed a huge sigh of relief.

On July 11, after the moving company had boxed and loaded the contents of my little apartment onto a truck, I turned in my apartment key and met my children at a Japanese restaurant. The time flew by in a swirl of surreal pictures, movements, and words. I felt ready to come apart, like a tower of precariously stacked blocks built on top of a washing machine that had just entered its spin cycle. I felt as though I might shake apart and tumble over in a crash of pieces that would scatter across the ground. We walked to the metro station; and there, in a country not our own, I wished my son well in his first semester at university before I said good-bye. Our hug broke, and I felt a gut-wrenching sob surfacing.

Always the peacemaker, sensing in an instant what everyone around her needed, Amanda chirped, "See you later, Mom!"

I laughed at her through tears.

Adam said, "I'll see you at Thanksgiving." He added, patting my tummy, "Good luck!"

I clung to him one more time then reached for Alexia and Amanda. We all stood there in a big group hug that I'll remember forever. My children held me as I fell apart before they patiently built me up again and stood me on my own. A heartfelt "see you later" was all the four of us managed to say as we walked away from each other.

The day Adam was born, I thanked God for loaning him to me to raise. He was a gift, and I knew the day would come that he'd no longer be a routine part of day-to-day life. There were similar prayers offered the days Amanda and Alexia arrived—prayers of gratitude for the privilege of being able to raise them while giving them back to God to protect physically, mentally, emotionally, and spiritually. Even though I'd always known they weren't mine to hold forever, I never imagined the scenario we were living.

From the moment I walked through its center, Vienna became a beloved city. On the day Adam took me to the Gloriette I was sure our family was where it needed to be. I had so many hopes and dreams for us upon arrival. Rather than our expatriate experience pulling Peter and I together though, our time abroad had only magnified the differences between us. There was sadness to relinquish the city I loved, but to be repatriating without my children was unimaginable torment.

∞ PART III ∞

In the courtroom, Alexia sat on the witness stand. As she was being badgered by an attorney to choose a parent, she began to cry.

I yelled, "Please! Everyone just stop! Think of her emotional well-being! Stop!"

She cried, "Mom," and ran to me. We clung to each other, and in the confusion of courtroom battle, everyone went silent. Had she just stated her choice? I stood holding on to Alexia, then arm in arm, we walked across the room to her father.

He stayed in his chair as I spoke. "You are half of her identity. You are a very significant part of her life. Her emotional well-being depends on your connection to her life, and I promise you I will include and involve you. I respect the bond my daughter has with you, and I will do everything I can to keep that bond intact for her. Alexia loves, needs, and deserves two parents in her life. No matter where you are in the world, no matter where she is in the world, you are her father, and she is your daughter. That bond is not broken, and your child is not lost to you. She's part of you, and you are part of her. She is part of me, and I am part of her. She deserves both of us."

Just like that, in my dream the judge understood who should have custody. The child was no longer going to be divided into two parts. With custody settled, life proceeded as normal. Alexia spent time with her father every time he was in town. I continued to video record her special events to keep him involved and included. When I couldn't video, I'd write him to make sure he knew what was happening in her life. As a teenager, she proved to be the challenge I'd anticipated she would be. Intelligent and beautiful, older than her years, we had our moments of conflict, always managing to smile in the end. Time without each other had taught us the privilege of having each other in our life. Yes, in my dream, we lived through ups and downs and filled our lives with each other, just because we could.

Chapter 47

To witness Viktor's farewell to his brother, who happens to be his best friend, was yet another tearful, gut-wrenching moment to endure. I knew the lifestyle these two men shared included large amounts of time in the other's company. The love and respect they had for each other was displayed openly in their embrace and their blessings for each other as they parted seemed never ending.

"It's the life!" Viktor said as he pulled himself together. "You take the good with the not so good."

We walked arm in arm to our room. It was our first night as a couple living together. As pregnant as I was, it felt overdue to me; but at the same time, it seemed very soon to be living as "one" again.

We'd managed to secure a ten-year visa for Viktor, which was more than long enough to finish raising Alexia before we would need to decide where we wanted to spend the rest of our days. Upon arriving in the States, Viktor entered the non-U.S. citizen line for passport control. When the officer questioned him about what he was doing in the States, he said, "I'm traveling here with my wife to start a new life!"

I was too far away to hear what was being said, but as soon as I was past my officer's desk, I was escorted to Viktor and the discussion taking place in the non-U.S. citizen line.

"Are you married to this man?" the officer asked me.

"No, I'm carrying his child though."

"You are not his wife?" he asked.

"No, we are not legally married."

"He told me you were his wife," he huffed, frowning at Viktor's passport and back at me as though we may not understand the seriousness of lying to a passport control officer.

"It's just a cultural thing. To him, I am his wife."

Viktor understood the conversation well enough to add, "A baby is more than a piece of paper!"

The officer didn't understand, and the frown on his face gave way to a scowl.

"The paper he's talking about is a marriage certificate. He thinks the baby we are having makes us more *family* than any piece of paper." The officer's evil eye relaxed a bit, so I kindly continued my explanation. "In Austria, I am called his *frau*. Literally translated, that means wife. It was an honest mistake. It's just a cultural difference."

He shook his head in a way that said, "I'm not buying that." He gave a nod to a colleague who promptly collected us. We were escorted to a holding area where we watched drug dealers lose their stash before they were taken away in handcuffs. In twenty-four hours we had gone from the historic and elegant Demel Café to a holding pen for criminals trying to enter the United States through the Los Angeles airport. Hours later, we were still surrounded by beat-up walls and dingy tile with a dirty glass mirror separating us from the officer deciding our fate. Thankfully, after he'd dealt with the worst of his problems, he seemed amused by our story. He had a much better understanding of the differences in international communities, which combined with his better sense of humor caused him to release us into the free world. Welcome to the United States of America, Viktor!

≈≈≈

I called the children daily during our time apart. Amanda was envious that I was able to shop in an American grocery store again. There were many things about the States that she never adjusted to doing without, and having a large selection at the grocery store was near the top of that list.

I'd heard that going back to the States after living abroad was even more difficult than leaving. In my case, having brought a significant part of Europe home with me, I repatriated just fine. Viktor looked for what was correct in life. He believed looking for flaws and mistakes, which are usually easy to find, was counterproductive to living correctly. Dwelling on the negative was just not his approach to life. Our days were upbeat, seeing only possibilities and opportunities for our brand new phase of life. It didn't matter that the week we'd spent with a realtor, looking for an apartment big enough for five, was completely fruitless.

"I really think we'll do better finding what suits us by ourselves," he said.

"What do you suggest?" I asked.

"Let's just walk through the neighborhoods we want to live in."

I was skeptical, but there was one part of town that we really enjoyed. The neighborhood was sentimental because it was the area we'd first spent time in as a couple in the States. After another dead-end appointment in a nearby neighborhood with our realtor one afternoon, we took off walking. There were plenty of apartment buildings in the area that we were interested in and a few listed phone numbers to contact for showings. I carried a clipboard, pen in hand and kept a record of addresses, first impressions, and numbers to dial. All the while and unbeknown to us, Viktor and I were being observed.

We were able to get a couple appointments to look at apartments over the weekend, but none sounded ideal. Too little space, too much money, or too little time on the contract—none were a perfect match; but we loved the location.

The following day, we went back to the same neighborhood for more scouting. We passed a gentleman who was watching us closely. We looked back over our shoulders to see that the man still had an eye on us, so we stopped.

"Are you looking for a place to live?" the gentleman asked.

"Yes! Do you know of any availabilities in this area?" asked Viktor.

"I do. I manage this building. It's private. You won't find any advertisements for this place. I watched you yesterday and thought you might be a good fit," he said, winking at us.

"Oh, ho! This is energy! Spontaneous is always a good fit and often what is *meant to be* in life," Viktor said.

The gentleman looked to me for translation as Viktor's accent was still very thick and his wit and wisdom, I was discovering, was seldom immediately understood.

"He said the spontaneous things in life are usually best," I tried to explain.

"Where are you from? Italy?" he asked Viktor.

"No, I'm from a little town called Arandjelovac. Do you know where Belgrade is?" Viktor asked.

"Of course. So you're from former Yugoslavia?"

"I am," Viktor answered, offering his hand.

"Pleased to meet you. I'm Herb," he said, extending a hearty handshake.

"I'm Viktor, and this is my wi . . . This is my . . ."

"I'm Viktor's partner, Paige," I said, reaching to shake Herb's hand as well.

"When's the baby due?" Herb asked.

"In about seven weeks," I answered.

"Well, you don't have a lot of time to set up house, do you?"

"No, we don't." I was smiling at his ever-so-keen observation.

"Would you like to see the apartment? I've got the keys right here," he said, looking at Viktor then me to make sure we'd understood.

"Absolutely!" I said.

Herb stretched a welcoming arm toward the door. We followed him inside and at first glance, knew it was all too good to be true. We were in Beverly Hills just a couple blocks from Rodeo Drive. The apartment was on our favorite street, on the lower level of the building (better with a baby stroller), with more than enough square feet to meet our needs and all for less money than everything else we'd looked at.

There were two full baths, and both had double sinks, so everyone would have their own sink again. I'd grown accustomed to the "water closets" with a spigot on the wall over a tiny little basin to wash hands, so the big bathrooms looked like a showy use of space. There was a long galley kitchen with more cabinets than needed and a tiled island with glass front cabinets hanging overhead to display china and crystal. Sitting in the corner of the living room was a baby grand piano, which was the first thing you noticed upon entering the foyer. I thought the piano was a sign the apartment was meant for us. Last but not least, connecting the bedrooms was a sun porch, which was ideal for the nursery.

Everything in town was within walking distance, which was important, as Viktor didn't drive. He intended to learn, but in the meantime, we'd found an excellent location. It was Saturday we met Herb on the street and looked at the apartment. It was Monday we signed the contract for it.

The high school nearby was very impressive, and their theater department looked like a "dream come true" for Amanda. She told me she wanted to continue swimming, so I looked into the programs offered and discovered they had a competitive swim team with a beautiful facility for practice and competition. It all just seemed unbeatable. The high school and junior high school were "blue ribbon" schools, just like the school Peter was touting near his home. I was satisfied that repatriating back to a more international community like Beverly Hills was a far better option for our daughters. It seemed going from a school full of different nationalities back to a small-town high school would be a step in reverse for them.

≈≈≈

It was July 27. Adam had one day left in Vienna, so he took his sisters for pizza and a stop at their favorite coffee house before they all took a walk through the Schönbrunn gardens. Amanda was crying because it was difficult to say good-bye to her brother and Vienna at the same time. She had no idea how well I understood her.

Adam was also near tears when I reached his cell phone. After the outing with his sisters, he made a trip to his girlfriend's house in spite of her absence that week. They said farewell earlier, but he just wanted to be in her room, surrounded by her quintessence one more time. Her brothers let him inside. He was planting notes for her, scattering them among her belongings that would soon be packed for university. On her desk, he left a piece of Swarovski crystal.

I wanted to speak with Peter before he left for Paris with our daughters. When I reached him, I let him know I'd be calling his phone to speak with the girls while they were in France. He was unresponsive.

"When will you be returning with the girls to the States?" I asked, unable to get any acknowledgement out of him in regard to speaking with the girls via his phone while they were on vacation.

He blatantly replied, "My attorney has advised me not to reveal any specific times or dates about our arrival."

"That is alienation."

"Don't get smart with me." His voice grew louder as he continued to yell at me about what constituted alienation. I knew again that his side of the conversation was for the *benefit* of those listening to him. I hung up.

I never got to speak to the girls during the week they were in Paris with their father. Peter's phone was turned off the entire time.

Adam landed in the States and called to let me know his flight was uneventful and he had arrived safely. I marveled at the normalcy of his actions when he was outside his father's presence. The decision to call me was out of a dutiful sense of respect that I valued immensely.

My attorney was able to get information in regard to when my children would arrive in California, so he set up an immediate court date. For the first time in nine months, I was awarded concrete and regularly scheduled time with my daughters as well as enough money to live normally without using assets. Peter was to back-pay the support he had avoided since our separation, and spousal support in an amount befitting our marital standard of living was ordered.

Chapter 48

It was August 5, when I first drove to Ventura to retrieve my daughters. Peter announced at the last minute he didn't want me to know where he lived. Court dates were approaching and I concluded he didn't want me to see the home he'd purchased or to know what area he decided he could afford. Despite that, my daughter's got the message that their father didn't want their mother to know where they lived. I could only imagine the reasons Peter gave them. I was instructed to meet them at an off-ramp of the interstate if I wanted to collect my girls. It was the first time they would meet Viktor and see their new apartment in Beverly Hills, so there was little that was going to keep me from being excited.

I arrived on time, but true to his nature, Peter did not. I had to step out of the car as it became too hot to sit in, even with the air-conditioning running. The highway clean-up crew nearby kept looking my direction. I couldn't see a guard, so I assumed they were not criminals. But the looks they were giving me eventually became too uncomfortable. Unsure of whether they pitied me pregnant in the heat or if they even noticed I was pregnant, I just decided to get back into the hot car to drive a little and cool everything off. I was still back at the intersection before Peter arrived with our daughters.

We stepped from our vehicles, but the girls' reaction to seeing me was very guarded as their father observed the entire encounter. I hugged them longer than they were comfortable before I opened the trunk for them to put their bags inside. With their father, they exchanged inflated expressions of "missing each other already", while I waited for Peter to convey his drawn out good-bye. He acted like the amount of time they would spend away from him was the end of the world. He pulled at their heartstrings with every bit of skill he could muster. I couldn't help but remember how he'd travel on business for weeks at a time, dashing out the door without giving a second thought to his adieus or to how the children and I would do in his absence. There on the side of the road though, he pulled them closer to him and spoke quietly so that I couldn't listen to the instructions they were being given.

The girls were going to be with me for a week before they flew out with Peter to help establish their brother at university in Indiana. I was joyous as we drove away, knowing I'd have six uninterrupted days with my daughters, and six nights to kiss them goodnight and tuck them in. They liked the idea of taking the scenic route down the Pacific Coast Highway. As the distance between them and their father grew, I watched them blossom into the girls I had raised. We stopped for pastries and a long conversation about them meeting Viktor, who was waiting for their arrival at our studio apartment. They seemed ready to meet him, almost excited that the time had finally come.

Viktor met us at the door, and as he stood face-to-face with my daughters, he had tears in his eyes. I don't think the girls noticed his emotion as they shook his hand. They were the primary reason he had closed his business and left his family and friends behind in Vienna. He believed girls needed their mother as much as a mother needs her children. Alexia was a little reserved, looking to me for translation at times. Amanda was nonchalant, as though meeting the father of a new sibling is something you do every day. I wanted them to understand the depth of love and sacrifice the man in front of them had given for them, but that was going to take some time.

For me, the moment felt like my senior prom. It was an anticlimactic event that I'd spent way too much time pondering and worrying about. There was small talk mixed with nervous smiles and shallow laughter before Viktor suggested we walk them around the sports complex of the apartment building. They were happy to see a swimming pool, a movie and party room, treadmills and every other imaginable piece of workout equipment in the gym, which overlooked tennis and basketball courts below. They thought it was great, but they were eager to be back in an American grocery store. I knew we dared not enter one of those before they had eaten, so we loaded up and drove to the Cheesecake Factory, another American treat!

Viktor slid into the booth. I chose the chair near him to give my pregnant belly the space it needed. Alexia found a way to separate us, sliding into the booth beside Viktor, thereby moving him down the bench and away from me. She centered herself between us, settled her hand into mine and smirked. Amanda watched her sister jockey for position without amusement. I delighted in all that was familiar having them with me.

The week was a whirlwind of activity getting our apartment established and taking part of each day for some fun, as it was still summer vacation. Viktor was happy to be on familiar terms with the girls, and they seemed to enjoy becoming acquainted with his expressions and customs.

"Can I call you V-doe?" Alexia asked.

"I'm not sure I like that. It doesn't sound very respectful. No, you may not call me that," Viktor answered.

I cringed a bit. Alexia had spent the past nine months having people around her bend over backward to please her, dancing to her tune to keep her happy—to win her.

"Well, I'll think of something else," she said.

"How about Viktor?" he said to her.

Resigned, she sighed and said, "Okay."

I watched their little "dance"—the eye contact, the comfort level of both—and couldn't help but wonder how curious my daughters must have been about the man their mother had chosen. All this time, they'd never known him.

≈≈≈

We'd been cleaning and grocery shopping before taking a little time for the girls to get a workout and show Viktor what they could do in the swimming pool. Amanda looked as natural in water as she did on land. I was the proud mom and coach again as we watched her glide through the water. Alexia raced her once and was shown no mercy, so she walked to the basketball court beside the pool and started shooting baskets. Viktor enjoyed being entertained by their athleticism.

The girls had paired up in basketball. It was clear they were discussing something. "Can we rent movies tonight, Mom?" they asked in duet.

"That sounds fun," I answered.

They ran back to the apartment to continue decorating their new bedroom, happy to have a plan for the evening. Viktor and I followed.

"We can't just watch movies tonight," Viktor whispered to me.

"Why not?" I asked. I knew Viktor well enough to know he was thinking something. He'd been observing our interaction for a few days, and the look on his face told me he sensed our time with the girls was not all it should be.

"I just think it's not good to go from work, to more work, to entertainment and then back to another chore that needs to be done before you break for more entertainment. It's all superficial. There is nothing in all this activity that touches a heart." He was looking for understanding and openness in me to continue. "I think unless you want mechanical children, you need to touch their hearts."

I'm sure the look on my face suggested he should continue, but the reality of it was, I was lost. We'd regularly filled our days with activity. Wasn't that what all good parents did for their children? They enthusiastically packed the day with an agenda so that at the end of every day, we could all see it was a day lived fully—a job well done. Accomplishment rewarded by entertainment was the norm.

"Mechanical children? That seems a little harsh," I said.

"It's not harsh. I want this . . ." he said as he intermeshed his fingers and brought his hands into one whole.

His understanding of what needed to take place and his lack of vocabulary to explain it was endearing.

"Unity," I said.

"Yes, that's it. Let me make a suggestion."

"Go right ahead." I'd watched him care for my daughters for months before he met them, but to see him in action thrilled me. Viktor didn't complicate life. When he had something to say, it was for a reason. My respect for his way of thinking had grown tenfold in the months I'd known him, so following him was natural.

"Step by step," he said to me before he walked to the hallway of the girls' room and began speaking. "All right. If there is going to be a cinema here tonight, we'll need a ticket taker and a concession stand."

The girls appeared in their doorway. I stood in the background, within sight and raised my hand. "I'll be the behind the scenes technician. We must have one of those too."

"Definitely," said Viktor.

Amanda was rolling her eyes as she apparently thought she was a little old for this game, but Alexia didn't notice her reaction.

"Can we go across the street to get stuff for the concession stand, Mom?" Alexia asked.

"Sure! Make a list before we go though. Just draw up your menu."

She giggled and got busy. If there was paperwork involved, Alexia was going to have a good time. She loved paper. When our little entrepreneur was ready, there were tickets, programs, and a poster for the concession stand that all included prices!

Amanda, Viktor, and I lined up to be admitted to the cinema. Alexia handed me my ticket with strict instructions to stay awake throughout the entire feature; otherwise, I'd be asked to leave the theater. We lined up again at the concession stand and all spoke at once, placing our orders on top of each other.

"He was first," Alexia said, pointing at Viktor.

It was my turn to be teary-eyed. Only weeks ago, he lived across the street from Vienna's historic opera house that he attended regularly; and now, he was content to play "cinema" with my daughters. He was first, all right. First-class, number one, and just *the best*.

≈≈≈

"Sweetie! Come out here so I can see you," I said to Amanda who was trying on some new jeans. We had dedicated a day to shopping for new school clothes, as they felt more comfortable shopping with me than they did with their dad.

"When I find something I like, I'll come out," Amanda informed me.

"Are you all right in there, Little Bit?"

"I'm fine!" Alexia answered. She was still too small for the line of clothing in the shop we occupied, but did manage to find one piece to try on. Though she had decided against it, she hadn't emerged from the cabin. I waited . . . and waited, grabbing Amanda's rejected pieces that were flung over the curtain. Amanda finally appeared with a satisfied grin on her face.

"What do you think?" she asked.

"Perfect! Turn around."

She spun in delight, gave a little wiggle of her rear, kicked a pointed toe up behind her, and bounced back behind the curtain. Alexia was sitting on the bench inside, playing with what I thought was her handheld Yahtzee game.

"Oh, NO!" Alexia screamed.

"What! What's wrong?" I heard Amanda ask.

I peeked through the curtain to see Alexia holding a cell phone with a frightened look on her face.

"Whose phone is that Alexia?" I asked.

"It's my dad's."

"Why do you have his cell phone?" I asked her.

"In case I need to call him in an emergency."

"If there is an emergency, you can use my phone. You don't need to have your dad's phone."

Amanda looked at me and dropped her jaw as she extended her neck in a "duh" gesture. It all clicked. *Ah, right . . . I would be the emergency to escape.* Trying not to let my fury show, I asked Alexia why she had just yelled.

"I think I just sent a text message to the wrong person."

"Who were you writing to?" I asked.

"I was writing to Dad."

"Okay. Is everything all right? Do you need to talk to me about something?"

"No, nothing like that, Mom," Alexia answered. "I'm fine."

"Who did you send the message to?" I asked.

In a sheepish voice, she said, "I think I sent it to Vienna."

Amanda grabbed the phone and started pushing buttons. She pulled up the text message Alexia sent and read aloud.

"'*I hope you slept well with Mel last night. I love you . . .*' Oh my gosh, Alexia! You sent this to Heidi!" she scolded.

It was almost four o'clock in the afternoon, which meant it was one o'clock in the morning in Vienna.

"Who is Mel?" I asked, confused.

"It's her stuffed animal that she sleeps with. Dad told Alexia he would miss her too much while we were with you, so she gave him Mel to sleep with so there would be a little *part of her* there with him."

"How sweet," I said, smiling at Alexia, trying, again, not to let my frustration with Peter's emotional head games on my children show.

"Alexia, I'm keeping the phone," Amanda told her.

"Fine," she answered.

We paid for the new jeans and made our way back to Viktor who was waiting in the food court. Amanda handed me the phone because she wasn't carrying her purse and had no place to stash it. No sooner had I slipped it into my bag than it began to vibrate and jingle. Pulling it out to answer, I could see it was a text message from Heidi. All I read before Amanda grabbed the phone from me was, "I haven't slept with anybody since I slept with—"

Amanda continued to read the message. I imagined what the rest of the text said and suspected my daughter would be shocked. But as sure as the sun was shining in Southern California, the blank stare on her face verified what registered in her mind and the disclosure was quickly shaken off. It appeared she wanted to pretend she hadn't seen it or, better yet, forget it entirely. I understood her. Oh, how I understood the ingenuity of self-deception and wanting so badly to believe in someone you'd put all your hope into.

I was casual, moving quietly through the mall with my daughters, but my mind raced. I imagined the scenario of Peter handing Alexia his phone for emergencies and the explanation that accompanied that exchange. I imagined my young daughter feeling guilty for leaving her pitiful and emotionally fragile father alone. My baby girl was the caregiver, intuiting a need to give her protector a "snuggly" to sleep with. It was a warped father-daughter dynamic.

We had just reached Viktor when Peter's cell phone rang.

Amanda answered, "Hello . . . Hi, Heidi . . . No, he's not here right now . . . Yes, I know . . . I'm sorry about that. It was Alexia. She was just playing with Dad's phone . . . No, it was Alexia . . . Mel is her stuffed animal that she let Dad sleep with while we stay with Mom . . . I'm sorry, Heidi . . . I'll try . . . I'm really sorry. I'll tell him . . . Yes, I'll tell him . . . . Okay . . . I'll tell him. I understand. I'll tell him."

Heidi was calling from Vienna in the middle of the night, sobbing, frantic, and crying the whole story out for my daughter.

"What did she say?" I asked Amanda.

Without missing a beat, Amanda, the actress among us, assumed Heidi's German accent and began. "May I speak with Peter, please? But he just wrote me! I don't know Mel! I've never known a man named Mel, and I haven't been with anyone since your father. Please tell him! He just left town! He didn't even say good-bye! I thought we would be married! I love him! Can I have his new phone numbers? Please tell him to call me! I love him so much!"

Amanda was dialing the phone before she finished Heidi's monologue and had barely caught her breath before she began speaking. Peter's assistant needed to pull him out of a meeting. Nonetheless, Amanda insisted she speak with him.

"Dad, you need to call Heidi . . . immediately!" she informed him. "I know it's the middle of the night! Alexia sent her a text message that was written for you, and it said, 'I love you.' She thought you were writing to tell her you loved her because you didn't say good-bye! . . . Please, Dad, call her now. The message said, 'I hope you slept well with Mel last night. I love you.'" There was a pause before Amanda continued. "It's not funny, Dad. Call her!"

Just as she closed her father's phone, it rang again. Amanda answered and started dealing with Heidi's distressed hysteria all over again. "I called him, Heidi . . . He's in a meeting right now . . . I told him to call you. He knows you're upset . . . I'm really sorry, Heidi . . . I don't know what to tell you . . . I'll tell him again."

Amanda dialed her father, and for the first time, I heard her take a tone with him that suggested she was the one "holding the reins" in the relationship with her father. Not in a dominant way, but just self-assured in a guiding and very emotionally composed manner. Rightfully, she was demanding *he* be the one to deal with Heidi.

There were a couple more calls from Heidi and as many from Amanda to her father. I imagine Heidi gave up hoping to hear from Peter, as he never confirmed to us that he had called her. Amanda did a beautiful job of picking up the pieces. I was irritated all over again, remembering all the times Peter let me do his dirty work in regard to social situations. Feeling protectiveness for my older daughter as the drama played out, I suggested the phone be turned off and put away. With the incident behind us, I couldn't help but chuckle knowing Peter's antics had come full circle.

Lunch was late and long as the conversation turned to life. The girls wanted Viktor to tell them about themselves! I suspected they were testing his awareness . . . or just curious to know his perception of them. Viktor told them about their differences, and then pinpointed some of their characteristics before he explained to them how important it is for us to know ourselves.

≈≈≈

Alexia was grinning at me when we woke up. She threw her arm over me, and we started talking. Between whispers and adjusting ourselves on the air mattress, which is not easy to do when you are eight months pregnant, we woke Amanda. During our first week with the girls, Viktor slept at the studio apartment to give Amanda and Alexia time to adjust to him in their lives. The girls and I had the new apartment to ourselves.

Having filled my cabinets with all their favorite breakfast cereals, it only took reminding them of the selection on hand to get them out of bed. After eating their favorite things to start the day, they strapped on Rollerblades and cruised around the empty apartment. Then they took turns playing the piano while the other danced. Before I knew it, they were both leaning into my pregnant belly, singing and hugging their little brother with their voices. "I love you. You love me. We're a happy family . . ."

We drove to the studio apartment to pick up Viktor before spending the day at Venice Beach. The girls enjoyed gliding along on their Rollerblades in the wide-open space of the cement walkway along the beach. We were "people watching" throughout our lunch at the sidewalk café. To go from being surrounded by the reserved nature of the Austrian public to the flamboyant characters of Venice Beach made us all feel like we were living on a different planet.

My doctor's appointment was late in the afternoon, and it was the first time the girls attended with us. They got to hear their little brother's heartbeat. All of us were ready to meet him, ready to be the happy family the girls were singing about that morning.

≈≈≈

Amanda was leaning into Marilyn Monroe's handprints as Viktor snapped a shot of her. "Ladies and gentleman, a new star!" Viktor encouraged her. In only a few days, he'd grown to love listening to her sing.

We made our way down the Walk of Fame and stopped inside the wax museum for a photo of all of us against a display we thought would make a nice background. The attendant behind the counter looked bored and was happy to snap a few shots. As we gathered to pose, Alexia reached up to Viktor's shoulder to pull him over. She caught herself and thought better of it, turning loose of him; but what was instinctive to her, thrilled me.

The girls wanted to introduce Viktor to Mexican food that night, and he was a willing subject. It was a week full of *firsts*, but a week that left me optimistic. We'd purchased new beds for the girls' bedroom, and after a joint effort attempting to assemble them, Viktor asked that he be allowed to work in silence. It was a labor of love, but he managed to build two sturdy loft beds. We added file cabinets underneath each bed, covered in planks of wood for their desks. The girls had fun choosing a harmonizing color scheme for their shared space. Beyond shopping to complete their bedroom and new school wardrobes, I'd shown the girls their respective potential schools.

It was a time of anticipation, spent enjoying each other while simultaneously preparing for the next phase of life in a new city. Most notable during our first week together were the new relationships that had blossomed between Viktor and my daughters.

≈≈≈

It was time to take the girls outside where Peter was waiting. He had arrived early to pick them up. Walking them out the door and over to their father waiting in his car across the street felt as unnatural as the past six days with them had been ordinary.

"What are your travel plans, Peter?" I asked.

Peter was reluctant to answer anything. "What do you mean?"

"When will you be with your parents? When will you be taking Adam to college? . . . So I know where to call to speak with the kids."

"We'll be flying to get Adam to campus." His answer was irrelevant to the questions I'd asked. Remembering his time with the children in Italy, London, and Paris, I knew there was a slim chance of actually reaching them while they were traveling with their father.

"When will you be back in LA?"

The girls were buckled into the car. Peter pretended not to hear me as he struggled to reach into the back seat to give them long hugs while I waited to find out when they would be back in town. The answer never came. Peter drove away, making me jump to keep my feet out from under from his rolling tires. The girls looked back, and I blew them kisses but didn't receive any in return. They were back to being *Peter's* daughters. I realized I had no idea what airline they were traveling on as the car pulled away.

I called them several times that weekend, but Peter's phone was turned off. The automated message stated, "At subscriber's request, incoming calls are not being accepted."

When I spoke to Adam, my words were inadequate in describing to him how difficult it was for me not being present to help him settle in at college.

"If anyone had told me a few years ago that I'd be ready to give birth the same time you were starting college, I would have never believed them!"

"That makes two of us," he answered.

"I'm with you in spirit," I told him.

"Thanks. I love you, Mom."

"Ditto!" There just weren't words.

Chapter 49

Court dates were postponed until the day after school started. My attorney and I arrived first, followed shortly by Peter's attorney. She had just spoken to Peter on her cell phone when she entered.

"Oh, my client is stretched so thin," she said. The compassion she tried to convey made me wonder if she'd ever considered a career in acting. "He is so stressed being a *single parent* with his big job. He's just called to inform me he'll be a little late."

And so it began—the twisting, the turning, the half-truths, and the flat-out lies. *Peter the single parent* by his own design, *Peter the victim* of his own imagination, *Peter the family man VP from a very family-oriented company* that was away from home as much as necessary for the company's bottom line.

Peter claimed status quo for custody of the girls. His attorney argued "ripping the girls out of the new school they have just adjusted to would not be in their best interest." After a status quo of full-time mothering to three children whose father was largely absent, she spoke as if the existing condition of the girls' new school, which they first attended just a day earlier, was foremost on the list of considerations.

The trial revealed that the girls were reporting back to their father very uncomplimentary stories. I knew they were trying to please him, but the number of incidents Peter's attorney spoke of let me know that every minute of the girls' time with me was being relived with their father. Conversations were misconstrued, and every opportunity to turn something into a threat to the girls' well-being was distorted to use in court that day. Naturally, I wanted to stand up and shout to the rooftops that Peter Sullivan had no idea what "well-being" was, but that would have been playing right into his and his attorney's hands.

The girls said they were forced to meet Viktor before they were ready. Peter introduced them to numerous girlfriends during the separation; and the girls, in particular, were very fond of all of them. They had rejected meeting Viktor for months after they learned about him. There were several times in Vienna that would have been appropriate for their introduction. But they continued to reject making his acquaintance even after they learned he'd be moving to the States in order for *them* to have two parents. Peter's attorney also spoke of the girls hating to spend time with Viktor and me because we held hands in front of them. When photographs were shown of our time with the girls, she quickly added the girls did not enjoy being photographed. My little actress and my little model did not like being photographed! Peter's attorney argued this with such conviction, I almost believed her.

Adam had written a declaration on behalf of his father, stating that he felt his sisters were better off in their father's home. Peter had been *sharing* all of the paperwork about the divorce because he didn't want to *keep secrets* from Adam. My attorney had strong objections to the fact that Adam even knew what a declaration was. When he spoke of parental alienation, the judge simply said, "I've never heard of what you are talking about." She gave the distinct impression she had no desire to learn what parental alienation was either.

In the end, it was my daughters who told the evaluator that they wanted to live with their father. Alexia came out of the room with the evaluator so distraught she could barely walk. When I reached to comfort her my arm was batted away by her father. He quickly escorted her to a friend that was to take Alexia home. It was payday for Peter. The tricks, the delays, all the effort he made securing his place in our children's lives concluded with the only judgment he would have ever accepted. So swiftly, so effortlessly, so indifferently, the judge gave primary custody of my daughters to their father and a nanny was hired to do what I thought I would be doing in the States.

The hearing was a surreal blur of words trapped inside marble walls. Nothing mattered. All the exhibits put forth containing sentimental memorabilia and letters of gratitude for me from Peter and my children were disregarded, irrelevant. The only thing that prevailed that day was the illusion of truth. Having foregone a face-saving abortion, casting doubt on me was easy as I sat there pregnant. My impropriety was on display, but Peter's merciless conduct was undetected. In fact, his aggressive and offensive tactics to win our children's loyalty were being rewarded. There was no convincing anyone that I was my children's emotionally stable parent. My role of being a stay-at-home mom was a mutual decision Peter and I made for our children before they were born. Now, eighteen years of mothering, simply gone in an instant—my efforts and all I'd invested of my life just vanished into irrelevance.

I don't recall getting home, but I remember being in the elevator, feeling the weight of the judge's decision crashing in on me. I couldn't cry, I couldn't breathe. I nearly collapsed, but Viktor held me up. With so much for the two of us to look forward to in the coming month, an emotional breakdown was the last thing either of us anticipated that day.

"Stop this!" he pleaded. "It's not good for the baby."

"How can this be happening? The courts were supposed to save my place in the girls' lives, not 'seal the deal' on the nonsense that went on in Vienna! This can't be happening. It just can't!" The tears broke, and I was wracked with sobs.

"Stop it!" Viktor yelled, trying to shake me out of it.

"You can't expect me to feel nothing. I've lost my children, and they were my whole life!"

Viktor couldn't understand what had happened either. He'd given up so much to be in the States so that my children and I would have each other, as usual. In his culture, there was respect for God, followed closely by respect for one's own mother. The bond between children and their mother was sacred. Even if their father had been around, the mother who carried them, gave birth to them, nursed them, and nurtured them was the person they would follow, no matter the circumstances. Though he didn't understand my children choosing to be with their busy father or a court system that would put their stamp of approval on such distortion, he knew the present moment was what mattered. The little boy I carried deserved better than to be subjected to a nervous collapse in the days before his arrival.

"As long as they are alive and well, you have not lost your children." Viktor held me and repeated himself until I could breathe. His words became my mantra, my strength.

As long as they are alive and well, you have not lost your children.

Chapter 50

My mother arrived, followed shortly by an earthquake. When the loud rumble of what sounded like a train coming at us hit, it was frightening, to say the least. Viktor jumped up, leaving the rest of us frozen in our seats at the restaurant. Amanda and Alexia were with us, and my mind flashed back to the charming days we spent together settling our home in Vienna. Oh, how far away the magic of that life seemed from all the unpleasantness we were dealing with.

Wanting to help mother in making sure I didn't exert too much trying to settle the new apartment, my sister had also joined the fray. We all cursed Peter's timing for the container of goods from Vienna. It was September 10 when the shipment arrived, and my due date was the twelfth.

On September 11, our phone rang at the crack of dawn.

"The United States is under attack." It was my brother-in-law telling us to turn on the television.

"That's not possible," said Viktor as I shook him to wake up.

It was another dose of *impossible*. We dug the television out from behind the boxes, and like every other household watching the reports that morning, we held each other and wept. Perspective was defined.

It seemed as though our little one knew the world had gone mad, and he wanted no part of it. My due date passed and a week later, I was still pregnant. Mother was waiting to meet her new grandson, and back home, my father waited for the safe return of his wife. My sister was also depending on the airlines to get her home to her husband. When air travel resumed, the two of them caught the first flight they could manage to find, and it happened to be only hours after baby Marko had arrived.

Viktor and I were on our own with a new baby in a city full of strangers, but I never felt alone. The three of us stayed at the hospital together the entire day of Marko's birth and made our way home by taxi the next day.

Sitting on the foyer table was a note from my mom and sister tucked inside a basket of bath supplies for the baby. The best gift of all was that we walked into a perfectly organized and spotlessly cleaned apartment. All we had to do was enjoy each other! In the days that followed, everything we needed was at the market across the street. We settled in to recover, our hearts bursting with joy. The bond we shared grew deeper, and balance began to return to our lives.

Life with Viktor as a new father was a feast of revelation. His connection to our son was something to marvel. Their bond was beyond hands-on-hearts-on. It was intuitive wisdom at work in visible form. I told Viktor while I was pregnant that I thought we were given a boy because the world needed more men like him. Watching him with his son, I knew that was true. I was aware of a different energy and could observe in the union he had to the new little person in our lives, how differently, how wonderfully our son would be raised.

We spent hours and hours talking about different cultures and their respective methods of childrearing—each time, of course, with our own philosophies thrown into the mix. That my first three children were not more resistant to shutting me out of their lives, for any reason, made me question everything about the way I'd raised them. I was completely open to new thoughts and the traditions of a new culture in regard to parenting. Even with so many years of motherhood experience under my belt, often I found myself the student and Viktor the teacher.

≈≈≈

Following childbirth, I was unable to drive. Wanting Amanda and Alexia to meet their little brother, I called Peter to ask if he would trade weekends for driving. He flatly refused. There was exuberant happiness in our apartment, and my daughters were not going to be allowed to be part of it, part of us, until I was medically released to drive myself.

Peter knew I wouldn't be able to handle my half of the drive on the weekend they were supposed to be with us, so that kept him from bringing the girls to us the following weekend as well. He relished the control he had under the circumstances.

The girls met Marko weeks later when I was finally able to drive to them for a regular evening visit. They held the baby for the first time in an outdoor café. The girls were sitting in iron chairs and their young arms were barely enough cushion to keep Marko's head from hitting the metal armrests. It wasn't homey, it wasn't comfortable. It was just harsh in every sense. Bright sunshine, cars driving by, people chattering, and children screaming—there was nothing sacred about the moment. It seemed so superficial for them to meet that way. However, I seemed to be the only one feeling such things. The girls squealed about every little detail of their brother.

"His hands are so big!" . . . "He looks like he already understands everything!" . . . "Oh, he's holding my finger!" . . . "Ah, I just want to stay right here." They were thrilled with baby Marko, and for the first time, they were able to look him in the eye and sing, "I love you . . . you love me . . . we're a happy family!" There were smiles beaming all around, and at the end of the day that was all that mattered.

Chapter 51

It wasn't enough that Peter won primary custody of the girls. His campaign to destroy my relationship with them continued. The custody order and visitation schedule meant Peter had to drive on Friday afternoon twice a month, and each time he let my daughters know what a hardship it was for him to drive thirty miles. I remembered the years I drove almost two hundred miles a day because Peter wanted to live near his place of work, in spite of our decision to put our son into a private school in a neighboring city. Now, a sixty mile round trip, twice a month, was just over and above what he felt should have been expected of him. During the entire year, Peter and the girls arrived on time only once. Often, they'd miss the whole evening and arrive in time for bed, or later. Over and over again, there was an excuse for their tardiness.

"The girls knew they needed to clean their rooms before we left the house." . . . "Traffic is horrible this time of day." . . . "The girls were hungry, so we stopped to eat and the service was so slow." . . . "We had a fender bender." They all carried cell phones they left turned off and usually, I was uninformed of what was transpiring. If I asked why no one called, they'd just say, "But Dad did call you!" More imaginary phone calls for the benefit of my children listening to him.

On occasion, Peter would make plans on one of my evenings with the girls; and together, they would call me.

"Well, I thought I'd take them to the concert Friday night," he'd say.

"That's fine. I'll just bring them home a little later on Sunday."

"No, they can't stay with you all day Sunday because they've got homework and chores to do."

"Well, when can we make up the time?"

"Listen, Paige, if you don't want them to attend the concert, that's fine." I'd hear the girls whining in the background, hoping for their mother to be "cooperative." There was no working with Peter, there was only giving in to him. So I did.

Peter thrived on conflict, competition, and winning; but there were no winners in the reality we all lived. There was nothing successful, nothing victorious about the antagonistic state we were forced to survive. Peter needed to conquer the "problem" once and for all, and he was obsessed with his mission. Every opportunity he could find was used to wear me down.

It didn't matter how much fun we'd have on the girls' weekends with us, Alexia would have her bag packed to return to her father's house the moment she was out of bed on Sunday morning. She would carry it to the front door with a defiant attitude and drop it where it could be seen all day long as a display of her eagerness to leave. More often than not, there was a morning phone call to "touch base" with her dad, and each time, he was informed that her bag was packed and she was ready to leave. She wanted her father to know that my efforts to please my daughters and make our home inviting had failed. Alexia would spend the rest of our day together trying *not* to have fun. I guessed one attitude was just easier for her on the days they returned to Peter.

As I straightened the girls' beds after their weekend with us, my hand brushed a note from under the pillows. "*I hate my fucking mother.*" It was the handwriting of Alexia, my soon-to-be-eleven-year-old. My sweet, innocent daughter was using language I had always forbidden in our home. The note went on, expounding on her hatred of her mother's fucking boyfriend. I looked at it in disbelief. How could a child who so fully and completely loved me throughout her life write such a note? How could she appear to enjoy herself in my presence, then think such thoughts in regard to me? The extreme contradiction in her behavior was truly mind-boggling.

In the months following the judge's decision for custody and visitation, Amanda developed an ulcer. I witnessed her handle her father's emotional needs on more than one occasion and, naturally, suspected what I witnessed was only the tip of the iceberg. Unable to manage Peter's roller coaster of instability myself, I felt incredible guilt over the fact that my daughter was now dealing with that black hole of emotional poverty in her father. She was also adjusting to a new school as well as the finality of her living arrangement. Even if she sensed a need for her mother, I knew that Amanda couldn't have told the evaluator she wanted to spend more time with me if her own life depended on it. Now, our time together was relegated to a couple evenings a week and every other weekend. She stuffed her feelings about everything, and her health began to show it.

≈≈≈

Adam's first trip home from university was Thanksgiving break. He was genuinely pleased to have a little brother. He held Marko and talked to him as though the baby was his peer. The girls stayed gathered around while Adam got to know his new sibling. It was also the first time for Viktor and Adam to meet.

Adam was as closed to Viktor as he was open to Marko. Another conundrum. Should I try to discuss it with him and help put tensions at ease or just pretend not to notice? It was also the first time Adam and I had seen each other since the declaration he wrote for his father was revealed. He never spent the night with us during his brief stay in LA, but over the next few days, there was time for conversation and taking steps toward much-needed healing.

I let him know he was entitled to his opinion, but that I could not agree with it. I also let him know that the court process as well as the paperwork and details he'd been privy to were matters he should never have been subjected to.

Adam was as good at shutting down conversation with me as his father had ever been. "You know Dad's holding all the cards. He's got the power, the money, the success, and the fame." He was letting me know that no matter what I did, how hard I fought or prepared, I was the underdog in a big way. And he was correct. His father never lost—NEVER! Following our first hearing, it was an additional year of forensic accounting, acquiring depositions, preparing documents, and dealing with court delays before trial dates were met.

Chapter 52

It was the best and the worst time of my life. Viktor and I talked and talked, spending the better part of every day together. We enjoyed life, our baby, and each other. He was absorbing a new culture, and every detail of it was fodder for his philosophical mind. In an attempt to continue his coffee house habit of newspaper and time to ponder what he took in, he had asked a couple of gentlemen on the street where he could find a café with good coffee and a quiet atmosphere for thinking. They laughed, reminded him where he was, and said, "We don't do that."

"You don't drink coffee, or you don't think?" Viktor jib-jabbed with them.

"Too much sunshine to sit and think!" they quipped before dashing away.

Nevertheless, the custom was a deeply ingrained habit of Viktor's. He found a few suitable spaces that became part of his routine. It was rare he accompanied me to visit the girls as he intuited their desire to have me alone. On the days we didn't see Amanda and Alexia, Marko and I spent most of our time with Viktor, who was determined to impress upon me how to take pleasure in life, regardless of the chaotic and fast-paced environment surrounding us. Our discussions about his perceptions of my country, as compared to his motherland, were especially intriguing. Often voices would rise, each of us convinced our way was best. Yet both of us remained flexible in combining cultural differences so that our household might be the best of both worlds. We invested in each other differently, but every day there was discovery and enrichment.

Peter was back to being full-time vice president, trying to make his mark in a new work environment, and the nanny was my replacement. I was able to pick the girls up from school a couple days a week, but those evenings were spent operating out of the car, as there wasn't enough time to make the commute between homes. We would go for a snack, find a place to study if they had too much homework for the night, pick a restaurant for dinner and before we knew it, our time for the evening was over.

Their activities didn't coincide, so most of the time I had them one-on-one. As frustrating as it was, in the beginning, to have Peter set up activities for the nights assigned to me for time with my daughters, I quickly learned that having them separate was much better. There was no need for them to keep up their façade of hatred when they were alone with me. Court had proven that our time together was being relived at Peter's house, so in the presence of each other, there was the threat that one or the other might enlighten their dad about a special moment or something amusing that had taken place with me. I could imagine Peter's face turning stone cold at the mention of any enjoyment the girls shared in the company of their mother or little brother. Neither Amanda nor Alexia trusted the other to keep quiet about our time together, each, I suspected, vying for favoritism from their dad. No better way to be the *best* in his eyes than to share his view in regard to me; or the reverse equivalent—no better way to make the other "less than" pleasing to their dad, than to explain cheerful stories that revolved around time with me. In any case, to say or do something nice for me in the other's presence was just too risky. But on their own with me, both of them were able to let their guards down. Relatively speaking, when that happened, it was time with the daughters I knew.

Often, our moments together seemed dreamlike. One night, Alexia and I just drove while Amanda was busy. We ended up parking on a hill that had a distant view of the surrounding countryside. We threw open the hatch on the back of my Highlander, ate snacks, and listened to music. We were out of sight, so when the refreshments were finished, we danced! We were sitting on top of the world just absorbed in each other. It felt like heaven to me. There was a connection between us that let me know Alexia was still able to identify with me; that our bond was not just a superficial whirl of "allowed" activity and small talk.

Amanda and I had an hour together during each of Alexia's horseback riding lessons. Near to the trail she rode was a pond, complete with a dock and adjacent playground where we could swing Marko. Amanda would strap Marko's carrier on and keep him tucked in close to her chest while we walked, chatting and photographing as we made our way around the entire pond. I savored the moments alone with each of them and hoped that their broken hearts were able to do the same.

When Amanda asked if she could audition for a new pilot and get into acting, I was more than happy to help her as I believed she had talent along those lines. The lessons were expensive, but I managed it. On studio days, Marko and I would drive out to gather Amanda then drive another two hours to the studio where I wandered through shops, trying to keep the baby entertained in his stroller. It was great time together, but Amanda wouldn't consider spending the night with me on studio nights, even though we drove right back past our apartment. She knew it meant Marko and I would spend around seven hours on the road those days, but that was my problem. I catered to her desires and spent those days doing what I needed to in order to have additional time with her.

For the most part, sacrifices I made to help them through the transition were not even noticed. Furthermore, it didn't matter how many hoops I jumped through to please them or how many hardships I had to bear. Their attitude was that I deserved whatever I might be going through; and they, as well as their father, deserved respect. If I asked for anything, it was too much. If I asked for nothing, my silence was touted as me caring only about my new family.

≈≈≈

The kids came for an early Christmas celebration at our apartment before they flew to their grandparents' for the holiday. I was allocated Thanksgiving and Peter, Christmas. As sad as it was to be separated from them during the Christmas break, I consoled myself knowing that dealing with their combined negativity would only ruin Viktor's first Christmas as a father, his first Christmas in the States.

Viktor, Marko, and I spent the holidays much like we enjoyed all our days, giving credence to Viktor's philosophy that every day is a special day. We each opened only one package on Christmas Eve, saving most of the excitement for Marko's first Christmas morning. But the next morning he napped before we finished opening gifts, so we went back to bed too. Why not? I didn't have a big Christmas dinner to prepare. There were no expectations whatsoever of me and there was something very liberating about that. We were free to shape the day as we wished, with coffee, gifts, a late breakfast, and a long walk down the boardwalk, the ocean at our side. It was just the three of us all day. Add a simple, albeit gourmet dinner of smoked salmon, Parmesan cheese, and figs. Some wine, a toast. A prayer of thanks.

To wrap up the holidays and start the year, we watched the Vienna Philharmonic's annual New Year's Day concert. It's a beautiful opportunity for the city of Vienna to share its sights and sounds with the rest of the world. But we watched unlike the rest of the world. Vienna was home. So great was our sentimental attachment to the city and the memories it held for us that by the time the program ended, both of us had tears running down our cheeks.

Chapter 53

Marko was in his stroller, and I stood behind him watching Amanda's track meet. I spotted Alexia across the field with her father. In fifty-degree weather, she stood there shivering, wearing only a little spaghetti-strapped top, sans a jacket of any kind. I waved to her and knew that she saw me, but she didn't wave back. She stayed by her father's side like a good little soldier; and not once, the entire time we watched, was she able to walk away from him to say hello to her mother or her little brother. I decided before the meet ended that I would walk over to speak with Alexia and say hello to Peter. The moment I started heading in their direction, Peter tucked my daughter under his arm, turned, and began walking away from me. The distance between us was too great for me to catch up to them without running and making a scene. In addition, they were moving quickly and we could have gone in circles for a long time. I left the meet without speaking an audible word to Alexia, hoping she was perceptive enough to hear all that was unspoken.

Amanda's end-of-year school concert inside the gym was the same scenario, only the distance between Alexia and I was shortened considerably. Still, she made no effort to come speak with me or give her little brother one of their customary snuggles. She was paralyzed beside her father all evening. Amanda slipped off the stage and sat beside me briefly to say, "Thanks for being here!" The lights were dimmed by then, and I was sure Peter didn't notice her talking to me.

I drove home in tears, wondering *how* this would ever end. *Would it* ever end? Should I try to wait it out? Let the kids come around on their own? Trying to reason with Peter was futile. But something had to *give*. I was witnessing my children's psyches literally being divided in two. Each daughter in one body, but with two "acts", two mind-sets, and two voices to maintain; and I felt it was too much for them to bear.

I couldn't ignore what was happening. Mentally, I struggled to balance the continual barrage of conflict. I knew that my daughters were struggling the same way, but without the same amount of life experience to help them cope. It was a difficult realization, but driving home that night, I understood that simply being present in my children's lives enabled Peter to continue his campaign against me. Sometimes it was subtle . . . and sometimes not so subtle. Much of it I was unable to witness, but what I did comprehend was how powerfully his poison worked. In front of my eyes, my children were being torn in two, emotionally and mentally. Everything in me knew it was time to release them from the mire of the caustic circumstances they lived in.

≈≈≈

I found the note on the kitchen table Sunday morning while Alexia and Amanda were with us for the weekend. Alexia's handwriting stopped my heart cold.

It read, "I'm telling Dad that Viktor touched me."

A day earlier, Viktor had hugged Alexia because she caught Marko from falling as he toddled near the hard marbled floor. Viktor thought it was sweet and caring of her to keep her little brother safe. He wanted to let her know how much he appreciated seeing that kind of reaction in her, so he gave her a sideways hug. It was the first time there had been spontaneous physical contact between Viktor and either of the girls, and the moment was a lighthearted, pleasant exchange. Naturally, with every glimpse of normalcy in the time we had together, my hopes would rise.

I knew the girls' environment with their dad was acerbic in regard to Viktor. Peter had been working to discredit him from the beginning. It was for that reason, to keep Viktor above reproach, that I never left the girls alone with him. It wasn't to protect the girls. On the contrary, it was to protect Viktor from ever being accused of exactly what Alexia was willing to suggest. Their minds were so distorted, and their allegiance to their father was so great, that in their desire to please him, I had assumed they were capable of lying about such things. Obviously, I'd been correct.

I was aware of the likelihood that Peter was capable of planting ideas in their minds that would help him defeat me, bring down Viktor, damage our relationship, and eliminate any hope of normal, continued contact with Amanda and Alexia. Peter wouldn't read or hear "Viktor touched me" and presume it was innocent. He was on a witch-hunt. A note like Alexia had written would bring Viktor into disrepute, supplying Peter with the conquest he pursued.

I was utterly shattered and at wits end. The carnage Peter inflicted into the hearts and minds of my children was not even a secondary consideration of his. He simply couldn't *feel* what he was doing to them. Worse yet, the courts couldn't see it—or wouldn't give a lot of credence to my claims since Amanda and Alexia were old enough to state where they wanted to be. I saw my children synonymous to "followers" who believed their existence was only perfected within a cult. Freedoms being the foundation of our culture, my children were at liberty to state their preferences, and according to their father, free to think their own thoughts.

When Alexia woke up, I asked to speak with her. She sat on the sofa, and I sat near her in the rocking chair. I held the note up to show her what I had discovered.

"Alexia, I don't think you realize how a note like this could hurt everyone?" She gave me a defiant stare from the sofa, and I glared right back at her. It wasn't often in the past year that I expressed disappointment in her, but that morning I was uncharacteristically stern with her. The look she received from me let her know I was completely letdown. I could see her softening, and tears began to well in her eyes. "I know Viktor has not touched you inappropriately because Viktor has never been alone with you. I have *never* left you alone with Viktor. Do you realize that?"

She shook her head, focused on me through the tears in her eyes, and her chin began to quiver.

"You have never been alone with Viktor because I was afraid something like this was possible. I didn't ever, *ever* want to be in a position of having to choose who to believe, so I kept you with me at all times." I paused, waiting for a response. None came, but a tear fell.

My words to her were slow and deliberate. "Alexia, you are playing with fire. Do you understand that there is no way I will stand by and let Viktor suffer while you and your dad play games with him? I will be gone. Maybe that's better for everyone. A note like this will devastate your future, Alexia! You will suffer just as much as anyone. It will ruin my life and wreck your little brother's future. Viktor would be shocked to know you could even think such a thing." I shook my head. "Alexia, what you intend to do with this note will put an end to everything! None of our lives would ever be the same. Especially yours."

I heard myself talking. *Put an end to everything* registered with me. I wondered if stopping the emotional tug-of-war going on around her was part of her motivation to suggest to her father that Viktor had touched her.

Her tears turned to sobs, and she apologized for writing the note. She grabbed it from my hand and ran to flush it down the toilet. I was beside myself to think she could even contemplate such manipulation. When the girls left that day, I had no idea if she would tell her dad Viktor hugged her. I suspected she wouldn't, but the potential for Viktor to be unjustly accused loomed over every weekend they spent with us. After that, progress in each relationship was thwarted because I couldn't relax or let down my guard.

My daughters had no idea what it would mean to them to grow up thinking they'd been sexually abused. As with any brainwashing, in time, the repetition of lies would become their truth. They had no concept of the misery that would ripple among our lives for years to come. I knew from our conversations that such offenses were almost unheard of in Viktor's culture. The news broadcasts and talk shows we'd seen on the matter were appalling to him.

I was caught in a crossroad of loss, but it felt more like I was strapped to the wrong track with a heavy train barreling down, my family's demise just a breath away. Disaster loomed over all of us. In sorting through my options, I knew there was only one thing I could do. I'd forever been accused of being overprotective of the children. Never could I have imagined that leaving them one day would be the best way to guard them from complete ruin.

Chapter 54

Viktor and his entire financial history were subpoenaed for court. Peter wanted Viktor to be the center attraction in our divorce proceedings that had become a three-ring circus.

"I really don't think he should be given any opportunity to let your divorce from an eighteen-year marriage be about me. The judge seeing me with you in that courtroom will only hurt you," Viktor said. "Your divorce must deal with your marriage, not your prospective future."

I knew he was right. The proceeding had to focus on the marriage, the marital lifestyle, and not Viktor's career or status.

As fate would have it, Viktor's mother received word that the kidney she had been waiting for was available. Without a second thought, Viktor caught the first flight he could back to Vienna to be with his family during his mother's transplant and recuperation. His brother faxed documents from the hospital for me to prove in court that Viktor was called away for a family emergency. He left the day before our trial began.

When my attorney picked me up for court the next morning, I informed him Viktor was in Austria. He raised his eyebrows in disbelief, took a deep breath, made some mental adjustments, and smiled. When it was made clear to the court that Viktor was absent, I noticed Peter whisper to his attorney, who immediately stood and asked for a warrant to be issued for Viktor's arrest should he ever return to the United States. She cited contempt of court.

The trial totaled five days. In regard to custody, it was an inflated version of the first trial. The girls implied that if they were placed in my custody, they would run away from home. Even if we could have proven some of the alienation and brainwashing tactics Peter had used, no judge in her right mind would place a child in the home of a parent that the child does not *want* to be with—especially if the possibility exists that the children could endanger themselves. My daughters had their reasons, believing their views were exclusively personal and worthy of respect. To them, my life was ruined and they wanted no part of it. They had been sheltered from too much throughout our marriage to understand the choices I'd made, much less hold them in high regard. My children were certainly not alone in that line of thinking. So, custody orders remained.

At the top of Peter's declaration was a document showing statistics of women in the workplace. I never received an opportunity to explain how Peter would rant about not having an ironed shirt in the morning. "I depend on you!" he'd yell. The times I did try to work were fraught with tension in our home because Peter needed to be able to focus on his career, which meant I ran the home and raised our children. Peter wanted and needed my undivided attention toward the details of his life. It was a life that exhausted both of us. A career of my own, or even a job, never meshed well with Peter's expectations.

There were stacks of documents put forth by Peter's attorney and her entourage. They used transport dollies to haul in file cabinet-styled boxes that lined the wall behind them. My attorney brought in one such box. Inundating their opponent, as well as the court, with paperwork was a tactic Peter's attorney had used throughout the entirety of the divorce. In the end, it all boiled down to a small stack of files.

Peter's declarations were replete with exploited half-truths. In addition, he recruited a couple mothers of our daughter's friends to write declarations, both of whom happened to have husbands that worked for him! The worst accusation from them was speculation—that I probably wanted custody of my daughters so that I would have built-in babysitters. He also acquired a declaration from another of his subordinates, a man I barely knew. The gentleman dined with us in our home and apparently, he felt I was "distant and absent" from the conversation and therefore, deficient in my ability to mother. The evening he joined us in our home for dinner was a last minute event that I managed to work out, but it left me exhausted. I didn't remember nodding off during the discussion that revolved around manufacturing, but it's quite possible I did. The gist of his observation was to open the door to conjecture about whether I might have done drugs. On one occasion, my attorney, who had witnessed a lot in his profession, just shook his head and said, "I've never seen anything like this." In spite of it, he advised me to take the high road.

In regard to financials, my attorney presented one discovery after another of Peter's manipulation and deceit. The forensic accountant we hired turned out to be worth his weight in gold. A large portion of stock options had been rolled over into a new investment to appear as though it had been received after the date of separation. Of course, Peter had a perfectly plausible explanation for it. Absolving himself by clarifying his intentions with lies and apologizing profusely was an instinctive part of Peter's persona. At the end of the day, assets were divided in half, maintenance was ordered, and I breathed a sigh of relief knowing my financial future.

Chapter 55

I could hear street musicians playing in the background as I pictured him walking down the Graben, holding a mobile phone to his ear. Viktor was still in Vienna with his family, awaiting our arrival. His mother had yet to meet her new grandchild. It was time for Marko, almost a year old, to make the long flight to meet Viktor's family.

"How are you?" I asked.

"This city is so beautiful and so peaceful. I'm asking myself what we are doing caught in nonstop conflict in California."

"I know something has to change. Everything in me knows it's time to let go, but I just can't imagine being away from them. It feels like I'm letting Peter win, but at the same time, I know nobody is winning in all this. There is no progress. We're all just less and less and less—mentally . . . emotionally . . . spiritually."

I was still trying to protect Viktor from the details of insanity and disconnection among my family, although there was no protecting him from his own intuition. Viktor was more certain than I that the only way to improve my relationship with the children was to distance myself from Peter and initiate a measure of harmony essential to calming the situation.

"This is not going to get better, Paige. It's going to get worse. I see what is coming, and it is going to get worse . . . for everyone."

The two-year ordeal had been exhausting in every way. Viktor's thoughts were the confirmation I needed. He had been a part of my life long enough for me to know that I could trust his instinct, as it was one of his greatest gifts.

≈≈≈

It was Adam's last night in California before returning for his second year of college. It was also the last night I would spend with all of my children, together in one place, for a very long time. We celebrated Adam's birthday at the restaurant of his choice before we drove down to the beach where I tried to make sense of what was happening for the kids. I made it clear in the final court hearing that I intended to move back to Vienna. It seemed Peter had told my children what was happening before I was given the opportunity. Nevertheless, I needed to explain my decision to let go. There was a lot of deliberation and emotion that went into the conclusion to move back to Vienna, and I wanted my children to understand. I didn't try to protect Peter. There was no way to explain why I was leaving without attempting to help them recognize what we were all being put through.

"I think you guys already know that the situation we're caught in is not working. I've made the most difficult decision I'll ever have to make in my life, and I hope one day you will understand it."

They were listening intently, eyes fixed on mine. Fighting to stay composed, I continued.

"You guys have been my life's purpose. You know that. Adam, do you know you're almost my age when you were born? We were in the middle of college, and I couldn't wait to have you. I wanted, more than anything, to be a mother; and I got my wish." Looking at my daughters, I added, "Then another . . . and another."

Alexia chimed in, grinning, "Third times a charm. You finally got one that looks like you." She'd heard it so many times, and I was happy to know it pleased her. I had the impression she was trying to change the subject, or just delay the inevitable. I pulled her to me. It was true. The ongoing worry that her resemblance to me would be a disadvantage to her, under Peter's roof, interrupted my concentration.

"You guys are the biggest part of what defines me and there is nothing I would go back in time to do differently because you've been the best part of my life." Already, I was blinking back the tears in my eyes. "There is nothing happening that makes me wish I'd chosen to spend my life any other way. There's a saying that goes, 'Better to have loved and lost than never to have loved at all.' That's how I feel, only my love for you goes on forever. I've lost a battle that should have never existed. I can't stop it from continuing even though I've tried. It's a struggle that none of us should be caught in, definitely a game I don't want to play anymore because it's so, so terribly destructive to all of us. There is just no way for any of us to thrive while we're caught in this conflict. I see how it is tearing you guys apart. I feel like there are two different people inside each of you, and I can't bear to watch this happening to you anymore. You also need to understand that I don't blame any of you for the things that have happened since your dad and I separated. Do you know that?" I asked, looking each of them in the eye.

The question was met with blank looks since they believed their actions were their own. I suspected they felt if anyone was to *blame* for all the turmoil, it was me. At the same time, I knew they felt a turning point. I was their safe place; the parent they could take for granted and the one they didn't need to worry about pleasing . . . and I was leaving. I focused on the speech I'd tried to memorize, as it was important to me that they understood *why* I'd made the decision to let go.

"I've loved raising you and being your mother. I thanked God the minute I knew I was pregnant with each of you, and that feeling of gratitude for you is endless. Whether you are *here* with me or *there* with someone else, you are my children, and I love each of you unconditionally. There is nothing you can say or do to me that will make me love you any less."

I hoped my feelings were sinking deep into their psyches. Their emotions had been so manipulated I wasn't sure they'd ever remember what it is to be loved unconditionally. When Peter demanded their loyalty, they intuited the condition—not to be treated the same as Mom.

"It's taken the past year to show me that frustrated people do not make good parents, and for that, I'm so sorry. I wish the three of you could know the mother Marko has, because she's a lot happier person. I regret that you didn't see me smile more because the three of you are my pride and joy. I've raised three amazing kids!"

That sentiment was met with not-so-humble agreement, and my composure broke. There were tears combined with laughter, but I was determined to finish.

"I've decided that being here only *enables* the conflict that is happening. Just being here lets all the bad stuff happen," I reiterated, looking at Alexia. The tears flowed freely by this point. The girls were crying too, but Adam's face was stone cold.

"I'm heartbroken that the situation has turned out like it has. I want you guys in my life just like our lives were before the separation. I'll forever want things to be normal for all of us. There is an open door for you in my life—always!" I needed a deep breath, but couldn't continue.

"Will you come back here?" asked Amanda.

"Of course! I'll visit you here, you'll visit me there."

"No, I mean will you ever live here again?"

"It's too early to say. I can't predict what will happen in the future. Your dad asked for a warrant to be issued for Viktor's arrest if he ever enters the United States again. I do know Viktor is not a man to be played with, so if he doesn't want to return, I hope you'll understand why. I also know

Marko does not deserve to grow up without his father. I wanted . . . Viktor wanted *so much* for all four of you to have both parents in your lives. He gave up everything so that the three of you could have both parents. He got a ten-year visa!"

They were all just staring at me like what Viktor had sacrificed was his parental obligation to them. There was no regret whatsoever showing on their faces for the way Viktor had been treated by them or their father. I took a deep breath and continued, "Viktor will get his business established again. Marko will be in school. We have to be realistic. Moving back and forth is not an easy thing to do."

Speculating about the unknown was not helpful.

"I know you guys feel tension and must realize that every week, there is some kind of conflict."

"But that's just life, Mom," Adam said.

"No, life can be peaceful. Life can be calm." I felt remorse at the realization that my children did not know a better way to live. Their expectation was that life is difficult.

"Life *should be* joyful and a lot easier than what we are going through right now. This struggle and tension we all live with is such an unsuccessful, unhealthy way of life. It is shaping you in ways you might not even realize yet." I paused, waiting for them to respond, affirm, deny, or comment in some way. Nothing. "You should feel perfectly comfortable walking over to say hello to me at a school event, but you don't. I understand your dad demands your loyalty." I shook my head and took another deep breath. "I hope you understand all this one day. You might not believe this, but I feel sorry for your dad. He needs assurance, but he's fighting for it the wrong way. I've tried to tell him, but that doesn't help either. Nothing helps and nothing is working . . . for you, for me, for Marko, for Viktor, or for your dad. Without me around, I hope your dad will be able to move forward. If that happens, it's the best thing for all of us."

The children just stared into space, listening. I'd just said something uncomplimentary about their father again, and that was consistently met with guarded and defensive posturing in them.

I desperately wanted them to grasp the reasons for my decision to let go. I hoped they would eventually comprehend what I was sacrificing for them and, above all, realize how much better their lives would be once they were no longer caught in the middle of contention. I expected in time they would come to terms with the necessity of my decision, but a glimpse into the future would have been nice.

I wanted to make certain that one day, when they were old enough to leave home, they wouldn't feel a sense of deliverance leaving *both* parents behind because they were sick of all the discord. It had to stop. They needed two parents in their lives and the freedom to *always* have both parents in their lives. I concluded they would be much more free to love me with an ocean between us.

Chapter 56

The judge refused to order a visitation schedule for the girls to be with me, at home in Vienna, without another round of evaluations. Peter's attorney had worked her expensive magic again.

"Please don't put us through that, Mom!" the girls pleaded. "We'll be fair. You'll have time with us. We don't need a court order to want to come see you. We promise—we'll be fair."

"Tell me what you think is fair. What can I plan on?" I asked them.

"We'll have summers and every other Christmas. Maybe spring breaks. We'll be fair, Mom. Just let us say when we're coming," Amanda begged. She was fifteen years old and definitely old enough to say where she wanted to be.

I knew what the girls wanted would be fair, but I also knew that unless it was what Peter wanted, my daughter's desires would likely not come to fruition. But there was no way to explain his control to them, and forcing evaluations would be taking ten steps backwards in my relationship with Amanda and Alexia. I wanted to move back to Vienna on good terms and not right after a big campaign against me for yet another round of court assessments that would, no doubt, yield the only outcome Peter would be satisfied with. I believed I stood a better chance at *normal* time with my daughters by letting time and distance work in my favor than I did hoping a court-appointed evaluator would detect the signs of parental alienation. The whole impression I had of the courthouse was a subdued public, accustomed to living a fast paced life of chaos, maybe even anarchy, yet eager to put their best foot forward. It was society at its peak of misrepresentation. I suspected the lives of the evaluators were not much different than the public they dealt with and couldn't bet on one of them being able to figure out the perplexities of our situation.

I'd also learned that Peter had spoken to the last evaluator, whereas I was not given the opportunity to meet with her. I couldn't restrict whom Peter might gain access to, and I couldn't negate his charm in winning the people necessary to prevail. Given our history, involving the courts for a permanent visitation schedule was a gamble I was not willing to take.

So sure that my absence would defuse the situation and calm Peter's aggression, I made the decision to just let the girls have their own voice, even if it was tainted by Peter's desires. My children were old enough to say where they wanted to spend their free time. It didn't take a genius to know that Peter's influence on whatever time they were to be with me would be part of the equation—with or without a court order.

≈≈≈

As I boarded the plane and waited for takeoff, my mind raced. No one should ever have to choose between two parts of themselves. All I could do was draw strength from tender memories of my older children. In my carry-on was a little heart shaped pillow Adam had hand-painted for me when he was a little boy. There were notes and cards from Amanda as well as her siblings. Wrapped in tissue was a little vase with a dried flower, from the time Alexia had placed a fresh daffodil in a small kitchen cup for me. The items I carried were too dear to be entrusted to anyone else.

I was tearful and deadened by the fact that the ordeal of the past two years had come to this. Yet there was an overwhelming sense of deliverance that calmed me as we ascended into the clouds. Peter may have been the "winner." Yet I knew the victory of peace and my desire for—my duty toward—mental and emotional health, for my children and myself, championed the entirety of our nightmarish divorce.

Chapter 57

It was a new year and several months had passed since my decision to return to Vienna. Viktor and I were sitting at our favorite Chinese restaurant, and the moment was quiet as Marko slept beside us.

"Can we talk?" Viktor asked.

"Of course."

"There is something I need to say to you."

"All right." His demeanor piqued my interest.

He took a moment to gather his thoughts, as well as some props from the table, before he began.

"This is your past," he said, placing a coaster on the edge of the table. "Everything about your life before we met is here," he reiterated, pointing to the coaster he'd just named the *past*.

"This is the present. This is me, our son, and a new life in one of the most beautiful cities on the earth." Viktor had placed the second coaster he called *present* on the opposite side of the table.

He took a serving napkin and slowly unfolded it before he crumpled it into a ball. He held up the crumpled paper, threw it into the center of the table between *past* and *present* and said, "This is you. You're not here; you're not there. You are nowhere. Look at all this space around you. You're not connected to anything. Right now, the way you are living, you're not good for yourself, you're not good for your present life, and you're not good for your kids."

I listened and understood fully as what he described was precisely how I felt.

"Please don't ruin your present trying to stay connected to your past," he said.

"But they are my children! I have to stay connected to them," I pleaded.

"Yes, of course, stay in contact with your children! You just can't let this fight for relationships with them consume you. It's not healthy for you. They are old enough to want a bond with you too, and when they do, you will be here."

I took a deep breath and tried to absorb what he was telling me. It was hard not being defensive in regard to my relationship with Adam, Amanda, and Alexia. I'd lost so much and the numbness I felt since arriving in Vienna was beginning to wear off and fester into irremediable grief that simmered with anger. The loss I felt was devastating. My emotions ran the gamut adjusting to life without them. I was conscious of it and tried to protect Viktor and Marko from it, but apparently, my effort fell short.

I knew Viktor was right and sensed he viewed me as a shell of the person he had hoped for in our life together. For two years, he had counseled, coached, and loved me through it all. He'd been more attentive than a partner should need to be, and I wanted very much to be in the present with him. I felt myself "half here" and "half there", physically present, but mentally distracted by thoughts of my older children. Even though baby Marko filled my days with activity and my heart with joy, my other children were not replaceable. Each was as much a part of me as the other and there was a void, a sense of purpose that could not be filled.

It was instinctive to do the right thing *for my children* and let go knowing their life would be easier and better. There were immediate benefits, for all of us, not to be caught in animosity. What I hadn't been able to measure was how difficult it would be. Even though life was peaceful in Vienna *and* I knew my children's lives were no longer divided, it wasn't easier or better not seeing them on a regular basis. It was a daily sacrifice.

When my daughters had no parent in their lives because Peter's business travel had resumed, I felt tremendous guilt but consoled myself with the fact that even when I was present and available for them, Peter never called me to stay with them when he traveled for business. He called a nanny, a grandparent, a trusted friend, or even a girlfriend; but not once did he ask me to be with my daughters in his absence.

There hadn't been enough time go by to forget the way things were. Remembering our year in Beverly Hills roused my conviction to end the conflict and help me stay focused on the moment at hand. Viktor and Marko deserved all of me. When Adam, Amanda, and Alexia wanted me, they would have all of me too. I felt time was on my side

Learning to live in the present was a new concept for me. Throughout my marriage, every decision we made, down to how much we spent on a can of peas at the grocery store, was with our future in mind. Every day was lived for the future, and vacation time was lost in order to stay on top of the career that would create upcoming posterity. While friends enjoyed their meals and family time in restaurants, Peter and I ate my cooking, as dining out was not in keeping with saving for the future. Our habit for hard work was expected to pay off, so that eventually, we'd have all we needed to enjoy our tomorrows. Only what we banked, by Peter's account, was never enough. In addition, time with Viktor had taught me that expecting a habit for drudgery to morph into an ability to enjoy life was quite improbable.

Viktor's approach to life was so opposite what I had known that every day felt like a holiday. When he came home in the afternoon, he would ask, "Did you enjoy your day?" as opposed to Peter, who asked, "What did you get done today?" To Peter, my worth was the tasks I'd completed; but with Viktor, I was appreciated, treasured even, for what I added to his life's big picture. It was a radical change for me to hear, "Come with me today! You can do those things later. Enjoy life!" Viktor was fully present every minute of the day, and that is exactly where he wanted me too.

When you're from a war-torn country, focusing on the past or living only for the future are two things you learn are futile. Viktor had learned long ago that the only thing a person can count on is the present moment; therefore, giving all your energy, all your mind, all of yourself to that day was really all that mattered.

The tenderness, love, and wisdom Viktor showered on me was nurturing. Yet, I'd emerged from the divorce so wounded that letting myself be fully replenished with the beautiful moments surrounding me was contentment that stayed just beyond my reach. Ending a bad marriage should not cost a full-time mother her children. Choosing life, love, and happiness over neglect and indifference should never be a crime. Acceptance of the loss and injustice, for my children and for myself, had eluded me. I knew it was time to embrace the life I'd chosen—the life that had been gifted to me.

Chapter 58

Wanting to deal with the issue of spousal support modification without attorneys, as I felt we'd spent a ridiculous amount of our estate on legal fees, I called Peter to discuss the matter with him directly. I reached him on his cell phone while he was driving.

"Can we discuss the modification?" I asked.

"Why are you going back to court for more child support?" he nearly screamed.

"What are you talking about? Peter, you know this is not child support. It's about maintenance. Your attorney should have told you that the amount ordered after our trial last December was temporary. You know this has to be modified."

"If you want to modify this, then come deal with it in court."

"I think it's better to deal with it ourselves!"

"It all has to be the way you want it, doesn't it, Paige?"

"Things were seldom the way I wanted," I reminded him, thinking the direction our conversation was taking was bizarre.

"It's all about you, isn't it?" he baited me.

I sighed in exasperation at his ability to project his own traits onto me. "Peter, if you can't have a rational conversation with me, then we can go back to court."

"Well, you've already cost us hundreds of thousands of dollars, and the girls need to be able to go to college."

"Peter! Your attorney and her entourage have charged more than double what mine charged, and you know it."

"Listen, if you need more money, get a job!" he sneered. I was silent, wondering if he was drinking or what might be going on as the conversation digressed. The judge had made it clear to everyone that a modification on spousal support would be necessary once my expenses in Vienna were taken into consideration. Peter knew this and had delayed dealing with it. Now, he was screaming. "You know how to clean houses! Get a job! If you want money, ask your boyfriend! Why *won't* your boyfriend support you?" he shouted.

"Peter, this is about what I'm due from our marriage. I exhausted myself supporting your career. We need to discuss this when you are in a rational frame of mind and are ready to make progress."

"Get a job! Move on! Let go! You can't get over me, so you just keep coming back for more."

For an instant, I pitied his inability to grasp the truth, as well as his need to think I couldn't get over him. My litmus test for divorce was the feeling of relief I had when I envisioned Peter with someone else. Before I left him, I knew it would never bother me to see him with another woman or be without him.

I heard another voice in the car.

"Is that the radio?"

"No, it's Amanda talking to Alexia."

At that moment I understood what it is to "see red."

"They are in the car with you? Oh, my gosh!" I screamed. "All of that ranting was for them to hear?"

I could almost hear Peter's smug face curl into a cynical smile in the silence that loomed. I wanted to curse him and make him know how evil and dark his mind worked. But that would only encourage more rage. In perfunctory fashion, I asked, "Can I speak with them."

"Which one do you want to talk to?"

Divisiveness was truly second nature to him in regard to dealing with our children and me.

"I'm not going to name one so the other can feel second. Just hand the phone back and let one of them take it."

"Amanda, it's for you," I heard Peter say.

Amanda grabbed the phone and quickly let me know they were in the middle of a game and couldn't be bothered. It was naïve of me to think either of them would feel comfortable talking to me. I wanted to explain. But I couldn't. Explaining what their father had just done made me a perpetrator of the sickness that gripped our family, a disease born of Peter's continued hostility. The situation was impossible to amend. My children remained completely contaminated by our toxic divorce.

Chapter 52

Before summer plans had been made, Peter bought Alexia a dog. It was made clear the new puppy was her responsibility. I viewed it as yet another tactic to keep her tied to his home. Time was shortened for us that summer in Vienna because the dog needed to be cared for and Alexia didn't want to miss watching the puppy grow. Regardless, the girls were coming to spend a couple weeks with me, and I was so excited for them to see their new home in Vienna. It had been almost a year since I'd seen them as they were with Peter over the Christmas holiday. I made plans to spend time doing all the things they loved to do. We were going to shop, paint pottery, spend afternoons visiting in the cafes, and do all the "girly" things they wanted to do. Our time at home would be spent looking through school papers and new photos they planned to bring. In general, the plan was to just enjoy each other.

The cost of their international flights fell to me. Travel arrangements were made for them to fly as unaccompanied minors, and we were all counting down the days we'd be together. Their suitcases were packed over the course of several days before they were to travel. I was thrilled to know they were excited enough about the trip to actually begin packing days in advance. When we spoke the day before their departure, all of us were nearly squealing with excitement.

"I'll *see you* tomorrow! See you! We're going to be looking each other in the eye! Try to sleep on the plane, sweetie. I'll be waiting at the gate!

"That's all right, Mom. You don't need to meet us at the airport. Dad wants to see where you live. He'll bring us to your house."

My heart sank. Peter was traveling with them.

"Your dad is coming?"

"Yah, he's got work in Vienna the next couple weeks."

Every ounce of anticipation drained out of me. It was bad enough that I had to settle for less than a couple weeks of my daughters' summer when most noncustodial parents I knew spent at least two months with their children. Peter was not going to *give* me time with the girls. If I wanted more time with my daughters, I was going to have to pursue it in court where he could sway evaluators and make the girls view it as all my fault they were being put through more court analysis and psychological evaluations. All Peter had to do was sit back and offer his sympathy to our poor children whose mother just would not respect their wishes.

I took a deep breath, knowing my disappointment couldn't show or be voiced lest we begin our time together for the summer at odds. To know their father would be in town the entire time my daughters were to be with me was almost too much.

Peter did bring them to my house. He didn't come inside the gate when I buzzed them in, so I went down to help the girls with their luggage. It had been over nine months since my daughters and I had been together. Despite that, our first glimpse of each other was as Peter held them tight, one in each arm, and the three of them stayed locked in a big group hug with me looking on. Again, Peter was whispering exaggerated sentiments of missing them already and reminding them he was only a phone call away. He held on to them, knowing it had been months since I'd seen them or held them myself. In his exploit was a reminder to the girls, and to me, that I was an outsider. My summer time with the girls began with me wanting to scream.

There wasn't a day that went by that the girls did not speak to Peter, at least once. He would invite them to join him for ice cream in the evenings. He made sure they understood his hotel room was empty, and he was lonely. The time my daughters and I had to enjoy, focus, and reconnect with each other was thwarted at every turn by Peter's blatant interference. His presence in Vienna continued to send the subtle message to my daughters that I was someone for them to fear. Kidnapping, I guessed. Peter had kidnapped their hearts, their minds, and their souls . . . all but their physical beings. He had long projected his ills onto me as though my thought process was similar to his. Nothing could have been further from the truth, but my daughters lived in the fog of Peter's reality. His alienation tactics were severe . . . . yet completely undetected by my children.

≈≈≈

Before the girls left town, Peter needed me to sign some papers that would set up a separate stock account. We met at the girls' favorite ice cream parlor, and it seemed we'd barely received our order before their bowls were empty. They wanted to shop across the street while Peter and I took care of paperwork. Naturally, there was opportunity for conversation while we took care of the mindless business of signatures and applications.

Peter began. "The girls are really doing great without you. They've moved on and are just happy."

"Their happiness and well-being are the reason I'm here."

Peter huffed, dismissing my statement.

Determined to make it through a bit of communication with him about our children, I listened as Peter told me about my daughters, as though they were people I didn't know. He literally described their personalities to me. He'd forgotten I knew them in my womb and was there for every detail of their childhood. Through his words, I was able to better comprehend how the mother my children had known was made null and void in their minds. I listened as he referred to himself as sole custodian as though that negated the fact that I was . . . is . . . always will be my children's mother. I tried to voice my thoughts about the girls, but to end our "conversation" Peter had one more thing he needed to let me know.

"You are insignificant to me," Peter said, trying to sound flippant.

Naturally, I was taken aback. I pushed away from the table. "Don't you know that was always the problem?" I asked him.

I remembered an evening he had his staff members interspersed throughout a dinner with the company's board of directors. He moved through the large room introducing staff, discussing their responsibilities, introducing their wives, and thanking each of them for a specific contribution they made to the "team." There was only one wife in the room who was not introduced to the company's board of directors that night. It was me, drained and bone weary from all that went into preparing our home and yard for that event, yet completely insignificant to him. It was so long ago, but in an attempt to offend me with words, he showered me with yet another new version of his reality.

Pretending to be distracted by the server, Peter avoided answering my question. A blonde wearing a tight mini-skirt walked by and caught his eye. He craned his neck, watching her, before he stood to leave and walked away without saying good-bye or paying the bill.

It was the first of many such summers with my daughters over the next couple years, each a reminder as to why I let go.

Chapter 60

Adam had begun seeing a therapist who happened to be the author of a book that promoted the value of a father's relationship with his children. I was kept uninformed of the sessions until it became clear that the good doctor had Adam on a prescription to wake up, a prescription to sleep, and a prescription to deal with the rest of the day. When I tried to set up an appointment with the therapist myself, he failed to answer his phone at the time I was told I would be able to speak with him.

I relayed my thoughts and concerns to Adam. I told him about my attempts to talk to his doctor as well. It didn't seem like good psychiatry to shut out any significant adult in the life of a child being treated. I wondered if the doctor needed the income to supplement his retirement. Knowing Adam's ability to be diplomatic, I'd hang up the phone after speaking with my son and wonder if I'd been able to get through on any level or influence him at all.

My answer came during the holidays when Adam showed up with more tablets than my elderly grandfather took. My son had become unreachable, and I had the feeling that a part of him was finished with both Peter and me. Adam was angry, and I knew he had every right to be. But I wanted my little buddy back! I wanted so badly for him to understand, but for him to understand, he would need to *feel*. Feeling was just too painful for him, so with the help of a therapist, he avoided it.

In the months before Amanda's graduation, I received an e-mail from Peter that "implored" me to be at her graduation. Again, I could imagine the conversations taking place in his home.

"I have *begged* your mother to be at your graduation, Amanda. I sure hope she shows up."

To Amanda, any sentence she heard along those lines would negate every desire I had to be there. At the same time, all the credit for my attendance would go to Peter as though I was at her graduation solely due to his display of concern for his daughter when he pleaded for me to attend.

I wouldn't have missed Amanda's high school graduation for the world. There was no need for him to implore me to be there, but Peter loved to be my crazy maker in every sense of the word. What was worse, five years after the separation, he still didn't care what kind of *crazy* he inflicted on our children.

Since my decision to let go and return to Vienna, Amanda had come to view her father as her hero, the man who rescued her when her mother left. Even so, she wasn't completely unaware of the fact that her life quality had improved immensely when I made the decision to let go. She met me for breakfast, just the two of us, the morning after her graduation celebration. Like the rest of her class on their final retreat together, she hadn't been to sleep yet. It wasn't easy trying to schedule time with her while I was in town for her graduation. We realized the morning after Grad Night was the only time we could be alone together. I held her hand on top of the table, and we just looked at each other.

So many words on her tongue and mine . . . so many unnecessary words. My eyes welled with tears. Being back in my daughters' environment, having been gone from it for three years was like sleep walking through an irrational dream. It was not supposed to be this way.

I nodded. She nodded. I nodded again and said, "Tell me," even though we seemed to be reading each other's thoughts.

"Thank you for making my life easier, Mom."

I broke. Through tears and sobbing and the realization that she understood what I did and why, all I could say was, "I love you."

She whispered, "I know."

Chapter 61

A year later, it was time for Alexia's summer visit, and with only two years before her graduation, it was decided she would spend five weeks with me that summer. It was the longest amount of time we'd been given together since the separation.

I received an e-mail from Peter asking for details of my plans with her, including dates and travel itineraries as well as phone numbers. His e-mail read as follows.

> *I also understand that you are planning to take Alexia to Milan for fashion week. I want to get your agreement that you will not enter her into any modeling assignments this summer, as I do not feel she is ready emotionally for that. I have discussed this with Alexia. She is not thrilled with this, but she understands.*

Peter had allowed her to visit a few modeling agencies in LA, yet he was telling me he didn't believe she was ready for modeling. Alexia's ambition of pursuing a career in fashion had grown from being the fantasy of a little girl to a self-assured belief she could succeed. It was a realistic goal and entirely plausible for her.

In the years since our return to Vienna, Viktor's talent agent business had developed to include models as well as musicians and athletes, so we knew our way around the world of modeling. Alexia had an advantage breaking into the business with us. I wrote back to Peter, assuring him we would abide by his wishes. And we would! To succeed, she would need the emotional calmness of his blessing.

Alexia arrived in Vienna, and within a few days, we were in Bratislava on our way to Milan. That evening, we were watching a concert while sitting in the plaza downtown, and a man approached our table. He asked if we were in fashion. I smiled, pointed at Alexia, and said, "She will be!" He introduced himself at that point and explained that he was a scout for two of the top agencies in Paris. He told Alexia she should get started in her modeling career. I found that incident very interesting. Our little American spotted by a scout who had been sent out to find Eastern European models.

During fashion week in Milan, there were models everywhere. In the trams, the cafes, the streets—they were everywhere! But it was Alexia turning heads. I deduced people were trying to figure out who she was. A guy peddling his bike down the street was watching her when he rode his bike into five pedestrians. The incident was quite a commotion, but it appeared no one was hurt. People were literally stopping in their footsteps to stare at her as we passed by.

"They're trying to figure out who you are."

Alexia beamed, saying, "They'll know soon!"

One instance I was thankful the loaded tram we'd just stepped off was on rails because the driver was turning a corner as he was twisting his neck to look backward so that he might watch Alexia walk away. The reaction she got from a city that loves its models and thrives on fashion was just one "taste" of her potential. Moreover, Alexia was completely at home and in her element.

It was walking down the street with Viktor and his client that Alexia was spotted by a gentleman involved in casting for the Armani shows. They all sat down together in the Armani Cafe for a coffee. During this conversation, Alexia was told she could and should cast for Armani's next teen campaign in September. He also told Alexia he'd like to see her cast for their upcoming perfume ad. To hear that coming from a man who is on the front lines of the business in charge of casting for Armani, you could bet Alexia had a great shot at beginning her career with an Armani campaign.

A dinner was arranged for her to meet more people. It was a lot for her to "wrap her head around" and a lot for us to be proud of as well. The plan was to contact the gentleman when she returned to Milan and let him introduce Alexia to the agency of his choice, which would put her in good standing with any agency.

Before we left Milan, we looked at several apartments but didn't make any deposits. Alexia needed to speak with Peter and let him know what she had decided. She was presented a golden opportunity, and it was being handed to her on a silver platter because Viktor and I were going to make sure she had all the support and instruction she needed to succeed.

Back at home in Vienna, she worked up her courage to call Peter. She let him know that she had decided to stay and model. She relayed the story of being spotted on the street by Mr. Armani's good friend and colleague.

Peter didn't even let her convey the sum of her encounters in Milan before he began yelling at her. "You're not staying there! You *will* be on that plane to come home in July. Do you hear me? You are not staying with your mother. With God as my witness, you will never live with your mother! I will have her arrested for kidnapping if you are not on that airplane, Alexia. Have I made myself clear? I will bury your mother in court before I ever let you live with her."

In one blow, he obliterated everything she had gained in her experiences over the past two weeks. Her psyche crumbled, her spirit was crushed, and her confidence disappeared. I utterly despised Peter for it. Later, he accused me of staging the entire meeting with Armani's casting director. Still, he assumed that I operated like him.

He always told me, "Our children know what they want." But when what they wanted didn't match what he wanted, he went ballistic. I couldn't believe that with the opportunity in front of our daughter, Peter was going to continue to be so selfish. It was the chance of a lifetime and unlike so many girls who arrive in Milan with no connections and no one to support them emotionally and mentally, Alexia had it all. We were prepared to live in Milan with her for a year or two. Viktor's clients could still meet with him, and the business would not suffer from that location.

I called my attorney for advice, and he let me know that if Peter would not respect Alexia's wishes, then a hearing would need to take place. At that point, Alexia would need to be able to go face-to-face with Peter and tell him she wanted to live with me. He asked if this was something she would be able to do. Frankly, I couldn't imagine it.

I knew Peter would do all he could to make our lives hell if Alexia was not on the plane to return to him. Dealing with emotional turmoil and court proceedings involving her father would have kept Alexia from a life, a mind-set, conducive to a successful launch in modeling. When Alexia and I discussed it, we decided she would go back, talk to her dad, and make him understand her opportunity. She also wanted to say her good-byes and pack more of her belongings before we returned to Milan with her. At that time, it seemed the best way to handle the situation.

I wrote Peter a long letter begging him to listen to his daughter, to give her a voice, to give her "wings." I reminded him that we had respected his wishes not to sign any contracts and hoped that he would respect us the same as we worked to help Alexia accomplish her goals. I tried to make him understand this was not about him or about me, but about what Alexia wanted. With Viktor and myself, her connections to the business were good fortune. Combined with her potential, it was a rare chance she'd been given. Her aim was to improve her portfolio with some recognizable ad campaigns before attending college in New York. In addition, it was a perfectly natural thing for a teenage girl to want to live with her mother.

I closed the letter with this paragraph.

She loves you with her whole heart. This isn't a competition between us. All of us—you, me, Kathy (Peter's wife), and Viktor—have our own knowledge, our own gifts, and our own unique dynamic to contribute to her life. I think she's a very lucky girl! Viktor will not let her fail in this. She'll do well, Peter. With your blessing, an easy transition, lots of support from those who love her there, she'll do very well. She's got an open door to the top. I pray for her, for you, and for your relationship with her in the future that you let her take it.

Peter wrote back asking for more details. I relayed the turn of events in Milan and closed that letter with the following.

Please take time to consider the things I've said. Anything that happens in modeling for her needs to happen with your blessing. I think your relationship with Alexia is at a very healthy place for her to even have the courage to tell you she wants to be with me. It's not about something that went wrong with you and Alexia, as you suggested to her. There seems to be something very "right" going on in your relationship, as she's comfortable telling you what she wants. She has a golden opportunity Peter. Please. Let her take it. You can do this!

I hope you and Kathy were able to make the most of some of your free time together this summer.

Paige

As Alexia passed through the security gate at the airport that summer on her way back to her father, she looked back at me and said, "I'll see you in a month!" She was determined to take advantage of the lucky break she'd received into the modeling world, and fully intended to talk her dad into letting her pursue her dream. But after much duress from him, she agreed to forego the modeling opportunity and graduate from the high school she attended rather than join the international school system again. By escalating the problems involved in custody, Peter was able to negate Alexia's motivation and the outcome was that her choice was simply stripped away from her. The safety net of not being allowed to make her own decisions had become a comfortable place for Alexia. I resented Peter terribly for crippling her confidence and robbing her of an incredible opportunity.

In the months that followed the "decision," I felt Alexia slipping away and prayed she wouldn't do something to hurt herself. Her determination to succeed in the fashion business was suffocated by new demands placed on her. Her zest for returning to us succumbed to her need for peace. It was harmony she wanted most, even if the price she paid for it was her dream.

After school had begun, I received the following e-mail from Peter.

Paige,

Thank you for your proposal from some time ago. Also, thank you for telling me to take my time and think about it. I have and, at this time, do not believe it is in Alexia's best interest to take her out of her school to pursue modeling full-time.

Peter

No one had even considered the possibility of Alexia not finishing high school, but Peter needed a good reason to deny his daughter her wishes. The international system in Milan was comparable to Vienna, and Alexia would have received a diploma similar to her older brother's.

I knew while we were in Italy with Alexia that the apartments we were looking at should include space for a baby nursery. Viktor and I had discussed the fact that our second baby would be born in Italy. Marko would learn to speak Italian quickly in the kindergarten, especially since it was a language Viktor spoke. It was an exciting time for all of us. But once the school year began, we resigned ourselves to the fact that Alexia wasn't coming back. We settled in to enjoy the rest of the pregnancy with the knowledge the baby would be born in Vienna sometime around Valentine's Day.

Chapter 62

That Christmas, while making their road trip to the Midwest, Alexia was spotted at a rest stop by a photographer based in Atlanta who told Peter that she should get into modeling. The photographer convinced them that he was her ticket to New York, so plans were made to shoot a new portfolio in Atlanta that would replace the portfolio Viktor and I had put together for her. She flew to be photographed in Atlanta, Georgia, from Los Angeles, California, hometown to actors in abundance who most certainly need headshots and updated portfolio photography. The trip was made with her father and her stepmother, all for the sake of a new portfolio and a different connection to the modeling business than Viktor or myself.

Alexia had looked forward to meeting her new little sister during spring break, but when the time came for us to make her travel arrangements, she balked at the plan. Peter had decided he wanted to use spring break to secure a modeling agency for Alexia in New York, and at the same time, visit some of the universities in the area. I was so disappointed she wouldn't be coming to meet the baby. In addition, I had concerns about Peter trying to take her modeling career into his inexperienced hands. Gracing the doors of the agencies that would be the right "fit" for Alexia in New York, with Peter and a mediocre portfolio, just didn't seem like a good idea.

"Well, sweetie, I'm disappointed. We didn't see you at Christmas. But we knew we would see you this month. Now, that has changed too."

"Don't you want to support my dream?" She asked, seeming to have completely forgotten Milan. And worse, what Viktor and I could do in the future to support her in that business.

"I'm trying to protect your dream, Alexia."

I didn't think Alexia was ready for New York. More importantly, I *knew* that Peter was not prepared to be the one taking her. I sent letters, coaching, giving the information I had about different agencies and, later, learned that none of them had even been read. Peter said he just didn't have the time. Had the trip been about his career, he would have made the time to prepare, but it wasn't about him. When all was said and done, I believed his trip to

New York with our daughter was to help her put the idea of modeling out of her mind. It worked brilliantly.

≈≈≈

Viktor and I were blessed with a beautiful baby girl earlier that year. We named her Kallie. At our age, she was "icing on the cake," a victory of sorts and an absolute delight. Adam would celebrate his twenty-fifth birthday the same year she celebrated her first! The gift of a daughter to raise was poignant, and I was elated with her arrival.

By Easter, shortly after Alexia's trip to New York, Kallie had developed a bladder infection that landed her in the hospital for a week. A month later, she had another one. The hospital staff determined she would need to undergo renal scans that clearly showed a reflux problem. We were assured it would be something she'd likely outgrow, but if not, the surgery to fix it had become routine.

In spite of being on nightly antibiotics, the infections arrived monthly. We would spend five to seven days in the hospital so that Kallie could receive IV therapy for her infections. I was thankful the hospital stay during the month of July was immediately before Alexia's summer arrival, as it ensured Alexia's time with us would not be interrupted by an infection or a hospitalization. It was upon returning from that week in the hospital in July, four days before Alexia was to be with us, that I received this e-mail from Peter.

Paige,

I am writing to let you know that I have decided that Alexia will not be coming to Vienna this summer. The reasons for this are as follows:

1. *Alexia has a number of school commitments this summer that are important as she heads into her final year of high school. Missing ten days in the midst of this makes it quite difficult to meet these commitments.*

2. *The first semester of her senior year will be a very hectic time as Alexia will need to apply to and visit numerous colleges in addition to her normal school activities (which includes a heavy*

course load). She needs to complete her summer commitments and be well rested as she enters the school year.

3. *Each time Alexia visits Vienna she struggles for up to six weeks to get back into the groove at home. This is a result of the physical and emotional toll of the travel and visit. She simply doesn't have the luxury this year of losing these six weeks.*

I have discussed my decision with Alexia. It would be very helpful to Alexia if you would let her know that you understand and only want what is best for her. Failing that, I would implore you to not stress her emotionally over what ultimately was my decision. Doing so simply puts her in the middle of two parents she loves very much. This is not a decision to keep her from seeing you or your family. In summary, while Alexia will not be visiting Vienna this summer, I know she and her brother and sister would love to see you if you are willing to make the effort. I sincerely hope that works out for you.

Peter

It was his last big chance to use her to hurt me. Too busy to make a phone call, too much better than me to show any courtesy and discuss it with me, an e-mail was all I received. With a sickly infant who needed to be near her doctor as well as the hospital she'd been in and out of over the past four months, I was supposed to fly to the States, risk my daughter's kidney, and live out of a hotel in order to spend time with my children. He made Alexia believe that if there were a *will* for me to see her, there would be a *way* for me to be there.

I called Alexia to make sure she was all right with the turn of events, because just the day before while I visited with her from the hospital, she was talking about packing Hot Tamales in her suitcase. The candy is difficult to find in Vienna and hot popcorn without Hot Tamales sprinkled on top, just isn't the same. Packing as many boxes as possible in suitcases and packages coming into the country is routine procedure. I realized Peter's letter had been written before that conversation.

In trying to discuss it, Alexia had little to say. I could hear Peter in the background, so I asked to speak with him. He had no desire for a conversation with me. His only desire was for Alexia to hear him.

"Why won't you come see your children?" he asked, in a voice that sounded as though he might be ready to cry.

No matter what I explained of my pregnancy or of Kallie's acute health issues, my words fell on deaf ears. Peter thoroughly ignored the impossibilities for me, even though he's well-versed in regard to conditions involving the kidney. For me, that Alexia was not allowed to meet her little sister for almost a year magnified Peter's indifference to life, love, and family.

≈≈≈

Alexia and I were on the phone looking at her senior photos that had been posted on the Internet, and she had visibly matured. I was teary-eyed because we hadn't seen each other for over a year. I remembered her smile as she turned at the airport and said, "I'll see you in a month!" as she waved good-bye. Yet there we were, over a year later, and I was weeping at the sight of her.

"It's almost over," she said.

Her foresight stopped me and brought a smile. "It's almost over," I repeated.

The difference in her appearance was subtle, but the development in her understanding of our plight had come full circle. Through it all, she became a little rebellious, but in light of Peter's crushing level of control, I was thankful a little rebellion was the worst of it through her high school years.

≈≈≈

For Christmas, Adam, Amanda, and Alexia flew to Vienna. It was the first time since Kallie's birth that I had all of my children in the same place and for me, that was bliss! But the interaction with each of them is different when the house is full and by Alexia's spring break of her senior year, she wanted alone time with *her mom*. We did need time together as the year she was going through seemed to be one drama after another. I thought a change of scenery that week would be beneficial for her. I gave her the itinerary I'd found and let her know I was willing to make the arrangements, but she would need to get permission from her dad. Peter never reimbursed me for the trip he cancelled and I didn't want to deal with that again. Naturally, her father didn't like the idea of her spending time with me, so I wrote him an e-mail.

Hello Peter,

Just a note to ask you to please let Alexia come for spring break. She was not allowed to come last year for her break. You took away last summer and there seems to be no good reason for you to keep her with you this break. I think she could use some time away from her social scene. Alexia and I had little time together at Christmas as there was a houseful and we'll have even less time together at her graduation. If she wants to be here . . . please let her be here!

Thanks,
Paige

I received Peter's "response" a couple days later.

Paige,

I received my bonus. Your part will be transferred to your account.

Peter

There was not one word about our daughter. I viewed it as egoism compounded by indifference. Our daughter is *his* daughter—our children are *his* children; and ad infinitum, that is what Peter Sullivan will believe. In his estimation, I forfeited my right to parent our children when I ended our abysmal marriage.

By the time Alexia graduated from high school, Kallie's health had improved enough to risk traveling with her. I discovered homeopathic tablets for the baby's condition that had helped her avoid being hospitalized. In light of that, I was comfortable making the trip.

Amanda and Alexia met us at the airport. They were hanging over the banister reaching for hugs before we made our way past the blockade. They were nearly singing, "Welcome to California!" when they handed me a bouquet of a dozen roses. I customarily welcomed them to Vienna with one red rose, so their gesture of a multi-colored dozen spoke volumes. Alexia drove and though it was the first time I'd seen her drive, it was the most natural thing in the world. She was an excellent driver, and I smiled at the thought of her *driving* her own life soon.

The evening of Alexia's graduation ceremony, all of my children and I walked away from the festivities together to celebrate at the restaurant of her choice. It was her wish that she celebrate at a later time with her father. I knew it was in part due to the short amount of time we had to be together, but walking away from Peter and his family caused me to remember the night of Adam's graduation when I was left behind. It was a full circle moment for my children and me. My spirits lightened as I sensed the weight of offenses over the years begin to fall away from us.

Chapter 63

It was a beautiful autumn evening in Vienna. Viktor and I were dining at one of our favorite Italian restaurants downtown. Perched on the edge of a quintessential street, it comprised all there is to relish in an outdoor café in Europe. We were enjoying coffee with our dessert when I noticed Peter walking down the street toward our table.

He still had business to tend to in Vienna, but no one had informed me he would be in town. Surprised to see him, I said, "Hello, Peter!" as he neared the table.

True to form, his head hung as he walked. There on one of the most exquisite streets in the city, he sauntered along unaware of the beautiful environment surrounding him. A colleague, clearly subordinate, walked beside him engaged in a lifeless conversation.

A little louder, I said, "Hello Peter!" He was close enough to touch if I'd been willing to risk crushing the flowers in their boxes that stood between the street and our table.

I watched the man I'd spent eighteen years of my life with walk right past me, completely unaware of my presence, and entirely detached from the energy of the atmosphere. It saddened me to see there was still no joy on his face or in his gait. I actually felt sorry for him, as he appeared to still be his own worst enemy. There I sat with all the things money can't buy, and Peter marched on, another day.

Viktor observed Peter until he could no longer see him. He was digesting more of my past as he contemplated what had just occurred. So many years with a man who had just brushed past without seeing me, without hearing me, without sensing me. There was nothing to say as I looked at Viktor while he watched Peter walk away.

I was overcome with gratitude and an overwhelming sense of thankfulness for the man sitting in front of me. He was a force of restoration to me during the worst time of my life. He lived his life so keenly aware, I knew it would be impossible for him to walk down a street and not feel my presence. His love was empowering and wholly experienced.

My eyes were filled with tears of joy when Viktor's gaze returned to me. He was silent, still taking in what had just occurred. I couldn't help but smile at the symbolic irony in the incident. With tenderness spilling over, I picked up his hand and brought it to my lips. In an eternal and authentic moment, I whispered, thank-you before I placed a heartfelt kiss in the palm of his hand. I closed his fingers on the kiss, sealing the completeness of my love, my life, into his hand.

Epilogue

It was seven years ago that I lost custody of my children. It was eight years ago that the bond I shared with them was broken. In that time, I have learned that the *only* thing I could have done to prevent what has happened would be to have stayed in an emotionally abusive and negligent marriage. My children would know a "broken" mother rather than the mother they know now.

Though we miss moments that should have been shared, I have maintained contact with all of the children. We cannot get back the time we've lost, but I believe the time given up created a much healthier environment for my children and myself. As they mature and grow in understanding and compassion, their respect for me is evident again.

Each of the children bare their own unique *scars* from the ordeal. Adam has emerged from the rubble of the divorce his own person. He stopped seeing his therapist and began to own his actions. He's matured and questioned everything about his life and come to his own truths. He sees both of his parents in himself and is able to appreciate what is good in each of us. My little buddy for so many years has grown to be a twenty-five-year-old man, and my son is now a friend I can depend on.

Amanda is twenty-one years old and minimally conscious of what she has endured, though dwelling on it is not her style. She is still full of life, energy, talent, and love. I suspect her busy schedule keeps her moving forward in a way that doesn't allow time to think much about the past. The last opportunity I had to be alone with her in Vienna provided a chance for us to have long discussions. The questions she asked helped me know the importance of writing this book.

Alexia's high school graduation is cause to hope for a newfound sense of independence in her. Throughout the remainder of her school years after I moved back to Vienna, I woke her in the mornings with a phone call and as much conversation as she had time for. Many of her friends don't have the relationship with their mothers that she has with me, and she's expressed her gratitude for the ability to talk to me about everything. Even though she was never allowed another mobile phone that worked internationally so that she had access to her mother, our connection stayed strong because I made the afternoon phone call from Vienna, to her mobile phone in California, a daily priority.

The girls seem to go through cycles of comprehension and are not free from the subtleties of parental alienation still living near Peter. I guess it's human nature, similar to married couples that begin to mirror each other. At times, they are angry and feel a need to punish me for my absence. When Amanda yelled, "You never leave your children!" trying to teach me what is right, I draw a line in hopes that one day she understands that spending a lifetime fighting, watching your back, and trapped in conflict, is not a life.

Friends ask them, "So your mother lives in Austria? How can that be? How does a mom do that?" Alexia has even gone so far as to say she doesn't want to be a mother because she's afraid she'd abandon her children. Her level of understanding still runs the gamut. Thankfully, I can ask her to look into the eyes of her younger siblings and tell me she believes they are not happy and loved children. Then I remind her, they are just like her in that they are *deeply loved* . . . by their mother. Even with an ocean between us, I'm as attentive in the lives of my older children as they let me be. We have the future for better times.

The counseling they receive is all one-sided. I have not been allowed to talk to a counselor, nor have any of their therapists ever returned my phone calls. Even though there was a court order for Peter to keep me informed about my children, that did not happen. The only communication between Peter and I in regard to the children was about itineraries and travel arrangements. Fortunately, all of them were old enough, willing, and able to communicate with me on their own after I released them from the "fight."

Lately they have told me, "Dad's over the divorce, Mom. We never talk about it anymore." I've even been told, "He was angry! Of course, he did things to hurt you." There are perfectly rational reasons and explanations for Peter's decisions and behavior; therefore, it is excused. Love does that, and I'm thankful my children are forgiving.

Peter will continue to make me as insignificant as he possibly can in regard to my children, and I have accepted that they will indulge him, to a degree. There is much at stake for them. As complicated as their challenges are in dealing with their parents, I believe they will always choose to have both of us in their lives to whatever extent is possible under all the circumstances.

What IS normal, in this situation? What can I hope for or expect? I've decided the answer must be *love*. When all is said and done, they know I love them, and I know they love me. Through the heartache and tears, the disappointment and the distance—there is still love. It is love that has been challenged, yet endures. It is love that is quieted, but has not been silenced. It is love that will never be negated as long as my children and I are able to keep each other close in our thoughts and in our hearts.

≈≈≈

So this is my story. In writing this book, I have to question whether I'm perpetrating the ills of parental alienation. Perhaps these pages should be tucked away, and I should go on, accepting my children's "truths" and perspectives. Yet, I have tried to teach each of them that indifference is unacceptable, and this book was written in that vein. Martin Luther King Jr. wrote, "Our lives begin to end the day we become silent about things that matter." At some point into their adulthood, I believe it is a disservice to keep the truth from children who experienced bond abuse. They have a right to know because their foundation is not complete without an understanding of parental alienation syndrome. When my children are ready, they'll have the other point of view in this book. Ultimately, this is their story as much as it is mine.

I wish for Adam, Amanda, and Alexia to be of sound mind, strong in their ability to delve deeply into their memories for answers in regard to their past and their futures. I would like them to experience life and connect so completely to their journey and those it includes that it is impossible for them to ever make a once-loved person an insignificant piece of their lives. It is my hope that they realize their choices, based on solid decision-making, should remain worthy of a measure of their respect. I wish for them to be mentally and emotionally whole with an ability to love fully.

I will continue to hope for the day that Peter is able to, at last, love them so correctly that they hear him say, "I am sorry I made it difficult for your mother to be in your life."

Parental Alienation or Bond Abuse

Some experts claim parental alienation has reached epidemic proportions. Others claim it is a term conjured for abusers to use in court custody battles. Whether you are a targeted parent who knows this syndrome is real or a child of divorce who was robbed of parenting you deserved, you have likely recognized there is a crucial need for awareness among the people involved in the dissolution of marriage involving children. Responsiveness on the part of all of us who have been a targeted parent is critical. Together we can rally for better legislation as well as improved training for evaluators, mediators, and judges, in order that they become more proficient in detecting this often disregarded phenomenon.

Our judicial system does little to discourage a "winner takes all" mentality, and our children have become the ultimate reward for heavy-handed litigation. Among alienating parents and their legal team, there is little empathy or conscience involved in winning custody by domination or manipulation in court. Nor is there any punishment, which is the reason parental alienation has become a political issue and has been dubbed the ultimate hate crime.

Parental alienation or bond abuse is considered to be a serious form of child abuse resulting in psychological injury to the child. Parental Alienation Syndrome occurs when the child becomes aligned with one parent, which leads to an impaired relationship with the alienated parent and, as a result, a loss of parenting. If you are like me, a targeted parent, you were likely blindsided by the experience. Additionally, attempts to communicate actually made things worse because it provided opportunity for my ex-spouse to rage and submit the children to more conflict and mistreatment.

In alleviating the life-changing impact of this abuse on your children, first and foremost, be the parent you know you are and the parent you want your children to know. Be true to yourself! Don't be intimidated by the alienating parent. Their lies are their own reality, but you should not let the lies define you. Keep being a loving parent with normal expectations of your children, which includes normal behavior toward you and other members of your family.

Focus on your own behavior by changing the way you react to the alienating parent. Limit contact and refrain from responding to their manipulation and alienation tactics as this limits their power. In many ways, your life is a daily trial in which you will need to display who you are. Your child needs your love, even if he or she is unable to receive it. Keep showing them your love and preserve the emotional bond you have with each of your children. Teach them unconditional love by your actions.

If you are the targeted parent, know there is hope if you are able to maintain contact with your child. Let them know it is your desire for them to have a good relationship with both parents and that obedience or loyalty to the alienating parent should not depend on their rejection of you. Likewise, if they are able to recognize parental alienation in their life and/or understand what they contributed to the experience the targeted parent suffered does not mean aligning with the targeted parent in the future.

It is out of illness, ignorance, and indifference to the human spirit that an alienating parent is able to employ their devastating tactics to undermine or negate their child's relationship with a parent. Every parent is part of his/ her child's identity, and when a child's love for a parent turns to hatred, they are in essence being led to hate a part of themselves. The disconnect in the abuser's person, in their being that is capable of provoking disintegration of a parent-child bond, is a void to pity in the abuser's character.

Make it your goal to ensure your children do not adopt the same indifference toward the people in their lives and especially toward themselves. Stay mindful of what your child is going through and know it is possible for a child to "break" under the stress. Help them stay connected to their feelings, and make sure they understand how important their own role will be as future partner and parent. Without an ability to connect with others, to feel what another feels, we are devoid of the human experience.

If you would like more information about bond abuse, parental alienation or PAS—Parental Alienation Syndrome, go to: *www.theparentectomy.com*

Questions for Discussion

1. Expatriation

    a. Would you consider taking an overseas assignment?

    b. Would your point of view in regard to living overseas change if you were in a troubled marriage?

    c. How would you feel about expatriating if children were involved?

    d. What was Paige's motivation to live abroad?

    e. What might have been Peter's motivation to accept an international transfer?

2. Living Abroad

    a. How did living in a foreign country affect the family?

    b. What life changes did each family member experience?

    c. What caused the couple's differences to be magnified while living abroad?

3. Separation

    a. Why might Peter's attorney have told him his wife would be begging to come home before the divorce was final?

    b. When Peter told Adam his mother would kill herself when she realized what she'd done by ending the marriage, what was his intention?

4. The In-laws

    a. Why didn't Peter tell Paige his parents would be arriving the weekend following their separation? How did their arrival encroach on the terms the couple had agreed to during separation in regard to the children?

b. Why was it important for Peter to have Paige's keys even though there were several sets between Peter and the children?

c. What motivated the grandparents' participation?

d. Do you suppose Peter had ever failed before?

e. How would the children's lives have been better, or worse, without the grandparents' presence?

5. Perpetrating Parental Alienation

a. How is parental alienation similar to a political campaign?

b. What motivation did Peter have to "win" his children?

c. Peter used a number of covert, subtle messages to influence his children. What were they, and how might they be more effective than overt persuasion?

d. How could Paige have communicated to the children that they were being manipulated without bad-mouthing their father and perpetrating Parental Alienation herself?

e. How would you deal with the phone calls Peter used to devise scenarios of conflict, enabling distribution of his propaganda for whomever was listening to his side of the conversation?

f. What were the repeated messages Peter used to induce loyalty from his children?

g. What elements are needed in laying a foundation for brainwashing? How were fear, isolation, and psychological dependence created?

h. How is the power of suggestion an important tool in controlling and aligning another person with yourself?

i. When the children were alone with their mother, their behavior was relatively normal. Together, they treated her with contempt. Why?

j. Is it possible to stop parental alienation from occurring when one parent is obsessed with winning and/or determined in aligning the child with him/herself? How?

6. Decisions

a. Peter was not willing to leave the home his employer was renting on his behalf. Other than staying with Peter, what could Paige have done differently?

b. Without knowing what parental alienation or bond abuse was, would you also be blindsided by the events that occurred?

c. In your opinion, was meeting Viktor a timely or untimely event?

d. How would the outcome of Paige's ordeal differ without Viktor and their baby?

e. Were there any cultural differences that you found intriguing?

f. How does a "winner takes all" mind-set shape our society?

7. The Judicial System

a. The judge stated that she had no idea what parental alienation was. From that perspective, would your verdict be different than hers?

b. If parental alienation or bond abuse could be proven, should it be punishable by law?

c. How does the mental and emotional abuse of parental alienation compare to other abuse?

8. The Aftermath

a. When Paige begins to see her children display behavioral changes that lead her to believe they will have mental and/or emotional problems if the environment they are in does not improve, what are her options?

b. To what length might a child go to please the parent they have aligned with? . . . or to escape the conflict?

c. In rising above parental alienation, Paige took responsibility to end the conflict. Would you do the same thing? Why or why not?